TONIGHT I SAID GOODBYE

2005 Edgar Award Nominee for "Best First Novel by an American Author"

"Michael Koryta hits the ground running . . . He's already so good, it's scary!"

—Steve Hamilton, author of *Ice Run*

"A terrific, first-class debut full of suspense, tension, tricks, and charm."

—Lee Child

"The 21-year-old author excels at building characters and story, making this one of the best mystery debuts this year."

—*Library Journal*

"This riveting detective novel should delight fans looking for new talent."

—*Publishers Weekly*

"A gracefully written, straight-ahead detective story with a welcome 11th-hour surprise."

—*Kirkus Reviews*

"Koryta is only 21, but he writes with the style of a seasoned vet . . . this is a writer to watch."

—*Globe & Mail*

"Michael Koryta makes an impressive debut."

—*Midwest Book Review*

"*Tonight I Said Goodbye* scores points by never underestimating the reader's ability to guess ahead, and all plot points, though unexpected, are never far-fetched. Koryta, winner of the 2003 Private Eye Writers of America's Best PI Novel contest, emerges fully formed in his first effort."

—*Baltimore Sun*

MORE . . .

CRITICAL ACCLAIM FOR MICHAEL KORYTA

SORROW'S ANTHEM

"Koryta's impressive second hardboiled mystery is a worthy successor to his debut, *Tonight I Said Goodbye*, an Edgar and Shamus finalist. . . . The 22-year-old author, who works for a PI and for an Indiana newspaper, displays credible insider knowledge of those professions as well as a gift for creating both sympathetic characters and a fast-moving, twisty plot."

—*Publishers Weekly*

"[A] work of rare profundity. The multi-layered and labyrinthine plot is worthy of Raymond Chandler or (more aptly, perhaps) Ross MacDonald. And that's more than mere hyperbole; Koryta is that good. *Sorrow's Anthem* is so good it'll bring tears to your eyes. And it's good on just about every level; as a crime novel, as a hardboiled mystery, and as a mainstream exploration of choices, consequences, and of individual responsibility. In the end, and as far 'anthems' go, this one never misses a beat."

—*Mystery News*

"Sometimes a book grabs you and stays in your memory long after the rest of the in-box's contents have been flushed away by new arrivals. Koryta's second mystery about Cleveland private eye Lincoln Perry has this kind of hold on me . . . Dashiell Hammett of *Red Harvest* would appreciate the tangle of high-level political and police corruption of *Sorrow's Anthem*, but anyone who mourns for lost friendships will add a more visceral reaction."

—*Chicago Tribune*

"Perry is an appealing fellow, and Koryta is a straightforward storyteller, but the real pleasure here is touring the back streets of C-Town. . . . Nominated for an Edgar Award for best first novel at the age of 21, Koryta is now 22, but *Sorrow's Anthem* is no sophomore slump."

—*The Washington Post*

MORE . . .

"A knockout private eye novel . . . this is a real winner for dedicated private eye fans, a great choice for those who can't get enough classic action."

—*Lansing State Journal*

"Quick pacing, sharp dialogue, and very human characters—the good guys and the bad—make Michael Koryta's debut a fine and satisfying read."

—S. J. Rozan, Edgar Award–winning author of *Winter and Night*

"A terrific, first-class debut full of suspense, tension, tricks, and charm. If you like Spenser and Hawk, or Elvis and Joe, or Myron and Win, you're going to love this."

—Lee Child

"An exciting debut that crackles with gunfire and terse, dead-on dialogue. This is noir, fresh and fine."

—William Kent Kruegar, author of *Blood Hollow*

"Michael Koryta's debut novel is the next must-read. The plot sizzles. Characters seem to jump right off the page. And in Lincoln Perry, he has created a hero whose investigative and personal intuition transcends the mythos of the fictional private eye."

—Andy Straka, author of *Cold Quarry*

"I'm hugely envious of a twenty-one-year-old who arrives fully formed as a writer of poise, style and, damn it, elegance . . . and he's crafted a narrative that sizzles on the page. My consolation is that I've witnessed the emergence of a unique talent—still madly envious, though."

—Ken Bruen, author of *The Killing of the Tinkers*

ALSO BY MICHAEL KORYTA

TONIGHT I SAID GOODBYE

SORROW'S ANTHEM

MICHAEL KORYTA

St. Martin's Paperbacks

This is a work of fiction. All of the characters, organizations and events portrayed in this novel are either products of the author's imagination or are used fictitiously.

SORROW'S ANTHEM

Library of Congress Catalog Card Number: 2005044597

ISBN: 0-312-93660-5
EAN: 9780312-93660-0

Printed in the United States of America

St. Martin's Press hardcover edition / February 2006
St. Martin's Paperbacks edition / January 2007

St. Martin's Paperbacks are published by St. Martin's Press, 175 Fifth Avenue, New York, NY 10010.

10 9 8 7 6 5 4 3 2 1

To my parents, Jim and Cheryl Koryta,
with love and gratitude

ACKNOWLEDGMENTS

My editor, Peter Wolverton, deserves the foremost thanks, as he remained confident that there was a book somewhere in the initial mess, and gave me the time and guidance I needed to see it through. Working with Pete and my agent, the supportive and insightful David Hale Smith, is truly a pleasure. Thomas Dunne, John Cunningham, and the rest of the team at St. Martin's Press are exceptional in every facet.

My early readers—Bob Hammel, Laura Lane, and Janice Rickert—were outstanding, and greatly appreciated.

My uncle, Kevin Marsh, of the Cleveland Metroparks Rangers, provided insight into his department and the Cleveland law enforcement community in general. He should not, however, be blamed for any errors made or liberties taken by this writer.

Thanks also to Don Johnson of Trace Investigations, and to Stewart Moon, Donita Hadley, and the rest of the *Herald-Times* gang.

During the year surrounding publication of my first book, a number of writers whom I greatly admire went out of their way to offer advice, encouragement, and support. Such opportunities were without question the highlight of the first-book experience for me, and I am greatly indebted to all of you.

As always, my family is most appreciated, and I need to offer a special note of thanks to my father, Jim Koryta, a Clark Avenue original who made the near west side of Cleveland a place of stories for me when I was young. It appears to have had a lasting effect.

PART ONE MEMORY BLEEDING

CHAPTER 1

I heard the sirens, but paid them no mind. They were near, and they were loud, but this was the west side of Cleveland, and while there were many worse places in the world, it was also not the type of neighborhood where a police siren made you do a double take.

"You ready, West Tech?" Amy Ambrose asked, taking a shot from the free throw line that caught nothing but the old chain net as it fell. Out here the nets were chain, not cord, and while they could lacerate your hand on a rebound attempt, they sounded awfully satisfying when a shot fell through, a jingle of success like a winning pull on a slot machine.

"Of course I'm ready," I answered, trying to match her shot but clanging it off the rim instead. This didn't bode well. Amy had been challenging me to a game of horse all week, and I was distressed to find she could actually shoot. I'd played basketball for West Tech in the last years of the school, before the old building was shut down, but it had been several months since I'd even taken a shot. Amy had become a basketball fan in recent years, more inspired than ever since LeBron James had arrived in Cleveland, and I had a bad feeling that I was about to become the latest victim of her new hobby.

"I hope you've got a better touch than that when you actually need it," Amy said of my errant effort.

"I was always more of a point guard in high school," I said. "You know, a distributor."

"So you couldn't shoot," Amy said, hitting another shot, this one from the baseline. She pointed at her feet. "You've got to make it from here."

I missed. Amy grinned.

"You've got an 'H' already, stud. Looks like this will be a short one." She was about to release her next shot when her cell phone rang with a shrill, hideous rendition of Beethoven's Fifth. She missed the shot wide, then turned to me with a frown. "Doesn't count. The cell phone distracted me."

"It counts," I answered. "You ask me, you should be penalized a letter just for having that ring on your phone."

She let the phone go unanswered. I took a shot from the three-point line and made it. Amy missed, and we were tied at "H." Her phone rang again, turning the heads of a few of the kids who were hanging out at the opposite end of the court. We were playing at an elementary school not far from my apartment.

"I'm not losing to you, Lincoln," Amy said as I hit another shot. She continued to ignore the phone, which was on the ground behind the basket, and eventually it silenced. After a long moment of focusing, she took the shot and made it, forcing me to try again.

We traded makes for a few minutes, and then Amy pulled ahead by a letter. We were both beginning to sweat now as we moved around the court, the mugginess of the August day not fading as fast as the sun. Amy looked like a teenager in her shorts and T-shirt, with her curly hair pulled back into a ponytail. A couple of boys who were maybe sixteen went past on skateboards and gave her a long, approving stare.

"Your shot," Amy said after she finally missed one. "Make it interesting, would you?"

I dribbled left and came back to the right, pivoted, and fired a pretty fadeaway jump shot that caught the side of the backboard and sailed out of bounds, a Michael Jordan move with Lincoln Perry results.

"That was embarrassing even to watch," Amy said.

"I won seven games with that move in high school, smart-ass."

"Really?"

"No."

Her phone began to ring again. I groaned.

"Just answer the damn thing or turn it off, Ace."

"Okay." She tossed the ball back to me and walked over to pick up the phone. While she talked, I stepped outside the three-point line and put up a few more long shots, missing more than I hit.

Amy hung up and walked back onto the court. She stood with her hands on her hips, her eyes distant.

"What's up?" I said, dribbling the ball idly with one hand.

"It was my editor. Big story breaking. He wanted to know if I had a good source with the fire department."

"Oh?"

"Involves your old neighborhood," she said. "Any chance you want to ride down there with me and do some reporting? Maybe you could hook me up with a good source or two."

I smiled. "You're way too suburban to be hanging out in my old neighborhood, Ace."

"Shut up." Amy likes to think of herself as tough and street-savvy, and she hates it when I hassle her about her childhood in Parma, a middle-class suburb south of the city. I was west side all the way.

"What's the story?" I took another jump shot and hit it.

"Murder."

"That does sound like the old neighborhood." I retrieved the ball and dribbled back to the top of the key, my back to Amy.

"Some guy set fire to a house down on Train Avenue with a woman inside. Dumbass was caught on tape, though. A liquor-store surveillance camera from across the street, I guess. When the cops went to arrest him this evening, he fought them and got away."

"Remember the sirens we heard earlier?" I said.

"That could've been the reason for them. Guy who set the fire lives up on Clark Avenue. I thought you grew up off Clark."

"That's right." I took another shot. "What's the guy's name?"

"Ed Gradduk."

The ball hit hard off the back of the rim and came bouncing straight at me. I let it sail past without even extending a hand. It rolled to the far end of the court, but I kept my eyes on Amy.

"Ed Gradduk," I said.

"That's how my editor pronounced it. You know him?"

The sun was all the way behind the school now, the court bathed in shadows. The ball lay still about fifty feet behind us. I walked across the court, picked it up, and brought it back to Amy. She was watching me with raised eyebrows.

"You okay?"

"I'm okay," I said. "Here's your ball. Listen, I'm sorry, but I need to leave. Consider it a forfeit if you want. We'll have a rematch some other time."

She took the ball and frowned at me. "Lincoln, what's the problem? Do you know this guy?"

I wiped sweat from my forehead with the back of my hand and looked off, away from the orange sunset and toward the shadows east of us. Toward Clark Avenue.

"I knew him. And I'm sorry, but I've got to go, Ace."

"Go where?"

"I need to take a walk, Amy."

She wanted to protest, to ask more questions, but she didn't. Instead she stood alone on the basketball court while I walked away. I went around the school building and out to the street, got inside my truck, and started the engine. The air conditioner hit me with a blast of warm air and I switched it off and lowered the windows instead. It was stuffy and hot in the truck, but the trickle of sweat sliding down my spine was as cold as lake water.

It's early summer. I'm twelve years old, as is Edward Nathaniel Gradduk, my best friend. We are spending this night as we've spent every night so far this summer: playing catch in Ed's front yard. The yard is narrow, as they all are on Clark Avenue, so we begin our game in the driveway. As the night grows late, though, the house and the trees block out the remains of the sun, and we move into the front yard to prolong things. Here, with the glow of the streetlight, we can play all night if we want to. The ball is difficult to see until it is right on you, but we've decided this is a good practice element, calling for faster reflexes. By the time we get to high school, we'll have the best reflexes around, and from there it will be a short trip to the major leagues. High school, to us, seems about as real a possibility as the major leagues this summer; a dreamworld with driver's licenses and cars and girls with breasts.

"Pete Rose is a worthless piece of shit," Ed says, whipping the ball at me with a sidearm motion. "I don't care how many hits he has."

"Damn straight," I reply, returning the throw. Ed and I are Cleveland Indians fans, horrible team or not, and if you're a Cleveland Indians fan you hate Pete Rose. You hate him because he is a star player in Cincinnati, a few

hours to the south, but more than that, you hate him because he ran into Ray Fosse at full speed in an All-Star game more than a decade ago and Ray was never the same after the collision. Thirty years after the team's last pennant, a player like Ray Fosse means a lot to Indians fans. He is another bust now, another hope extinguished, but for this one we get the satisfaction of blaming Pete Rose.

"My dad said he'd like to see Pete Rose come up to Cleveland and go into one of the bars," Ed says. "Said he'd get his ass kicked so fast it wouldn't even be funny. 'Cept it would be funny, you know? Funnier than shit."

Ed has a way of talking just like his old man, which explains the persistent profanity. My own dad would clock me if he ever heard me swearing like we do, but when I'm with Ed, it's safe. Cool, even. A couple of tough guys.

"Damn straight," I say again, a tough-guy phrase if ever there was one. "I wish I could be there to see it."

"Pete'll never come to town," Ed says. "Doesn't have the balls."

Ed lives on Clark Avenue, and I live with my father in a small house on Frontier Avenue, just south of Clark. Our wanderings carry us as far east as Fulton Road, and a favorite spot is St. Mary's Cemetery on West Thirty-eighth. Sometimes Ed and I run through the cemetery at night, telling each other ghost stories that start out seeming corny but end up making us sprint for home. Ed's mother is always at home; my mother has been dead since I was three. I have a framed picture of her on the table beside my bed. The first time Ed saw it, he frowned and asked why I had a picture of my mother in my room. I told him she was dead, flushing with a mix of shame and anger—ashamed that I was embarrassed to have the picture out, and angry that Ed was challenging it. He looked at it ju-

diciously, touched the edge of the frame gently with his finger, and said, "She was real pretty." From then on, Ed Gradduk has been my best friend.

My dad's at home now, probably asleep in his armchair with the Indians game on the television or the radio, whichever is broadcasting tonight. We don't have cable, so we still listen to a lot of the games on the radio. I'm allowed to be at Ed's house because his mother is home. Ed's father is probably down at the Hideaway, playing cards and drinking beer. He might come home soon, toss the ball around with us for a while and tell jokes, or he might not come home at all. Ed will pretend he doesn't care if his dad hasn't shown up by the time we go to bed, but he'll also alternate glances between the clock and the street until he falls asleep.

"Pretty Boy Pete Rose," Ed sings, jogging back until he is on the sidewalk and rifling the ball at me so hard I take a step back and hold my glove up with both hands, feeling silly, but thankful I am able to see the damn thing before it can drill me in the nose.

"Tougher than usual tonight," Ed says, seeing my near disaster with his throw. He points skyward. "One of the streetlights is burned out."

"You wanna go in?" I say.

He scowls. "Nah, I don't want to go in this early."

I toss the ball in and out of my mitt and wait for him to make a decision. He scuffs his sneaker on the ground and eyes the garage thoughtfully.

" 'Member when my dad was painting the house?" he asks. When I nod, he says, "Well, he couldn't do it till he got home from work, and by then it was already almost dark. So he bought a spotlight to help him."

"You still have it?"

"Yeah. He never really used it, said the paint always

*looked different during the day and that pissed him off.
But I think he kept the light."*

"We bring that out here, maybe we can even see well
enough to hit wiffle balls," I say, liking this suggestion.
"It'd be like playing at the stadium in a night game."

"Come on." Ed drops his mitt to the ground and starts
for the tiny, one-car garage that sits behind the house. I
follow.

There used to be a floodlight attached to the garage,
but it, too, is broken. The overhead door is down, and we
have to go in through the side door. Ed's a step in front of
me, but even so I can smell the gas as soon as he pulls the
door open. Most old garages carry the smell of fuel with
them, but this is different, just a bit too strong. There's music playing, too—Van Morrison singing "Into the Mystic."

Ed is fumbling against the wall for the light switch,
oblivious to the smell. He can't find the switch, reaching
with a twelve-year-old's short arms, so he steps farther
into the garage. I move with him, and now I'm inside the
dank little building. The fuel smell is still potent. I'm
wearing my mitt, but I slip it off my hand and let it drop to
the concrete floor. The baseball is clenched tight in my
right hand, my arm pulled back a bit. I've never been
scared of the dark, but for some reason I want out of this
garage.

"I can't find the damn switch," Ed mutters beside me,
and then there's a click and the little room fills with bright
white light. For a second it's too bright, and I close my
eyes against the shock. They're closed when I hear Ed begin to scream.

My eyes snap open and I take a stumbling step backward, trying to get out of the garage, thinking that there is
an attacker in here, some sort of threat to make Ed
scream like that. My back hits the wall, though, and in the

extra second I'm kept in the garage my eyes finally take in the scene.

Ed's father's Chevy Nova is inside the garage. The driver's window is down and upon the doorframe rests Norm Gradduk's head. His face is pointed toward the ceiling, his skin puffy and unnatural. It takes one look to tell even me, a child, that he is dead.

Ed runs toward the car, shrieking in a pitch higher than I would've thought he could possibly reach. He extends his arms to his father, then pulls them back immediately. He wants to help him; he's scared to touch him.

"We gotta call somebody," I say, my own voice trembling. I step closer to the car despite a deep desire to get as far from the scene as possible, and now I can see inside. There's a bottle of liquor in Norm Gradduk's lap. One of his hands is still wrapped around it. On the stereo, Van Morrison sings of a foghorn blowing, "I want to hear it, I don't have to fear it . . ."

Ed turns and runs past me, out the door and into the yard. He's still screaming, and after one more look at Norm Gradduk, I begin to shout, too. Inside the house, Ed's mother yells for everyone to keep it down out there.

It takes the paramedics seven minutes to arrive, and about seventy seconds for them to tell Ed and his mother that there is nothing they can do.

CHAPTER 2

I still knew the house, although I hadn't been inside in years. Word of mouth brought me the news that Ed had bought his childhood home, and while I could no longer remember the source, I remembered hearing about it. The house had never been a showpiece—nothing in our neighborhood was—but when Ed's dad was alive it had been the best on the block, hands down. He'd spent hours on it, painting and repairing and weeding. My own father had always been impressed by it, telling me on many occasions that while Norm Gradduk had his faults, he took pride in his home, and there weren't enough men around who still did that.

It was evident that Ed intended to match his father's devotion. The house looked bad, with a sagging porch roof, a broken window on the second story, and paint that had forgotten whether it was pale yellow or white and decided to settle on grimy gray. A ladder was leaning against the west side of the house, though, and it was clear that someone had been scraping the peeling paint off that wall with the idea of applying a fresh coat. A stack of discarded scrap wood near the porch was evidence of new planking laid on the floor. No doubt the porch roof was next on the list.

No police cars were in the driveway or at the curb when I arrived, but I saw a black Crown Victoria parked on the street two blocks down. They would be there all night, watching for a return that would surely not occur. I parked my truck facing them, and then I walked through the yard and up the front steps. Maybe someone would be home. A girlfriend, or a roommate. Hell, he could be married by now for all I knew.

My footsteps were loud on the new porch. I stood there and looked around for a minute, lost in memories, then nearly fell back off the porch when someone screamed at me from inside the house.

"Go away, go away, go away," a woman's voice screeched. "I told you filthy bastards to go away!"

I started to heed the command, but then the voice jarred something loose in my memory, and I stopped and turned to the closed front door.

"Mrs. Gradduk, it's Lincoln Perry," I said, speaking loudly.

Cars passed on the street, and a few blocks down some kids were yelling and laughing, bass music thumping in the background, a party building. The streetlight flickered and hummed, and I stood with my hands in my pockets and waited. I waited until I was sure she was not coming to the door, and then I reached out and knocked. I'd hardly laid my knuckles to the wood when the door swung open and a thin woman with hollow eye sockets and deep wrinkles stood before me.

"You son of a bitch," she said. Her voice was as thin as she was; you could hear it fine but it always seemed on the verge of breaking, maybe disappearing altogether. If you didn't know the woman, you'd associate those vocal qualities with old age or a lifetime of cigarettes. But I knew that the voice had always been the same and that she'd never smoked. Her hand rested on the doorknob, and her forearm and wrist were the sort of severely thin that made me think of starving children in Africa and black-and-white footage of Holocaust concentration camps. Her skin hung draped from sharp, angular bones in the same fashion as her sleeveless dress, creased and puckered and wrinkled. Her blond hair was gray now, filled with split ends and tangles. Looking at her, it was hard to believe that she had once been a beautiful woman. Not that many years had passed, but it seemed she'd aged ten with every one that had gone by on the calendar.

"Evening, Mrs. Gradduk," I said. Evening. As if I'd dropped by for a glass of lemonade and a chance to discuss the weather and the kids.

She tightened her hand on the knob, and I couldn't help but stare at it, waiting for the bones to splinter.

"What the hell do you think you're doing here?"

A fine question. I licked dry lips and ran a hand through my hair, my eyes on the fresh planks beneath my feet.

"Well?" she said.

"I didn't know you were living here, too," I said, just to fill the silence with something.

"I asked what you want."

I straightened up and looked her in the eye again. "I guess I'd like to find Ed. Maybe I can . . . maybe I can help him."

"Help him? *Help* him?" She took a half step out onto the landing, peering up at me, her mouth twisted with distaste. "You're the one to blame for this, you know? He made one mistake and then you *ruined* him. He was never the same."

"That was a long time ago," I said. "I can't fix that. But I hear Ed's in a lot of trouble now. I'd like to find him."

She leaned back and glared at me. "You even spoken to him in the last ten years?"

It hadn't been ten years, but I also hadn't spoken to him. I didn't answer, just stood there awkwardly before a woman who'd once baked me cookies and was now look-

ing at me as if she'd like to sink her teeth into me, pour
venom into my veins.

"What the hell do you think you can do, you asshole?"
she said, and I was struck by her language, the stream of
profanity. In all the years I'd known Alberta Gradduk, I
couldn't think of one time I'd heard her swear. "The police
have it all on tape. He did it, you know. He set that fire and
burned that girl up. And you want to know why he did it?"

I didn't answer.

"Because it's what he turned into after you turned your
back on him. He made a mistake. People make mistakes.
And you were supposed to be his friend. His best friend."

"I did what I was required to do, Mrs. Gradduk. I'd
taken an oath, and it didn't stop with friends."

"What do you think you can do now?" she said, and
while there was still hostility in her voice, there was also
a hint, however vague, of hope.

"I don't know." Down the street, the shouts and the
music were getting louder, the party picking up steam. I
took a glance at the Crown Victoria at the curb, saw the
streetlight reflecting off the tinted windshield, then
looked back at Ed Gradduk's mother.

"I know attorneys, and I know the police," I said. "I'm
an investigator now. I don't know what the situation was,
but I do know he's only doing himself more harm by running. He needs to come in and get legal help, get some
people behind him. I can help him with that. Right now,
he's just getting himself into more trouble."

"And you'd know all about getting him into trouble."

"Listen," I began, but she wasn't having it.

"Get away from my house," she said, stepping back inside. I saw for the first time that she was barefoot, the
veins on her pale feet standing out stark and thick and
purple against the skin.

"I can help him if I can find him," I said, and somehow I believed it, though I had no reason to. "Where would he go, Mrs. Gradduk?"

But she closed the door then, the old windowpane rattling as it slammed. I heard the bolt roll shut and the security chain slip into place. For one wild moment I was ready to lean back and slam my foot against the door, kick it again and again until it was open and I could grab the crazy old bitch and shake her and tell her that it wasn't my fault, it had never been my fault, Ed had screwed up and I'd had no choice but to be the one who made him accountable. It's tough to raise that kind of anger and conviction over something you're not entirely sure you believe, though. I turned and walked back down the steps.

His closest friend was Scott Draper. It had been me once, but that was long in the past, and Draper had lingered as a presence in Ed's life while I had not. At least four years had passed since I'd seen Draper, but he wouldn't be hard to find; the Hideaway on Clark Avenue had been in his family for three generations, and unless the building had crumbled around him, he'd be there now.

To get there, I had to walk west down the street, past the Crown Vic. I was about ten feet from it when there was the soft purr of a power window, and a drawling voice said, "How's it going, partner?"

"Fine," I said, walking past, but then the door opened and one of the car's occupants stepped out onto the sidewalk in front of me. I pulled up and looked at a cop whom I'd never seen before. If he knew me, he didn't show it.

"Nice night, huh?" he said, leaning against the car. I glanced in the vehicle, trying to see the face of the man in the passenger seat, but it was too dark.

"Fine night," I said, trying to step around him and continue on my way. He stepped with me, though, and I pulled up again.

"Mind my asking what your business with Mrs. Gradduk was?" He was tall enough that I had to look up at him, into a face that was set in a hard scowl, dark brown eyes looking at me coldly. It wasn't the eyes that held my attention, though, but his nose. It was swollen and purple, the bridge askew beneath the puffiness, the discoloration spreading into his eye sockets. He'd had his nose broken very recently. Probably by Ed Gradduk, if Amy's information about his fight with police had been accurate.

"Expressing my condolences," I said. "Heard her son had a run of bad luck today."

"Or caused one," the cop said. "What's he got to do with you?"

"I'm his priest," I said, and stepped away one more time. He reached out and put his hand on my arm, but I twisted free and kept going.

I should have stopped and talked to him. I should have explained the situation for exactly what it was, tell him that I was an old friend with no idea what I was doing here, chased by bad memories. Tell him that I'd been a cop, too, maybe swap a few stories about long nights on stakeout duty. Everything about the evening had suddenly become surreal, though, twisted and strange. And so, even while I told myself to stop and clear the air, I lengthened my stride and pulled away. He did not pursue me.

I walked west on Clark for several blocks, past the Clark Recreation Center, an ancient brick building that had started as a bathhouse around the turn of the century. For decades now it had been a rec center, and I remembered many furious basketball games played on the small court inside, a handful of onlookers watching from the balcony that ringed the court. Tonight a group of Hispanic teens sat on the steps and watched me go past. The neighborhood was shifting more and more toward the Hispanic and Puerto Rican populations now, but it had been even when I was growing up. Beside the kids was a vacant lot, nothing left but a concrete pad where a house had once stood. I remembered the house, and seeing the lot empty made me feel much older than my years.

The Hideaway was just west of the rec center, tucked in a narrow building with a crumbling brick facade and a PABST BLUE RIBBON sign hanging in the window. I hesitated on the cracked sidewalk for a moment, looking up at the familiar structure. First place I'd been served a beer. I was fourteen—something the bartender had been well aware of—and I'd knocked the neck of my bottle together with Ed's before I'd downed it. Budweiser, of course. That's what you choose to drink when you're fourteen; it's got to be called the King of Beers for a reason, right? I'd spent countless hours in the place growing up, and I remembered the interior of the bar as well as my old house. Upstairs, there was a storeroom and an attic, but those windows were dark tonight. Whatever business had been next door was gone, the space empty now. I went up the steps and entered the bar.

Inside, the room seemed long and narrow, with cramped booths lining the walls and cigarette smoke hanging in the air. A broken jukebox sat beside a pay phone on the back wall. This was the dining room, and although I could remember some booths as the permanent residences of local boozehounds, I didn't remember anyone doing much dining here. A Hideaway cheeseburger was considered a real risk; the sirloin steak, for no one but the foolish or suicidal. They could pour a cold Bud or PBR, though, fill a glass with Jack, and that's all anyone there tended to need.

Through the doorway to my left was the bar, a long expanse of oak lined with vinyl-covered stools, the way a bar is supposed to be. Behind the bar was a massive shelving unit with liquor bottles stacked in front of a long mirror, and at the end of it stood two pool tables. Both were in use now, and only a handful of the barstools were occupied. A white kid in a sleeveless shirt and toboggan-style hat was manning the bar. Summer, and he's wearing a toboggan. Tough.

"What can I get you?" he said.

"Your boss," I answered, and he frowned.

"'Scuse me?"

"Scott Draper still own this place?"

A slow nod. "Uh-huh."

"Well, go get him."

He didn't like the commanding quality of my tone, but he responded to it, walking out from behind the bar and toward the steps at the rear of the building. He paused on the first step and looked back at me.

"Who's here for him?"

"Lincoln Perry." The guys at the bar were watching the exchange, but my name didn't seem to mean anything. It had been a while since I'd spent any time in the Hideaway.

The kid went up the stairs and I settled onto a stool with a split vinyl cover. The television above the bar had the Indians game on, the Tribe down two in the bottom of the seventh with bases loaded and the cleanup hitter at the plate. First pitch was low and away, but he swung and caught air. Second pitch, same location, same result. Third pitch a heater right down the middle and he sat on it for called strike three.

"Lincoln."

I looked over my shoulder. Scott Draper was as I'd remembered—tall, thick, and bald. He had a natural sort of muscle; as far as I knew, he'd never set foot in a gym, but he could probably bench-press a Honda if he needed to. He'd been shaving his head since we were kids.

"Long time, brother," he said, extending his hand. His voice was warm, but his eyes didn't show anything one way or the other.

"Has been," I said, shaking his hand, his palm rough and calloused against mine. "Good to see you've kept the place running."

"Would've closed down a year ago, but I couldn't convince these drunks to go home," he said loudly. The men beside me laughed, one of them giving Draper the finger. Regulars.

I gave it a half smile, then said, "You heard about Ed?"

He let his eyes linger on mine for a moment, then looked up at the television, a beer commercial playing, and picked up a pack of cigarettes that lay on the bar. I didn't think they were his, but nobody said anything. He shook one out, took a Zippo from one of the guys at the bar, and lit it.

"I heard," he said when he'd taken his first drag.

"It doesn't sound good," I said.

He shook his head and blew smoke at me. "Not good. Some serious shit, is what it is. Murder. Plus arson, but at that point who cares?"

I nodded. "Cops come down here?"

"Not long ago, actually. Asked a lot of questions, I told 'em where they could stick it, they made some noise about building inspections and liquor licenses, you know, trying to be heavy about it. Then they left."

"They caught up with him and he got away, is the way I hear it."

"That's the way they tell it, yes." He put his eyes back on the television. After a brief period of silence he flicked them back at me. "And what's it got to do with you, Perry?"

"Not a damn thing."

"But you're here?"

I nodded. "Figured if I could find him, I might be able to help him out."

He raised an eyebrow, amused. "Help him?"

I wasn't sure if he was entertained by the notion that I would try to help Ed, or that I thought I could.

"I don't know how," I said. "But he's not doing himself any good taking off like this. They'll catch up with him eventually, and then it'll go harder than ever."

The game was back on, taking the attention of the drinkers at the bar again, so we were alone even in the group. Draper put out his cigarette and frowned at me.

"You haven't said a word to him in all these years, have you?"

I shook my head. "Tried once," I said, and then, after a beat of silence, "but not very hard."

"And yet you drive down here as soon as you hear about this shit? Feel the need to involve yourself?"

I understood his disbelief, because I was feeling it, too. But all I could do was nod.

"Well, I guess that's a hell of a nice thing for you to do," he said. "But I don't know what to tell you, Lincoln. I don't know where he is. If he shows, I'll tell him the same thing you'd tell him—to go turn himself in."

"If anybody can get in touch with him, Scott, it's you. I'd like to talk to him."

He kept his eyes on the television but I could see the muscles in his chest and shoulders tighten.

"Listen," he said, "you already know how I feel about the way you dicked Ed over to help your career. But you've stayed out of the neighborhood and out my bar since then, and, shit, we were friends once. Because of that I thought I'd do my damnedest to be cordial when you showed up here. But you're making that awfully hard, Lincoln."

"I appreciate the attempt at cordiality," I said, "however poorly executed."

"Please don't make me . . . ," he began, but before he could get any further, Ed Gradduk came down the stairs that led up to the storeroom and shouldered his way past the crowd at the pool table.

CHAPTER 3

I watched Ed walk toward us, and when Draper saw my face, he turned and swore under his breath.

Ed was wearing jeans and a white T-shirt. There was blood on the shirt and a nasty gash over his right eye. His hair was tousled and long, and beneath it his face was tan and smooth. Not yet thirty, and facing life in prison, if the jury went easy.

"A friend in need," he shouted as he approached, and it took only those four slurred words to let me know he was hammered. "Where does that put me, Lincoln? I'm in need, my man, that's for damn sure. But you a friend? Shit."

Draper put his hand out and caught Ed's shoulder, trying to turn him and send him back up the steps, but Ed shrugged it off. His movements and his speech showed he was drunk, but his blue eyes were sharp and piercing. When we were kids, people used to take us for brothers, with the same dark blond hair and bright blue eyes.

"What are you doing here?" he said.

"I heard you were in some trouble."

"Some trouble? You jerking me off, man? Some *trouble*?" He looked at Draper and laughed wildly, but Scott didn't crack a smile. He was glancing at the door, probably thinking that a cop could step inside at any moment, that there might be one watching the bar from the street.

"He's taking a few hours to get himself together," Draper said to me, eyes still on the door. "Had to get his mind in order, sober up, cool off. Maybe call an attorney, maybe get his hands on a car and bail." Draper snapped his eyes back to me and now they were hard and unfriendly. "I'm not going to make the call, Lincoln. Wasn't when he showed up, and I won't now."

"Nobody's making any calls just yet," I said. Ed was watching me with a leering grin, swaying like a sailor on board a pitching ship.

"The hell you doing here?" he said, and his voice was filled with wonder and not anger. "I mean, *damn,* Lincoln. You just gotta be there when I go down, huh? Gotta soak it up, savor it?"

I met his eyes, and I waited for my own response, waited for the words to form themselves into something that would get through to him, tell him how it had been for me, tell him why I'd had to do it. The words didn't come, though. After eight years of waiting for them, I shouldn't have been surprised.

"Good luck, Ed," I told him, and then I turned and walked for the door.

He started after me, and when Draper tried to pull him back, Ed told him to stay the hell inside. I pushed the door open and stepped out into the cooling air, stood on the sidewalk with my hands at my sides and my eyes on the ground while Ed joined me. He took out a cigarette and lit it, and we stood there together in silence. The smell of the alcohol was heavy on him, but somehow I had the sense his mind was sober right now.

"They execute a guy for murder in Ohio, don't they?" he said.

"Sometimes."

He nodded and smoked some more.

"Sometimes they don't," I said. "Depends on the circumstances. What are yours?"

He laughed, and it was a menacing sound, so empty it chilled me to the core.

"What are my circumstances?" He laughed again. "Oh, man. You don't even want to hear about it, Lincoln. They are not clean. I can tell you that. They are not clean."

He began to walk down the sidewalk then, swaying and weaving but moving fast enough, and he motioned for me to follow with a jerk of his hand. I shot a glance down the street, looking, as Draper had, for a police presence. When I saw none, I followed.

"My circumstances," he said around the cigarette, "are a little difficult to explain. I hear there's a videotape of it, though, and that's all the jury needs to see. If a picture is worth a thousand words, then what's a video against words from an ex-con? Probably worth a million of those. A guy like me could run the world dry of words, still not have enough."

The breeze picked up, rustling the trash and gravel on the sidewalk and sending dust and bits of fine dirt into our eyes. I blinked against it, ducked my shoulders, and put my head down.

"What happened, Ed?"

He worked on the cigarette for a while, and when I glanced at him the gash above his eye was brighter than it had been, the wound opening up again and spilling more blood.

"In the beginning," Ed Gradduk told me, "it was all about money. The revenue stream, as my old man would have called it. I found one, buddy. It was already there, but I got my piece of the action, played my role, and took my cut. All you can ask, right?"

I didn't answer, and we walked on in silence for maybe a block, Ed sorting out his thoughts.

"So it was money," he said. "A lot of money to some people, less to others."

"And to you?"

"Enough to me. It was enough. But then . . ." The menacing laugh came again, and with it the temperature seemed to drop ten degrees. "Then it stopped being about money. Got personal."

"Why?"

He stopped walking and looked at me, tilting his head to the side.

"A man told me a story."

I raised my eyebrows. "What story?"

"The one he didn't want to tell," Ed answered. "And I do feel bad about that. It was hard on him, because he knew it'd be hard on me. Stuff like that, well, it doesn't tell easy, Lincoln. But I guess that's how it goes. The stories that matter most are the hardest to tell."

"Did you kill the woman?"

He blew smoke wearily. "I did not kill the woman. And I don't give a damn if they have a video or a picture or a thousand eyewitnesses to whatever it is they say happened, Lincoln—that's not how it went down."

"I can help you, Ed," I said, and he raised his eyebrows and snorted. "I can help you, but you've got to tell me the whole score. Give me the names, give me the facts, lay it out there."

His eyes had drifted past me, over my shoulder and into the houses behind me. He pointed at them with his cigarette.

"Andy Butcher used to live in a house up that street. 'Member him? Crazy little shit. We were standing out in his front lawn that day the bus from the Catholic school went by." He laughed and smiled, seemingly carefree, just another guy out for an evening stroll. What murder charge? Nope, not me.

"The bus from the Catholic school goes by, and one of those shirt-and-tie boys tosses a bottle at us? You remember it; I know you do. Little prick throws a bottle at us, and it hits the grass instead of the sidewalk, doesn't bust. And Andy, shit, he picks it up and takes off running. Bus must be doing twenty miles an hour, but he catches up to it."

I remembered it, the scene playing through my head now like a movie clip: Andy Butcher sprinting after the bus with the bottle in his hand; the bus slowing because a car had just swung out of a driveway in front of it. Andy making a jump right at the side of the bus, Ed and I standing back in the yard with our mouths hanging open, staring in amazement, as Butcher hooked his left arm through the half-opened bus window and hung there, clinging to the side of the moving bus while he brought the bottle in with his right hand and smashed it against the stunned Catholic school kid's face.

"Man, we ran like hell," Ed said.

I nodded, and somehow I wanted to smile, even though this was no time to reminisce. "We did," I said. "The bus driver got out, started chasing us, screaming about getting the police."

We'd gone probably twenty blocks that day before any of us had the sense to cut in one direction or the other, get out of the driver's line of sight. Ran through a few yards until we collapsed in a heap, laughing our asses off and exchanging high fives.

"Butcher, he was one hell of an athlete," Ed said. "Never played an organized sport in his life, but he could catch a moving bus and hang in the window. Amazing."

"Ed, you've got to tell me what happened," I began, not wanting to talk about Andy Butcher anymore, but he held up his hand and interrupted again.

"People talk about memories like they're the best things in the world, Lincoln. They love the word, love the feel of it, say it with this breathlessness, all nostalgic and shit. *Memories,* they say. Oh, how I love those memories."

He tossed his cigarette to the pavement and ground it out under a well-worn Nike. "Sometimes, they hurt." He looked up at me. "Memories, I mean. I know there are good ones, but bad ones? Man, that's the worst. You'd do whatever you could to put them away, drive them out of your mind, lock them out for good. But you can't do that. They'll keep coming back, and, Lincoln, those suckers can *hurt.* It's like your memory's bleeding, you know? And you can't do anything but give it some time, wait for it to clot. Can't stitch it up. Just got to wait it out."

"Ed"—I tried to fill my voice with some of the commanding tone I'd used on the bartender—"give that talking-in-riddles shit a rest, all right? Maybe you didn't want to see me down here, but I came, anyhow. And if you want my help, I'll do the best I can. But you got to tell it to me."

He started walking again, and while his steps seemed a little surer now than they had when we'd left the bar, it still wasn't difficult to tell he was drunk. His eyes looked sober, though, and his face had a serious cast that told me his mind was—finally—very much in the moment.

"You don't need to be a part of this, Lincoln," he said. He still moved with shuffling steps, his feet seeming not to come off the ground at all. It was the way he'd walked when he was twelve.

"I know that."

"I went to the prosecutor," he said. "You know what he told me?"

"I don't know, Ed."

"Told me to go home and keep myself out of trouble. Told me he had enough problems without a con like me coming to him with wild schemes and rumors. You believe that? The man's paid with taxpayer cash, Lincoln, and he sent me out of his office. Told me to stay out of trouble."

"Why'd you go to the prosecutor?"

"I'll tell you something else—I tried to do it the right way. The *legitimate* way, you know?" His eyes had a milky cast to them again, wandering, fading back into the recesses of his booze-addled brain. "I tried. And they sent me home and told me to stay out of trouble. Then I said the hell with it. I'll get them to take a look one way or the other, right? Because, Lincoln, the man needed somebody to bring it back to him. One way or the other."

A car was drifting up the street behind us. I was looking at Ed's face, but he turned to glance at the car, and when he did, his eyes went flat.

"Shit."

I turned and looked myself, and when I did, I echoed him. It was the Crown Vic that had been parked outside his mother's house. The cops realized we'd seen them, and the driver punched the accelerator, closing the gap with a squeal of rubber. A flashing bubble light came on at the top of the windshield, and Ed Gradduk ran.

"Don't run—let them take you in, and we'll go from there," I yelled, but he ignored me. I ran after him and tried to grab him, hating the cops for showing up just when Ed was beginning to explain things. My hand caught a piece of his shirt, and when I tugged it, he spun off-balance before twisting away from me. The loss of balance sent his right foot off the sidewalk and into the street. I saw him glance up at the minivan that was traveling in his direction, then back at the Crown Vic coming from the opposite side. He looked at them both, then tried to run across the street as I lunged after him again. He made it a couple of steps, but there was too much alcohol in his bloodstream for such rapid movements, and halfway across Clark Avenue his feet tangled beneath him and he went down.

The Crown Victoria driver had been pushing it, trying to get in front of Ed and block his path across the avenue. When Ed fell, the driver didn't slow immediately, his reaction time poor. When he finally did register what had happened, he locked up the brakes, but far too late. The car rode the skid into and over Ed Gradduk.

I stood on the curb and screamed something that was supposed to make sense but came out like the howl of a wounded animal, and then I ran into the street, too. Ed's body lay under the car, and the stupid son of a bitch in the driver's seat put it in reverse and backed up, rolling the front wheels over Ed once more. I screamed again, and then the car was in park and the cops were clambering out it, shouting at me to keep back. I ignored them and ran toward Ed, reached under the car for him.

I had my hands on Ed's shoulders when the cop who'd been driving grabbed me and tried to pull me back, shouting at me to get out of the way. I spun and put my right fist into his stomach without thinking about it, then crawled back under the car while he doubled over. Ed's body was only partially covered by the front end of the Crown Vic, and as I tugged him free, I knew he was dead—blood was flowing from his nose, mouth, and even his ears, the flesh ripped and scraped, bits of the skull stark and white against the blood and torn skin. I got only a glance before the second cop wrapped his arm around my throat and pulled me back, pushing the barrel of his gun in my ear.

There was more shouting then, but I don't remember what was said. Some of it was directed at me, some of it was from me. The cops were shoving me away, and I was screaming in their faces. The middle-aged woman who'd been driving the van from the opposite direction got out of her vehicle, took one look at Ed, dropped to her knees, and vomited in the street. More cars had gathered now, and people were standing on the curb, watching the scene. One of them was moving forward, and I turned away from the cops in time to see Scott Draper just before he threw a punch at my head.

"You shoved him!" he screamed. "You shoved him!"

"He ran," I shouted back, and he swung at me again as the cops tried to get in our way. "I tried to *stop* him, you stupid bastard."

He was still trying to get at me. I grabbed him by the shoulders and knocked him backward onto the pavement. I would have gotten a punch in if the cop who'd been driving the Crown Vic hadn't caught my wrist. He slammed me onto the ground next to Draper. That's where I remained while they put the handcuffs on— facedown on the street, my right cheek against the road, my left eye watching a trickle of Ed Gradduk's blood work its way toward me, cutting a determined path over the pavement as if its last mission were to touch my flesh.

CHAPTER 4

They let me go home around midnight. Charges of interference and obstruction had been threatened but I had not been booked. The cop who'd been in the passenger seat, a guy named Larry Rabold, lightened up once he learned who I was, but his partner, the one who had stopped me on the sidewalk, was not so fraternal. His name was Jack Padgett, and he didn't show any desire to let bygones be bygones once he found out I had been a cop. They talked to me for about an hour, asking all about Ed, particularly what information might have been exchanged in our brief conversation. They seemed unconvinced by my claim that I hadn't spoken to him in years.

"Why the hell did you come running down to his house as soon as you heard the news, then?" Padgett had asked. It was a good question, one I'd already failed to answer earlier in the night, and I still hadn't come up with anything satisfactory. They'd both been intrigued by my description of how things had gone down with Ed and me a few years back, and I knew they'd check it out and see if they could find anything to indicate I'd had contact with the man since then. They would come up empty, though.

Once I was kicked loose, I called a cab to take me back to my truck. Clark Avenue was dark and quiet save for a few stragglers on the sidewalk and one woman waiting for a bus. I stood at the curb and stared up the street to where my oldest friend had died a few hours earlier. They'd hosed the blood off the pavement, and the night heat had already baked it dry.

I climbed inside the truck and started the engine, sat there listening to the traffic noise, and wondering if I'd be able to drive without seeing visions of Ed running into the street. I took a look at the clock. It was time to go home and go to bed.

I drove to my partner's house.

Joe Pritchard lives on Chatfield, maybe three minutes from the office. He was in the neighborhood long before I arrived, and it was through him that I learned of the gym I own when it went up for sale. Recently dismissed from the police force and with no real career plans, I'd purchased the gym and moved into the building. Joe's retirement a few years later had led me into the PI trade.

His house is a brick A-frame that is common in the neighborhood, two blended triangles with a chimney rising along the front wall. I once heard that the houses were all products of Sears Roebuck kits that became popular as the neighborhood expanded following World War II, but I don't know if there's any truth to that. The neighborhood around Chatfield has been maintained better than most, although the majority of parents send their children to private schools rather than enrolling them in the public system. That was the case when I was growing up, too, but my father couldn't afford it—and had no desire to send me to one of the private schools even if he could. If I couldn't make it in a public high school, he often said, how the hell was I going to make it as a cop? Even then, it was what I told everyone I was going to do, and my father was right—four years at West Tech were invaluable to that career acclimation.

Joe's house is the shining star of a nice block, with a perfectly manicured lawn, gleaming windows, and a cobblestone path between the house and the sidewalk. Quite the homemaker, our Joe. Most of the backyard and a stretch between the driveway and the house are filled with beautiful flower gardens, heavy on the impatiens. There's a garage behind the house, stocked with rakes and hoes and potting soil and fertilizer, and if you want to find Joe on a Saturday or Sunday afternoon, you need only look in the yard or in the garage. When we'd worked the narcotics beat together, it hadn't been that way. Joe's wife, Ruth, tended to the flowers and yard as if they were her reason for living, but Joe never did much more than shovel the driveway, and then only in the heaviest snows. It was winter when Ruth died, and when spring broke the next year, Joe hated the idea of seeing her flower gardens fail to appear in the fashion to which the neighbors had become accustomed. Now I think he spends more time on them than Ruth ever did.

He met me at the door with a wary look, but it was clear he'd still been awake, which I'd expected. Joe is late to bed and early to rise and always alert despite that. There are some qualities you don't leave behind after thirty years of police work. Poor sleeping patterns are among them.

"It's after midnight," he said, closing the front door and following me into the living room, "and you wouldn't show up here at that time just for small talk. So that makes me think this is case-related, and that troubles me. Why? Because the only cases on our plate are small-time, and you wouldn't need to discuss them at this hour. So I'm guessing you've decided to involve yourself in whatever shit went down with your convict buddy."

Took him maybe ten seconds to reason that out.

We sat in the living room and I asked him if he'd seen

the news, if he'd seen the footage of Ed Gradduk on his way to do murder. He told me that he had.

"You remember anything about the guy?" I asked.

His eyes flicked off mine momentarily. "You kidding me? It was the first case we ever worked together, LP. And in all the cases we've worked since, I've never seen you so locked in. You were robotic about it. I liked working with you, could tell you had ability, but at the same time I was a little concerned about your emotional stamina. You seemed burned-out already, like an old cop who's hung on five years too long."

I nodded.

"I remember it didn't go the way you'd expected it to go," Joe continued. "And the kid took a fall. But that wasn't your fault. He had options. Not your fault he decided against cooperating."

I was silent.

"There's more to it than you ever told me," Joe said. "And it involves the girl."

I looked at him, surprised. He was waiting for a response.

"There's more to it," I said. "And it involves the girl. But not in the way you're thinking."

He shrugged. "Whatever. That's not the issue of the night, though. Tell me what happened."

I took him from Amy's phone call to the scene in the street to my interview with Padgett and Rabold. I realized halfway through the story that I was rubbing my temples, trying to drive away a headache that I didn't consciously feel.

"I'd ask you why you ended up going down to Clark Avenue," he said when I was through, "but I expect you don't really have an answer for that."

"Accurate expectation."

Joe stared at the muted television. It was tuned to ESPN Classic, as it always seems to be, and the network was airing a basketball game between the Bulls and the Jazz from sometime in the late nineties.

"Rough seeing a guy die like that," he said. "Especially when it was a guy you used to be close to."

"Uh-huh."

"I'm taking it this abbreviated conversation with Gradduk meant something to you. Makes you, what, curious? Skeptical?"

"Makes me think the guy could have been set up."

"But he told you it was all on tape."

"Well, it is all on tape. Amy, Ed, and the cops all agree on that point. You just said you saw it on the news."

"So he murdered the girl."

"He said he didn't."

"But the police have a tape of him setting this house on fire. The same house from which a body was recovered."

"Yeah."

"Cut-and-dried," he said, but I knew he was too good a detective to buy that for even a minute.

"Who was the woman?" I asked. "I don't even know her name."

"Anita Sentalar. They had a long feature about her on the news tonight. She's a thirty-seven-year-old attorney, good-looking, intelligent, single."

"And the connection to Gradduk?"

"Undisclosed, as of yet."

"Maybe she was already in the house, dead."

He snorted. "Oh, yeah, I like this idea. Someone else kills her, leaves her in the house, and Gradduk just happens to come by and set fire to it, concealing the body? What, he's trying to do someone a favor by torching the place? Insurance on that dump wasn't worth a thing, from what I've heard."

"What's the tape show?"

"Shows him going into the house and coming back out. Shows his face pretty clear. Shows his car, and apparently they could zoom in enough to get a plate number off it."

"And the fire?"

"House went up about twenty minutes after he left it. There was a small explosion of sorts before the flames, I guess. Fire investigators think he used a timer and an incendiary device."

"Twenty minutes? Damn, Joseph, that's a hell of a lot of time."

"Camera didn't show anyone else going into the house after him, though."

"Camera had a panoramic angle on the house? Covered every side at once?"

He sighed. "Just the front."

"So a dozen people could have waltzed in and out the back door during those twenty minutes?"

"Maybe. But what's Gradduk doing in a vacant house in the first place if he's not the guy who set it on fire?"

"That," I said, "is what I'd like to look into."

Joe sighed again and leaned back in his recliner, rolling the footrest out and up. I was sitting forward on the couch, elbows on my knees, watching him. Joe was the best cop I'd ever worked with, and he was my business partner. If I was going to get started with this thing, I wanted his support, for both reasons.

"He told me he went to the prosecutor, Joe. Said he went there and was sent home. At the very least, I want to talk to the prosecutor. See what Gradduk went in there with."

"If he sent Gradduk home," Joe said, "it was probably with good reason."

We sat together in the dark living room and watched the muted old basketball game, Michael Jordan slicing his way through the lane, tossing in off-balance shots and drawing fouls.

"This guy Gradduk," Joe said, "was not the kid you re-member growing up with. He'd done time, and it looks like he should have been doing some more. Shitty brakes on a Crown Vic saved him the agony of years in a cell, and saved the taxpayers the cost of putting him where he belonged."

I didn't answer.

"Regardless of what he said to you, the man appears to have murdered someone, Lincoln."

"Appears."

"Why does it matter?" He grabbed the remote and snapped the television off. "If he did kill her, or didn't? He was never convicted of the crime, just suspected of it. The man is dead, LP, and dead he is going to stay, with or without your involvement. And, whether you choose to believe it or not, you did him no wrong. Not tonight, and not the time before that."

I sat and thought about everything I wanted to say to that, how I wanted to tell him that it went back to walking the same sidewalks and fighting the same guys and chas-ing the same girls, that it went back to twelve years of a bond that you simply can't match upon reaching adult-hood, not even with your partner.

"Ed never caught a break in his life," I said. "From the cradle to the grave, the guy was taking it on the chin. Did he earn it sometimes? Sure. Every time? Hell, no."

"And he's gone now. Can't help him anymore."

"It's not about helping him. It's about making sure someone else isn't getting away with something far worse than any of Ed's sins."

Silence.

"I watched him die tonight, Joe. A few hours ago. I watched it happen. And tomorrow morning when everyone turns on the news or opens their paper, all they'll think is—'Good, the guy was a killer and he got what he deserved.' "

He sighed and shook his head, looked past me out the dark window toward the rows of flowers his wife had planted and he still tended. You do things for the dead, even if you don't have to. Maybe because you don't have to. Joe knew that as well as anyone.

He stared at the window for quite a while, then turned back around and picked up the remote. He turned the television back on, settled into his chair, and put his attention on the game.

"We'll go see the prosecutor," he said, and that was all he said until I got to my feet and let myself out of the house.

CHAPTER 5

When my alarm went off at six that morning, I grabbed it, tore the cord from the outlet, and threw the clock into the closet. Then I remembered why I'd set the alarm so early in the first place. For a long moment I remained in bed, eyes squeezed shut, trying not to think about what I'd seen the previous night and what duty it had provided for me this morning. Sleep is a temporary shield, though, and I'd slipped from behind it. I got out of bed and went into the shower. Twenty minutes later I was out the door and on my way to break a heart that had been broken too many times already.

Allison Harmell lived in North Olmsted. Fifteen years earlier she'd lived on Scranton Road, a neighbor but not a classmate. Allison's parents came up with the cash to send her to a Catholic school, but she'd hung out more with the West Tech crowd than with her friends from school.

She was an accountant now, recently resigned from one of the large national chains to work independently. I'd learned this in the same way I'd learned everything else that had happened in Allison's life in the last eight years—through letters. We didn't talk on the phone because the silences that inevitably slid between us never felt as comfortable as they should have between old friends. We used to meet for drinks occasionally, always at a hotel bar in Middleburg Heights, in a room filled with strangers, but now those meetings had gone by the way-side, as well. These were the rules of contact that had developed between us as the years had passed, and while they were always unspoken, they were also rigid.

She worked out of her house, I knew, so I didn't have to rise so early simply to catch her at home. I was more interested in catching her before she turned on the television.

She came to the door within seconds of my knock, but she wore a robe and had her hair in a towel.

"Lincoln," she said, lifting a hand to her temple. "What in the world . . ." Halfway through the question she answered it for herself. "Something's wrong."

I nodded. "Yeah. Something's wrong."

Seeing her again, I regretted that I'd designated myself as the messenger. I'd known it wouldn't be any fun for me, but it had also seemed better than letting her hear it from some idiot television news reporter or as overheard conversation in a grocery store checkout line. Now I was struck by just how difficult the disclosure was going to be.

"He's in trouble," she said, stepping aside from the door. "I've already heard. But, Lincoln, he couldn't have killed that woman. He couldn't have."

"He didn't," I said. "But that doesn't matter anymore. Not where he's concerned."

I was inside the house now, following her through a tiny dining room and into a kitchen that smelled warmly of brewing coffee. Allison sat on a kitchen stool, the robe sliding off slim, bare legs.

"What are you talking about?"

"Ed's dead." I was standing in the kitchen doorway, tall and rigid, hands hanging at my sides.

"No. Dead? No. He's just in jail, Lincoln. They were going to send him back to . . ." The attempt died then, and she shut up and stared at me.

"It happened last night," I said. "I was there when he died. The cops came after him and he ran into the street. He was drunk and he couldn't make it across. They hit him with their car."

She didn't say anything, just reached up and slowly unwound the towel from her long blond hair. It fell to her shoulders, some of the wetter strands sticking to her neck.

"Three years and seven months," she said. Silence for a moment, and then: "That's how long it's been since I talked to him. I figured that out when I heard about the fire on the news last night. We saw each other once when he got out of jail, and then no more."

There was another long pause before she said, "So then I shouldn't be sad, right? Not really."

She started to cry then, softly and without theatrics, just a quiet supply of tears that she'd occasionally wipe with the back of her hand. I didn't move toward her. For a long time we remained like that—her crying on the stool, me standing with my hands at my sides in the doorway.

"Shit," she said eventually, sniffing back the last of the tears and shaking her head. "He's dead and I'm mad at him for that. Make any sense?"

"Yes."

She barked out a laugh that was still wet with tears and shook her head again. "Good. I'd hate to seem crazy."

The silence that followed lasted a few minutes. Then she took a long breath and said, "Now are you going to tell me how you ended up with him when he died? Because if it's been almost four years since I talked to him, it had been a lot longer for you."

"It had been longer."

"Tell me," she said. "Tell me why you were there, tell me how he looked, tell me what he said. Tell me how it was when he died."

Thirty minutes later we were still in the kitchen. The coffee had finished brewing but sat unpoured, and Allison's hair was air-drying and fanning out a bit with static. I was still standing in the doorway, refusing to cross the threshold and join her in the room.

"Did you believe him?" Allison asked.

"When he said he didn't kill her?"

"Yes."

"I believed that before he said a word. Ed was a lot of things, Allison, but a murderer wasn't one of them."

"People change. Especially when they . . ."

"When they spend years in jail," I said for her. She winced, but it wasn't because she'd stopped the sentence to protect my feelings. It was a whole lot more personal than that.

"Yes," she said. "That changes a person."

"Not that much. I don't believe it changes someone that much. But then I've never been to jail." I paused a second before saying, "For more than a night, that is," as if that detail mattered.

"He hadn't been in any trouble," she said. "Nothing since he got out. I watch the papers for his name."

"You have any idea what he *was* doing since then?"

She shook her head.

"Me neither," I said, and something in those two words made her cock her head and frown at me.

"You're going to find out, though, is that it?"

I shrugged.

"Are you?" she prompted.

"Would it be wrong if I did?"

She shook her head, her eyes watching me with a measure of pity. "No, Lincoln. But it's too late to make amends."

"You think that's what it's about? I don't have to make amends, Allison."

"Right," she said. "We never did. But I'm not sure you ever believed that."

"I did. I do."

She smiled slightly. "So tell me again why you went after Ed last night?"

"I wanted to help a friend."

"He wasn't your friend, Lincoln. Not anymore. Hadn't been for years."

"He's my friend."

"And you're his," she said. "That's what you wanted to prove. To him, to Scott Draper, to anyone who ever knew the two of you. To the whole damn neighborhood, whatever's left of it."

I looked at the wall behind her.

"I'm not discouraging you," she said. "I'm just reminding you of what you came here to tell me—he's dead."

"His name's not. It's still going strong right now, and headed in the wrong direction. You want the city to remember him as a killer?"

"No."

We were quiet for a while, and then she asked if I ever saw anyone from the old neighborhood.

I shook my head. "Some people sent cards or called after my dad's funeral. That was the old guard, though, most of them over fifty. As far as the kids we grew up with, no. You?"

She smiled at me the way you smile at someone who's just asked an utterly absurd question.

"No, Lincoln. I'm not thought of too highly around there."

"Neither one of us is, Allison."

She tried to make her tone light. "We did what we had to do, right? Just didn't work out the way anyone wanted it to. No regrets, Lincoln. No regrets."

There wasn't much more to say after that. I stayed in the kitchen with her a while longer. She finally poured the coffee. I drank mine while she cried over hers. She was dry-eyed again when I left.

"You look good, Lincoln," she said as she walked to my truck with me. "It's been a while since I saw you, too, you know."

"I know." I turned to her and gave her a hug. She squeezed me tightly and her fingernails bit into my back. I pulled away when I felt the first fresh teardrop on my neck.

"You're still the most beautiful woman I never wanted to sleep with," I said, and she laughed not because that was funny but because she knew it to be true.

She watched me climb into the truck, then motioned for me to put the window down. When I did, she said, "Call me, Lincoln. Tell me what you learn."

Her voice held both a note of pleading and one of command. It was a blend I'd heard before.

*T*he house is dark because the sun sets behind it, the long shadows in the room making it seem later than it really is. I'm on the couch. Allison is on her knees in front of me. Her elbows are braced against my thighs, her hands clasped. It's as if she is praying to me, and in a sense she almost is. Tonight I have been called upon to be a savior.

"You know I'm right," she says. "I've talked to him until I simply have run out of things to say. He's not listening. And he won't listen."

"He might," I lie. "You can't give up on him this easily, Allison. He loves you the same as ever. He's just . . ."

"He's just killing himself," she finishes for me. "You're trying to turn a blind eye to that, Lincoln, but you know it's true. You're the one who told me what Antonio Childers is like."

I turn away from her and stare at the wall. Antonio Childers is one of the great social menaces in our city, a drug dealer who is also a suspect in nearly a dozen unsolved homicides. For several months now, Ed Gradduk has been working for him. It started as petty shit, muling and couriering mostly, but it's escalated. Ed's in construction, had a run of bad luck with lost jobs and bad bosses, and apparently he found an alternative income source. I haven't seen much of him recently; I'm working nights for the Cleveland police, putting in as much overtime as possible, trying to get noticed and get promoted. That's how you make detective, I know, and that's what I intend to do.

"He's going to get killed," Allison repeats, and I avoid looking down directly into her face.

"I know," I say softly. Allison and I have had this conversation before. Ed and I have had this conversation before, too. He told me to keep my eyes on the other side of the street when I pass him in my cruiser, and otherwise things would be normal. I told him it couldn't work that way. We haven't spoken much since.

"He's gone all the time now," Allison says. "We've had calls at all hours of the night. Once a guy sat in front of the house in a van for hours, just waiting for Ed to come back."

They still live on the near west side, which is part of the problem. Childers has recruited Ed because Ed knows the neighborhood well, knows who to talk to and who to avoid, and works the streets with all the familiarity you want from a foot soldier. For the life of me, I cannot reason out how this began, how Ed could possibly have allowed himself to get involved with Childers.

"There's only one way to get him to listen," Allison says, and she reaches out and squeezes my upper arms to emphasize her point. "You told me you could arrange things if it came to that. I'm telling you it has come to that."

"Shit, Allison." I shake my head. *"He's got to talk for it to work. If he doesn't . . ."*

"He will. Trust me, Lincoln. If it comes down to a choice between freedom and jail, between me and a cell, he will make the right decision. You know he will. But until he's faced with that choice, I'm afraid he's going to keep looking at it as a game."

"He's got to talk," I repeat.

"He'll talk. He may not care enough to save himself right now, but if we press him to that point, Lincoln . . . if we put his back to the wall, he'll have to."

"We'll save him despite himself," I say sarcastically, but she nods with an equal amount of sincerity.

"Yes," she says. *"That's exactly what we'll do. But I need your help. You have to be involved, have to make sure he has the options. Are you sure you can do that?"*

I run my tongue across dry lips. *"I'm sure. There's a narcotics detective named Pritchard. Joe Pritchard. He's got a good reputation, supposed to be a hell of a cop. And he's got a serious hard-on for Antonio Childers. He's not going to send a small player like Ed to jail when he could trade that conviction for information about Childers."*

"So you'll do it."

I take a long look at her face, then look back at the window, the glass dark with growing shadows.

"Lincoln," she says, *"Ed is losing his life here. He's going to be killed or he's going to get sent to jail by someone else, someone who will see that he's kept there a long time. You know talking is not doing any good. We have to force to him to walk away from this."*

I swallow and get to my feet, step around her and into the middle of the living room, heading for the door.

"I'll call Pritchard tonight."

CHAPTER 6

When I got to the office, Joe had the little television on top of the tall filing cabinet tuned to a news station. I watched while a grim-faced announcer stood on the sidewalk on Clark Avenue, recounting the "brutal end to a tragic tale" that had occurred there the night before.

For a moment the screen was filled with a picture of Anita Sentalar: a smiling, beautiful young woman who appeared to be Puerto Rican. She had glossy dark hair framing a fine-boned, mocha-skinned face, and kind, intelligent eyes.

The next face we saw was a different extreme. Old, sour, and angry. Red-rimmed eyes narrowing on the camera in a glower. This was Anita Sentalar's father.

"What comment do I have on the death of Ed Gradduk?" he said, responding to the question he'd just been asked. "Are you kidding me? My comment is, fantastic. Good. Street graves are just what guys like that deserve. It doesn't bring my daughter back, though."

They switched from the Clark Avenue report back to the studio, where the anchor explained that no relationship between Gradduk and Sentalar had as yet been disclosed, and then told us we were about to see some "horrific footage" of the fire that had killed the female attorney on Train Avenue. I moved closer to the television screen and watched carefully.

The liquor store security camera had provided a crisp, black-and-white image of the sidewalk in front of it, and, in turn, the house across the street. It was a run-down home, a crumbling structure that had been left untended and empty.

The footage showed a man who walked down the sidewalk right in front of the liquor store, and the camera got a clear look at his face. It was unquestionably Ed Gradduk, and he was smiling while he crossed the street and disappeared along the side of the house.

"Now we'll move ahead seventeen minutes," the news anchor said, and the black-and-white footage jumped to a new clip. After a short pause, white flames showed themselves inside the house across the street, spreading with astonishing speed, licking their way up the walls and over the eaves.

"Plenty of time for someone else to have burned that house," I said.

"Sure," Joe answered, but he kept his eyes away from mine.

I turned the television off and sat down behind my desk. Joe looked at me and raised an eyebrow.

"Still a man on a mission?"

"If that means am I still going to see the prosecutor this morning, then, yes. But you don't have to come along if you don't want to get involved."

"If you're involved, I'm involved. You know that."

I gave a small nod.

"A guy called for you about an hour ago," Joe said. "Said it's about Gradduk."

"Give a name?"

"Scott Draper."

"Shit."

He frowned. "Why's that bad?"

"He's the one who took a swing at me last night, accused me of pushing Ed into the street. Ed had spent the evening hiding in the guy's storeroom, soaking himself in bourbon."

"Amy called, too. She sounded upset."

"I disappeared on her last night," I said. "I'll call her now."

I had to listen to about a five-minute lecture from Amy before I even had the chance to get a word in, but then I explained my situation. When I was done, I switched from taking all the questions to asking a few of my own.

"Any progress on the arson aspect?" I said.

"Fire investigators are still giving it a look. They'll probably make an announcement pretty soon, but they're waiting for lab results. Whoever did it was pretty good. Place went up in flames real fast and burned real hot."

"Now that Gradduk's dead, they'll probably write the case off," I said. "Say that justice has been served, if accidentally."

"I guess."

"You know who owned the house?"

"I think the city owned it, actually. Some urban-renewal deal. They buy up vacant property and mortgage foreclosures, fix them up, and put low-income families into them."

"I see. Who are the cops on the case?"

"Fire officials are assisting with the arson end of things. A Cleveland homicide cop is working it, too. Guy named Cal Richards. You know him?"

"Yes, but not well. He's supposed to be a hell of a good cop. Closes cases fast, and when he closes them, they're flawless."

"That sounds like the man," she said. "He did seem a little intense."

"Sure," I said, "the way a shark seems intense when it's about to feed. Is the coroner's office working to find out whether the victim was killed by the fire, or dead beforehand?"

"Lab results will take a while, but I think Richards suspects she was already dead."

"I expected that."

"The city fire investigators are swamped right now. Something like ten fires in the past two weeks, and more than half of those could be arson. They've got to check them all out. This one gets priority because there's a victim, but, still, they're spread thin."

"Maybe Joe and I will spur things along when we go visit the prosecutor today."

"Prosecutor?"

I told her of Ed's veiled comments about his interaction with the prosecutor.

"That guy is maybe the most popular person in the city right now," she said. "Hasn't announced his candidacy for mayor yet, but it's almost a sure thing that he will run."

"Think he'll win?"

"Probably. The way the city government's been leaking money the last few years, voters don't want another politician in there. They want an ass-kicker, and he fits that mold."

"You know him?"

"Fairly well."

"And?"

"And I think he's a politician," she said, and I could imagine her grin even though I couldn't see it. "Nice enough guy, sure. But that's in a face-to-face scenario. You leave his office and I bet the mood shifts real quick."

I'd never dealt with the current prosecutor, Mike Gajovich, directly, but I knew the crime rate had gone down on his watch and the conviction rate up. I'd heard grumblings that the conviction rate had more to do with petty drug arrests than anything else, though. When the

city budget had reached crisis status in the last year,
Gajovich had made himself something of a local hero
with his outspoken criticism of the current mayor, who'd
made cuts to police and fire department personnel even
while he was adding high-paid consultants to his own
staff. Gajovich's brother was in the department, as well,
and most of the cops I knew loved the guy.

"You have an appointment to see him?" Amy asked.

"No."

"Then you need my help. I'll call him and ask if he'll
agree to see us for a few minutes. My guess is he will.
Right now the guy is soaking up media attention whenever possible. You know, catering to the political bid next
year."

"Call him," I said. "We'll triple-team the poor bastard
and see if we can't get somewhere."

Amy called back within ten minutes and told me
she'd arranged a meeting with Gajovich at ten. I
thanked her and told her we'd meet her at the Justice Center. When I passed the news along to Joe, he
looked grim, but he stood up and slid his suit jacket over
his shoulder without a word of complaint.

"Last chance to back out," I said.

"I had my last chance the day before I asked you to be
my partner," he said. "I've been kicking myself ever
since."

"That's what I like most about working with you," I
replied, "the constant support."

The Cuyahoga County Prosecutor's Office is located
in the Justice Center, a twenty-six-floor building of
little aesthetic appeal that stands on Ontario Street,
casting a shadow over Cleveland Browns Stadium. The
building is also home to the police department's down-

town headquarters, but I decided not to drop in and say hello to the chief. There was no love lost between the two of us. The prosecutor and his minions were on the eighth and ninth floors of the building. Amy, Joe, and I took the elevator up and sat in the lobby together, waiting. Amy assured us we'd get in to see Gajovich without trouble.

"Trust me," she said, "I deal with this guy on a regular basis, and, happy family man or not, he's got wandering eyes. You tell him I'm on my way to his office, and he's on his way to greet me."

"Journalism at its finest," I said.

Amy shrugged. "Hey, not my fault most of our elected officials are lecherous jerks."

She made good on her promise. Hardly had the secretary gone to alert her boss of our arrival before Mike Gajovich stepped out into the lobby with a big grin on his face, looking right at Amy.

"What a lovely surprise," he said, walking toward her happily, and immediately my respect for him plunged. Prosecutors are supposed to be like cops, dodging the press whenever possible. I never trusted a cop who went out of his way to be friendly to a reporter, and the same notion lingered here.

Gajovich stepped right past Joe as if he didn't see him, offering his hand to Amy. When she took it, he covered her palm with both of his, still with that grin on his face.

"Gosh," I said to Joe, "it's almost like this guy doesn't recognize one of the most decorated cops in department history."

Joe didn't respond, looking bored with the whole scene, but Gajovich took his hands away from Amy's and looked at us for the first time. "I'm sorry," he said. "Are you gentlemen waiting to see me?"

"We're with her," I said, jerking a thumb in Amy's direction.

"Hey, that's great," he answered, his face making every word a lie. "How come you didn't tell me you were bringing backup, Amy?"

"Slipped my mind," she said. "This is Lincoln Perry, and that's Joe Pritchard. They're private investigators now, but both of them were cops at one time."

"Joe Pritchard, of course." Gajovich shook hands with Joe as if my partner had been sculpted from pure gold. "You're a law enforcement legend in this city. A pleasure to finally meet you." He turned to me and offered a limp hand. "And Lincoln Perry. I think I remember hearing about you, too."

"Got booted from the force for a night of drunken disorderly conduct and an assault on one of our better-known attorneys," I said helpfully. Hate to be forgotten.

Gajovich managed a smile. "I wasn't sure of the circumstances, and I doubt they're the reason for your visit now, so we don't have to get into it."

"Right."

"Come on back into my office and we'll have a talk. I'm really swamped today, but I promised Amy I'd clear a few minutes." He winked at her, and I wanted to kick him in the ass.

We went back into an office that wasn't particularly impressive aside from a gold-embossed nameplate on the desk that looked as if it weighed thirty pounds.

"Say, Amy, who's this new reporter covering the city beat?" Gajovich said, sitting down behind his desk and stretching his arms behind his head. He was in his late forties but looked ten years younger, with tousled blond hair and freckles that gave him a bit of Tom Sawyer charm. He was smooth and confident, and despite his leering at Amy I could see why people tended to like him.

His bearing suggested a genuine quality, and in government and administrative circles that's not something you
see every day. If and when he made a run for the mayor's
office, I wasn't going to bet against him.

"Andrew?" Amy said. "He got promoted from fea-
tures. Why, don't you like him?"

Gajovich grinned at Joe and me. "Can he spell my
name right? If so, then we're good."

He laughed, and we all joined in, as that was clearly
the thing to do.

"Hell," Joe said. "Could you blame him if he
couldn't?"

We all laughed some more then, just yukking it up to
start this meeting.

"So I should probably be nervous," Gajovich said,
leaning forward.

"Why?" Joe said.

"Two private investigators *and* a reporter? You kidding
me? This is a threatening group." He gave us the grin
again, and we all returned it. My face was already starting
to ache. In my business we don't do so much smiling so
early in the day. "What's on your minds?"

Amy turned in her chair and motioned to me. "It's really Lincoln's show. I'm along for the ride."

"Well, let me have it," Gajovich said, still showing us
his perfect teeth. We'd put him in such a good mood that
some lucky bastard was probably going to get a plea bargain this morning.

"Do you know a guy named Ed Gradduk?" I said.

The smile dissipated slowly, ice melting in the sun.

"Ed Gradduk," I repeated when he didn't answer.

Gajovich let out a sigh that nearly cleared his desk of
paperwork and leaned back in his chair. "You mean the
murderer?"

"I mean the guy who got run over by one of Cleveland's finest last night," I said. "Far as I know, nobody'd convicted him of murder yet. Or is that not required around here?"

"Getting fired in disgrace didn't do a whole lot to change your attitude, did it?" Gajovich said.

"I got fired quite a while ago, and that's got nothing to do with why we're here." Even as I spoke, I was amazed at how quickly the tone had changed. I mentioned Gradduk's name; Gajovich and I were adversaries. That fast, that simple.

He looked at Amy. "You know, I would have appreciated it if you'd given me an idea of what to expect here."

She spread her hands. "Hell, Mike, I didn't know what to expect. I'm just an interested observer."

For a minute no one said anything. When the silence was broken, it was by Joe.

"So I'm confused. Where's the hostility coming from?"

Gajovich didn't look away from me. "There's no hostility," he said. "Sorry if I gave that impression. Here's the deal: I'm not a big fan of this Gradduk fellow. He came into my office not long ago with some crazy idea, criticized me for not supporting him, and a few weeks later I find out he's an arsonist and a killer."

"What crazy idea did he come to you with?" I said.

"That's what you're here for?" Gajovich said.

"Yes."

"And what's your interest?"

"That of a concerned friend and citizen. You know, one of those taxpayers who provides your salary. And one who plans to vote in the next election."

He ran a hand through that boyish blond hair and smiled at me, but there was no Tom Sawyer in it this time. "I'm not a guy to screw with, Perry."

"Didn't come in here with the intention of screwing with anybody. Came here with a pretty simple question."

"You know," Gajovich said, "a lot of people forget that I am still a practicing attorney. That's what a prosecutor is, of course, an attorney. And people also forget that any legal conversations I have are protected by attorney/client privilege. They're private."

"Including the one you had with Ed Gradduk," Joe said.

Gajovich nodded. "Yes. I don't know what Gradduk told you, or what you heard. And I don't really care. Here's what I do know, and what I do care about: Gradduk was a criminal. He came in here with a record, and when I sent him away, he promptly went out and killed somebody. I regret that he was killed in that accident, and not just because it was an embarrassing moment for our police force. I regret that he was killed because it robbed me of the opportunity to see him prosecuted, to see him put back where he belonged."

"Hard-nosed," I said. "That'll appeal to the voters. You might pound on your desk with your fist, though. Add a little emphasis."

"Go to hell," Mike Gajovich told me.

For a long time we all sat there and said nothing, just traded stares. Outside, a printer was grinding away and women were laughing.

"I suppose this is the end of our meeting," Amy said at last.

"I suppose so," Joe answered when Gajovich didn't.

They got to their feet, but I stayed where I was, meeting the prosecutor's glare. Joe had his hand on the doorknob when Gajovich finally spoke again.

"I heard there was a stack of charges pushed under the rug for you in that Weston fiasco, Perry."

"People say the craziest things," I said.

"A situation like that can get messy."

"He threatens without threatening," I said. "Damn, but you are savvy, Mr. Gajovich. A politician's politician, I'd say."

"If I were you, I'd go back to your office and leave this one alone. That's all I'll say. Gradduk was a loser, Perry. So I'm not surprised to hear he was your friend. But losers don't have power, and losers don't attract sympathy from people who do have power. They attract trouble and then they're stomped out. You remember that."

CHAPTER 7

Amy went back to work and Joe and I went back to the office. I spent most of the ride burning over Gajovich's words, but even while they'd angered me, they'd helped me. I knew now I was going to have to return Scott Draper's call, after all. My knowledge of Ed's life effectively ended seven years before he died. I needed to talk to someone who'd been close to him, and Draper was the best option I had.

"Lincoln," Draper said when I identified myself, "thanks for calling me back, man. I wanted to apologize. That thing in the street, it was bullshit. The cops told me what happened, told me you didn't push him. From my angle, it looked like something it wasn't. Still, I should have better sense than to pull shit like that. I'm sorry."

"Don't worry about it."

"Look, you got a few minutes? Time to run down here and grab a beer?"

"A beer in the morning?"

"Doesn't have to be right now. Whenever you have a chance."

"I'll come down around noon."

I'd just hung up the phone when the door swung open and Detective Cal Richards stepped into the room.

He was a tall, lean black man with a face that was all hard angles and edges, like a wood carving. He wore black slacks with a blue shirt and matching tie, and a badge was clipped onto his belt. None of that stood out as much as the scowl on his face, though.

"Gentlemen," he said, easing into one of our client chairs. We have two standard client chairs and a set of wooden stadium seats from the old Cleveland Municipal Stadium, and he gave those a curious glance as he sat.

"How are you, Detective?" I said, offering my hand. He didn't take it.

"How are you, Detective?" he mimicked. "I'm a little pissed off, Perry. Pissed off that somehow you got kicked loose last night before I had a chance to talk with you, but for that I can blame an incompetent sergeant who thinks he's got authority just because he's old. But lest you think all the blame's headed in that direction, I'm also pissed off at you. I just got off the phone with a source who informed me you intend to run a parallel investigation into the Sentalar death without bothering to contact me."

I pulled my hand back. "That's not true."

"You're not investigating?"

I hesitated, and his gaze turned even more unfriendly. "I stump you with that one, Perry? I can speak slower."

Beside me, Joe was grinning. I gave him a glare and then looked back at Richards.

"I am not investigating in any sort of official capacity, Detective. Ed Gradduk was a friend of mine. A close friend, a long time ago. I saw him on the night that he died, and he talked with me briefly. You already know that from the police reports, I'm sure."

He nodded. "And now you want to fool around with this, compromise my investigation?"

"I have no intention of compromising anyone's investigation, and if I *am* investigating, I promise it won't be 'fooling around,' Richards," I said, a touch of hostility creeping into my own voice. "I'm pretty good at what I do. I was going to contact you this afternoon, so don't get all bent out of shape over my failing to notify you of my interest. It's a waste of our mutual time."

He loosened his tie and leaned back in his chair. "You interfere with this and I'll take you down hard, Perry. You know that, because you know my rep."

"And you know mine."

A slight smile played on his face. "Oh, yes. Yes, I do know your rep, friend." He jerked his head at Joe. "And your partner's, of course. Thirty years of distinction. You, Perry? Not so many."

"Should be enough," I said.

"It is enough," he said, "provided you don't get clever with me on this."

"Anything I know, you'll know, too."

He chewed on that for a while before speaking again. "Your buddy's been dead less than twenty-four hours and already you're on the move and concerning people. Makes me wonder what you know."

"Not a damn thing," I said. "And your source for this information couldn't be more obvious, because the only person we've talked to today is Mike Gajovich."

Richards smiled then, and something about the look made me think that if I had to pick just one man in the city that I would never cross, he would have to be close to the top of the list. Something in that smile spoke of a to- tal self-confidence and dangerous intuitiveness that few men possessed, and I knew at that moment that never in Cal Richards's life had he acted simply because it was what another man told him to do.

"Listen," he said, "Mike Gajovich has hardly given me the time of day before this morning. Then suddenly we're best friends and he wants to keep me apprised of something that could jeopardize my investigation. You want to know how I responded to that? By losing whatever respect I ever had for the man. Because as soon as he tells me this, I know he's made the call only to save his own ass. Why? I don't know. But don't think I'm buying it."

Joe looked at me and grinned as if to say, Isn't this guy a scream?

Richards said, "Here's what I'm going to tell you: Stay away from the Anita Sentalar murder investigation. I don't like freelancers stepping inside. However . . . if you want to dig up every last damn thing you can about Ed Gradduk's recent past, go for it. I know you two are capable investigators. It's very simple: You don't interfere with my work, and I won't waste my time on you. Sound fair?"

"Sounds fair," I said after pausing long enough to make his eyes narrow. "But can I ask you if there's anything to suggest the victim even knew Ed Gradduk?"

Richards took a deep breath, his broad chest filling with air. "I'll get back to you on that one."

"Come on."

He shook his head. "Sorry, Perry. That's the very thing I've been busting my ass on all day, and while I have a start, I'm not to the point where I want to throw around theories. When I nail their relationship down, I'll let you know."

"But they did have a relationship? Not total strangers?"

"Not total strangers," Richards said. "But I'm not taking more questions. Just stay the hell away from my murder investigation. You want to look at Gradduk, fine. Not Sentalar. Clear?"

"Clear."

He shifted his eyes to Joe. "You were a hell of a cop, Pritchard. Everyone knows that. I'm trusting you to keep your cowboy partner's heart in the right place."

"I'm usually too concerned with keeping his head out of his ass, but I'll try to worry about the heart, too," Joe said.

Richards turned back to me. "Now we're going to have an official talk. This is my murder investigation, and that incompetent asshole Padgett took it upon himself to conduct an interview with you and then put you back on the streets last night without ever bothering to check in with me. I've already put the fear of God into him, but I still need to hear what went down."

And so I told it again, a story I was already growing weary of telling. Richards asked more questions than anyone else had, so it took longer to tell, but in the end I couldn't provide him with anything more.

"Were you with Padgett and Rabold when they went to arrest Ed Gradduk?" Joe asked Richards when I was done.

He shook his head. "No. They got the tip from the liquor store owner, it seems. Not too surprising, considering those guys have worked that neighborhood for years. They got hungry for a headline, went in alone, and botched the arrest. Gradduk got away, and then your partner saw how well it turned out."

I willed away an image that came with sounds of squealing brakes and crunching bone.

"Yeah," I said. "I saw."

Richards got to his feet, and this time he offered his hand to me. "I owe you a shake. But take me seriously with this, and don't get in my way on this investigation." He released my hand. "I forgot how damn young you are. Have you even hit thirty yet?"

"Not yet, but I'm about to take a swing."

He pursed his lips and whistled noiselessly. "You must have been the youngest detective in department history."

"No. But I was close."

"Ever miss it?"

"Just pissing off the brass," I said, and he almost smiled before he left.

I t was harder for me to walk into the Hideaway this time. It had given me a moment's pause the night before, standing at the threshold of a building filled with memories. But that night I'd had a mission, and at its end was a chance to see an old friend. This time I would walk out of here alone.

Only a handful of people were at the bar when I stepped inside—two guys and three women, all of them smoking cigarettes and drinking Budweiser. When I opened the door, I sent sunlight spilling into the dark room, and everyone turned and squinted at me, expecting a familiar face. Those were the faces you saw most in the Hideaway, and that antiquated the place maybe even more than the ancient building itself. The kid from my last visit was behind the bar again, and Scott Draper was standing beside him, talking softly over the counter with an older guy who wore jeans and a silk shirt. I moved toward them, but before I got to the bar, someone spoke from behind me.

"The hell you think you're doing in here, prick."

I turned to see an old man with an ugly scowl set on his fleshy face sitting at one of the little tables across from the bar. He was maybe sixty, with thick gray hair and red-rimmed eyes, and he was staring at me like he wanted to break his beer bottle over my head.

"Good to see you, too, Bill," I said.

"Kiss my ass."

Bill Foulks had been in the neighborhood for every one of his sixty-some years on the earth, and as far as I knew, he'd never left for more than a week. He'd worked at one of the meat shops in the West Side Market when I was a kid, and he'd been one of Norm Gradduk's closest friends.

"Somebody invite you here, asshole?" he said. "You haven't had the balls to hang around here since you busted Eddie, but now that he's dead you think it's okay? Think something changed? Well, nothing has. Get the hell out."

I was opening my mouth to suggest Bill get his fat ass off the stool to make it easier for me to throw him through the window when Scott Draper stepped over.

"Give it a rest, Bill," he said.

Foulks looked at him with wide eyes. "You shittin' me, Scott? This prick's the guy—"

"I know damn well who he is," Draper said, his voice low and cold, "and I don't need to hear your opinion on him, either. Lincoln's here because I asked him to be."

Foulks gaped at him in disgust. "You telling me you *want* the son of a bitch down here?"

Draper wouldn't look at me. "He's here on business," he told Foulks, and then he motioned for me to follow him back into the dining room. Foulks glared at me and showed me his fat middle finger as I left.

I followed Draper into the dining room, which was empty. On the wall all along this row of booths were pictures of the neighborhood through the years. I was in one of them, standing with Ed and Draper on the steps outside the bar the day we graduated from high school, and I was pleasantly surprised to notice the picture still hung above the old booth where we'd all carved our names. I took a step toward it, wanting a closer look, but Draper took my elbow and guided me away from it and into another booth.

"What can I get you to drink? On the house, of course."

"Whatever's cold and in a bottle."

"Be right back." He went back out to the bar, and I heard him talking in low tones with Bill Foulks. I wondered what Draper was saying. Probably not giving me a hell of a lot of support. *He's here on business.*

When Draper came back to the dining room, he had a bottle of Moosehead Canadian in each hand, and the guy in the jeans and silk shirt trailing behind him. Draper handed me one of the beers, then nodded at his companion.

"This guy was Ed's boss," Draper said. "I was just filling him in on what happened last night."

I looked at the stranger with interest now.

"Jimmy Cancerno," he said, offering his hand as he slid into the booth beside Draper. He wasn't as old as I'd originally thought, probably no more than fifty, but he carried himself with slouched shoulders, and his thinning hair was shot with gray.

"You want anything to eat?" Draper asked me.

"You kidding me?" I hadn't eaten in many hours, but the Hideaway food wasn't going to improve on an empty stomach.

"What? Food's better around here now, Lincoln. We made some changes."

"So the grill got cleaned?"

He grinned. "Some of the changes are still on the list. But we got new pickles."

"Dill chips?"

"*Spicy* dill chips. They were on sale, of course."

Cancerno watched this interplay without interest. We were jammed together in one of the tiny booths, hunched over an old wooden table. Above the booth we sat in today was an old black-and-white photograph showing Draper's grandfather sitting on the hood of a big Oldsmobile, probably taken around 1950.

"Bar's been here a long time," I said, looking at the picture.

"Better than a half century," Draper said. "My grandfather opened it when he got back from World War II. Dad took over when he came home from 'Nam. Family tradition called for me to fight a war before I could run the show, but then my old man died before I had the chance, so I took over."

"Died too young," I said. David Draper had died from lung cancer a few years after we graduated from high school. He'd smoked better than a pack a day for forty years and spent the rest of his time working in a bar that was generally so hazy with smoke it was difficult to see the television screens.

"Hell, all of our dads did," Draper said. "Yours was the oldest when he went, and he was still too young."

Draper took out a pack of cigarettes, shook one out for himself, and offered them to me. Apparently his father's illness had done nothing to deter Scott's habit. I declined, and he lit his own, then immediately set it on the edge of the ashtray.

"They put Ed in the ground this week," he said, and his brown eyes were flat. "I haven't decided if I'm going out for it or not. Wouldn't make a bit of difference to Ed."

I didn't say anything.

"Poor bastard," Draper said, sighing and lifting his cigarette back to his lips. "But in a way, it's almost better, you know? Things would have been ugly for him, Lincoln. You know that."

"If he didn't kill her, we could have proven that, maybe gotten him back out."

"We?"

I shrugged. "The police, then. I offered to help him, but it's too late now."

Draper drained a third of his Moosehead in one swallow and wiped his mouth with the back of his hand. He was wearing a white T-shirt that hugged his muscles closely, a thin silver chain hanging over the collar.

"I got to admit, I was pissed off at you last night, and I mean good," he said. "It's for the best that they put you in the police car. I was blaming you for it, even if you hadn't shoved him. I mean, he was fine upstairs until you showed up."

I sipped my beer and kept silent. Ed had been anything but fine, hiding out in a bar, drunk, with a cop's blood on his shirt, but if Draper wanted to tell himself he'd played the role of a protector, I wouldn't challenge it.

"I'm past that now," he said. "Blaming you, that is. You showed up, right? And I know you showed up 'cause you wanted to help him. That took some serious balls, Lincoln."

I leaned back, trying to clear some space in the little booth. He watched my face carefully, smoking his cigarette. Then he shrugged. "I think Ed had to appreciate the effort. And if he was going to go down that day, well, must have been nice for him to have an old friend by his side as he went."

I thought of Ed's drunken run into the street, the clumsy way his feet had tangled, the screech of brakes that were doing too little, too late.

"Sure," I said. "Must have been nice."

Cancerno hadn't said a word during our exchange, just sat and sipped a whiskey on the rocks.

"How long had Ed worked for you?" I asked him.

"Six months, maybe?" He shrugged. "Scott's the one recommended him to me." He gave Draper a look that had more bite than the whiskey in his glass.

Draper met it coolly. "I'd recommend him to you again, Jimmy."

"Hell of a thing to say, considering." Cancerno scowled.

"Pretty broken up about Ed, huh?" I said, the small booth feeling smaller to me with every word Cancerno said.

"I supposed to give a shit?" he said, eyes wide. "I hardly knew the guy. He was just a carpenter and a painter, same as a dozen other guys. 'Cept a dozen other guys don't bring the cops to my door."

"That bothers you," I said, and his gaze narrowed.

"Yeah. It bothers me. I'm a guy that likes his distance from the cops, asshole. That's all you need to know."

"Easy, Jimmy, Lincoln's not challenging you." Draper's tone made it clear that if I *was* challenging him, I'd better stop it.

We drank for a bit, none of us speaking. Draper finished his cigarette and took the pack out, but didn't light another one.

"You guys were gone, what, ten minutes before he got hit by that car?" he asked.

"Not even that."

"But enough time to talk a little, right?"

"We talked. He was pretty drunk. His mind was going places without taking me along."

"What do you mean?"

"Seemed like he was talking to himself as much as he was talking to me," I said. "He'd hint at some stuff but not get specific. When I asked questions, he jumped in new directions."

Draper stared at the table, sliding the pack of cigarettes back and forth between his fingers.

"He was into some trouble," I said, and Draper looked up. "You know anything about that? Who he was dealing with?"

"As far as I knew, he was clean and had been for

years." Draper stood up. "I'm going to grab another beer. Be right back."

He slid out and then it was just me and Jimmy Cancerno in the booth. Cancerno worked on what was left of his whiskey and looked bored.

"Was he a good worker for you?" I asked.

He spoke over the glass. "Good as any of them. Showed up on time and went home on time and billed for the time he'd worked. We do things a little different on my projects, see. Not a lot of paperwork. Pay in cash. It was a good job for him."

"What kind of projects was he working on?"

"Fixed houses, mostly. Was supposed to be fixing the one he burned down. It was a small job; I wouldn't have made much off it. Now I'm likely to get sued thanks to the son of a bitch."

"I thought the house was empty."

"It was," Cancerno said as if he were explaining something to a child. "But the property company that owned the place wanted it fixed. So they could sell it, right? Go figure."

I leaned forward, suddenly glad Cancerno was here, after all. "But he had a reason to be on the property, then?"

Cancerno hacked something up and re-swallowed it. Attractive.

"We hadn't started the work on that house yet, but he knew it was coming, and he had the keys. Could be he went over to get a look, maybe think about what materials would be needed."

"Well, that's pretty damn important," I said. Cancerno looked as if he couldn't care less.

"That's better beer than I remembered," Draper said, sliding a fresh Moosehead across the table to me and dropping back in the booth. "I sell it, but I don't drink it much. Might have to change that."

I didn't touch the bottle. "I need to know what that girl was to Ed."

Draper raised his eyebrows. "That's what the cops said to me. I can only tell you what I told them—I have no clue. I asked him last night when he showed up here, and he ignored me. Just said he didn't kill her and asked for a drink while he figured out what he needed to do next. Told me to get my ass back downstairs because the cops would be looking for him soon and he needed me to deal with them. I'd hardly sent them away before you showed up."

"So you've got no ideas at all," I said.

He shook his head, his eyes sad. "Wish I did, Lincoln. Wish I did."

"Who else was he close with?" I said. "Was there a girlfriend, anything like that?"

"He wasn't seeing anyone." This time Draper's answer was confident. "Worked a lot and came in here and drank and watched baseball. That was really about it. The last couple weeks, he hadn't even been in here."

"He told me he went to the prosecutor about something, Scott."

He frowned. "He went to the prosecutor?"

"Yeah."

He shook his head again. "Can't help you. Like I said, he'd been out of sight for the last few weeks."

I was frustrated with the lack of help. I'd counted on Draper knowing more. I wasn't sure if he was really this clueless or if he just didn't want to let me know anything, which was also quite possible. It would be foolish to assume his old bitterness had been washed clean in twenty-four hours.

"He hung around with a guy named Corbett a lot," Draper said, thoughtful as he sipped his beer. "One of Jimmy's guys."

I looked at Cancerno, who nodded. His glass was empty and he'd been looking at his watch.

"Mitch Corbett," he said. "He was Gradduk's boss on the work sites. An old-timer. Mitch is a good guy. Between his opinion and Scott's, I actually felt good enough about hiring that son of a bitch Gradduk that I gave him a raise."

I took a long drink, letting the cold beer soothe the anger that had risen with Cancerno's words, then said, "Would Corbett know if Ed had a reason to be in that house the day it burned?"

Cancerno nodded. "Probably. If he'd had a legitimate reason, Mitch would've given it to him."

"I'd like to talk to him, then."

"To who? Mitch?"

"Yes."

Cancerno smiled humorlessly. "Me, too, kid."

I frowned at him, not getting it.

"Corbett hasn't shown up for work in two days. And the son of a bitch won't answer his phone, either." Cancerno got to his feet. "Do me a favor, right? You talk to Corbett, you tell him he better give me a call within the next forty-eight hours if he wants to keep his job. I don't have the patience for his shit on top of this deal with Gradduk."

Cancerno said something to Draper before he walked toward the door, but I wasn't really paying attention. I was thinking about Mitch Corbett with a sense of unease. His boss had delivered the news of his absence casually enough, as if Corbett had been known to miss a few days of work before. I didn't like it, though. It came too close to everything with Ed.

With Cancerno gone, Draper turned to me. "Sorry about that. He came down here just ahead of you, wanted to see what I knew about Ed. He's pretty angry about it all, and blaming me because I was the guy who sent Ed to him in the first place."

"This guy Corbett," I said, "you think he was pretty tight with Ed? Might know something about whatever Ed got himself into?"

Draper shrugged. "Better chance Corbett will know something than anyone else I can think of."

"And you don't think it's strange the guy's missing?"

"A little early to say he's *missing,* Lincoln. Dude blew off work, is all."

I nodded, but by now I was convinced I wanted to look for Mitch Corbett. When I got up, Draper followed me to the door. "I appreciate you coming down here," he said. "I felt bad about the way things happened out there. We were all friends, once."

"Yes, we were." Draper had never been as close to me as he was to Ed, but we'd spent enough time around each other growing up. I stepped onto the sidewalk and leaned back, looking up at the old brick building.

"You going to keep the place going, Scott? It's the last of the old neighborhood bars."

He leaned against the doorframe. "Hell, yeah, I'll keep it going. It's all that's left of what this neighborhood used to be—a bunch of Poles and Czechs who worked hard and drank harder. Three generations in my family, I'm not going to let it go under that easy." He gazed up the street. "Clark's changed, man. Changes more every year. The Hideaway stays the same."

A flier stuck to the old wooden door read: SEE FOUR ON THE PORCH LIVE ALL SUMMER.

I pointed at it. "What's Four on the Porch?"

"A band with one good-looking black girl who can sing and three drunk white guys with no apparent talents," Draper said. "They're fun, though."

"So even the Hideaway's not staying entirely the same. Live music is new."

Draper gazed at the poster. "Yeah, it is. I've got to find

some way to make money, though. Not enough of the old crowd left. Have to bring people in somehow." He shifted his eyes to me. "And I guess you're doing okay, with both of your businesses going. The gym and the detective thing."

"I'm still afloat. That's all I can ask for. How'd you know about the gym?"

He stopped looking down the street and met my eyes. "Ed told me. He kept tabs on you, as they say. Didn't talk to you, maybe, but he knew your score."

I gave that half a nod. "I had that feeling."

*M*y father's funeral is on a Tuesday, and it rains. I have the week off for bereavement leave, but I've already decided to go back to work on Wednesday. Better to keep my mind occupied. The turnout is small, maybe because of the weather, or maybe because my father had been a fairly quiet man who'd kept to himself. My sister, Jennifer, is there, as is my father's sister, his only sibling. Since flying in from New Jersey, she has spent most of her time telling me how proud of me my father was, how many times he called her and told her of this pride. I appreciate her effort, but it bothers me slightly, because I know she is not being honest. My father was proud of me. I know this. He would not talk of his pride, however—not to my aunt, to me, or to anyone else. It was not his nature. My successes are my own, and while he enjoys them, I know he wouldn't speak of his pride in them. The quality I most respected—and envied—of the man was his humility.

We stand huddled together near the casket, staying close because it is hard to hear the voice of the minister over the rain pounding on the umbrellas. I don't have one, and I've declined offers. After five minutes of it I am thor-

oughly soaked, my suit saturated, my hair plastered against my skull. I like the smell of the rain on the earth they've dug up to make room for my father's bones. It is a fresh smell, one with some promise to it, and while it seems misplaced in this setting, I am grateful for it.

"Dear family and friends, please accept my sincere sympathy in your grief over the passing of Thomas Perry," the minister says, struggling to make his voice heard. He is an older man, and he looks frail and ill. I wonder what it feels like to make a business of funeral speeches when you're in such condition.

"Thomas was a devout man, one who knew his maker well during his time on earth, and I am sure Thomas knows Him even better today," he continues. "We are aggrieved that we shall not see him again in his earthly being, except through the eye of memory. Today that memory brings sadness, because the pain of loss is so near. But I promise you that sadness will give way to the pleasant remembrance of him as he was in the fullness of his life, and someday, hopefully soon, the memories will bring a loving smile in place of an aching soul."

While he speaks, my eyes wander. I do not wish to stare endlessly at the casket, and I cannot keep my eyes on the ground, as everyone else is doing. As I scan the cemetery, I become aware of a figure under a tree on a hill some fifty yards from us. He is the only person other than me who does not have an umbrella, but he stands tall, oblivious of the rain pounding at him. Surely, he cannot hear a word of what is being said, but he stands there anyhow, removed from the group, but present. He is a young man, average in height and build, and there is a familiar quality to him. I look closer, and he lifts his own face and meets my gaze. It is Ed Gradduk.

Four years have passed since I last spoke to Ed, and

then it was in an interrogation room, him giving me cold eyes while I told him I couldn't buy any more time—either he talked or went to jail. He went to jail. Stayed three years.

I stare in his direction for a while, then look back at the minister, who is concluding what he had promised would be a brief message. He said it would be brief because that was the unassuming nature of my father, but I think the ever-intensifying rain has played some role in the decision.

"With sure and certain hope, I commend Thomas Perry's soul to the mercy of God, his creator. May he enjoy forever the company of God together with his loved ones who preceded him in death," he says, and I think of my mother and smile for the first time in several days.

"In your loving kindness, please keep Thomas in your memory, as he kept you in his heart during his time with you," the minister concludes. We file up to the casket then, one at a time, and drop a flower on its rain-soaked surface. I go last, and when I have laid the carnation on the casket, I turn my eyes back to the hill in time to see Ed Gradduk disappear over it, walking away without a word.

I call him that night and leave a message. He doesn't call back. The next day I return to work.

CHAPTER 8

"**B**ut you say his boss didn't seem particularly concerned," Joe said.

I shook my head. "No." I was back in the office, filling Joe in on my conversation with Draper and explaining my interest in locating Mitch Corbett.

"So maybe he's a guy who's been known to sleep or drink through a few workdays in the past."

"Maybe," I admitted.

Joe sat behind his desk with his feet propped up on the edge of it. "And maybe there's more to it."

"Either way," I said, "I'd like to know where he is, because I'd like to talk to him."

Joe nodded and swung his feet down from the desk, pulled his chair closer to the computer, and clicked the mouse a few times, opening up one of our locator databases, probably.

"I know you won't want to hear it," he said, "but learning that Gradduk was working on that house doesn't do anything to help his case."

I frowned. "What are you talking about? It gives him a legitimate reason to be on the property the day the house burned."

"Also gives him a reason to choose the house as a good place to dump a body."

I hadn't considered that. He had a point, but I shook my head anyhow.

"I'm convinced he didn't burn that house, Joe. The tape would have been worthless in court with that twenty-minute lapse between the time he left and the time it went up in flames, and there's a reason for that—too much reasonable doubt."

"So if he didn't burn the place, why'd he run when the cops came for him?"

"Panicked," I said. "That's my best guess."

The printer began to hum and he pointed at it. "There's an address match for the only Mitchell Corbett I could find in this city. Says here he is forty-five years old. Looks like he lives just off Fulton Road."

"That sounds right," I said. "Same neighborhood as Ed and Draper." It felt as if I should include myself in that sentence, but several years had passed since I could. It wasn't just that I'd moved out of the neighborhood, I also hadn't so much as stopped by the Hideaway for a drink or even walked the sidewalks.

Joe got to his feet. "All right. Let's see what Mr. Corbett has to say."

The house was a small, one-story structure tucked on the back of a lot that was large for the neighborhood. Corbett had obviously used some of his trade skills on his home—a new carport and fresh paint and trim made the tiny house look nicer than its larger counterparts.

I parked in the driveway, which was empty.

"If the man's home," Joe said, "he's home without a car." The street parking in front of the house was also vacant.

"Let's take a look, anyhow," I said.

We got out of the car and walked up to the front door. The mailbox was an old-fashioned style that hung on the wall next to the door, and as we approached, I could see the lid was held open about two inches by the large stack of mail that had been jammed in the small container.

"Nobody's taken the mail in for days," I said.

"Three newspapers on the ground." Joe pointed at the rolled-up papers that lay in front of the door.

I pulled the storm door open and rapped on the wooden front door with my knuckles. The sound was loud and hollow. I let the storm door swing shut and stepped back. We waited. Nobody came to the door, and no sound came from inside.

"There's definitely no one home," Joe said. He was gazing up the street.

"Let's walk around back."

We went to the right and stepped out of the sun and into the shade of the carport as we moved toward the backyard. Joe stopped and put his hand on my arm.

"Check out the side door."

A door led into the house from the carport, and this one didn't have a storm door protecting it. It was closed and looked solid enough to me. For a moment I couldn't tell what had attracted Joe's interest. Then I saw the heavy black scuff beside the knob.

"Looks like somebody kicked it," he said, stepping closer. He bent beside the door and ran his fingers along the frame, then twisted the knob and pushed inward. The door was locked, but it gave a little and there was the sound of cracking wood. Joe grunted with approval and pointed.

When I leaned in beside him, I saw a split in the door-frame. It was yielding a bit to Joe's pressure. A few jagged splinters still protruded from the frame, indicating the damage was recent. There was no dead bolt on the door, just a simple but fairly new spring lock.

"Whoever kicked this door open assumed it'd be easy because there wasn't a dead bolt," Joe said, releasing the knob. "The lock was stronger than they thought, though.

They kicked it harder, and it opened, but it split the frame."

"Kick it open," I said. I was suddenly sure we would find Mitch Corbett inside, but in no condition to talk.

Joe frowned. "Are you crazy?"

I answered by lifting my own foot and driving my heel into the center of the door. The crack in the frame widened with a tearing sound and the door swung open. It hit the wall and bounced back toward us. Joe put out his palm to stop it from swinging shut. He stared at me.

"This is not the way I like to do things, Lincoln."

"Sorry, but I've got a bad feeling about this one."

I stepped past him and into the house. The side door led into a small kitchen that smelled of lemon Pledge. It was clean and tidy, no dishes stacked on the counter, no bag of chips open on the table. No body on the floor.

Joe had stepped into the house behind me, his complaints ceasing for the moment. Together we moved out of the kitchen and into the adjacent living room. A few issues of *Sports Illustrated* were on the coffee table, and an empty beer can was on the floor beside the couch. I picked the can up and studied its top. It was bone-dry, the contents not recently consumed.

I replaced the can as Joe walked past me, down the narrow hall that led out of this room. I trailed. He opened a closed door and stepped into what turned out to be a laundry room. There was nothing inside but a washer-dryer combination, water heater, a few mops and brooms, and a cat's litter box. We moved out of that room and continued down the hall, past an empty bathroom and on to another closed door on the right. Joe and I hadn't spoken since entering the house, and now he opened this door without a word and held it while I walked into a small spare bedroom furnished with a ragged couch and a thrift-shop-quality desk. We left that room and went on to the last room in the little house, this door closed, too.

This was the main bedroom, and it, too, held nothing other than the expected. A small desk was in the corner of the room, and I pulled a few of the drawers open, but found nothing more interesting than a videotape for the continuing-education programs at Cuyahoga Community College.

"Satisfied?" Joe said. "No corpses, no signed confessions of setting up Ed Gradduk."

"Also no Mitch Corbett," I said. "And somebody broke into this house not long ago."

"Could have been him, Lincoln. Have you ever locked yourself out of your apartment?"

"It wasn't him. And you don't think so, either."

"I want to get out of this house," he said. "Your door-kicking approach to investigation leaves something to be desired."

We walked back out the way we'd come in and closed the carport door behind us. It still locked, but even a slight bit of pressure would pop it open now. Good thing the owner was a carpenter.

J oe spotted the tail before I did, which was embarrassing because I was driving and should have been paying more attention to the mirrors than him.

"Check out the black Jeep Cherokee behind us," he said when I was at a red light. I shifted my eyes to the mirror and found the vehicle in question. Its windshield was tinted but I could make out two occupants in the front seat, both male.

"Yeah?"

"It was parked up the street from Corbett's house," he said. "Maybe five houses down and across the street. Right where I'd put it if I was watching the place."

"And it pulled out when we did?"

"Uh-huh."

The light went green and I pulled away. The Cherokee stayed with us, lingering a few cars back but always pulling closer when we neared an intersection, so there was little chance of losing us at a red light. It's the way you drive when you're working one-car surveillance.

"Well, hell," I said.

Joe grunted.

"I'm growing curious," I said. "You?"

"We could lose them easily enough," he said. "But that wouldn't tell us anything."

"Exactly. So what's our move?"

He scratched the side of his head and sighed. "I suppose I'll shadow the shadowers."

"Tough to do when you're in my car."

"Take me to the office and pull in at the curb. Make it look like you're dropping me off. I'll go back in the parking lot and get my car. Then you swing around the block. When you pull out, I'll fall in line behind them."

It took us five minutes to get back to the office, and the Cherokee was still with us. When I pulled up to the curb in front of the building, the Cherokee slid into a street parking spot about a hundred feet back.

Joe gave me more instructions. "I'm going to stand on the sidewalk and talk to you for a bit, make it look more casual, like we're oblivious to them."

"Okay."

I sat with the engine idling while he stood beside the truck, leaning in the door with his hand on the roof.

"I'll stay here until traffic thickens up," he said. "That way you'll have to wait to pull back into the street and it won't look like you're just killing time."

Joe was the best details cop I'd ever known, and he was proving it again today. When the cars had backed up at the red light in front of us, he slammed the door shut, waved at me, and walked into the parking lot with his hands in his pockets. I stayed at the curb till the light changed and the waiting cars slid through the intersection, then pulled back into the street. The Cherokee pulled with me.

I made a right turn on Rocky River Drive even though I had no place to go but home, which was in the opposite direction. There was a gas station on the north side of the street, and I swung in there and topped off the tank. The black Cherokee cruised past the gas station and pulled into the parking lot of the strip mall behind it. I went inside, paid, and came back out to the truck. When I pulled onto Rocky River again, this time headed back toward the office, the Cherokee slid out of the parking lot and followed, with Joe's Taurus behind. We were a regular caravan of curiosity.

I turned left onto the avenue, passed the office, and drove the seven blocks to my building. It wasn't quite five yet, which meant the gym office was still open. My manager, a sharp-tongued, gray-haired woman named Grace, smiled when I stepped inside. I'd lost track of the Cherokee by this point, but I was sure Joe still had them.

"Hey, boss," Grace said. "Off early today?"

"We've already purged the city of crime," I said, trying to go with her good humor even though my mind was elsewhere.

"That easy, huh?"

"You bet." I took a protein shake from the cooler behind the desk. I hadn't eaten lunch, and my stomach was aware of it. "I'm going to run upstairs and change clothes, then come down for a workout. Is it crowded in there?"

"Mobbed. Six people instead of our usual three."

"Funny."

I went up to my apartment and changed into shorts and a sleeveless T-shirt, then came back down to the gym, cell phone in hand. Joe would call me when he had something, I was sure. I just didn't know how long that would take.

I was halfway through my third set on the bench press when the phone rang. It was Joe.

"We're all still watching your building," he said. "I've got a plate number from them. You want me to bail and use the plate number to see who they are, or stick around and see what they do?"

"It's up to you. You're the one wasting time on them."

"I'll give it another hour."

I finished my chest workout and moved on to back exercises, pausing occasionally to talk with some of the gym regulars. Grace had closed the office and gone home, but the members could still come in after hours by using the keycard entrance at the front of the building.

It was nearly six when Joe called back. I was done with the weights and doing some stretches before going out for a run. I paused to answer the phone.

"You taking off?" I said.

"Don't have to make that decision, because they already lost interest in you."

"They left?"

"Uh-huh. And I followed. All the way to the police station."

"What?"

"You heard me. They're cops. Pulled into the officer parking lot and got out of the car. One of the guys was plainclothes, the other was in uniform. He went in the building while the plainclothes guy went home."

"Recognize either of them?"

"I was too far away to place them, if I actually knew either one. I'll use the plate number to get a name tomorrow."

"If Corbett's absence has attracted police interest, why

hasn't he been released as a missing person yet?" I said. "And why are they watching his house instead of going out looking for him?"

"And," Joe said, "why does it appear they are doing it while off-duty?"

We didn't have the answers for those questions. Not yet, at least.

CHAPTER 9

There were twelve Corbetts in the Cleveland phone book. Mitchell was listed, but I was pretty certain he wasn't going to return home anytime this evening, so I didn't bother to call him. The rest of the unfortunate Corbetts in town got the Lincoln Perry dinner-hour-telemarketing approach to investigation, however.

Of the first five names on my list, only three were home, and none of them had a relative named Mitch. One woman, Dorene Corbett, responded to the question by asking if I was planning to reunite her with her birth father. When I said that wasn't the case, she was disappointed.

"I thought maybe you were from one of those reunion shows," she said. "You know, like the ones they've got on *Oprah* now and then? I like those shows."

"So you've never met your father?" I said, trying to follow her conversation.

"Of course I have. But I thought maybe you were looking for someone with my name who hasn't."

"I see."

"There's another Dorene Corbett," she said. "I got her name off the Internet once. But she lives in Georgia. Try Georgia, okay?"

I assured her I would try Georgia, then hung up gratefully and continued working through my list. On the seventh try, I found a gentleman who had indeed heard of Mitch Corbett.

"Listen," Randy Corbett said as soon as I'd asked my question, "I'm tired of this. I don't talk to Mitch no more and he don't talk to me. We never seen eye to eye on a damn thing, I don't know where he is, and I don't care. Haven't talked to him in more than a year."

"But you are related to him?"

"I'm his brother, you jackass. You don't know that, then why the hell you calling me?"

"When I asked you if you knew Mitch, you said you were tired of this. Has someone else been asking about him?"

"Just the police," he said. "Shows what kind of good family I got, only time I hear about my own brother is when the police are looking for him. My mother's probably rolling in her grave right now."

"When did the police ask about him, sir?"

"This morning." He paused. "And if you're not one of them, who the hell are you?"

"A private investigator."

"Can you tell me what he's done? 'Cause the police wouldn't."

"As far as I know, he hasn't done anything other than blow off work. I'm just trying to track him down because he might know something that could be useful to me in another matter. Are you sure you don't have any idea where he would have gone?"

"Absolutely not. We ain't what you'd call close brothers, mister. And I'm all the family that old boy's got."

"Did he have good friends out of town? Someplace he liked to vacation, maybe?"

Randy Corbett let out a snort of derision so long that I thought he might faint from lack of oxygen before he finished. Apparently my question had been some kind of funny.

"Someplace he liked to vacation," he said at last. "That's good. Mister, Mitch ain't got enough money to make it to Sandusky, let alone someplace worth going. I can't tell you where he is, but I'd be mighty surprised if it's any farther away than the east side."

I'd hardly finished my Cleveland Corbett roundup when the phone rang. It was Amy.

"How you holding up?" she said.

"I'm up," I said. "That's all you can ask, some days."

"Right. You had dinner yet?"

"Hadn't even considered it. Hell, I never ate lunch, either."

"How about I pick up a pizza and stop by?"

"Sounds good. You got something on your mind or just worried about me?"

"I'm always worried about you," she said. "But I'd like to talk some things over, as well. Maybe you'd care to tell me a little more about your relationship with Gradduk? Like why you hadn't talked to him in eight years?"

"We can go into detail when you get here, Ace. For now all you need to know is I went cop and he went con. Worlds collided."

Amy arrived with a box of pizza and a bag of breadsticks about twenty minutes later, and we sat in the living room with the lights turned low, eating off paper plates. I knew Amy had come largely to get the rest of the story I'd promised her about my relationship with Ed, but to her credit she ate nearly half a breadstick before asking for details.

"So you went cop and he went con," she said. "That's all you gave me this afternoon. Now I want the rest."

I gave her the rest while we ate the pizza. She sat on the couch with her legs curled under her and didn't interrupt with questions until I was done, which is unusual for Amy.

"Man," she said when I was through, "that had to be hard on you, Lincoln. Sending your best friend to jail when you'd actually set out to help him."

"Had to be hard on him," I answered, "being sent to jail by his best friend."

"Did you really believe he'd talk?"

I nodded. "I was sure he would. Maybe that was because Allison did a good job of convincing me, but, yeah, I thought he'd talk to stay out of jail. Don't get me wrong, I expected he'd be bitter at first, but I thought maybe later . . ." I shook my head and sighed.

"What?"

"I had this vision of how it would go," I said. "There'd be a tense period, sure, but then he'd clean his act up and we'd begin to relax again. Things would get back to the way they used to be. He'd marry Allison, and sometime, maybe a couple of years down the road, we'd be out having a few beers, laughing, and then he'd turn serious. He'd lift his beer to me and say . . ." I stopped talking.

Amy set her pizza down. "He'd say?"

"I don't know. Thank me, I guess," and even as I said it I felt small. It had come out as if in my mind the situation had been more about me than Ed. Or was that not just in the way I'd phrased things?

"It sounds like this neighborhood is a tight little community," Amy said. "Kind of unusual now."

I nodded. "It's damn unusual. And most of the neighborhood isn't that tight, at all. It's a pretty transient area, now. But there are a few families scattered around that are vestiges of what it used to be. That's the group that stays close. Ed and Scott Draper were both third-generation in the neighborhood. Everyone that had been around for a while knew their families well. I was an outsider at first; we didn't move into that neighborhood until after my mom died. But my grandpa had lived in that neighborhood for most of his life, and my dad grew up there. When my mom died, my dad pulled a career change, became a paramedic, and said he wanted to live close to MetroHealth, because that was where his ambulance ran out of. I think in reality he just wanted to go back to familiar ground, because he was feeling a little lost. It was kind of like going home to him."

"How'd your mother die?"

"Killed by a drunk driver."

She winced. "I'm sorry. I knew she'd died when you were young, but I never knew how."

"Right. I was only three when she died."

"You remember her at all?"

"Vague things. I can still hear her laugh in my head even now, but the only really clear memory I have of her face is the way she looked the day I fell down the stairs. I nicked my head on something, and it just bled like crazy. I can remember her standing at the top of the steps and looking down at me with this utterly terrified expression. That one's just frozen in my memory."

"I didn't know your dad was a paramedic."

"Yeah. He'd been working as a plant manager in Bedford, making good money. Decided he wanted to do something else, and that was what he picked. We ended up back in the city, and I fell in with Ed and Draper, grew up around the families that had been around there for generations, and for a while I was part of the club. In a way, it was like growing up in a time warp. The neighborhood I got to know was more like the neighborhood of the fifties and sixties, before all the blue collars moved to the suburbs and the houses around there started turning over faster than apartments."

"And you're not part of the club anymore?"

I shook my head. "Far from it, Ace. The old-timers hate me. It was an unusually loyal group because it was getting smaller every year. They looked out for each other. They didn't send each other to jail."

I pushed out of the chair and went into the kitchen to pour a fresh glass of water.

When I came back, Amy had closed the pizza box and was sitting upright on the couch, less like a cat and more like a human for a change.

"I have a tip for you," she said. "It will be in the paper tomorrow, but you deserve to hear it early."

"Yeah?" Something about her attitude was a little off suddenly, something in the way she kept her eyes away from mine while she talked that made me uneasy.

"I got a call from a guy today who read my first story about Gradduk and said he could tell me when Sentalar and Gradduk met."

"That's pretty huge," I said, dropping back into my chair.

She nodded and took a sip of diet Coke but didn't say anything immediately.

"Well, where was it? Where'd they meet?"

"At a bar on Lorain," she said. "This guy, he's a bartender. Told me that he remembered both Gradduk and Sentalar as soon as he saw their pictures. According to him, they met in the bar about two weeks ago."

"He get a sense for whether it was a friendly meeting, romantic, or professional?"

She pushed the diet Coke can around the coffee table with her fingertips. "He said Gradduk was making a pass at Sentalar, and she was trying to get him to leave her alone."

I frowned. "That doesn't sound like Ed."

Amy pushed the can aside and rummaged in her purse until she found a notebook. She flipped it open, said, "These are direct quotes from the bartender," and began to read.

"The guy, Gradduk, he kept putting his hand on her arm, leaning down to talk real soft to her, pretty intense. And she shrugged him off a couple times. I remember once she said, 'You don't have a prayer.' And then he said, 'I'm not taking no for an answer.' And she answered that he was going to have to take no for an answer. They talked for another minute or two, and then she pulled away from him and said, in a loud voice, 'Just leave me the hell alone.' That was when I stepped in and told him he needed to listen to the lady. And he ignored me—well, didn't say anything to me—but he did get up and walk off. And as he was walking, he looked back at her and said, 'You know I'm not going away.' "

Amy closed the notebook and returned it to her purse.

I shook my head. "I don't believe it. This is some loser just hoping to steal fifteen seconds of fame by making up a story or fabricating what he really saw."

Amy raised her eyebrows. "He remembers the incident pretty damn clearly. And Cal Richards was very interested. I called him and filled him in late this afternoon, and he said it actually meshed nicely with the picture he was developing of their relationship. Thanked me for my reporting, like all of a sudden I was his favorite person."

"What's the picture he's developing?"

"He wouldn't tell me a whole lot of it, obviously, but he did say Anita Sentalar's phone records showed numerous but brief calls from Gradduk in recent weeks. And apparently the guy she works with, the partner in her law firm, said he knew Gradduk had shown up at the office a few times, and Sentalar had asked him to leave."

I sat with a half-eaten breadstick in my hand and felt myself beginning a slow burn toward anger. This wasn't fair to Ed. Not by a long shot. It was just a snippet of a weeks-old conversation in a crowded bar, but it would convict him in the public's opinion even more than he already was.

"You can't run that story, Amy," I said. "It's ridiculous. That's an unsubstantiated, one-sided account of a conversation that may never have even happened."

This time her eyebrows arched so high they almost joined her hairline. "Excuse me? I *can't* run that story? Like you're my editor or something? This story is huge, Lincoln, and it's good journalism. I'm the first person to provide *any* sort of account of a relationship between Sentalar and Gradduk. It's the biggest scoop I've had in months."

"Biggest since I gave you the story of your life, you mean?"

Now the eyebrows lowered and her eyes narrowed. "What's that supposed to mean? That because you gave me a good opportunity once, you're allowed to dictate what I do and do not report?"

"You can't run that story," I said. "It'll make Ed look like some sort of a psycho stalker, and that's absurd. If you'd ever known the guy—"

"Known him when he was twelve, like you did? Give me a break, Lincoln! You don't even know who he was anymore. Think about it: The last two times you even spoke to Gradduk, he was in the process of being arrested. And justifiably so."

I shoved off the chair and walked back into the kitchen, wanting to get away from her, the hostility building so quickly that I was afraid of losing my composure. I stood in the kitchen with my back to her for a few minutes, cleaning already-clean dishes, taking slow breaths, and keeping silent. Eventually, she stood up and gathered her things. She left the living room but did not follow me into the kitchen, walking instead to the door.

"It's been a long time since you knew him, Lincoln," she said.

"I knew him well during a time when boys become men, Amy," I said, stepping out of the kitchen so I could see her. "I think a person's character is pretty well established by then."

"You *arrested* him, Lincoln! What sort of character assessment were you making then?"

"There's a difference between a guy being willing to move some drugs when he's broke and a guy who's a sexual predator and a murderer, Amy." My voice was rising now, the towel I'd been drying the dishes with clenched tightly in my hands.

"You hadn't seen him in *eight years.*"

We stood there facing each other with cold stares, a pair of gunslingers in a dusty street.

"I've got to get back to work," she said eventually, turning and putting her hand on the doorknob. "I didn't want to run the story without telling you what I had first. But it's running, Lincoln. And it's the right thing for me to do."

"Obviously. It'll strengthen your résumé for the tabloids."

She jerked the door open so hard I was surprised she didn't dislocate her shoulder, stepped through it, and slammed it shut. I threw the dish towel at the door; it hit with a splat and left a smear on the paint as it slid to the ground. Count on me to come through with the childish gesture.

After a minute, I sighed, walked over, and picked up the towel. I cleaned up the rest of the mess in the living room, washed the rest of the dishes, turned the lights off,

and stood at the window. I stared through it without seeing anything. Worlds collided, I'd told Amy. They certainly had.

*T*he interrogation room is about the size of a bed-
        room closet in Shaker Heights or Pepper Pike.
        They got a table in here somehow, and it seems to
take up the entire space. If you attempt to walk around the
table, you have to flatten yourself against the wall. This
spoils any hope of a pacing-and-shouting routine like on
TV cop shows, but that's probably just as well.

Sitting across from my oldest friend, the room and the
table could not feel smaller to me. I'm not in uniform and
he's not handcuffed, thankfully, but even so the scenario
feels wrong in a way I couldn't have imagined before I
found myself here, wrong in a way that makes my stomach
roil and my hands tremble so much that I jam them under
the table so he can't see.

"Ed," I say, "I can't delay things anymore. If you don't
talk now, there won't be a plea bargain. You'll do jail
time. A few years of it."

His eyes are locked on mine, cold and unwavering. He
has several days of beard on his face, but he still looks so
young he could have just come from having a high school
yearbook photograph taken instead of a mug shot. I don't
want to know what I look like.

"Dammit, Ed," I say after a few minutes of silence.
"There's nobody listening right now. No recorders, nobody behind a mirror, none of that shit. It's just you and
me. Tell me something. Anything. Anything that I can take
out of this room and use to get you protection."

He leans back, folds his hands neatly, and rests them
on the table. His face is serene, his eyes indicting. His
mouth shut.

"You're going to go to jail," I repeat. "They've got you

*with possession of cocaine and intent to distribute. Got
your conviction boxed and sealed and wrapped with a
ribbon. Any leeway you might have had is going to be
thrown aside to make you regret not talking. They're going to go after you hard because you spoiled their plans."*

No response.

"You want to see Allison through a piece of glass, Ed?"

Not a word..

*"Come on, Ed," I say, and I hope the sense of desper-
ate pleading isn't as clear in my voice as it is in my heart.*

His eyes still on mine, he shakes his head slowly.

*"What are you worried about? You think Childers will
kill you? He's not that powerful of a force. We'll protect
you and Allison while we put him in jail. Once he's in jail,
the rest of his boys won't be a threat. They aren't loyal to
Antonio; they're scared of him."*

*I'm hoping the reference to fear will get through to
him. Surely, this is the reason he isn't talking—he's afraid
of Antonio's retaliation. But for two full weeks I've had
cop after cop and attorney after attorney promising Ed
he'll have total protection if he talks, and he has not.*

*I look at my watch. Ten minutes late for my meeting with
Pritchard and the deputy prosecutor already. This is it. My
last chance in the box with Ed Gradduk. My last chance to
produce what I have promised—testimony that will put Antonio Childers behind bars. My last chance to save Ed
from prison, from Childers, from the potentially deadly
impact at the bottom of the slope that his life has become.*

*Ed has not spoken, nor has he removed his eyes from
mine. They bore into me with all the intensity of a butane
torch. He wants me to feel them. Wants me to feel what he
has refused to say with words. I have betrayed him, my
oldest friend. He wants to surround me with that knowledge, drown me with it.*

"I'm trying to help you here," I say. "Damn you for not accepting that. You've gotten in over your head, brother, and you have got to get out. I'm offering you a hand here. But you've got to reach out and take it."

Silence that settles over me like a lead cloak.

"I just want to help you get your life back to where it needs to be, Ed. Try to understand that, could you?"

He speaks then for the first and only time.

"You, Lincoln, should have tried to understand. Before you brought the rest of these cops and prosecutors and judges into it. Before you took away any room I might have had to maneuver. To breathe. That's when you should have tried to understand."

A knock on the door. Neither of us speaks. The knock is repeated.

"Will you talk?"

He shakes his head.

A third knock, this time louder, more insistent. I hear keys jingling. They're about to come in, to take him away, and after this it is done. He will be on his way to jail. I will have sent him there.

A key slides into the lock.

"I'm sorry," I say.

The handle turns. The door opens.

"I know," Ed Gradduk tells me, and then he is gone, back in handcuffs and out through a steel door that clangs shut behind him and leaves me alone in a little interrogation room with my head in my hands.

CHAPTER 10

Live in an apartment along a busy city street long enough and you learn to tune out traffic noise. In the time I'd been in my current building, the roaring motors, squealing brakes, and harsh horns of the busy avenue below had gradually become just background noise.

When I woke the next morning, however, the sounds penetrated into my brain in a way they would usually not. I was lying half-awake in bed when a car out on the avenue slammed on its brakes. There was a brief shriek of tires skidding on pavement, but no subsequent crash as I've heard on other mornings. The tires were enough, though. I opened my eyes wide, fully awake, then closed them again as I recalled Ed in the street, the Crown Victoria blasting into him.

The image sickened me. I lay with my palms pressed over my closed eyes, as if the added pressure could drive the memory from my mind. I thought of the way his body had snapped, his shoulders and legs moving in toward the car even as his waist headed in the opposite direction. That was the last position I'd seen him in, for all of a fraction of a second, before his body was sucked beneath the still-moving car and disappeared.

And the sounds. I would never forget the sounds. A muffled *whomp* of impact after the scream of tires and squeal of brakes. A wet popping as the tires passed over his body, like a champagne bottle opened underwater.

And then the same sound, but duller, the champagne gone flat this time, as they'd passed over him again.

I pushed out of bed and went to the window. It was just past seven, traffic building to its rush-hour peak. I watched the cars move and I thought of Ed Gradduk and the blood that had been hosed off the pavement on Clark Avenue, how quickly it had dried. A thousand cars must have passed over the spot already. More than that. I wondered if any had slowed.

The light up the street changed and the cars beneath me moved again, the procession passing through the intersection by our office a few blocks west. They moved quickly during the green-light cycle, then backed up again when it went red, came to a stop under my window, impatient drivers craning their necks and looking ahead to count the cars, try to figure out if they'd make it through the light in the next cycle, if they'd get to the office before the bagels were gone and the first pot of coffee cold.

I left the bedroom, left the apartment, walked down the steps, and out into the parking lot. The gravel was cold and sharp against my bare feet. I wore nothing but a pair of gym shorts, but I walked around the building to the front sidewalk, stood there, and stared at the street as curious motorists gazed back at me.

You can see something happen right before your eyes, something profound and important and consuming, and yet you can somehow miss really *seeing* it. I knew this from years of taking eyewitness testimony. The eyes bring information in and the brain processes it. Simple enough. Except that when the eyes tell the brain that they have just seen something go wrong, badly wrong, the brain doesn't want to process it that way. If at all possible, it rationalizes, offers a sense of perspective or understanding that the eyes don't have. The brain, you see, exists to explain. You can't discourage it from doing that.

But then there's memory, that obnoxious little bastard of the subconscious. Memory holds the scene, holds what the eyes have shown. And, down beneath the conscious layer, memory holds it accurately. Holds the picture without the perspective. When I was a cop, that's what we tried to get to. It takes a trigger, generally, something that affects the senses in such a way that it provokes the subconscious into action. Something like the squeal of tires I'd heard this morning.

J oe was at the office when I arrived, a cup of coffee from the corner doughnut shop in his hand. His computer was humming through its preliminary motions, and he looked at me with surprise as I stepped inside. Joe usually beats me to the office by at least half an hour.

"You run the Jeep plate number yet?" I said.

He sipped his coffee and shook his head. "Just got here."

"It's going to belong to Jack Padgett or Larry Rabold."

"Because they're working on Gradduk's case, so interest in Corbett wouldn't be unreasonable?"

"No," I said. "Because they killed Ed Gradduk."

"Right. But that was an accident . . ." He stopped when I began to shake my head.

"I'm not so sure it was."

He watched me with narrowed eyes and took a few swallows of his coffee. "That's a hell of an allegation, LP. And I don't understand where it's coming from. Gradduk ran in front of their car. You saw it happen."

"I know. They backed up over him, Joe. After they'd already hit him. And at the time I assumed they were just trying to clear away from the body."

"Probably they were."

I shook my head again. "They'd rolled the front tires

right over him. I heard the sound it made; they had to feel the rise of the tires. They knew they'd run him over, but they backed up anyhow and went over him again. I think it was to make sure he was dead."

Joe took a long, slow breath. "Come on, LP. Think about how fast that happened. Imagine if you'd been the driver. Hell, he was probably more horrified by what he'd done than you were standing there watching it. His first impulse was going to be to move away from Gradduk. To try to take it back, in effect."

"They didn't slow until after he fell. He went down and they kept going for a second or two, then hit the brakes. By then they were way too close to stop without hitting him."

"They were going fast because they saw he was running across the street."

"They were going fast because they didn't want him to make it across the street."

He shook his head. "If you'd come to me with this theory the night it happened, maybe I would have bought it. But not now. You've had too much time to consider it, restructure what you saw until it gave you something to work with."

"Wrong. When I saw it happen, I assumed it was an accident because that's the way my brain was trained to think. You don't expect cops to intentionally run a man down, so you assume that they didn't. But they did."

"No, Lincoln. They didn't."

"Answer me this, then: Why did Padgett and Rabold go to Ed's house to make the arrest in the first place?"

"Richards said they got the tip from the liquor store owner."

I nodded. "Exactly. They got a tip even though it wasn't their case. And rather than follow police protocol, which they both know from years on the force, and pass the tip along to the detective on the case, they went down alone. And Ed fought them and ran. Why? If he was innocent, why'd he run?"

"Maybe he wasn't—" Joe began, but my look shut him down and he looked away and nodded. "Right. We're assuming he was."

"He told me he was," I said. "And I believed him. Still do."

"It's a hell of a thing to suggest. You're talking about two cops, LP. You know what you're going to get started with this?"

"I've got an idea."

"I don't know a thing about Padgett, but I've been around Larry Rabold more than a few times. Seems like a nice guy. Solid cop, too."

"Run the plate number," I said. "See if I'm wrong."

After a long pause, he turned away from me and logged on to his computer. Private investigators in Ohio have access to the motor vehicle bureau's database, and it isn't hard to run a license number. He was busy for a few minutes and then looked up.

"The Jeep is registered to Jack Padgett."

We sat and looked at each other.

He groaned and rubbed his face with his hands. "Shit, Lincoln."

All I could do was agree.

The first thing I wanted to see was a copy of the officer's incident report from the botched arrest of Ed Gradduk. Such reports aren't public record, not the details at least, but that's the advantage of having worked with the police department. We could always find some old friend who was willing to help out with the minor stuff. Well, Joe could, at least. I had my contacts at the department, sure, but Joe was a legend. He had friends with the police he hadn't even met yet.

He made a few calls and got a promise that the report was on its way. When he'd hung up, he lifted a newspaper off the desk and held it in the air. "You read Amy's article yet?"

"No."

I'd almost forgotten about Amy's discovery, thanks to my preoccupation with Padgett and Rabold. Now I took the paper reluctantly. A glance at the front-page, above-the-fold headline was almost enough to make me put it down: MURDER SUSPECT WAS UNWANTED PRESENCE IN VICTIM'S LIFE.

I read the article, then folded it so the front page was hidden and stuffed it in the garbage can.

I couldn't call it editorializing, because it wasn't. All Amy had done was take her quotes and lay them out there: Gradduk allegedly had an unpleasant exchange with Sentalar at a bar; Gradduk apparently made numerous calls to her office and residence; Sentalar's law partner, a guy named David Russo, said the dead woman had viewed Gradduk as a nuisance and seemed at times to be afraid of him. Amy had written what she'd been told, and I supposed the television news stations were cursing her for beating them on the story. That didn't make it any easier for me to read.

"What do you think?" Joe said.

"I think it's bullshit."

"Has to be some fact to it, LP. Has to be."

"Sure, there might be some fact to it, but without explanation or context the readers are going to take one look and make a snap judgment that Ed was some sort of stalker."

Joe smiled wanly. "And that's Amy's fault?"

"I didn't say it was her fault."

"But you're thinking it."

I stood up and walked over to the fax machine, checked the display to make sure it was on. No sign of the incident report yet.

"You know she couldn't have enjoyed writing it about your old friend," he said. "But it's her job."

"She talk to you?"

"No. I'm just seeing your reaction and warning you to take a step back. You're from a police and PI background, LP. You build an investigation one day at a time, then produce your result. Amy doesn't have that luxury. When she has a productive day of investigation, she has to slam it into the next day's paper, or she's considered a professional failure."

"But it makes him look—" I began, and Joe interrupted with a snort.

"It makes him look bad? Makes him look like something he wasn't? Spreads misconceptions, encourages unfounded gossip? No shit, Lincoln. Welcome to the world of the media. You'd think you'd never encountered it before."

"I've encountered it."

"Exactly. So think about that and then ask yourself if you'd be this mad if it hadn't been Amy breaking the story."

The fax machine ground to life then, sucking a blank page from the feed tray and pumping it through. I grabbed it as it came out and saw a Cleveland Police Department cover sheet. This would be the incident report.

It was seven pages long, and I ran it through the copier before I read it, so Joe and I could take a look simultaneously. The incident report had been written by Sergeant

Jack Padgett the morning after Ed's death. It began with the tip.

On the afternoon of August 12, at approximately 3:45 P.M., I received a phone call on my cell phone. The number is one I frequently distribute to witnesses, informants, and others who could be of assistance to police business. The caller identified himself as Jerome Huggins of the Liquor Locker on Train Avenue. Mr. Huggins asked me if I was familiar with a fire on Train Avenue. He said the fire had occurred the previous day. I told him that I knew about it. He then told me he believed his security camera had captured information that would be of value to the police. Mr. Huggins chose to call me because I had previously worked with him on a robbery that had occurred in his business a few years earlier. I told Mr. Huggins that I would stop by to look at his film.

Upon arriving at the Liquor Locker, I was shown to a small television monitor by Mr. Huggins. He then played the portion of tape that he found relevant. Some of this tape showed the fire, other segments showed a white male entering and leaving the vacant house shortly before the fire began. In one segment the man's vehicle was visible. I asked Mr. Huggins if he thought the man in the tape was familiar, and he said he did. He identified the male as someone from the neighborhood. He suggested the man's first name was Ed, but he could not recall the last name. I obtained the license plate number from a careful study of the tape. I then called in to dispatch and asked them to run the plate match. They informed me that the plate was registered to an Edward Gradduk. I then asked Mr. Huggins if he believed this individual could be the man he identified on the tape, and he told me that he believed that to be true. At this point myself and Officer Rabold took the surveillance tape to be entered as police evidence and went to locate the suspect, Edward Gradduk. At this point myself and Officer Rabold believed we had probable cause to suggest that Mr. Gradduk had trespassed on private property shortly before a criminal act of arson was committed at that property.

" 'A criminal act of arson,' he says." I looked at Joe, who just grunted and continued reading. I dropped my eyes back to the paper.

Dispatch informed me that Edward Gradduk's home address was on Clark Avenue. Together with Officer Rabold, I proceeded to this address in order to determine if the suspect was home. His vehicle, a Ford sedan, was found to be in the driveway of the residence. Officer Rabold requested that he remain outside to watch the house in case Gradduk tried to leave from the back, and I approved. I myself entered the house with permission of an older white female who identified herself as the mother of Edward Gradduk. We stood in the kitchen and waited for Edward Gradduk to come down the steps. He came down at his mother's request and seemed immediately to resent me being in the house. I told him that I wanted to speak with him about a fire on Train Avenue and asked if he would be willing to come to the police station for questioning. At this point the mother grew hostile, shouting at me and insisting that I leave. Edward Gradduk told me he wanted to call an attorney. I said he could call an attorney to meet him at the police station but that I would be taking him into custody as a suspect in an arson and homicide investigation. It was at this point that Edward Gradduk struck me in the face with his right fist and exited the residence through the front door. Officer Rabold had been watching the rear of the property and did not see Edward Gradduk leave.

The report went on to describe the arrival of backup, the delegation of duties in the search for Gradduk, and the medical condition of Padgett, whose nose turned out not to be broken, just bloodied. There was a mention of their encounter with me, followed by a concise description of the "accidental" death of Ed Gradduk, which was described as "unavoidable contact during pursuit of a fleeing homicide suspect."

I'd finished the report before Joe, so I flipped through the pages again until he'd read the last page and set it aside.

"The detail is a little sparse for an incident report that resulted in a suspect's death," he said. "But other than that, it doesn't seem especially unusual."

"Other than the tip."

"I don't see anything particularly odd about the tip. If Padgett knew this guy Huggins from a previous robbery case and from working in the neighborhood, it's not surprising that he'd get the call. If there's one breed of businessman who appreciates his local street cops, it's the liquor store owners."

"I still don't like it."

Joe shrugged. "I'm not telling you to like it. Just saying it isn't enough to base such a serious charge on, and wondering what you've got planned from here."

"I want to talk to Huggins, and I want to talk to Alberta Gradduk."

Joe nodded, looking not too subtly at our stack of active case files.

"If you're worried about the paying clients, I'll work it alone. Dock me for a couple vacation days."

He rolled his eyes and stood up. "There's nothing on our plate that can't hold a day. And no limit to the trouble you'll get into if I leave you to go at this alone."

PART TWO OUT OF THE ASHES

CHAPTER 11

We were at a stoplight on Lorain, on the way to the Liquor Locker, when Joe asked me to explain what had really happened with Ed all those years earlier. I was sure he'd wanted me to volunteer it myself, but the truth was, I kept forgetting he didn't know. I had few secrets from Joe.

It didn't take me long to explain it, and that felt wrong, somehow. It seemed as if it should take hours, not minutes.

"So you and his girlfriend were trying to bail him out of a situation he wouldn't bail himself out of," Joe said when I was through.

"Yes."

He grunted but didn't say anything else, just stared out the window and watched the houses and storefronts go by.

"I should have been up front about it back then," I said. "But I hardly knew you, and . . . well, it wasn't something that was easy to tell."

"And you're still feeling guilty about it."

"About not telling you?"

"No. About what you did to your friend."

"I betrayed him, Joe."

"Only to try to help him."

"No."

He turned his head, but I didn't look at him.

"It wasn't about his girl," I said. "I didn't want to be

with Allison. But I can't pretend I went with her idea for purely noble purposes, either."

"So what else was there?"

"I wanted to be the hero."

He was quiet for a moment, then said, "I see."

"I wanted to help him, sure," I said. "But I also wanted everyone to know that I'd been the one. Allison, Draper, Ed's mother, everybody. I wanted to be the savior."

"That's not what you became."

I laughed sadly. "No. People called me a lot of things when it went down, but none of those terms were mentioned."

Joe was silent till we were on Train Avenue, then spoke without taking his eyes off the road.

"What you just said, LP . . . that's every young cop's story. That's what they all want, at first—to be a hero. I've seen enough of them to know that's the truth. And I've been there myself. Young cops want to be heroes."

"And old cops?"

"Just want to understand," he said. "Just want to know the truth, and then disappear again. Fade to black."

Directly across from the Liquor Locker was a charred concrete foundation that was all that remained of the home where Anita Sentalar had died. Or at least where her body had burned. Joe pulled his Taurus up to the curb across from the liquor store and we both eyed the burn site. Little was left. It had burned, as Amy had said, real hot and real fast. Most of the crime-scene tape that had been used to rope the area off had been knocked down now by curious neighbors or kids. My window was down, and as Joe turned the motor off, I could almost imagine that the acrid smell of stale ashes and smoke was still in the air. A lazy wind blew between the old houses on either side of the ruin, whistling softly as it passed over the jagged concrete formations that remained.

"Hell of a strange place to dump a body," Joe said, "whether he had access or not. It's a crowded city street. Setting the place on fire discreetly wouldn't have been easy."

"The good news is, Ed wasn't looking for a place to dump a body, and he didn't burn the house, so that's not an issue."

"Sure."

We got out of the car and walked across the street and into the liquor store, a place that felt as spacious as an air-plane bathroom. There were three shelves filled with cheap booze and two coolers along the far wall that held cold beer. I saw four bottles of champagne on the end of one shelf, the most expensive a twenty-dollar bottle of Asti. A black guy with a fleshy face and several chins sat at the cash register and watched us look around. He had a toothpick stuck in the corner of his mouth.

"You looking for something in particular?"

"Had a couple questions for you," Joe said, stepping up to the register, but I stayed where I was, scanning the walls. There, in the back corner of the room, was one camera. It pointed toward the front of the store, at the door. I pivoted slightly and found another, mounted where it had a good view of the cash register. Now that I'd located both of the interior cameras, I followed their an-gles with my eyes and found what I'd expected—neither looked out across the street. I left the building while Joe introduced himself to the cashier, then stood on the side-walk until I found the third camera, a little one pressed up under the eaves, angled so its lens pointed across the street, directly at the charred concrete blocks that had once been part of a house. The camera was black and clean, the bolts holding it in place firm and without rust.

I went back inside. Joe gave me a curious look and stopped talking. The black guy worked the toothpick over to the other side of his mouth and glared at me.

"Are you Jerome Huggins?" I said.

He nodded. "I am. There a reason you so interested in my security cameras?"

"Yes. You're the guy who provided the tapes of the fire to the police, right?"

It was hot in the cramped little store, and beads of sweat stood out on Jerome Huggins's bald head and ran along his jowls. A tiny fan sat beside the register, blowing warm air into his face.

"That's right," he said. "And as I was just asking your friend here, what the hell does that have to do with you?"

"We're private investigators," Joe said, reaching for his wallet.

Huggins waved him off. "I don't give a shit what kind of badge y'all got, I don't think I want to be talking to you. If you're private investigators, who you working for?"

"Hell of a security system you've got in this place," I said, waving my hand around the room. "Two interior cameras, one exterior. I've been in banks that had less coverage than that."

"This ain't Brecksville, boy," Jerome Huggins said. "We got kids out there with big guns in their hands and small brains in their heads. Got to be prepared."

"How long you had those cameras up?" I asked.

"Two years," Huggins answered, chewing on the toothpick now with enough pressure to make his jaw muscles bulge.

I leaned on the counter, my face close to his, and smiled.

"Jerome," I said, "you are full of shit."

He wiped his sweaty jowls with one hand and spit the

toothpick onto the floor at his feet.

"'Scuse me, boy?"

"Those cameras are almost brand-new, Jerome. I'd be willing to bet if we pull them down and have someone from the manufacturer come here and take a look, we'll find out they were made in the last year. I'm guessing they haven't been up for more than a month."

Joe took a few steps to the side and stood peering up at one of the interior cameras, seeing what I already knew.

"I suggest," Jerome Huggins said, "that you boys be getting the hell out of my store now."

I shook my head. "Not yet, Jerome. Not till you tell us when those cameras went in and who told you to put them in."

"Kiss . . . my . . . black . . . ass," he said slowly, straightening up on his stool.

"You really buy those two years ago?" Joe said, voice casual.

Huggins looked at him with distaste but nodded.

"Where'd you get them?" Joe asked, still friendly.

Huggins's chest rose as he took a deep breath. "From a catalog."

"Any chance you'd have a receipt?" Joe said.

"Get out," Huggins said. "Now."

I put my palms on the counter and leaned in to him. "You're a lying piece of shit, Jerome. Those cameras are new, and you put them up because somebody told you to do it. Isn't that it?"

"I put them up because I like my security." His hand dipped under the counter. "Same reason I keep this." He brought out a small Smith & Wesson revolver, wrapped his fat fingers around the stock, and rested it gently on the counter, pointed my way. "I think it's time for you to go home."

I stayed where I was and stared at him. I stared at him

for a long time. Long enough for him to begin to concentrate on it, to focus on meeting my eyes. When it seemed he was properly absorbed with that, I swept my left hand across the counter and knocked the revolver out of his fingers with one sharp, swift motion. He came up off his stool and swung at me clumsily. I avoided the blow and reached across the counter to grab him by the throat. Joe swore and put his hands on my shoulders, pulling me back.

"Tell me if it was like I said, Jerome." I tightened my grasp on his throat and he gagged, his eyes wide and white, his hands tugging at my fingers, trying to free himself.

"Get off him," Joe said, his hand finding a pressure point between my neck and shoulder as he pulled me back. I released Jerome Huggins's throat and stepped away from the counter. He stood still, rubbing his neck and breathing heavily.

"Yeah, you best get him off," he said to Joe. "This boy here got crazy eyes, man. Crazy eyes. I see 'em come in here like that sometimes, ready to kill over something ain't nobody else even understands. I see 'em. And you know what they get next? They get dead, my man. Dead."

"Who told you to put the cameras up, Jerome?" I said. "You tell me that, and we're gone."

He shook his head. "You're already gone, brother."

I wanted to say more, but Joe was pushing me toward the door.

We went outside and across the street. Joe unlocked the car but didn't get inside, choosing instead to lean on the hood and stare at me.

"The cameras are new, Joe," I said. "They set Ed up."

The wind came across the empty lot and blew his tie up in his face. He smoothed it down and kept staring at me, silent.

"You know I'm right," I said. "You saw the cameras, and you heard Huggins, and you know what it means."

"I'll tell you what else I saw. I saw you lose control, Lincoln. Fast."

"You call that losing control? Please. That was pretty damn restrained. If I'd lost control, I would have broken every bottle of booze in that asshole's store and then put him through the window."

"Macho," Joe said. "Cool."

"Go to hell."

For a minute he was quiet. Then he said, "You know what I would've put in my report if we were still on the force? I would've written that my partner needed to be removed from the case because of an excessive emotional involvement. I would've written that your judgment could not be trusted on this case, that you were a liability to yourself and everyone around you."

I put my hands on the car roof and leaned against it, meeting his eyes.

"We aren't on the force anymore, Joe."

"That doesn't mean you can do *that*," he said, pointing across the street at the Liquor Locker.

"These bastards set my friend up for a murder, and then they killed him!" I said, my voice tight and loud, my hands pressed hard against the car. "Don't tell me what I can and cannot do. I'm here to settle the damn score, okay? And if I've got to settle it by kicking in doors and slapping a piece of shit like Jerome back there around, that's what I'm going to do. You don't like it, then get the hell out of here and go home. I'll finish this alone."

"You think this is the way to go about it? You're even shouting at *me* now. There's a way to investigate—"

"They set my friend up for a murder and then they

killed him!" I screamed it this time and punched the roof of his car. "You want to talk about protocol and manners? Are you *kidding* me?"

Joe stood up straight, every muscle rigid, his eyes flat and small. He did not speak.

"I don't need to hear about what you'd write in your damn report if we were still on the force," I said, my voice softer now. "We're not there anymore, and this isn't a case somebody dropped on my desk. This is the best friend I ever had, Joe, and he's dead. Don't tell me to treat it like it's another day at the job. It's not."

He took a deep breath, moved his eyes to the street, but stayed silent.

"You want to go home, go home," I said. "I'm going to see Alberta Gradduk."

He stayed where he was. I turned and walked away from him, east down Train. It would be a long walk to Ed's old house, but I had plenty of fuel to burn.

I'd gone maybe three blocks when Joe pulled up beside me and stopped, the motor idling. I looked in at him. He didn't turn to face me, just kept his eyes on the street while he popped the door locks open and waited for me to get inside.

Her face had taken on a grayish cast that reminded me of the Cuyahoga on a cold March morning. Her eyes were rimmed with red lines and her breath was stale with cigarette smoke and bourbon. I stood on the steps and stared at her, tried to remember her as she'd once been, an attractive woman who rarely drank and didn't smoke. It wasn't easy.

"I told you," Alberta Gradduk said, "to go away. I didn't want to see you back here. Why won't you leave us alone?"

"It's not 'us,' anymore, Mrs. Gradduk," I said. "Your son is dead. And I don't give a damn what you think of

me, or where you want me to go, or how much you want
to be left alone. I'm here to find out what really happened
to Ed, and I'm not leaving."

For a moment I was sure she'd slam the door in my
face again, but she didn't. Instead she turned away from
the door and walked back into the house on unsteady legs.
She left the door standing open, though, and Joe and I followed her inside.

Stepping over the threshold and into the house was like
walking into a museum, a place designed to freeze the
past and preserve memories. I remembered every turn
and doorway and room so well I could have navigated the
house blindfolded, though I hadn't been inside in fifteen
years.

Joe and I sat on a dirty couch with our backs to the
street while Alberta took an armchair across from us. She
shuffled with a pack of cigarettes and an empty glass on
the coffee table for a bit but didn't do anything with either.

"It's been a long time since I was in this house," I said.
I'd been obnoxious and commanding out on the steps,
trying to get in the door, but I didn't really want this conversation to be contentious. If I could somehow convince
Alberta Gradduk to talk with me as the old family friend
I still felt I was, it would be a much better scenario. "Ed
had clearly been doing some work on the place."

"How's what we did in our home any business of
yours?" Alberta snapped.

"You like being back in the house, then?" I said, ignoring her comment.

She rolled an unlit cigarette between her fingers. "I
hate this house."

"You didn't want Ed to buy it?"

"Ed didn't care what I thought of that." She looked up
at me and glared. "Why are you bothering me with all
this? You think asking questions about this stupid old

house is going to help anything? They're burying my son in three days, you know. Burying him." She rolled her eyes over to Joe. "What are you staring at?"

He smiled the smile of a patient priest in a confessional, passing no judgment. "Just listening, ma'am."

"This is my partner," I said. "His name's Joe Pritchard. He was a police detective for a long time. I thought he could help us here."

She looked at Joe contemptuously. "I hate the police, mister. Every one of you."

He looked at me as if to say *nice icebreaker,* but didn't speak.

"Ed got set up," I said, leaning forward, bracing my elbows on my knees. "I'm sure of that, Mrs. Gradduk. I want to prove it to everyone else, though."

"Like anybody cares." She waved her bony hands at me in disgust. She was in the same dress she'd been wearing when I'd come to the house two days earlier.

"We don't want to bother you, ma'am," Joe said. "We're really just hoping to help. Could you tell us what happened when the police came to arrest your son?"

She set the cigarette back on the table and scowled at it. "Marched in here like he owned the place, that's what he did. Didn't knock, just opened the door and walked right in."

I raised my eyebrows. "The cop didn't knock? Are you sure?"

"Of course I'm sure, I was sitting right in this room. I had the paper out, but I couldn't tell you exactly what I was reading in it. I heard him come up on the steps and I put the paper down, thinking I'd have to go to the door when he knocked. But before I could even get out of my chair, he was inside."

"What did he say?" Joe asked.

"Not a damn thing at first. Just looked at me all surprised, like he hadn't imagined finding me in my own house. I asked just what the hell he thought he was doing. He asked what I was doing here. What *I* was doing here, like I didn't belong and he did. That's when Ed came in."

"Where had Ed been till then?" I asked. I could remember sitting on the floor in this room with Ed, watching television. When we were in third grade, he'd had a model train that ran around the floor, and we used to run the track under the couch and pin its skirt up so the trains could go through our makeshift tunnel. Beside me was the door that led out to the front porch, where we used to sit in the evenings and listen to Norm Gradduk's stories, watch him play solitaire and drink Stroh's beer.

"I don't know, I didn't follow him from room to room," Alberta said, her voice high and whiny, like a child's.

"So what happened when Ed saw the police officer?" Joe said.

"When Ed came in, he pointed the gun at him and told him to get his hands in the air."

Joe and I exchanged a glance. "Ed had a gun?" Joe asked.

Alberta was disgusted. "No."

"But you said he pointed a gun . . ."

"That's right. Pointed it at Ed."

"The cop had a gun out?" I asked.

"That's right."

"He had a gun out when he came into the house?" Joe said.

"That's right."

We looked at one another again. An unannounced entrance, with gun drawn. This was certainly not the situation that had been presented in Jack Padgett's incident report.

"What happened then?" Joe said.

"He told me to go upstairs and leave them alone. He said he needed to be alone with Ed. I yelled at him and told him to leave. He told me to go upstairs, but Ed told me to stay where I was. They kept shouting, and then Ed hit him in the face. Hit him hard. He hit him and I yelled and then Ed opened the door and ran."

"Did it seem like Ed knew the cop?" I said.

Her eyelids went up slowly, as if it took a concentrated effort.

"You know," Alberta Gradduk said, "you're just like your father."

"Excuse me?"

"Just like him," she said, and I could tell that it was no compliment.

"What does my father have to do with this?"

She stared at me unpleasantly. "People have their own problems. They should be allowed to deal with them privately. I never liked meddlers."

"I'm not meddling, Mrs. Gradduk; I'm trying to clear your son's name. I'd like to think you'd support that attempt."

"I want you to leave."

"You haven't answered all my questions yet."

"And I'm not going to!" She shouted this time, her eyes wide and angry, a spray of spit following her words. "I don't want you here. I don't want you to come back. Just go away and leave us alone. We'll be fine without you and your judgment."

I started to open my mouth to tell her I wasn't judging anyone, but then I saw it was going to be wasted effort, and I shook my head and stood up. Joe followed suit.

"That's right, get out," Alberta Gradduk said, her voice back to its natural state, that weak, raspy whisper.

"We're going," I said, pulling open the front door. "You have a good day, Mrs. Gradduk. I'm sorry about Ed."

We were back at the car when I turned to Joe.
    "He came in without knocking or identifying himself, gun drawn," I said. "Seemed surprised and bothered to find the mother there. Once Ed showed up, Padgett told Alberta to leave them alone in the room. Ed told her not to."

Joe was silent.

"They came to kill him," I said. "Padgett didn't expect Ed's mother to be there. She threw him. Her presence saved his life, at least right then. Ed saw the situation for what it was, and he ran."

Joe's face was empty, his eyes hard. I knew I had him now, though. Joe came from a family of cops, and he'd devoted most of his life to being the best cop in the city. If there was one thing he could not stomach, it was the idea of a corrupt police officer.

"You ready to ride with me yet?" I said.

His smile was cold as he held up his car keys. "Hell," he said. "I'm driving."

CHAPTER 12

Our timing was bad. If we'd been five minutes later getting back to the office, we would have missed Cal Richards. Instead, we pulled into the parking lot just as he was climbing into his car, ready to leave. When he saw us, he got back out and leaned against the trunk of the unmarked Taurus, a smile on his face.

"Gentlemen. How fortunate that you've returned. I didn't want to miss you."

"What's up?" Joe said.

"You mind if we go up to your office?" Richards said, stepping away from his car. "Hot as a bastard out here."

We went in the building and up the steps, Richards walking silently behind us. Joe unlocked the office door and we went inside. Richards sat down across from us and cleared his throat dramatically.

"So, I've been out of your office for less than a day and already I've got a complaint about your behavior."

"From?" I said.

"Jerome Huggins. I talked with the man less than an hour ago. He told me a couple of white-boy private eyes were down this morning, giving him grief. Said the old guy of the duo was cool enough, but the young guy was, well, maybe a little headstrong. Jerome didn't seem to think fondly of him."

"A lot of PIs in this town," I said. "Could be anybody."

Richards rolled his eyes. "Let's not waste time on the

bullshit, okay? I didn't come down here to bust your balls over this, Perry. I'd be justified in doing that, but I don't want to. I know you're investigating your friend's past, and I got no problem with that. I just want to have some idea of where I can expect you to be turning up."

"What were you doing at the liquor store?" I countered.

He ran a hand over his bristle-short hair. "Wanted to verify some things with Jerome, is all."

I grinned. "You lie, Detective."

"Pardon?"

"You're too good not to have a problem with the cameras at that place," I said.

Richards sat expressionless for a minute, until Joe began to laugh softly.

"You confused him, LP. Called him a liar in the same breath as you complimented him. Man doesn't know what to do now."

Richards allowed a small smile. "Weighing my options, for sure. And I'm going to play along, Perry, and acknowledge that, yes, I am way too good not to have a problem with those cameras."

"Any idea who told Jerome to put them up?"

He shook his head. "Not yet. Jerome's sticking hard and fast to this tale that they've been up for years. One look tells you that's horseshit, but I'm not ready to put him in the box and sweat him yet. Just curious, is all. Jerome'll be there when I need him."

"I see."

"What about you?" he said. "Any idea who's at the other end of Jerome's puppet strings?"

I gazed across the room at Joe, who met my look with flat eyes. After a moment's hesitation, I decided to trust Cal Richards.

"I think your cops set him up. And then I think they killed him. Intentionally."

Cal let out a long, slow breath. "You want to run that by me again?"

I told him about the discrepancies in the incident report and Alberta Gradduk's account of the botched arrest, and I told him about Padgett and Rabold watching Mitch Corbett's house.

Richards didn't like it. Not a bit.

"Those guys are longtime cops, Perry. Maybe not the best on the force, but they've been around. That's a bold-ass suggestion you just made, implicating them in a conspiracy. In murder."

"They set him up, Richards. They set him up and they took him down. Ed was innocent."

He sighed. "Look, Perry, I'm going to give you this because I think you deserve to know. Think you *need* to know. I exercised a search warrant on Gradduk's house and on his vehicle. You know what I found? Trunk of his car was filled with bottles of a chemical accelerant and a couple hundred feet of industrial fuse. More of the same in his basement. Also in the basement were two home-made timing devices, designed to run about fifteen minutes before touching off the fuse. Just right for the fire on Train Avenue."

I was shaking my head even before he was done. "They weren't his, Richards. Someone planted that shit. Hell, Padgett and Rabold had ample opportunity."

"I've also got a guy who will testify to selling Gradduk the fuse cord. He recognized him from the picture and will swear to it in court."

"No," I said again.

He leaned forward, elbows on his knees, and looked hard at me. "I'll tell you what else I've got—a coroner's report on the victim. Sentalar was burned pretty badly, but not so badly that you can't tell that she didn't die from the fire. She had a bullet in her, first, one right in the center of her forehead. Medical examiners can tell me without a doubt that it was a thirty-two-caliber round. Only one gun is registered to Ed Gradduk, Perry. Also a thirty-two. Now missing."

I shook my head but didn't speak. Joe said, "Can they get a specific ballistics match on the bullet?"

"No. Bullet blew out the back side of her skull. If we had it, we might get a precise match, but the fire took care of that. It was in the rubble somewhere, and the fire department guys didn't locate it. Not that I blame them for that."

"He got set up," I said. "Ed got set up, Richards."

Richards nodded. "He got set up. But not framed for a murder. He killed that girl, Perry. But I think he got set up in having his picture taken while he was doing it. And I want to know why."

"But Padgett and Rabold—"

"Are a couple of good ol' boy cops looking for a hot collar," he said. "That's all they are. Believe me, I'll take a good look at this guy, Corbett, and I'll burn those two good for working a surveillance on him without letting me know. But in the end, I think they're just looking to make headlines. If they're guilty of anything, it's holding out on a tip. I bet they were given some real detail about this, but they don't want to pass it off because it'll go to me and they'll miss the glory."

I got out of my chair and walked to the window, stood with my back to him, my hands clenched at my sides.

"I know he was your friend," Richards said. "But he killed her. I'm almost sure of it."

I didn't answer. He sat there for a while, then said good-bye to Joe and left. When the door closed behind him, it was quiet. I stayed at the window. Joe let a few minutes pass before he broke the silence.

"All right, LP. It's not what you wanted to hear him

say. But that doesn't mean the work we did in the morning was for nothing. Let's get back to that now, get focused."

I turned away from the window, still angry. "He's convinced Ed killed her, Joe. He just shrugged off everything we gave him on those cops."

"He didn't shrug it off. He's a good detective. Maybe as good as you. He'll take what we gave him and blend it with what he's got, and he'll keep moving. Hell, did you expect him to leap in the air and click his heels at the idea Gradduk was set up by two of his own cops? Come on."

I gave that a grudging nod and returned to my chair. "Okay. I hear you. So what's our play then? Start with the cameras?"

He tugged at his tie and frowned. "I don't think so. The best way to get the truth about them is probably to break Huggins down, and I think we can do that by connecting him to Padgett and Rabold. I'd rather start with a hard look at those two. I want to know where they're from, how long they've been cops, what cases they've worked, who they drink with, who they sleep with. First things I want to look at when I'm investigating sleazy cops are their conduct evaluations."

"Think we can get those?"

He allowed a rare cocky smile to slide across his face. "I can get the chief's checkbook if I want it, LP."

"Then make the call. But you're forgetting about something."

"Oh?"

"Mitch Corbett."

He let his breath out loudly and nodded. "Shit, you're right. I had forgotten about him. If he's important to Padgett, he needs to be important to us."

I told him what little I'd learned with my phone calls the previous night.

"His brother wasn't helpful," I said, "nor was he fond

of Mitch. Could be the truth, or it could be a smokescreen he's putting up because his brother's hiding out at his place."

"All right," Joe said. "Let's do it like this: You work Corbett this afternoon. Get everything you can. And I'll do the background on Padgett and Rabold."

Family hadn't proved particularly helpful in my quest for information about Mitch Corbett, and I didn't know any of his friends other than the dead one. That left me with coworkers. Jimmy Cancerno was Corbett's boss, but he hadn't appeared to be too interested in cooperating the previous day. I decided I'd drive out to Cancerno's construction company anyhow, talk to whomever I could find, and see where it led me. If Ed and Corbett had become friends on the job, it stood to reason there had been a couple other guys in the mix.

Pinnacle Properties, Cancerno's contracting company, was located on Pearl Road, just south of Riverside Cemetery. On the other side of the interstate was MetroHealth, where my father had worked as a paramedic for years. MetroHealth was home to the city's busiest emergency room, and that had provided a constant sound track to the neighborhood when I was growing up. As I drove, an ambulance siren was wailing a few blocks away, and as soon as it faded, I could hear the thumping of helicopter blades as a medical chopper headed north for the landing pad on the roof of the hospital.

Pinnacle Properties was housed in a long prefabricated warehouse that gleamed in the afternoon sun. A small office was built into the front of the warehouse, and a half dozen cars were in the parking lot. I got out of the truck and walked into the office.

A young, blond girl with a good smile was behind the only desk inside. I told her I was looking for Mitch Corbett, just in case she had more up-to-date information than I did.

"Hmm," she said, "Mitch hasn't been working this week. I don't know what that's about. I can radio out to the site and see if he showed up late today, though."

"Tell you what, you tell me where those guys are and I'll drive out and have a word with them myself. If Mitch isn't around, I can always talk to . . ." I frowned, thoughtful, then pointed at her for assistance, as if I'd drawn a momentary blank on the name.

"Jeff."

"Right, Jeff." I smiled at her. "I'll talk to Jeff if Mitch isn't around. Where are they?"

She gave me an address on Erin Avenue. I thanked her, returned to my truck, and drove north on Pearl until it became West Twenty-fifth Street just past Clark Avenue. A left turn onto Erin Avenue, and then I slowed down to look at the house numbers. I found the one I needed without bothering to look at the address; a Pinnacle Properties pickup truck was parked in front of the house. The home itself was a narrow, two-story duplex that had seen better days. A pile of trash and debris was at the curb, and a weather-beaten sign stuck in the weed-riddled front yard claimed the house as a NEIGHBORHOOD ALLIANCE ACQUISITION.

I parked across the street and walked over and up the driveway. I could hear a stereo going inside, Lynyrd Skynyrd's "Gimme Three Steps" playing just as I was on my way up the three front steps of the house. Then the side door opened with a bang and a thick guy with red hair and no shirt stepped outside, followed by a Hispanic man with chiseled muscles. Each held bulging garbage bags in their hands as they marched down the driveway. They tossed them on top of the pile, and both bags promptly rolled off and fell on the sidewalk, something inside one of them shattering. The Hispanic guy turned around, indifferent, and spotted me standing at the door. The redhead was replacing the fallen bags to the top of the garbage heap.

"This is private property," the Hispanic guy said. "You got a reason to be up there?" His companion turned around at that and gave me a curious glance.

I left the front door and walked down to the driveway to meet them. "How's it going? I'm looking for a Jeff?"

"You got him," the redhead said. "Jeff Franklin." He pulled off a thick work glove and offered me his meaty hand. We shook, both of us squinting against the sun that shone down uninhibited by any trees. The Hispanic guy spat on the sidewalk and looked bored.

"My name's Lincoln Perry. I was hoping you could help me find someone."

"Yeah?"

"Mitch Corbett."

Jeff Franklin gave me an interested look as he pulled a red bandanna from his back pocket and wiped his face with it. His barrel chest was soaked with sweat beneath a mat of curly red hair, and his upper arms were all freckles.

"Mitch's missing, I'm afraid," he said. "Hasn't been in for a few days."

"Is that unusual?"

He nodded. "Very. I've worked with him for more'n a year and I can't think of a single sick day he took. Man's a hard worker."

"What're you, a cop?" the Hispanic guy asked, then spat on the pavement again.

"No. Just someone who needs to talk to *this* man." I nodded pointedly at Jeff Franklin, making it clear that I had no interest in the other guy, nor any desire for him to stick around. Before he could object to that, Franklin handled it for me.

"Go on inside and help the rest of the guys, Ramone. We got a lot to finish up today."

Ramone shrugged and went back up the driveway, shoulders slouched, swaggering. Jeff Franklin watched him and sighed, then tucked the bandanna back in his pocket.

"Can I ask why you're needing Mitch?"

There was something about Jeff Franklin that I liked. He carried himself confidently but without pretense, and I had the sense he would reciprocate straight talk with more of the same.

"I'm a private investigator. And I was a friend of Ed Gradduk's a long time ago."

Jeff Franklin gazed at me with sad eyes. "Let's you and I go sit down. You want a Coke?"

I started to shake my head, but he was already gone. He went out to the pickup truck, dug two cans of Coke out of a cooler, then walked back up the driveway and over to the sagging front porch. He sat down on it, opened one can of Coke, and handed the other to me.

"Ed was a good man," he said after he took a drink. "He'd only worked with us for about six months, but you get to know a fella pretty well in six months of work. And I liked him."

"I did, too."

He drank some more of the Coke, then muffled a belch and studied me. "You think he killed that woman?"

I shook my head. "No, I don't. And that's why I'm here."

"Looking for Mitch? What's he got in it?"

"Maybe nothing. But I won't know till I ask him. And I'm a little concerned that he's missing. I was told he and Ed were pretty close."

"They were." Jeff Franklin tugged the bandanna out of his pocket again, held it idly in one hand, the Coke in the other. "Mitch and Ed took to each other. Mitch was about twenty years older, of course, but they had a similar sort of personality, you know? Laughed at jokes nobody else thought was funny, noticed things nobody else noticed. Yeah, they got along, all right."

"How long have you known Corbett?"

He chewed on his lip absently while he thought about it. "I guess almost two years. That's how long I've been working for Jimmy, and Mitch was on when I got the job. He's the crew supervisor."

"Longtime construction worker, then?"

"All his life. Went into the army and came out a demolitions specialist, hired on with Jimmy. Been with him ever since."

"You say he was a demolitions expert?"

Jeff started to nod, then stopped and narrowed his eyes. "You thinking about that fire?"

"Maybe."

He shook his head. "Mitch is a good man, mister."

"So was Ed."

"I agree. And that's why I like to think neither of them had anything to do with it."

"You seen Mitch since Ed died?"

"No, I haven't. Last time I saw Mitch was the day before all that got started." He crumpled the Coke can and looked at me. "You think those two were into something together, don't you?"

"Could be. You got any ideas?"

He shook his head, and I believed him. He looked as if he would love to help me if he could.

"I need to talk to somebody who was close to him," I said. "Hell, close to either of them. I'm starting from scratch here. Take what I can get."

Jeff Franklin frowned. "I dunno what I can tell you. We all worked together, but not much was said other than the usual, you know? Sports and trucks and women and such. I got four kids, so when it's quitting time I'm done and gone. Didn't have much chance to hang out with the rest of the boys. Mitch and Ed ran around together some, I know, but that's about it."

"You don't know anyone else that Corbett spent time with?"

He chewed on his lip. "Well, this isn't a person, but he had a volunteer job in the evenings and on weekends, working down at some gym on Clark Avenue. Refereeing basketball and keeping the kids in line, that sort of thing."

"Clark Rec Center?" I said, and he nodded.

"It ain't much," he said, "but it's all I got for you."

When I left, Jeff Franklin asked me to call him if I learned anything about Mitch, and I told him that I would.

"Nobody around to worry about Mitch," he said. "No family to speak of, and not many friends. Man kept to himself. I keep wondering if we shouldn't talk to the police, but everybody else told me not to sweat it. Said Mitch was fine and that he'd be back when he got ready to be back."

He cocked his head at me. "But you know? I'm not feeling so sure about that anymore."

CHAPTER 13

Clark Rec had been a special place to me as a kid. Even then, it had been a relic from another time, but that was what made it special. There's an indoor pool, which is damn exciting to a Cleveland kid during the winter, but it isn't the stainless-steel tank and glaring light of your modern YMCA pool. It's a narrow lap pool, the floors tile and the walls painted with murals, everything lit with a sort of mellow aquamarine glow, skylights filtering in some natural light from above. I learned how to swim there, and, when no adults were looking, how to do one hell of a cannonball.

There's a basketball court, too, and it seems like a cage in a way, the court sunken and bordered closely on every side by stone walls. There aren't any bleachers for spectators alongside the court, but a balcony rims it, and that's where you'd sit if you wanted to watch, looking down on the action. CLARK WARRIORS is painted across the side of the balcony, a nickname that probably used to apply to the rec league team, even though I always connected it to West Tech High School's Warriors when I was a kid. I learned to shoot in that time warp of a gym, learned how to watch the offensive player's midsection to avoid being faked out on defense, how to box out for a rebound, run the fast break.

Out in front of the court is a room filled with picnic tables and games like air hockey and Ping-Pong. This is the room I entered from the street when I came from my talk with Jeff Franklin. Kids were coloring with crayons and construction paper at one of the picnic tables, a trim black woman standing over them. I moved left, looking for a less occupied adult, and then I couldn't resist walking down to peek in at the old pool. Brightly colored fish were painted on the walls now, along with two signs declaring that it was illegal to carry a firearm into the building. There was also a photograph of a young girl, the word MISSING written above her head in bold, black font. I took a deep breath of the chlorine-scented air, shook my head, and walked back into the front room.

It was surprisingly quiet. Maybe a dozen kids were huddled around the tables, but there wasn't the jumble of voices and loud laughter that you usually hear when kids are gathered together. The black woman was kneeling beside one of the children, a girl of maybe eight who had tears on her cheeks. The woman whispered soothingly to her, and the girl nodded and sniffed. She had long brown braids and big eyes and she looked tired. There'd probably been some sort of an argument or fight between the kids. The woman had probably responded to it by ordering a silent period. That would explain the odd quiet in the room.

Killing time till the woman was available, I walked over to the table and stood a few feet behind the group, glanced over the shoulders of the kids, at their artwork. What I saw made me raise my eyebrows and step closer. One of the girls had drawn a group of people with frowns and big blue teardrops on their faces. A child's rendition of anguished, grieving people. Above that group she'd drawn clouds, a woman hovering in them, a halo on her head. The boy beside her was working with a pencil instead of crayons, and he had some real artistic ability, more talent at nine or ten than most adults would ever have. His sketch was of a graveyard. A cluster of small headstones surrounded a larger monument. All of the stones were drawn with hard, dark lines, the earth beneath them and the sky above them shaded a light gray. The only color on the page was on the petals of the few flowers he'd drawn near the large monument, their bright hues standing out stark against the black and gray background. It was a hell of a good picture for a child of that age, and I was captivated by him as he worked, handling the pencil so naturally and confidently. He'd probably never had any formal training.

I looked back and forth at the two pictures, then at the weeping girl at the far end of the table. The room was as silent as the empty gym I'd been in a moment earlier. The black woman finally spotted me, whispered a few final words in the girl's ear, then walked around the table to talk with me. Her name tag identified her as Stacey, and her face was about as cheerful as the artwork on the table.

"Welcome to Clark Rec," she said in a low whisper. "What can we do for you?"

I forced a smile, which felt out of place in the room. "I used to spend a lot of time here, growing up."

"A nostalgia visit then?" she said, no return smile.

"An unintended one," I admitted. "But the real reason I'm here is to ask about a guy named Mitch Corbett. I heard he does some volunteer work around here."

"That's right." She was looking with concern at the girl she'd just left, who was now wiping at her eyes with the heels of her hands. "Mitch is a big help with the basketball leagues. Has been for years. These kids would tell you he's also the best air hockey player in the world."

"When was the last time you saw him?"

Her expression immediately became alarmed. "What's happened?"

"Nothing's happened. I'm a private investigator, and Mitch Corbett might have some background information that could help me in a case. I've been hoping to catch up with him, but I haven't had any luck."

She folded her arms across her chest and took a step back. "I see. Well, I don't know what to tell you. He isn't scheduled to he here until next weekend."

"When did he work last?"

"Saturday."

Saturday was four days ago, before the fire on Train Avenue.

"So that was the last time you saw him?" I asked.

"Yes. Are you being honest, sir? Are you sure nothing's happened to Mitch?"

"I don't know of anything that has," I said, which was as honest as I could be.

"Thank goodness." She laid her hand over her chest. "The last thing I want to have to tell these children is that something happened to Mitch."

I nodded my head in the direction of the picnic table. "It's none of my business, but the mood over there looks pretty somber. So does the artwork."

"It's a sad day. The children just found out they lost a friend. I had to tell them about it. I suggested they draw some pictures to express how they feel. It's good for them to have a way to release what they're feeling. At this age, they sometimes do that better through pictures than they do verbally."

"I'm sorry to hear that. But the picture idea sounds like a good one."

"They seem very involved with it."

I was looking at the girl with the brown braids. She had finally picked up a crayon and returned to her picture. Her lower lip was pinched between her teeth as she steeled herself against further tears.

"Was the child who died especially close to the girl you were talking with?"

Stacey shook her head. "Lily has a family situation to deal with, as well. I think she just got overwhelmed by it all today. And the friend wasn't a child."

"No?"

"No. It was an adult. You might have heard about it on the news. The poor woman who was killed in the fire?"

I stared at her. She watched me with raised eyebrows.

"Have you heard about that?" she asked.

"Anita Sentalar? The woman who died in a house fire on Train Avenue?"

"Yes. It was awful, wasn't it?"

I looked away from her, back at the kids and their pictures. "Anita Sentalar worked here?"

"No. But she came by one day last week and spent an afternoon with the kids. She was very sweet. They all loved her. She was supposed to come back today. That's why I had to tell them."

"Why was she here?"

"Well, actually, Mitch brought her by. The kids love Mitch. He's always around. That's why you scared me so much when you asked about him. I couldn't bear to have to tell them something had happened to Mitch, too."

In the pauses of our conversation, I could actually hear the squeak of crayons and pencils on paper. It was that quiet.

"Do you know why Anita Sentalar was with Mitch Corbett?" I said. "Were they a romantic couple?"

She shook her head. "I'm fairly certain they weren't. He said he was showing her the neighborhood."

"Showing her the neighborhood," I echoed.

"Staaaacey." A long whisper, this from the girl with the brown braids.

Stacey started back around the table and motioned for me to follow. The girl with the braids asked if she could go to the bathroom. Her face was flushed and streaked with dried tears. Stacey told her she could go. When the girl left, we stood at the edge of the table where she'd been seated. I looked down at her picture. This one was perhaps the most disturbing yet. It showed a tall house with almost a dozen windows, carefully drawn, gleaming with bright colors. At the top of the house, though, a ragged black hole had been drawn in the roof, orange flames around it.

I frowned and pointed at it. "You told the kids how Anita Sentalar died?"

Stacey shook her head. "No. I thought it was a bit too scary for them. I'll leave details like that up to the parents. I just said she was dead, and that we should all be grateful we got to spend a day with her."

"Then how'd this girl know to draw a fire?"

"Like I said before, Lily has had a family crisis this week. They were all set to move into a new house by the end of the month. She was so excited. Then their house burned down."

"It wasn't the house on Train Avenue?"

"No. It was right here on Clark. Just a block down the street, actually. But it was one of Anita's houses."

"Pardon?"

Stacey held up a finger, indicating that she wanted me to wait, then walked across the room to a rack on the wall that held a collection of papers and brochures. Enrollment forms for various rec center leagues and activities, that sort of thing. She selected a brochure, crossed the room again, and handed it to me.

The front page of the trifold brochure showed two pictures of the same house. The photograph on top was of a crumbling building with faded paint and broken windows. The lower photograph showed a shining home, fresh paint, new glass, completely restored. THE NEIGHBORHOOD ALLIANCE it read. RESTORING PRIDE TO THE WEST SIDE.

"There's a picture of her on the inside," she said.

I opened the brochure and saw a few more before-and-after pictures of houses, and a small block of text explaining that the Neighborhood Alliance was a Cleveland community effort to improve housing options on the near west side with the aid of federal funding. Run-down houses were being restored and then sold to low-income buyers with the assistance of federally insured mortgages. There was no picture of a woman, though.

Stacey was leaning over my shoulder. "Maybe it's on the back."

I closed the brochure and turned it over and stared at a small headshot of Anita Sentalar. The picture was familiar—it was the same shot that had been on the front page of the newspaper the day Sentalar's body was pulled from the ruins of the house on Train Avenue. Beneath the photograph was a caption labeling her the director of the Neighborhood Alliance.

"This is why Corbett was showing her the neighborhood," I said. "Because she was involved with the urban renewal project?"

"Yes."

"And Corbett's working on the houses," I said, remembering the Neighborhood Alliance sign outside the house where I'd found Jeff Franklin.

"Is he?"

"Yes." I was still staring at Sentalar's picture, thinking about her in this building with Mitch Corbett just a few days before she'd died.

"The fire on Clark Avenue burned one of this group's houses down?" I said.

"That's right. Lily's family was working out the purchase details. They've never had a house before, always small apartments, and there are four kids. They were so excited. It broke my heart to hear what happened, but Anita promised them she would make arrangements for them to buy another house. That's why Lily was extra-sad to hear Anita was dead. I'm afraid she thinks her family's house died with her."

The girl came back then, still long-faced, and pulled to a stop in front of us.

"Who's this?" she asked Stacey, pointing at me.

"He's Mitch's friend," Stacey answered.

The girl swiveled her head to face me. "Our friend died," she said.

I knelt next to the table, bringing myself down to her level. "I'm very sorry to hear that. I know how sad that must make you. One of my friends just died, too. It's tough."

"How'd he die?" she asked, a child's blunt curiosity getting the best of her.

"He got hit by a car," I said, and then for some reason added, "It was right on this street. I'm still sad about it, so I know how you feel today."

"I'm sorry. You have to be careful crossing streets."

I nodded. "Look both ways, right?"

"Right." She climbed back onto the bench seat and picked up a crayon. I straightened up, then noticed that Stacey was staring at me.

"Your friend was killed on Clark?"

"Yes."

"Ed Gradduk?"

"Yes."

Anger flooded her face. "Don't you know? He's the one—"

"Who's innocent," I finished for her. "Yes, I do know that. And I think you might have helped me start proving it."

CHAPTER 14

The lot on Clark Avenue was bare, the grass withered by heat, the soil baked dry. All the debris had been scraped clean, leaving only a decimated foundation behind. The scarred concrete surrounded by cracked, dried-out soil looked like something you might find alongside a lonely desert highway.

I remembered the house, though. Two stories, pale blue paint, white latticework around the bottom of the porch. I'd never been inside, but I'd walked past it almost daily for several years. The old guy who'd lived there when I was a kid had owned a snowblower, the only one on the block, probably. In the winter he'd do his own driveway, each next-door neighbor's, and then the sidewalk all the way up to the stop sign. Wore a big furry hat with earflaps that made me think of spy movies set in Moscow. Smoked a cigar while he worked the snowblower. Waved at everybody.

This winter, if it snowed enough, the drifts might fill in the old foundation, cover it up completely, until you couldn't tell there'd ever been a house there. I stood above the blackened stone and thought about Lily, the girl with the braids. It was supposed to have been her family's first house. Four kids, Stacey had said.

I walked around the yard, my shoes raising a cloud of dry dust as I moved. Stood in what had been the backyard and gazed out across the top of the foundation, took in a now unobstructed view of the avenue. Two days ago I'd walked hurriedly past, hardly pausing to glance at the vacant lot, as I'd gone in search of Ed Gradduk. Ed had actually been the one to come up with the Russian spy identity for the guy who'd lived here when we were kids. Called the old guy Agent X, the house, KGB Headquarters.

That was all a long time ago.

I left the yard and walked back up the sidewalk toward my truck, lyrics from an old Springsteen song dancing through my head. *I heard the voices of friends vanished and gone.*

Good song, I used to think.

Joe was on the phone when I got back, but hung up quickly.

"You were gone a long time, LP."

"Yeah."

"Anything productive to show for it?"

"The house on Train Avenue was owned by something called the Neighborhood Alliance, an urban renewal project. Anita Sentalar was the director of the Neighborhood Alliance. Cancerno's construction crew is working on the houses, with both Ed and Mitch Corbett involved. Another one of the group's houses burned down last week. A place on Clark Avenue. Corbett was a demolitions expert. Knew how to start an effective fire. He was with Sentalar last week."

"You were gone three hours," Joe said, "and that's all you got?"

I gave that one a bit of a smile.

"No, I've got to give you credit," he said. "That's impressive. Even in that clipped monotone you recited it with. Now run through it again. This time with details."

"Maybe work on the voice, too? Try a sweet soprano?"

"That's going to be different from your normal voice?"

It took me a little longer to tell it to him with the details. I walked him through my afternoon, trying to recall anything of significance that had been said in either my conversation with Jeff Franklin or with Stacey at the rec center.

"The second fire seems like a big deal," I said. "And Corbett's a demolitions expert, now missing? Who was waltzing around the near west side with Sentalar just a few days before she turned up dead in one of those fires?"

"Suspicious as hell," Joe said. "But doesn't necessarily clear your friend from the mix."

"I'm not saying it does. But the best way to clear Ed is to find the person who *did* kill Sentalar. Right now, Corbett's looking like an awfully intriguing fit."

"Doesn't mesh well with your theory about Padgett and Rabold, though. At least, not yet."

I nodded. "Not yet. But we've still got Padgett camped outside Corbett's house. That establishes some sort of connection. You get anything useful on the background checks?"

He waffled his hand. "Nothing like what you brought back, but still some interesting notes. They're both lifelong Cleveland residents. Padgett is single, previously divorced, and Rabold's married and has a kid. Both of them seem to live a bit beyond the means of a cop's salary. Padgett drives a new Jeep and owns a bass boat that must go for about thirty to forty thousand. His house is modest enough but he's also part owner of a time-share down on the Florida Gulf Coast. Could be he's just good with money. Rabold's house cost him almost three hundred grand, with a mortgage for only half that, and his wife doesn't work, just helps out at the kid's school library."

"You think they're on the take?"

"Reasonable candidates for it, at least."

"What about their history on the force?"

"Working on that. You remember Amos Lorenzon?"

"Of course," I said. "He was the first cop I rode with when I was out of the academy. Good guy, but I learned fast not to ask too many questions. They seemed to make him nervous."

"They probably did. Hear too many questions from a green rookie and you start to feel like you're working alone. Anyhow, Amos is a desk supervisor now, reads a lot of the conduct evaluations and keeps tabs on the patrol guys. I called him and told him what I wanted."

"I bet you made him awfully uncomfortable with that request."

He nodded. "Yeah, I imagine so. But he told me he'd pull the records and get back to us. He'll be more cautious about dispensing the information than some of the other guys I could have called, but the difference is he'll also keep his mouth shut. That's important."

"He'll keep his mouth shut," I said with a grin. "I remember when he had surgery and it was six months before anyone found out why he'd been gone for those two weeks. Said it was nobody's business, so he just took his personal days and didn't mention the medical reason. Talk about private."

"Right. That's why I chose him for the job. I expect we'll hear from him tomorrow."

"I want to see Jimmy Cancerno again today," I said. "He worked with this Neighborhood Alliance group, and he hired both Ed and Corbett."

"Call him, then."

I grabbed the phone book and looked up the number for Pinnacle Properties. The secretary there had bad news: Jimmy was out for the day. I asked if she had a cell phone number for him, and she said she couldn't give that out. I harangued her for a few minutes and got nowhere, then hung up.

"What about your buddy?" Joe said when I told him the problem. "The one who owns the bar."

Another flip through the phone book, this time for the Hideaway. A minute later I was speaking to Draper.

"Sure, I've got his number," he said after listening to my request. "How about I give him a call instead of you, though. Chances are I can get him to come down here and talk to you, whereas he might just tell you to go to hell and hang up."

"Good," I said. "Call me back, Scott. And thanks."

"Anytime, Lincoln."

It was only a few minutes before my phone rang.

"Jimmy'll be down in twenty," Draper said. "He wasn't real pleased with the idea, but I told him you're a stand-up guy."

Was there a hint of sarcasm in his voice, or had my imagination dropped that in? I wasn't sure.

"Thanks, Scott. We'll be there. I appreciate it."

"No problem. Want me to throw a couple cheeseburgers on the grill?"

"Maybe next time."

I hung up again and looked at Joe. "Cancerno's on his way to Draper's bar. You want to come along?"

"Let's go," he said, standing up. I thought about thanking him right then, but it felt awkward, so I didn't. I just walked out the door beside him, the two of us stepping together in silence.

We got to the Hideaway five minutes before Cancerno showed. Draper wasn't working the bar, and he came out to sit with us. He had a bottle in his hand and three glasses stacked atop one another. He dropped the glasses on the table and poured about three fingers of Scotch into each one. He slid a glass over to me.

"Glenlivet," he said. "Still the favorite?"

"It's a good one," I said. "And so is your memory."

"You work in this business, you better remember drinking tendencies." He pushed the second glass over to Joe, who shook his head.

"Too early for Scotch?" Draper asked.

"He doesn't drink anything but water," I said.

Draper, who had probably been nursed on light beer, regarded Joe with astonishment. "*Nothing* but water?"

"He exaggerates," Joe said. "I also drink milk."

Draper handled the dilemma by dumping the contents of Joe's glass into his own and draining a good portion of it in one swallow. Draper drank Scotch the way most men drank beer.

"So, tell me what's up," he said. "Why you need to see Jimmy?"

"You ever heard of the Neighborhood Alliance?" I asked.

He frowned and scratched his shaved head. "Ed did some work for them, I believe. They're buying up houses all over the neighborhood."

"Right. And it looks like Cancerno's guys are fixing most of them."

"Could be."

"The woman who died in the fire," I said, "was the director of the Neighborhood Alliance. I want to ask Cancerno what he knows about her, and how Ed might have come across her."

"Huh." Draper sipped some more of the Scotch. If I'd hoped he was going to offer an opinion on the matter, I was wrong.

Cancerno arrived then, again in jeans and a silk shirt, and again looking decidedly unpleasant. He nodded curtly at Draper and glowered at Joe and me.

"All right," he said, pushing into the booth beside Draper. "What the hell is this about?"

"Mr. Cancerno, this is my partner, Joe Pritchard." I pointed at Joe.

"Terrific. Now let me repeat—what the hell is this about? I got shit to do this afternoon."

"Remember the woman who died in the fire?"

"The one Gradduk killed?"

"The one who died in the fire," I said again.

"What about her?"

"She was the director of something called the Neighborhood Alliance." Suddenly I wanted to test Cancerno, curious as to whether he'd be honest at all or just lie to avoid continuing the conversation. "You ever heard of that group?"

His lip curled at one side. "Of course I've heard of the group. My guys are fixing all their shit-hole houses."

Okay, he had no problem with blunt honesty.

"What can you tell me about the organization?" I said.

"Not much. I don't mind their business, you know, just my own. They want me to get the houses fixed up so they can sell them again, and that's what I do. It's some sort of a government project, city or county. They buy up houses that are all beat to shit, run-down and empty, neighborhood eyesores. Then they fix them up so they're decent again, livable, and they put poor people in them. Got the Feds to insure the mortgages and finance it and all that crap. Supposed to make the neighborhood downright charming."

"If you're doing a fair amount of work for them," Joe said, "you must have known Anita Sentalar."

Cancerno shot him a glare that would have rattled anyone except Joe, who received it with a blank expression.

"I *must have* known her?" Cancerno said. "Afraid not, buddy. You don't know as much as you think. This is the first time I'd heard that the dead chick had anything to do with the Neighborhood Alliance. Guy who handled the contract with me was a consultant, you know, someone who actually knows a little something about construction. They aren't going to let some little girl with a law degree contract out house repairs."

"What was the consultant's name?" Joe said.

"Ward Barry. He does a lot of work with HUD on those types of projects. Used to be a city engineer. You want to know about this woman, you talk to him. I never said word one to her."

"What about Ed Gradduk?" I said, "Would he have had an opportunity to meet her?"

Cancerno scowled. "I don't know how, unless she came by the work site to see what was going on. I suppose that's possible. I sure as shit never introduced him to nobody. Glad of that, too. I'm dealing with enough grief just for hiring the son of a bitch."

I took a deep breath and sipped a little of the Glenlivet, felt the smooth burn work.

"Okay," I said. "That makes sense, Mr. Cancerno. How many houses are you working on for the Neighborhood Alliance?"

"We got the whole contract. So however many they buy up for the first two years of this, that'll be how many we work on. Probably got ten done already, another half dozen in the work stages."

"There was one on Clark Avenue," I said. "It burned down about a week ago. You know anything about that house?"

For once, Jimmy Cancerno looked interested, but before he could speak, Draper put himself into the conversation for the first time.

"One burned on Clark?"

I turned to him and nodded while Cancerno gave him a surprised look, as if he'd forgotten Draper was at the table. "Yeah, it did. A few blocks east of here."

"I heard about it," Draper said. "Didn't know it belonged to that Neighborhood Alliance deal, though." He picked his glass up again to take another drink, but it was empty. He set it back down and poured it half-full again.

"Were you working on the house on Clark?" I asked Cancerno.

"Nah, we haven't worked any on Clark."

"It was a Neighborhood Alliance property," I said. "I'm sure of that."

He shrugged. "Like I said, we work on them in the order those people tell us to. I can believe they owned the place, but we hadn't started on it yet."

"Don't you think it's a bit odd," Joe said, "that two of the group's houses would burn in a week's time?"

Cancerno coughed. "Would be odd if I couldn't blame it on Gradduk." He paused, then said, "Shit, I just realized what that means. If the little bastard *did* burn the other house, I'm going to have to deal with that, too."

"You have any idea," I said, "who might have had a problem with this Neighborhood Alliance group? Anyone else bid on the project and lose, anything like that?"

"No. Like I said, I just worry about my end of things."

I nodded. "Must be a nice chunk of cash in it. You said you're getting all the work for two years?"

Cancerno snorted. "A nice chunk of cash? Gimme a break, pal. I wish I'd never made the bid. I'll be lucky to break even on this."

"Really?" I said, surprised.

His scowl darkened. "Yeah, really. You don't believe it, I'll be happy to show you my books."

"No need for that."

For a moment it was quiet, and then Cancerno said, "Well, is that it?"

"I guess so," I said. "We appreciate your time, though. And we'll be talking to this Warren Barry."

"Ward Barry. And don't tell him I gave you his name. Last thing I need on my hands now is somebody else that's pissed off at me over Gradduk."

He stood, then turned back to the table. "You have any luck finding Corbett?"

"Not yet," I said.

"But you tried?"

"Yes."

He nodded. "Well, you find him, you can tell him I tore up his paycheck today. He ever wants to go back to work, it'll be for somebody else."

Joe and I got up, too, and headed for the door. I turned, expecting Draper would have followed us, but I saw he was still hunched in the booth, the whiskey glass in his hand.

"Thanks again, Scott," I said.

"Huh? Oh, right. No sweat, dude." He nodded at me, then stood up and walked out with us. I pushed open the heavy front door and stepped into the heat, the sun glaring off the cracked sidewalk, shimmering on the street. Draper stepped out behind us and let the door swing shut. He squinted down the avenue.

"Interesting," he said, "that the house that burned down here was connected to the one up on Train."

"Yeah," I said. "Interesting."

"It was a scene out here, I'll tell you that," he said. "All the trucks going by, people wandering up the street, looking to see what the hell was going down. I could see the smoke, even from here."

"That's a serious fire."

He nodded. "First fire I'd seen since the one when we were kids. Remember that one? We were standing with your old man."

I hesitated, thinking, then placed it. "Right, the pawnshop fire. Shit, that's a long time ago."

"We were still in elementary school. I remember we were coming back from the rec center, walking with your dad. He'd come up to walk back with us because it was at night. When we came out, all the sirens were going."

Draper looked at me and grinned. "Sorrow's anthem, right?"

"What?"

"That was what your dad called it, the sound all those sirens made."

I laughed. "Damn, Scott, you're reaching back for that one."

"Well, I remember it. Because it made sense, you know? You had the ambulance, the fire engine, the police cars. All those sirens have a little different sound to them, and blended together like that, it's like some sort of crazy song. Sorrow's anthem, your dad called it. Yeah, I remember that night."

I did, too, now that I stopped to think about it, and it made me sad. I'd stood on the street with Ed, Draper, and my father. Only two of us were still alive. I could remember the tense electricity that seemed to go up and down the avenue that night, the fire at the pawnshop going strong, sirens all around us. It made sense that my dad noticed the sirens, of course, and that he had a name for the sound. He spent his career in an ambulance.

"There was another fire that summer, too," Draper said, rubbing his bald head with the palm of his hand. "Hell, maybe two?"

"Yes. There were a couple, you're right. And they were

arsons. Everybody was worried about them. But it gave people something to talk about other than . . ."

"Other than what?" Joe said when I stopped talking. He and Draper were watching me with curious looks.

"Other than Ed's family," I said slowly.

Draper frowned, then nodded. "Shit, that's right. That was the same summer Norm killed himself."

Joe and I were looking hard at each other.

"Gradduk's dad killed himself the same summer that a bunch of fires went up around this neighborhood?" he said.

"Yeah."

"And now the son's dead, and there are more fires," Joe said.

The dull tingle I'd been feeling at the base of my skull from the Glenlivet seemed to be spreading. Draper was quiet, watching us.

"You have any idea how that old arson case turned out?" Joe asked.

I shook my head. "Nope. But all of the sudden I'm awfully damn curious."

CHAPTER 15

Joe wanted to call Amy, have her run a search through the paper's computer archives for the old fires. I discouraged him from that by saying I didn't think the computer database went back that far, but in reality I just didn't feel comfortable calling her for a favor. We hadn't spoken since she'd stormed out of my apartment the previous night, and I wasn't inclined to ask for her help right now, especially when we could handle it ourselves.

"So what's the alternative?" Joe asked.

I sighed. "I guess we'll do what a couple of tough-guy PIs like us should never have to do."

"What's that?"

"Go to the library."

Trust a librarian to do in twenty seconds what an investigator might take hours to accomplish. I'd hardly begun to explain what we were interested in before the librarian, a tall, gray-haired woman, was clicking away on her computer.

"We've got something called the Cleveland News Index," she said. "You can actually access this from the Internet; you didn't need to come all the way down here."

"Oh," I said, feeling like a moron.

"The news index has citation information from the local newspaper as well as three local newsmagazines. It goes back more than twenty years. Now you said you were looking for information on arson fires on Clark Avenue?"

"At least one was on Clark," I said. "But there were two others in the same summer."

"I'll just do a keyword search for 'arson' and 'Clark Avenue' and see what we get."

I told her the year the fires had happened, and she ran the search. A few seconds later she smiled and turned the monitor to face us. There were fifty records, and the screen showed us the titles of the articles and the dates and sources. I scanned through the first page and shook my head. She clicked the mouse and sent us to the second page of results. This time I saw what I wanted: *Pawnshop destroyed in arson fire.* I asked her to print that record, and then I kept reading. Six entries below that was another of interest: *Third west side fire in two weeks raising neighborhood concern and police interest.*

The librarian printed both records, then took us to a microfilm machine. She found the appropriate canisters of film in their storage area, brought them out, and loaded the machine.

"You want me to print copies of the stories for you, or would you prefer just to read them on the viewer?" she asked.

"Print them, please."

She did, then handed us three pages, and returned to her desk. Joe and I stood in the center of the room and read through the articles together. The first was brief, detailing the timing of the fire on Clark Avenue and saying that while no one had been injured, the pawnshop was a total loss. The next article was much more interesting. It connected the fire on Clark to earlier fires—one on Fulton Road and another on Detroit. Three fires in three weeks, the article said, all to properties owned by one man, Terry Solich. The reporter said Solich had declined an interview request and also mentioned that Solich had previously been charged with possession of stolen goods, although the case was dropped.

"You ever heard of this guy?" Joe asked.

I shook my head and started to respond, then stopped when my eyes caught on another name, further down in the story: *While fire investigators are sure the blazes are the result of arson, neither they nor police would reveal whether there were any suspects. Det. Matthew Conrad of the Cleveland Police Department said he has worked closely with fire investigator Andrew Maribelli on the case.*

"Conrad's dead," Joe said.

"You sure?"

"I was at the funeral."

"Damn. Do you know the fire investigator?"

He shook his head. "Nope. But I think it's time we made his acquaintance."

We called the fire department switchboard first, because nearly two decades had passed, and it was entirely possible Maribelli no longer worked with the department. We were in luck, though—at least at first. Maribelli was still with the department. He just wasn't interested in talking with us.

"I got to be honest," he told me when my phone call had been routed through to him, "I don't feel too comfortable talking to you guys when there's an active police investigation."

"The fires happened almost twenty years ago," I said. "How active can the investigation be?"

"Police department requested my old files about six hours ago. So it feels pretty damn active to me. Now what's your interest, exactly?"

"Who requested them?" I said, ignoring his question to

ask another of my own. "Was it a detective named Cal Richards?"

"Nope. It was an officer named . . ." There was a pause while he thought about it or looked for his notes. "Larry Rabold."

"Larry Rabold requested your old file," I said, and Joe's eyebrows lifted when he heard. "And you still had it? After seventeen years?"

"I keep my notes on any major case that we don't close. And we never closed that one. I told this Officer Rabold what I could remember about things, and then I dug out my old notes and made copies for him."

"No arrests were made in the case?"

"Listen, like I said, I'm not going to talk to you guys when I don't know who the hell you are and the cops are suddenly looking into this thing again. I'm not trying to be a bastard about it, but I'm also not going to change my mind."

"No problem."

I hung up and looked at Joe. "He doesn't want to have anything to do with us. Reason is that he believes there's a renewed police interest. Rabold interviewed him and asked for copies of the old case file this morning."

Joe slipped his sunglasses on and nodded. "When I did my background check on Rabold today, I got his shift information. He's supposed to be off-duty today, but he's out working on a seventeen-year-old arson case? Hardworking sons of bitches, him and Padgett."

"If it's his day off, he might be at home. Maybe we could drop by, see if he's around."

I said it casually, as if I were suggesting we stop off for a beer on the way home.

Joe frowned, considering it. "We'd be tipping our hand a little early, maybe. Showing our interest."

"I'm betting Jerome Huggins informed these guys of our interest hours ago."

He hesitated only briefly. "All right. I guess it's time to ante up, anyhow. No matter what his response is, it should tell us something."

Larry Rabold's home was on the stretch of West Boulevard that ran between Clifton and Edgewater Park—a historic neighborhood, and damn high rent. The house was a large Victorian, and through the yard you could see the bright blue sky and swath of water from the lake. A wraparound porch offered nice views, and as we walked up the sidewalk toward the house, I could see a boat with a bright multicolored sail out on the water.

"How many cops you know have a porch with a lake view?" I said as we turned up the driveway.

"Counting this guy, the total is one," Joe said. "Although I'm beginning to hesitate to call him a cop."

A two-car garage was set behind Rabold's house, and a black Honda Civic was parked outside it, another vehicle partially visible through the open garage door. We walked up a cobblestone path lined with a nice flowerbed. The front door had a fancy brass fitting in its center, with a protruding key. Joe reached out and turned the key, and a bell rang somewhere in the house. The key probably cost fifty bucks more than a button. Class.

"Hell of a place," I said, thinking about the big price tag and the small mortgage and the wife that worked as a library aide.

Joe didn't say anything. No one came to the door. He reached out and turned the brass key again, the bell grinding away as he did it. This time, when the bell died off, another sound replaced it. A high, shrill wail. It went on and on. Joe looked at me, brow furrowed, eyes concerned.

"What the hell is that?"

The wail picked up in pitch, a sustained cry of anguish. I stepped forward and twisted the knob. Locked.

"He's got a kid," Joe said. "Maybe she's throwing a tantrum or something."

Even as he said it, the sound changed, the wail becoming a soft shriek, then disappearing into a series of rapid, choked sobs. An electric chill rode down my backbone at the sound, all my muscles going rigid. There is someplace deep in the brain that recognizes the emotion behind a human noise, spreads it to the listener, and the emotion I was now feeling was terror.

"What the hell's going on?" Joe said for a second time, but I was walking away from him, moving around the side of the house. There'd been a car in the driveway, and whoever drove it in probably hadn't walked all the way around to the front door. There'd be a side entrance.

There was one, just a few steps away from the Honda. The knob turned this time, and the door opened. I stepped inside with Joe behind me, found myself standing in a narrow room with a coatrack on one wall and a few pairs of shoes on the floor. The room smelled of fresh bread and incense or candles, something with a vanilla scent.

"Hello?" I called. "Is everyone all right?"

That was when everything that had been restrained in the wailing noise broke loose, and it became a scream. The sort of scream that dances through nightmares and horror movies and hopefully never touches your real life.

I ran toward the doorway, my hand creeping back toward my spine before I remembered that I was unarmed. The narrow coatroom emptied into a fancy kitchen with a granite-topped island and brand-new appliances. As I shoved around the island and moved toward the screaming, I noticed a block of knives on the counter and paused long enough to grab one. It was a simple kitchen knife with about a six-inch blade, but I felt better with it in hand. Whatever had provoked that scream couldn't be good.

Out of the kitchen and into the living room, with Joe behind me. The scream reached a hysterical level, a pitch that made me want to cover my ears and run in the opposite direction. Maybe that was the idea. I stood in the middle of the living room with Joe and looked around. The scream was here with us, but I couldn't see anyone. It seemed to be coming from the couch, but the couch was empty.

I stepped over to the big blue couch, grabbed one end with my free hand, and tugged it away from the wall.

A young blond girl, maybe fifteen, was cowering behind the couch. She was wearing shorts and a T-shirt, her knees pulled up to her chest, protecting her. Her face was paler than the cream-colored wall behind her head, and her eyes were like nothing I'd ever seen before, not even in my days as a narcotics detective when I'd been face-to-face with people in the throes of drug-induced convulsions and fits. Her eyes held nothing but terror, and I was so frozen by them that I didn't even realize she was fixated on the knife in my hand until Joe took it away from me and threw it across the room.

"Stop," he said to the girl.

I don't know how he did it with just one softly spoken word, but she stopped. The girl went silent and stared at us, her chest heaving, and only then did I notice the blood on her shoes.

It was fresh, still sticky, but only on the ends of her shoes, as if she'd dipped her toes into it, like someone testing the temperature of water in a swimming pool. Joe saw it, too.

"Where is he?" he asked, understanding something that I hadn't begun to consider yet.

She didn't speak—couldn't speak, probably—but she

lifted a shaking hand and extended her index finger, pointed it at the floor.

"Basement," Joe said, and stepped away. I went with him.

There was an open door at the other side of the living room, beside a staircase that led up to the second level. Once we were closer, we could see carpeted steps leading down. I noticed a few tacky crimson smears on the carpet. She'd come up this way.

Joe went down first. I followed, wishing he hadn't taken the knife from me. My heart was thumping, my hands clenched into fists, my muscles tense. We reached the bottom of the steps and came out in a finished basement room with another couch and television, a bookshelf on the wall. Everything looked normal. Joe was still looking in that direction when I turned right and went around the wall.

There was a pool table there, and a dead man beneath it. The body was slumped on the floor, the legs exposed and the torso shoved under the table. Blood was pooled around the body, more of it on the wall behind the pool table, along with bits of flesh and tissue, splattered remnants of a large-caliber gunshot blast.

I opened my mouth to say something to Joe, but he was already beside me, inhaling a long, sharp breath between his teeth.

"The girl," I said. "Get back upstairs. Get an ambulance down here, a doctor or therapist or someone to help her."

He turned and went up the stairs, his footsteps loud, the wall beside me trembling as he hurried back up to the living room.

I moved forward.

The blood was still wet in the center of the pool, sticky at the edges. It had puddled against the man's legs, and a coppery smell was heavy near the body. I dropped to one knee beside his legs, and as I did, the smell came up stronger, overwhelming me, and I gagged. I leaned forward, lifting a hand to my mouth as I choked, thick bile rising in my throat. I fought it down, closed my eyes, and covered my mouth and nose. I was not a homicide detective, and while I'd seen bodies before, I hadn't seen so many that my brain and my body were trained not to react. I took a few seconds with my eyes closed, concentrating on slow, shallow breaths, and then I felt ready. I opened my eyes and leaned under the pool table.

It was Larry Rabold. Three-quarters of his face was visible, but the upper left corner, beginning above his cheekbone and extending to his eye and temple, was gone. Blown away. A bloody mess of pulp left in its place, no skin or bone visible.

He'd been shot once in the face, a close-range shot with a high-caliber gun. I'd seen small-caliber gunshot wounds before, and this was not one of them. The close range was obvious both from the extent of damage and from a speckling of tiny hemorrhages on his cheek and jawline. That's called stippling or tattooing, and it's the result of burned powder and fragments driven into the skin. You don't get those marks when the gun is held far away from the victim.

When I could finally bring myself to look away from his face, I realized he'd been shot twice more. There were large holes torn through his torso, one in the chest just above the heart, another in the stomach. Blood still leaked out of the chest wound, and a part of his insides, some thin black organ, ran through the mess. I felt the rise of vomit again, but then I realized the black strand I was looking at wasn't part of his body, at all. It was a wire.

I leaned forward, the desire to understand what I was looking at overriding the nausea, and then I noticed that half of Rabold's shirt had been pulled free from his pants. He'd had it tucked in, but the right side was free.

There was a ballpoint pen in my pocket. I took it out and reached out to Rabold's body, gingerly slipped the tip of the pen between his shirt collar and his neck, and pulled it back. The collar slid away from his neck only an inch or so, but it was enough. Clipped to the inside of Rabold's collar was a seed microphone—an extremely tiny, extremely sensitive microphone that is used for covert recording. Son of a bitch.

I moved the pen away and let Rabold's collar fall back in place, then rocked onto my heels and thought about it. A seed microphone like that could be outfitted with a wireless transmitter that sends the conversations to an off-site recorder, but those units were sophisticated, rare, and damn expensive. Far more common was a setup where the microphone ran back to a tiny digital recorder, some of them as small as a nine-volt battery, concealed somewhere on the body.

Sticking the pen out once again, I slid it beneath the free end of Rabold's shirt and lifted. The bottom of his shirt rose a few inches, and I cocked my head, straining to see. There, against Rabold's pale, fat belly, was the end of the microphone cord, leading to . . . nothing. At the end of the wire a bit of bare copper was exposed. The wire had been cut, and whatever recorder it had led to was missing.

The proximity to the corpse got to me then, in a sudden, overwhelming wave. I slid back out from under the pool table and stood up. I made it three steps toward the stairs before my vision blurred and it seemed my heartbeat was suddenly coming from my temples. I put my left hand out and found the wall, leaned up against it, and bit down hard on my lip. The burst of pain cleared my head.

I kept one hand on the wall while I went up the stairs, my knees unsteady until I was near the top. When I came out into the living room, Joe was sitting on the floor beside the couch. The blond girl was still curled up, breathing in ragged gaps. I couldn't see her face, just the jerking rise and fall of her chest. Joe's hand rested gently on her knee. Her own hand was wrapped around his wrist, painted fingernails biting into his flesh.

I stood and stared at Joe. His eyes were distant. Cop eyes. Cop mode, now. I needed to get back into it, myself.

"You make the call?" I said.

He nodded, said, "Is it . . ." but didn't finish the question, because he didn't want to say Rabold's name. Not with the girl who was probably Rabold's daughter a few feet away.

"Yeah," I said.

I couldn't look at the girl anymore. I walked away from them, to the front of the room, and peered out the window, waiting for the police. I stayed on my feet. Somehow, it felt stronger than sitting. I needed to feel strong, right then.

CHAPTER 16

By the time Cal Richards got there, we'd learned Rabold's daughter, Mary, had probably been home for almost thirty minutes before we'd arrived. A neighbor remembered seeing her drive in, alone, and told the cops this in a high, hysterical voice that Joe and I could hear plainly from where we stood beside one of the squad cars. When we had the timetable for the girl's arrival, our imaginations could handle the rest of the sequence. She had probably gone downstairs, seen her father, and gone into shock. She'd made it back upstairs, but then the terror had overwhelmed her. She couldn't think to call the police or even leave the house. Instead, in that shock, in that terror, she'd hid. She'd crawled behind the couch and curled into a ball and waited, with her father's body in the basement beneath her. I'd never heard of anything like it, but then I'd never seen anything like the scene in Rabold's basement, either. His daughter was sixteen.

Richards came onto the scene early, because Joe had requested him with the initial call. They'd sent out another homicide team first, but Richards was given control once he got there. The other cops knew Cal, that was for sure. Mary Rabold was gone, taken away in an ambulance, a detective riding with them.

Richards came out of the front door of the house about twenty minutes after he'd gone in. He walked through the yard to where we stood beside the evidence tech's van. Three cruisers were parked in front of the house now, along with the evidence van and Cal's unmarked car. Neighbors stood across the street, but there was no media presence yet. That wouldn't last long.

"Let's walk around the house, gentlemen," Richards said. Somehow his face was even more impassive now than normal. He'd seen what I'd seen in the basement, but somehow he managed to keep it off his face, shut it down, and trap it inside him. I couldn't do that—not in the same way that he could, at least. Maybe that wasn't the worst thing in the world, though.

We followed Richards back up the driveway and around the black Honda that was parked there. A screened-in porch was off the rear of the house, and a couple of uniformed cops were working it and the yard, taking photographs and scanning for evidence. Richards stopped around the corner, out of their way but also out of sight of the watchers on the street. He leaned against the wall, pulled out a cigarette, and lit it. He took a few drags, flipping idly through the notebook he held in his hands.

"This gets messy," he said. "Dead cop. Murdered in his home, found by his daughter. Kid can't even talk now. Wouldn't say a word. Just stared with those eyes, man . . . those eyes." He took another drag on the cigarette, a long one, then tapped it out against the wall and carefully put it into his jacket pocket. Couldn't contaminate the crime scene.

"Messy," he said again. "All right, you tell it to me, boys."

We told it to him. While we talked, the uniforms continued to move around the yard, combing the grass and taking their pictures. Everyone was silent. Back out on the street, there was some mild commotion, doors opening and closing, voices raised. This would be the media arrival.

"He was wearing a wire," I said when Joe and I had gone through the basics. It was the first Joe had heard of it, and his face registered surprise. Richards, on the other hand, was impassive.

"Was he?" he said.

"Come on, Cal. You were down there. You saw it."

He frowned and looked away, not liking it that a civilian had been on the scene first.

"He was wearing a wire," he admitted. "And it was cut. The recorder's gone. Do you have it?"

"No."

He gazed at me hard, and I said, "Are you insane? No, Richards, I didn't steal a recorder off the man's corpse."

"Okay."

Joe was watching with interest. "Rabold's a street officer," he said. "What the hell's he doing wearing a wire? And in his own house?"

"I can't tell you that," Richards said, "because I don't know."

"He was requesting files on old fires this morning," I said. "And now he's dead. You think that's unrelated?"

Richards's face showed nothing. "I'm not a guess-maker, Perry. I'm a detective. We'll see where it goes."

"Sure."

"Look, you know we're going to need to sit down and get an official statement recorded," he said. "And we're going to have to separate you. Makes me look bad if I keep witnesses together for an interview. Baker'll handle that. You'll be seeing both of us, but I'm going to have to give you up to him now."

"Who's Baker?" I asked.

"My partner."

"You actually have one?"

"We're a good team," Richards said, "provided we spend plenty of time on separate courts."

He took us around to the front of the house, and as we cleared the corner, I saw Jack Padgett shoving his way through the crowd, snarling at a uniformed officer to get out of his way. He was in street clothes, jeans and a brightly colored golf shirt, and his face was flushed with fury.

"Shit," Richards said. "The last thing I need is that crazy bastard in my crime scene."

He moved toward Padgett, who turned to look at him and spotted me. His face darkened, and he stepped forward, shoulders squaring and rising, like a boxer stepping away from the ropes.

"What's this guy doing here?" he said, pointing at me.

Richards reached him then and said something that I couldn't hear. Padgett answered, his own voice softer, and all I caught of it was an obscene reference involving my mother. Then Richards had his hand firmly on the taller man's shoulder and was guiding him away from us, back toward the ring of cops watching the perimeter of the yard. Inside the house, the evidence techs were probably still hunched over the body of Padgett's partner. I wondered when he'd heard, and where he'd been. Crooked cop or not, having your partner murdered had to hit deep.

Richards had disappeared into the crowd before I remembered that I hadn't told him what I'd learned about Sentalar and Corbett. A few hours earlier, that was huge news. A few hours earlier, Mary Rabold's father was still alive.

Joe and I spent a while talking to Baker, a short guy with a military haircut and a sunburn, but Richards never returned. Baker took us back to the station and interviewed us separately, on tape. Then we filled out a witness form, and he told us we could go.

"What about Cal Richards?" Joe asked. "Is he coming down here?"

Baker shrugged. "Don't know. He told me to get your statements on tape and get back down to the scene, myself. Didn't say anything about holding you for him."

"He knows where to find us," Joe said.

A patrol officer drove us to my apartment. Joe's car was going to be searched by police, of course. They might not think there was a gun in the trunk or bloody fibers on the floor mats, but they had to check.

When the cop dropped us off, we stood together in my parking lot and looked at each other. It was evening now, the sun gone, the night air beginning to cool. A few cars were in the gym lot, but it was quiet outside.

"That poor damn kid," Joe said.

"Yeah."

He sighed and ran both hands through his hair and over his face. "What the hell is going on, LP? What was your friend into?"

I shook my head. I didn't have any answers. It was just twelve hours ago that I'd stood on the street in front of this building and formed my idea that Rabold and his partner had killed Ed intentionally. Now Rabold was dead. That didn't change my previous theory, but it sure as hell complicated it.

"You tell any of the other detectives about Corbett and Sentalar?" Joe asked.

"No. It's Cal's case. He's the only one who would have understood what it might mean. I'll tell him."

"Okay. We'll tell him in the morning. Get some sleep, maybe some dinner. A few hours of normal life, get our heads back together. We'll see where it stands in the morning."

"They shot him three times, Joe," I said. "Blew a piece of his face off, shot him in the chest, shot him in the stomach. That's not a killing for killing's sake. It wasn't a hit, a guy getting whacked just to be eliminated. There's a lot of anger in those wounds."

"I wonder if his wife is with that girl yet" was all he said.

"I hope so. You want me to give you a ride home?"

"No, thanks."

"You sure?"

"Oh, yeah," he said. "I need the walk tonight."

He left, and I went upstairs and took a long, hot shower, my muscles slowly loosening under the spray. I dried off and changed clothes. By then it was almost ten, well past dinnertime and closer to sleeping time for normal people. Since I clearly wasn't normal, I thought I'd go ahead and eat breakfast for a very late dinner. I fixed an omelet but couldn't find any appetite for it, ended up tossing it in the garbage, and drinking a glass of orange juice.

After a while, I took a bottle of Beck's out of the refrigerator and went up on the roof. There's a trapdoor with folding stairs in the ceiling just outside my apartment that provides access to the roof, and I've dragged a couple of lounge chairs and some potted plants up there. It's a nice place to spend a summer evening.

I sat alone, listening to the traffic noise and sipping my beer and thinking about old friends and a terrified sixteen-year-old girl hiding behind a couch. When the beer was empty, I went back downstairs to get a fresh one. I stood at the door for a moment, hesitating, then grabbed the cordless phone as well and took it onto the roof with me. The connection had some static up there, but you could hear well enough for a conversation. I set the beer down unopened and dialed Amy's number.

"Hey," I said when she answered, "you asleep yet?"

As soon as she recognized my voice, she launched into me.

"You know, you're a real jerk, Lincoln. I shouldn't have walked away last night as easily as I did. The more I think about it, the more pissed off I get. I mean, I don't walk into your office and tell you how to do your job, and that's basically what you did to me last night. Yes, I realize Gradduk was your friend, but the moment I start changing my approach to reporting based upon friendships is the moment I sacrifice whatever professional integrity—"

"One of the cops that tried to arrest Ed was murdered today," I said, interrupting. "I spent the whole day trying to prove he and his partner set Ed up, and then I found out he was dead. He was shot three times, in his basement. Joe and I found the body. His daughter had already seen it. She was hiding behind the couch upstairs. She couldn't talk to us. Couldn't get a word out."

Silence, then: "You at home?"

"Uh-huh."

"I'll see you in ten."

She hung up.

Fifteen minutes later gravel spun and tires squealed below me—Amy's trademark entrance. I'd left the door to the steps unlocked, and now I heard it open and close, and then Amy was knocking at my apartment door.

"I'm up here," I called down to her. The steps on the trapdoor creaked as she worked her way up, and then her head poked above the surface of the roof and she shot me a concerned look. I didn't say anything. She marched across the roof, took the bottle of beer out of my hand and downed a third of it, then gave it back to me.

"Okay," she said. "What the hell happened?"

It took me a long time to tell it. It had been that sort of day. When I was through, she sat quietly and stared out at the night sky.

"I'm sorry, Lincoln," she said after a while. "That's an awful, awful thing to experience."

"For the daughter."

"And for you. Awful for you because you had to see both the body and the daughter. I bet it was almost harder to see her."

"Yeah."

"You heard any ideas on what happened?"

I shook my head. "Not yet. We gave our statements and they sent us home. I'm kind of surprised you hadn't heard about it."

"I left early today because I worked late last night."

"Right." I didn't want to bring up her article. Some-where between Larry Rabold's living room and basement I'd lost my capacity to be angry over something like that.

She brought it up, though. "Look, Lincoln, I didn't suggest Gradduk was some sort of perverted loser who killed the woman because she'd rejected him. I just put out what I knew—"

"And let the readers determine he was a perverted loser who killed the woman because she'd rejected him," I fin-ished, but there was no hostility or bitterness in my voice.

"I'm sorry if that's how you feel," Amy said softly.

"It's okay, Ace. I didn't like it. I still don't. But you did your job, and you'd do the same thing again, and I guess it's easier for me to take because I know that's the case."

"I think your day mellowed you out, Lincoln."

"That's one word for it." *Hollowed* was another one, but I didn't want to say that out loud.

We sat together and watched a few courageous stars try to make themselves visible in a sky clouded with a city's light pollution. Traffic hummed along the avenue beneath us. I finished the beer and wanted another, but didn't get up.

"So Anita Sentalar knew Mitch Corbett," Amy said. "And he's been missing for a few days. A couple cops were looking for him, too. The same cops that killed Ed Gradduk and filled an incident report about it with lies. And now one of those cops is dead. Is that the gist?"

"Basically."

She leaned back in the lounge chair and made a light clicking noise with her tongue. "What a mess."

"That's what Cal Richards said."

"Well, he was right. What's your plan now? I assume you haven't decided to take up permanent residence on this roof."

"Some nights, it doesn't seem like that poor an idea. But I'll probably come down eventually. And when I do, I'll have to get back to work. Because we haven't done anything yet. Generated a hell of a lot of questions today, and got damn few answers to go with them."

"Where do you start?"

I raised my eyebrows and stared at the sky, wondering that myself.

"I suppose we'll have to start with the fires," I said. "I don't know what connects fires that happened almost twenty years ago and fires that happened last week, but it seems something does. The only link we had is dead now, though."

"Well, if you need any help, just ask."

I started to thank her, then realized she could actually help. I reminded her about the house that had burned on Clark Avenue and explained again that it had belonged to the same group that owned the home on Train Avenue.

"I want to know more about the Neighborhood Alliance," I said. "Run them through the paper's archives and fax me any article that mentions them, would you?"

"Sure. And I'll see if we ran a story about this fire on Clark."

"Thanks, Amy."

Her face was lost in shadows, but even so her eyes looked intense. "That's pretty damn interesting, Lincoln. Two fires to these houses in one week, both of the homes vacant?"

"There's more," I said, remembering now details I'd left out the first time. "Mitch Corbett has a background in demolitions. He's experienced with fuses and explosives, would have a good idea of how to go about setting a fire."

"You think he killed Anita Sentalar?"

"Could be. But why the other fire?"

"Arson for profit?"

I shook my head. "These houses are old, broken-down homes in a low-rent neighborhood, Ace. Insurance claims on them wouldn't be worth a damn."

"So why the second fire?"

I shook my head. "Like I said before, I'm coming up with questions, not answers. That has to change."

She didn't stay long after that. When she left, she gave me a hug, and somehow the softness of her hair and the smell of her seemed to cleanse some things from me, like the coppery odor of Larry Rabold's blood and the chilling sound of his daughter's scream. There was no more discussion of her article, and I knew there wouldn't be again. It was done now, and I was glad. True friends are precious, and lost friends are the kind of ghosts that never wander far away. I knew too much about both ends of that.

CHAPTER 17

Andrew Maribelli was a tall, thin man with a shock of gray hair that was combed over to hang long on the right side and was trimmed short on the left. It gave him an off-balance look, as if his head were always tilted. His chest was broad but his shoulders were small, pointed knobs of bone. The starched blue shirt he wore looked like it had been pulled over a door, all broad and flat with those pointy shoulders at either end.

When he stepped into his narrow office in the Cleveland Fire Department headquarters on Superior Avenue at eight that morning to find me sitting behind his desk and Joe studying a framed photograph on the wall, he handled it well enough.

"Gentlemen," he said, closing the door gently behind him, showing no real confusion, "while I always do encourage my guests to get comfortable, I prefer to know when they're arriving. You know, so I can tidy up the place."

I stood up and came around the desk, and Joe turned to face him. When I'd called Joe at seven that morning to suggest we take a run at Maribelli, he'd been in favor. Putting our interest where Rabold's had been right before he was killed could be a productive venture. And probably a risky one.

"I'm Lincoln Perry. I spoke with you on the phone yesterday."

He frowned. "Uh-huh. And I told you—"

"I know what you told me," I said, "and it doesn't matter anymore, Mr. Maribelli. Because the cop whose interest you were protecting is dead. He was murdered."

He winced. "Shit. I'd heard that a cop . . . but I didn't know, I mean, I didn't hear the name, right? Didn't know it was that guy."

"It was him," I said. "He was shot in his basement. We found the body."

Maribelli sighed heavily and moved past me, squeezed around the desk, and dropped into his chair.

"We were cops, too," Joe said, and Maribelli looked up as if noticing him for the first time. "I was one for thirty years. So was my father. So was his father. So this matters to us. A cop gets killed, we don't like it. And we want to know why it happened."

Maribelli's reservations about talking to us the previous day had been strong enough, but there's a sense of brotherhood between people like cops and firefighters, and we were counting on it helping us here. He studied us for a moment, silent, but then he nodded and leaned back in his chair.

"You said you found the body?"

"That's right," I said.

"I'm sorry."

I nodded.

"If my old case is so damn important, though," Maribelli said, "why do I have PIs down here instead of a homicide detective?"

"Things go the way we expect," Joe said, "and you will have a homicide detective down here. Anything we produce, they'll get. But slowing down our work isn't helping them. Not a bit."

"Well, what do you need?" Maribelli leaned back in his chair and clasped his hands behind his head. "Those fires the officer wanted to know about, they happened seventeen years ago. Three fires on the near west side, all in a short time during the summer, all to property owned by a man named Terry Solich. But I assume you've already got that much."

"We read the old newspaper articles," I said. "According to them, you investigated the fires, determined them to be arson."

He nodded.

"What can you tell us about the investigation?"

"Speculation was that Solich was being burned out of business. He ran a couple pawnshops around that neighborhood, was generally regarded as a pretty shady operator. Police theory was that he either pissed off the wrong guys, or somebody was trying to muscle in on his action. They thought Solich knew who was responsible, but he wasn't saying. That was frustrating to the police and me because by the time the third business went up in flames, it was becoming a pretty big pain in the ass. Scaring people in the neighborhood, getting a lot of media attention. We wanted to put it to bed, and Solich wasn't helping us at all, even though he probably could have."

"And you never did put it to bed?" Joe asked.

Maribelli started to shake his head, then stopped. "Well, we did and we didn't."

"Meaning?"

"No arrests were made, but we had a suspect who looked good for the fires. By the time we got onto him, though, he was dead. Killed himself."

"Killed himself," I echoed. "You remember the name?"

"Wouldn't have yesterday, but since I just looked this over with the cop, I can tell you. Suspect's name was Norman Gradduk."

He pronounced it *gra-duke* instead of *grad-uk,* but that

didn't lessen the impact of the name. I felt something inside me tighten.

"How'd you come to him as the suspect?" I said.

"Tips from the neighborhood. One of the beat cops down there had his ear to the ground, passed some news back to Conrad, the police detective. He and I had been looking at another guy, a guy we'd interviewed in another arson case about a year before, same neighborhood. Word around there was that it was this Gradduk guy, though. Time we came around to see him, he'd been dead a few days already. Shit got crazy that fall, Conrad was busy and so was I, and the case went cold. Best suspect was dead, anyhow. Fires had stopped."

"What do you remember about the fires themselves?" Joe said.

It was a good question. Like any specialist, Maribelli remembered more about the details of the case than the generalities of it.

"All three were set using a small explosive and a kerosene accelerant," he said without hesitation. "The guy ran fuse cord around the building and sprayed the walls down with the accelerant. That ensured that when the place went up in flames, they weren't going to be put out until the building came down. I suspected he was using a timing device, too. The fuse cord he used was fast-burning stuff, you couldn't just touch a match to it and run away, have the place blow a few minutes later. It wasn't as fast as Primacord, that shit the military uses that goes up at something absurd like ten thousand feet in a second, but it was too fast to use with a match-light technique."

Joe and I exchanged a glance. It was the same method Richards had described to us.

"We're not sure what, if anything, these old fires have to do with a few recent arson fires in the same neighborhood," I said. "But what you just described sounds like it fits with the new fires, and some of those old names are popping up again. You mentioned the tip came from a beat cop in the neighborhood. You remember who it was?"

He groaned and looked at the ceiling. "Shit, I'm not the best with names. Yesterday morning my wife asked me to sign a card for her sister, and I wrote 'Dear Alice,' when the woman's name is Allison. You should've heard my wife. She pitched a fit." He looked back at us and grinned. "Or bitched a fit, maybe. That's a little more like it."

"The name?" I said.

"Yeah, yeah, I'm working on it. Oh, man. Seventeen years ago, this is asking a lot." He screwed his face up, an expression of intense effort, but then sighed and shook his head. "I'm sorry, but I can't think of it."

"Wouldn't have it in the old files, something you could reference?"

"I went through the file yesterday. I don't remember seeing that cop's name in it. Maybe it's in Conrad's notes, if you can track them down. But it wasn't in mine. I had most of the technical stuff."

I didn't want to put a name in his mouth rather than have him offer it, but I had to ask. "Could it have been Jack Padgett?"

He frowned. "Could it have been? Sure. Could have been a lot of things, though. I honestly can't remember."

"All right. What about the suspect you'd been looking at before you got the tip on Gradduk?"

"I know that one. Guy's name was Mitchell Corbett. Local guy, had a background in demolitions, had been a suspect in an earlier fire, like I said."

I turned and looked at Joe, who was gazing back at me.

"You know," he said, "we really need to find that son of a bitch."

♦ ♦ ♦

We started with an information broker in Idaho. The term "information broker" was code for a government spook and a hacker. The guy was ex-CIA and knew how to get into most of the computer databases that you aren't supposed to be able to get into. There are a handful of guys like this across the country, and while it's not commonly discussed, any private investigator worth a damn knows one or two of them. You don't ask for help from a guy like that on a routine investigation, though. That kind of help is for a special case, only. There are a couple of reasons for that: risk and cost. Make a habit of having information you shouldn't have, and you'll get into trouble eventually. And guys like our man in Idaho don't work cheap. When Joe made the call, he did so knowing that our nonexistent expense account was going to take a serious hit. He didn't hesitate to do it, though.

Joe asked for an activity check on Mitch Corbett's credit cards and bank accounts. If he'd made a credit card purchase, we'd know where and when. Same for the debit card, same for an ATM withdrawal. It was the right place to start. The guy in Idaho told Joe to give him a few hours to work on it, then he'd call us back.

I checked our fax machine and found a dozen pages waiting in the tray. Amy had remembered my request. She'd sent a few articles about the Neighborhood Alliance, along with a complete list of the Alliance's properties, compiled from the recorder's office database. The early articles were trivial things—a few clichéd quotes about rebuilding a sense of community by rebuilding houses, a mention of Sentalar as the director, and damn little else. The last article was more significant, however. Just two months old, it explained that the Neighborhood Alliance, with the assistance of funding from the city and a fifteen-million-dollar HUD grant, was going to be con-

verting the old Joseph A. Marsh Junior High School
building into apartments, all of which would be rented at
low rates to people who met limited-income require-
ments. The old brick school, which was now close to
ninety years old, had stood empty for more than a decade.
Like West Tech, it had been closed shortly after I passed
through its halls. I had that effect on a school, apparently.

West Tech, which was an equally historic building, had
also been converted into apartments within the last few
years. I'd been in the building once just to see how it
looked, and I was impressed. They'd somehow managed
to turn the school style into something that was so unique
it was appealing. The tenant mailboxes were positioned
between the old locker bays, the gym had been converted
into a workout room, the auditorium was available for
special functions. Upstairs, the classrooms had become
apartments—some of them two levels, with spiral stair-
cases and wide banks of windows. While the rent wasn't
aimed at the lower-income tenants the way the Joseph A.
Marsh project seemed to be, it had gathered a lot of fa-
vorable publicity when it was completed. I wasn't surprised to see that a similar idea had been pitched for the
Joseph A. Marsh building.

"Whatever money was tied into the Neighborhood Alliance for the houses just got kicked up to the big leagues,"
I said to Joe, and showed him the article. "There's a
fifteen-million-dollar grant involved in this one alone."

While he read the article, I looked through the
recorder's-office list Amy had included. It showed that
the Neighborhood Alliance currently owned nine houses
in addition to the school building, all on the near west
side. Two of the nine were vacant lots now, I knew, the
houses that had once stood on them turned to ashes. The
ninth house on the list had just closed on a sale a week
before, for the inspiring sum of thirty-two thousand dol-

lars. That made me shake my head. Nine vacant houses, crumbling mortgage foreclosures, probably, in the neighborhood I'd grown up in. I thought of the old black-and-white photos on the wall in the Hideaway, the houses and businesses tall and solid, clean and well maintained, the men and women standing in front of them with some pride.

"Interesting," Joe said, finished with the article. "Considering what your friend had to say about cutting in on somebody else's revenue stream, this would seem to have some potential. We've got a couple hours to wait and see if our guy in the mountains can get a line on Corbett. I suppose we could find that consultant Cancerno mentioned, the HUD guy."

I shook my head. "I think we'll use the time to go see Terry Solich, ask why my dead friend's dead father would have wanted to burn down his businesses. Or why Mitch Corbett would have."

"Guy didn't help the cops all those years ago," Joe pointed out.

I smiled. "Right. But the cops didn't break his arms, either. I'll get him to talk."

"What did I tell you about control?" Joe said. "We don't need to start by breaking arms, LP. Not when the man has fingers."

CHAPTER 18

Terry Solich had liver spots on his face and on his bald head, and his sunken eyes were rimmed with dark circles. It was closing in on noon, but he opened the front door of his house wearing a robe, with a pot of coffee in one hand and a ceramic mug in the other.

"You gotta be kidding me," he said. "How many times I have to tell you people, I'm not going to join your stupid neighborhood watch program."

"We don't live around here," Joe said.

"And the neighborhood looks damn peaceful already," I said.

"You bet your ass," Terry Solich said.

Five minutes later we were sitting on the backyard patio. A sprinkler was hissing out in the grass, casting a fine spray on a row of flowers that grew along the fence. A little terrier ran in circles out on the lawn, barking at nothing in high, incessant yips.

"I moved out of that damn neighborhood fifteen years ago," Terry Solich was saying. "I'm retired now. I got grandkids. Why can't you just leave me alone?"

He'd made the mistake of offering coffee before we'd gotten to the point of our visit, and right now I figured that was the only thing preserving our interview. Solich was a cranky old bastard, but he wasn't so low as to throw us out of his home before we'd finished our coffee. Manners.

"We're not trying to bring you any trouble," I said. "But you might be able to help us stop some. We just want to know why your businesses were burned, Mr. Solich."

He scowled and slurped his coffee. "How the hell am I supposed to know? Punk kid vandals set a place on fire, then come by and tell me why they did it? Is that what you think? Okay, here's why they did it: Their parents didn't love 'em and the schoolteachers didn't, neither. Satisfied?"

"Your businesses weren't burned down by kids, Mr. Solich," Joe said, friendly but firm.

"You don't know that."

"But you do," Joe said. "So why don't you explain it to us?"

Solich's only response was a belch.

"Seems there were some rumors about you selling stolen merchandise out of your shops," I said. "Any chance that had something to do with these fires?"

Solich put two fingers in his mouth and cut loose with a whistle that made my hair stand on end. The crazy little terrier bounded over, gave Joe and me cursory sniffs, then settled down beside Solich, licking his hand.

"I'm retired," Solich said again. He crossed his legs over bony knees, tightened the belt on his robe.

We waited. Five minutes passed, and Solich was silent. We didn't push him, though, because it seemed he was working up to it.

"I'm not answering any questions about what I sold twenty damn years ago," he said eventually.

"This isn't about what you sold twenty years ago," I said. "We don't care, and to be honest, the police probably don't, either. We just want to know why someone burned three of your pawnshops down."

He sighed and scratched his head. "I did have three, didn't I? Most I ever had. Started with a little dump over on Superior, moved into a bigger space, then got another, and another. Yeah, I was doing all right. Making money." There was a wistful quality to his words. "Yeah, I guess I can tell you. I suppose it don't do no harm now. Time's passed."

"Yes, it has," I said.

He drank some more coffee. "People brought me quality items, and I bought them, no questions asked. That was the way I did business. Should be the way everyone does business. Over the years, though, I guess I got a pretty good handle on things. Paid better than some of the other guys, got more merchandise, moved more merchandise."

"Swag," I said. "Stolen goods."

His lips curled slightly. "Merchandise."

"Right."

"Anyhow, the market in that neighborhood, hell, in most of the west side, was mine. Had been for a few years, and it wasn't changing. There was another guy moving in, wanted my network. Wanted me gone. I told him to screw, he burned down my shops. Simple as that." Solich drank some more coffee, then reached down to re-fill his cup.

"You've got to give us the name," Joe said.

Solich frowned.

"We aren't going to drag you into it," Joe said. "But we've got to know."

He sighed. "You two were worth a damn, you could figure it out, anyhow. But I'll save you the trouble, because I don't matter to him anymore, so I doubt he'll come out here to give me grief. Guy's name was Jimmy Cancerno."

I leaned forward in my chair. "Cancerno? He's in the construction business."

Solich regarded me with amusement. "Man's in a lot of businesses. Owns half a dozen pawnshops on the west side, too, though from what I hear he's moving more into the cash loan operations now." He made a sour face. "I never liked that."

"Canerno wanted you out of business, so he burned you out?" Joe said.

Solich nodded. "Uh-huh. That was back when Jimmy was an up-and-comer. I suspect he's long outgrown my sort of thing now."

"Why didn't you tell the police?" I said. "Just because you didn't want them looking at your business operation?"

"Wasn't too worried about that, since everything that would've been there to look at was burned up. I just didn't want Jimmy to come any harder than he had. Man made his point, and I took it."

"You think Cancerno would've done more than burn down your buildings?" Joe said.

Solich cocked his head at Joe. "You don't know much about Jimmy, do you?"

"No, I don't."

"Well, the man is one ruthless son of a bitch. Didn't take me but one fire to figure that out, but he didn't let it rest there. He didn't want me to step out of his way, he wanted me to run out of it, and not look back. And he got what he wanted."

"So what exactly is Cancerno into?" I asked. "Swag sales, loan-sharking? That it?"

Solich's sunken eyes went wide, his eyebrows arched. "What *isn't* Jimmy Cancerno into? Back then he was a punk kid, and swag and loan-sharking was about all he had. Man's gone big-time since then, though. From what I hear, at least. If there's an illegal enterprise on the near west side that he doesn't run, I'd be surprised."

"Organized crime, then," Joe said. "Is he connected?"

"To what, the Italian mob?" Solich shook his head. "Hell, no. That goombah shit isn't Jimmy's style. Too independent for that. He's got his hand in everyone's games, but he keeps his distance. In that neighborhood, though, he's the boss. Ain't a damn thing goes down between Clark Avenue and Fulton Road that doesn't get his stamp of approval first."

We sat quietly for a moment, Solich stroking the terrier's head, the sprinkler hissing away over the flowerbeds.

"You said you didn't tell the cops anything because you didn't want Jimmy to come at you harder," I said. "What exactly does that mean? Do you think he'd kill?"

Solich turned to me with solemn eyes. "Mister, there's a reason I retired."

We stayed for a while longer, maybe ten more minutes, but Solich seemed to grow increasingly uncomfortable. Toward the end he was almost wincing every time we mentioned Cancerno's name. I had the feeling he was beginning to regret being as forthright as he had been. Fifteen years of sitting on the patio in Parma and watching his dog and grandkids had lulled him into a sense of comfort. Now we'd come along and rattled him. I was glad we'd gotten to him first, though. I doubted he was going to be as cooperative with the next group that showed up asking what Solich knew about his old neighborhood and the people who ran crime in it.

"Do you buy his description of Cancerno?" Joe asked as I drove us back to the office. He spoke loudly, trying to be heard over the roar of the wind ripping through the cab of the truck.

"Yes. It didn't seem like he was bullshitting us. Besides, it fits. Cancerno told me something the first time I met him about not liking the police in his business, and there was more to it than a general privacy concern."

"If the guy's everything Solich says he is," Joe said, "then this thing is jumping up a few weight classes. Organized crime, even if it's limited to a neighborhood. And, shit, if Cancerno was burning people out of business, the level he was playing at twenty years ago wasn't too light-weight, anyhow."

"Do we take a run at Cancerno?"

Joe shook his head emphatically. "No way. Far too early. Nothing to gain, and plenty to lose. I still want Corbett. What that guy knows about things both past and present could probably go a long way toward helping us straighten this out."

Back at the office, a message from our spook in Idaho was waiting. Joe called him back immediately, but it wasn't good news. No activity on any of Corbett's accounts in the last ten days. He had two credit cards and a debit card and used both regularly. He'd stopped ten days ago.

"Tells us a couple things," Joe said after he'd related the news to me. "One, Corbett might be dead."

"Then why were Padgett and Rabold looking for him?"

"Because they didn't know he was dead," Joe said. "But that's not the only possibility. The other possibility is Corbett's on the run, hiding from somebody. And if he is, he's smart. He's not using plastic because it can be traced. If that's the case, it tells us something else, too."

"What's that?"

"That he expects the guys chasing him might have a pretty broad reach. Pretty good resources, if they can trace a credit card."

"Right. Doesn't help us find him, though."

Joe nodded and sighed. "On to the next option, then."

"Wearing out shoe leather."

"You got it."

We spent five hours at it and got nothing. For the rest of the afternoon and into the evening, Joe and I worked the streets together, trying to find someone who could put us in contact with Mitch Corbett. We went to his brother's house and almost got the cops called on us. We went back to the Clark Recreation Center, got them to give us a phone list of the other volunteers who'd worked with Corbett, then went through it looking for someone who could help. Nobody could. We canvassed Corbett's neighborhood, hitting twenty-five houses. Everywhere we went, with the exception of the brother's house, we heard the same speech. Mitch Corbett was a nice enough guy, kept to himself, and, no, he hadn't been around for a while. Not for a few days, at least. No, not sure how to get ahold of him, where he might have gone.

"Shit," I said as we walked back to the car, "this has been a total waste, Joe." We'd devoted most of the day to Corbett and had nothing to show for it. Meanwhile, a half dozen other aspects of the investigation sat untouched.

"We had to try," Joe said. "He's got answers, LP. You know he does."

"Other people might have had answers, too. Instead we just lost time."

We walked back to the car in a silent, shared frustration. The humidity had been building throughout the day. Even in the time it took to walk from the car to the house and back, I'd begun to sweat. Heavy purple clouds hung on the horizon to the northwest, out over the lake. Hopefully, they'd work their way down and into the city, dump some rain on us to cut the heat and humidity that had been increasing for days. It was hard to tell in August, though.

Sometimes the storms pushed in off the lake late in the day, other times they simply passed along with a few teasing drops.

Back in the Taurus, Joe started the motor and cranked the air-conditioning up, blasting warm air out of the vents. He'd left his cell phone sitting on the console, and now he picked it up and checked the display.

"Missed a couple of calls."

"You know, the damn things are portable for a reason," I said, still awash in my frustration over a fruitless afternoon's work.

Joe didn't answer, just put the phone to his ear to play the messages. I stared out the window, tilting my face away from the hot, dusty air that was surging out of the vents. I gazed up the street at Corbett's empty house, saw the stack of newspapers piled against the door, the mail bulging out of the box. Where the hell had he gone? And what did he know?

"That was Amos Lorenzon," Joe said, breaking into my thoughts as he lowered the cell phone a minute later. "He wants to meet us. As soon as possible. He said he got something from the conduct reports."

"Only a day late."

"Yeah." Joe's face was intense. "He said it was big, LP. The kind of big that made him afraid to say a word about it over the phone."

Amos Lorenzon met us at Bartlett's Tavern on Lorain Avenue. Several people were at the bar, but Amos sat at a tiny table in the corner of the room, secluded. It had been a few years since I'd seen him, but he hadn't changed much. The real shock was seeing him out of uniform. I tried to think of another time I'd seen him without the blue on and came up empty.

"How are you, son?" he said, shaking my hand. Amos

had always called me son when we'd ridden together, but it had never been in a derogatory fashion, and I didn't mind hearing it again.

"Doing fine," I said. "Good to see you again."

While he exchanged greetings with Joe, I pulled a third chair up and we all sat down. The table between us was about the size of a beer coaster. The bartender, a middle-aged woman with a hoarse voice, shouted over the music to ask Joe and me if we wanted a drink. We both declined.

"I hope you guys understand I wouldn't have done this for just anybody," Amos said. His skin tone was light for a black man but looked darker here in the shadows. There was gray in his fuzzy hair now and deep wrinkles across his forehead. He wasn't tall, but he was built like a fire-plug and had the strongest hands of anyone I'd ever known. More than once I'd seen him put what looked like a casual hand on the shoulder of a drunken disorderly and immediately bring the man to his knees with one squeeze.

"We know that," Joe said. "And you should know how much it's appreciated."

"We'll pay you whatever you think is fair," I offered, even though we had no client to bill for the expense. I didn't want Amos to feel like we'd taken advantage of him.

He scowled. "Great idea, son. It gets around that I released this information, I'm in deep enough *without* it looking like I took a bribe."

"Fair point."

"What have you got?" Joe said.

Amos gazed at the crowd around the bar, wary even though there was no way they could have heard us over the Pearl Jam that was pulsing through the speakers. This wasn't any sort of police bar, and I had a feeling that was why Amos had selected it. He was nervous about the information he was about to offer us.

"I went through the conduct evaluations like you

asked. For both Rabold and Padgett. Same day I'm doing that, Rabold gets killed."

Silence.

"Didn't think you'd have a whole lot to say about that," Amos said. "But I don't like it."

"When I asked you to check out the conduct reports, I didn't know the guy was going to get killed," Joe said. "Now what do you have?"

"They've had their share of criticism," Amos said. "Rabold got busted eight years back for letting a guy slip him a few hundred in cash in exchange for not arresting him for drunk driving. The guy talked about it at a party when there was a city official in the room, and Rabold got his ass chewed good on that. No suspension, though; it never made the papers so it was all done quietly. That was about the only serious knock on Rabold other than general complaints about laziness."

"And Padgett?" Joe said.

"He's a different matter." Amos shifted in his chair, pulling closer to the little table. "Never gets a positive review, but he's been around so long and he's so loud and overbearing that I think some guys are intimidated by him. He's had nearly a dozen complaints of excessive force over the years, but none of them developed into anything. Internal affairs investigated a rumor of him taking bribes over some swag sales about ten years back, but they cleared him."

"Swag sales," I said. "You know if that involved a guy named Cancerno?"

"I don't remember any names being mentioned on that. It was just a few sentences saying he'd been checked out and cleared." Amos stopped talking and sipped the glass of water that was on the table, his eyes on the bar again. I glanced over my shoulder and saw we were getting a stare from the bartender as she poured someone a fresh draft. Three guys sitting at a corner table in a bar, drinking nothing but one ice water between them. This was probably the most suspicious behavior she'd seen in a while.

"Tell you something else I found out that I don't like," Amos said. "When I asked records to pull those conduct evaluations for me, the girl there said something about Rabold being a popular guy. I didn't know what she was talking about and said so. She told me there have been a couple requests for his evaluations in the past few weeks—one from internal affairs, another from the FBI."

"FBI," Joe echoed. "Wonderful. She have any idea what it was about?"

"No. But like an idiot, I decided I'd pursue it a little bit. I called a guy I know with internal affairs, asked him what he knew about Rabold. The man got seriously bothered. Wanting to know what the hell I was asking about Rabold for. I told him I was doing conduct reviews and was curious, but he didn't buy it, and if he checks me out, I could be in some trouble. That is, if you two tell anyone I passed information along to a couple civilians."

"We're not telling anyone," I said. "But this guy didn't give you any idea of what's going on with Rabold?"

"No. And he's a guy I know well, too. A friend, almost. So his reaction surprised me." Amos lowered his voice another level, which made him practically inaudible. "The records girl gave me the name of the FBI guy who requested Rabold's evaluations. Name was Robert Dean. I checked him out just enough to find out that he's with the RICO task force."

Joe looked at me and raised his eyebrows. "RICO task force, and Rabold wearing a wire?"

"Sounds heavy," I said. "And the RICO angle could bring Cancerno into the fold easily enough."

"Wire?" Amos said.

"Rabold was wearing a wire when he was killed," Joe said. "You think he could have been working for internal affairs? Maybe setting up Padgett?"

Amos leaned away from the table and held up his hands. "I have no idea, man. None."

We were all quiet for a bit, thinking it over. Then Joe asked Amos if that was all he had.

"I'm not done yet," Amos said. "But before I keep going, I want to ask you boys a straight question and get a straight answer in return. Fair?"

Joe and I nodded.

"All right. Now, Pritchard, you didn't tell me what this was all about, and I respected that. But I remember some things, maybe more than you two think I would, and I've got my own ideas. Does this have something to do with Ed Gradduk getting killed?"

Joe left the answer to me.

"Yes. That's what it's about, Amos."

He pursed his lips and frowned. "I was afraid of that. I remembered what happened between you and that guy before you made the jump to narcotics, son. Remember it didn't go easy on you."

"I made my own bed on that one, Amos."

"Sure, son. But I remember, is all I'm saying. And I heard about it when he got killed a couple days back, but I didn't think of it right off when Pritchard called me."

We waited.

"There was a harassment complaint filed on Padgett more than fifteen years ago," Amos said. "Of the sexual nature. Claim was that he'd drop in on this woman time to time, make her perform for him. Seemed he had something on her, or maybe just intimidated her, because she let it go on for a while."

He paused, then said, "The woman was Gradduk's mother."

For a long time the only voice in the room was Eddie Vedder's as he wailed over the guitar and the drums.

"You think there was bad blood going back a long time with those two, don't you?" Amos said.

"Looks like it," I answered, my voice flat.

"Looks like an awful mess, is what it looks like," Amos said. "One of the cops that ran that kid down in the street was harassing the kid's mother years ago? Man, that's a shit storm waiting to happen."

"What were the details?" I said. "That's a substantial complaint, but Padgett's still on the force all these years later. It never came around to bite him."

"That's the hell of it," Amos said. "The Gradduk woman wouldn't make out a complaint herself. Wouldn't tell anyone a damn thing. The complaint came in and the department saw what a hellacious pain in the ass it could be, realized they had to go heavyweight with it right at the start, so they sent it up the line to the attorneys, who talked to the woman. She wouldn't tell them anything. Without a victim stating she'd been victimized, all they had left was a rumor. It died a quiet death and got shoved under the rug. Stayed there, too."

"At least till now," Joe said, and Amos grimaced.

"Wait a second," I said. "If Alberta Gradduk wouldn't say anything about it, then who made the complaint initially?"

"I got that." Amos slipped a piece of paper out of his back pocket and scanned it quickly. "I'm not giving this to you, because I want all this exchange to stay in the mind and not on paper; you know, protect myself. We get done, this sucker's going down the toilet back in that bathroom."

We waited while he searched for the name. After a minute, he had it.

"The original complaint was filed by a friend of the

family. Went right in to the chief, himself. Guy who made the complaint was named Thomas Perry. Says he was with a city ambulance team."

Joe looked at me. "Shit, Lincoln. Was that your—"

"Father," I said. "Yes. That was him."

CHAPTER 19

My father had not been close to the Gradduks. He hadn't much in common with Norm, and Alberta had always been in the house, out of sight. The only member of the family my father had regularly seen was Ed, because Ed had always been at my house. There had been times when just the two of them were together, though. Times that had been difficult for me to understand at first, when I was young.

They used to play baseball together in the front lawn of Ed's house on Tuesday evenings, the only weeknight my dad was home for dinner. I stumbled across them by accident once, watched them with shock for a few minutes, then retreated, feeling hurt and left out. My father had seen me there, though, and that night he came into my room to talk. Told me he needed to spend some time alone with my friend now and then, that Ed was feeling the loss of his father heavily. He said he was glad I was mature enough to understand that. It was a subtle, kind way to let me know that if I didn't like the two of them having some time without me, I needed to grow up. I took the lesson.

And so they spent time together, occasionally. But I'd never considered that my father might have been hearing things from Ed that I was not. I was Ed's best friend; my father was an old guy. If anyone knew secrets, it was going to be me, right? Wrong.

Long after Joe and I left Bartlett's Tavern I was still stunned. I wondered what exactly my father had known, wondered why Ed had told him and not me. But maybe there are things you can tell your best friend when you're a fourteen-year-old male and things you can't. Admitting that your mother was being sexually harassed might have fit into the latter category. And I didn't have to wonder why my father had never told me—if he felt strongly about keeping his own problems quiet, and he did, then he felt stronger still about keeping the problems of others quiet. Thomas Perry was not a man who passed neighborhood gossip along. He was the brick wall that brought it to a halt.

You're just like your father, Alberta Gradduk had said, scowling at me. *I never liked meddlers.*

So he'd meddled. But how far? He'd made a complaint to the police, obviously, had instigated an investigation into Padgett. But then what happened? Did Padgett go away, or did he linger? What had his contact with the Gradduks been over the years? What had put him at Ed's house with a gun in his hand three days ago? And why the hell wouldn't Alberta talk? She'd been cooperative enough until I'd asked if she knew one of the cops, and then she'd thrown us out.

These were the questions that ran through my head as Joe drove us back to the office. It was growing late now, the sun a fading red mass at the end of the avenue, the day gone. We didn't have much to show for it, either. More questions, maybe. Not a lot of answers. That seemed to be the pattern.

Joe went upstairs when we got back to the office, claiming he was just going to shut his computer down. I knew he was probably going to get to work on the paying cases we'd been neglecting for days, though. I said goodbye and walked back to my apartment. When I got there,

I didn't go upstairs, but kept walking east down the avenue. I walked until I got to the West Park library, then went around the building and lifted myself up onto the cool stone wall that bordered the steps. I could hear laughter from the little park that's just down the street from the library, kids playing tag or chasing the season's last fireflies, maybe.

Leaning back until I was flat on the wall, I cupped my hands behind my head and looked up at the night sky. I listened to the kids and remembered how it had felt to be one of them on a hot, muggy summer night. They're all special when you're a kid, three months of treasures strung together before you're sent back to school. There's nothing quite like that when you reach adulthood. I closed my eyes and breathed deeply, feeling the stone cold on my back. Ed and Draper and I used to sit on the concrete steps outside the Hideaway late into the summer nights, saying hello to the regulars that went into the bar, watching for any girls that might pass by on the avenue. It seemed like a million years ago, and like yesterday.

I was bothered by how much had gone on without my knowledge. Norm Gradduk had been a suspect in the neighborhood fires the summer he'd killed himself, his wife had apparently been harassed by a cop, and my father had made a complaint about the cop's behavior. It had all happened right around me, along the streets I'd walked every day, to the people I knew best in the world. And I hadn't known a damn thing about it.

My phone vibrated in my pocket. I thought about letting it go, not wanting to lose the brief moment of peacefulness to whoever was calling, but I took it out of my pocket and checked the display. It was Amy's work number.

"How you doing, Ace?"

"Okay," she said. "Did you get those faxes?"

"Yes. Thanks a lot."

"Anytime. Did you see the recorder's-office list, though?"

"Uh-huh."

"Good. Remember how I added that note that said there hadn't been any other fires to the Neighborhood Alliance properties?"

"Yes."

"Well, you can erase that. I heard a fire run called in on the police scanner ten minutes ago. It's a house on West Twenty-fifth. The same one on the list I faxed you."

I sat up.

"You there?" Amy said.

"Yes."

"Ed Gradduk didn't start this fire."

"No."

"But another Neighborhood Alliance house is burning. So what the hell's going on, Lincoln?"

"I don't know." I dropped down from the wall. "But I'd like to see for myself." I walked away from the library, back toward the avenue.

"Are you going down there? To the house fire?"

"Seems like I ought to."

"Want me to meet you down there?"

"If you'd like."

I thanked her, hung up, slipped the phone back into my pocket, and quickened my pace. I wanted to get to West Twenty-fifth while the house was still burning. And I wanted my gun.

had the Glock in its holster and the key in the ignition of my truck when Amy called again. I started the truck and answered the phone as I pulled out of my parking space.

"I'm on my way, Amy."

"It'll be a shorter trip then you thought."

"What do you mean?"

"You're not going to believe this, Lincoln, but we've got another fire going now. Another Neighborhood Alliance house. It's on Hancock Avenue."

"You're sure?"

"Positive. They just called it in. We've got two fires going at Neighborhood Alliance houses now. Two in about twenty minutes, Lincoln. Who's doing this? And why?"

The annoying thing about hanging out with a reporter is that she tends to keep asking questions, even when she knows you don't have the answers. I told Amy I'd call her back, and I pulled into the street and hammered the accelerator, the big truck's exhaust roaring. While I drove, I dialed Joe's home number and put the phone back to my ear. It took six rings before I remembered that he'd still be at the office. I disconnected and called him there. He answered immediately.

"Something strange is going down, Joe."

"Yeah?"

"Two house fires just started on the near west side in the last half hour. They're both Neighborhood Alliance houses."

Silence.

"This isn't Ed Gradduk's work," I said, echoing Amy's obvious statement.

"Where are you?"

"On my way to Hancock Avenue. It's fresher."

"You think it's going to do one damn bit of good for you to stand on the sidewalk watching that thing burn?"

"I don't know, Joe. But I'm sure not going to sit at home and wait for Amy to call me with updates. This has to be arson. Somebody might have seen something, just like Gradduk was caught on tape with the last fire. The time to try to talk to people is now, while they're all out on the street watching the show. It'll be easier than trying to knock on doors tomorrow, hoping to find out who was home when the fire got started."

He grunted, which was the best acknowledgment of support I could hope for. "You want me to meet you down there? Work the crowd as a team?"

"I don't know yet. Let me get an idea of what the situation is and call you back."

"All right." There was a long pause, and then he said, "You got any bright ideas as to what this could be about?"

"No."

"Me neither."

"I'll call you back, Joe."

A quarter mile away from the fire on Hancock, I could hear the sirens and see the smoke. I got within two blocks of the house before I ran into a roadblock of police cruisers parked sideways in the street, keeping traffic away from the fire. There was no parking at the curb on this side of the street, but I pulled my truck in anyhow, rolling the passenger-side tires up onto the sidewalk to get as much of the vehicle out of the way as possible. I left it there, sitting at an angle, half on and half off the sidewalk, and then I began to jog toward the house.

I jogged into view just in time to see the porch roof fall in under the deluge from the fire hose. Two trucks were working on the blaze, one parked in the street and one pulled into the narrow driveway. Neighbors stood huddled in little groups of five or six across the street, watching with a mix of horror and excitement. The flames seemed to have been beaten back by the water, but thick black smoke continued to pour out of the second-floor windows. When the roof of the porch caved in and collapsed, one woman screamed and covered her eyes, while a young boy beside her clapped his hands and bounced up and down on his toes, eyes wide, soaking up a scene that was much better than whatever show he'd been watching on television before the sirens had interrupted and drawn him out of the house.

The temptation was to stand there with them and watch the blaze, stare with awe as the old house—first burned and now soaked—continued to crumble to the ground. I put my back to it, though, and looked at the crowd instead.

Maybe twenty-five people were watching, staying in small groups, but I didn't see any familiar faces. I approached the woman who had covered her eyes when the porch roof fell in and pulled out my wallet, letting it flip open to expose my private investigator's license. Showing a license, any type of license, is often a great way to convey authority and convince people to give you more than cursory attention, and in this situation I figured it would be the only way to get this woman to look away from the fire.

"Ma'am, do you live around here?" I said, showing the license for all of two seconds before snapping the wallet shut and returning it to my hip pocket. She looked at me and blinked, surprised by my approach and not following the question. She was about thirty, with shoulder-length, blond hair and an ample stomach and abdomen pinched by a belt. I assumed the boy beside her was her son, judging from the way she kept pulling him back onto the sidewalk and out of the street.

"Do you live around here?" I repeated once I had her attention.

"Um, what? I mean, yeah, I live, you know . . ." She waved a hand behind her that could have indicated any of ten houses, and her eyes began to drift back to the fire.

"When did this get started?" I said, stepping closer, trying to command her attention.

"Like, five minutes ago?"

The kid beside her, who was maybe ten, was looking at me with far more interest than his mother, and he shook his head impatiently. "No, it was longer than that. Before the end of the inning. We were watching the Indians game."

"Were you out here before the fire department got here?"

She looked from the kid to me and shook her head. "No. Well, like, about the same time. We heard the sirens, right? So I went to the window and looked out, and I saw the house was burning. We came outside right when the fire trucks were pulling up."

My phone was vibrating in my pocket, but I ignored it and stepped closer to her, fighting to hear over the sound of the hoses and the shouting firefighters and neighbors.

"Any idea how it got started?" I asked.

"What? No. I mean, nobody lives there, so it couldn't have been like a cooking fire or anything." We were standing close now, our faces huddled together, and her breath came at me with a heavy smell of pickles that made me want to lean back.

"Was there any sort of explosion?"

"I don't know. Jared had the TV on so loud . . ."

Another man who'd been standing near us, a tall, lean guy with an Indians baseball cap and a scraggly goatee, now interrupted.

"Yeah, there was an explosion. Well, you could hear it go up, at least. Kind of a *whoosh* noise."

I turned to him. "Where were you when it got started?"

He pointed at the house immediately to my left. "Right there, smoking a cigarette on the lawn. I was the one who called it in." He looked at me curiously. "You with the police?"

"I'm an investigator."

"Oh, fire department?" he said, and rather than answer the question I threw another back at him.

"How long had you been on the lawn?"

He tugged at the goatee with his fingers. "Oh, ten minutes at least."

"You notice anything going on across the street? See anybody walking around, maybe sitting in a car watching the place, anything like that?"

One of the fire hoses changed direction now, approaching the house from a new angle, and the breeze caught the spray and carried some of it across the street, brushing over us like raindrops blown off a tree's leaves. The smell and taste of the smoke was heavy in the air.

"I didn't notice anything," the man with the goatee told me as the fire captain shouted that it was time to go inside the house. I turned away long enough to see three of the firefighters approach the porch in full gear, armed with axes.

"The house has been empty for a while, right?" I said.

"Oh, yeah. Couple months, now. I never seen nobody over there, though. Probably was a neighbor kid or something. You know, playing with matches."

More sirens were coming from the east now, growing steadily louder, and the kid who'd been fidgeting around us the whole time covered his ears with hands. His mother had turned away from me completely to refocus on the scene across the street. My phone was vibrating again, buzzing against my leg, and I held my finger up at the man with the goatee, asking him to wait a minute, then stepped away and pulled the phone from my pocket. The display showed it was Amy's work number. She hadn't even left yet.

I answered and said, "I'm down here, Amy. Get in your car and drive instead of calling me for updates."

"Lincoln, this shit is getting out of control. There's another one burning now. Clark and West Thirty-sixth."

"What?"

"You heard me. We've got three houses up in flames, all of them in under an hour. All Neighborhood Alliance properties."

The sirens were close now, making me wince. I hunkered down on the sidewalk, elbows on my knees, and covered one ear, fighting to hear Amy.

"We've got two reporters out now, and my editor asked me to stay here and coordinate with the field reporters," she said. "Not my choice, but I'm going to have to stay here."

"This is insane," I said. "Three of them burning at once?"

"Hate to be a pessimist," Amy said, "but do you really think it's going to stop there?"

"Maybe not." Even as I said it, I realized I was wasting time standing here talking to the neighbors. "Shit, Amy— you've got the list of all the Neighborhood Alliance homes right there, the one you sent me."

"So?"

"Well, it looks like someone's working their way through the same list, right? Opportunity knocks."

"You're going to try to catch up with whoever's doing this?"

"You said it yourself, Ace—it's probably not going to stop at three. And there's a chance I might be able to get ahead of this guy."

CHAPTER 20

Amy read the list to me and I wrote the addresses down with a pen and paper borrowed from one of the neighbors watching the fire. Then I hung up and returned to my truck. The first house on my list that wasn't already in flames was on Erin Avenue, a few blocks north of Clark and not far from Mill Park. There was another house on Erin, too. I figured I'd start with the one near the park and then move east.

Soon I was far enough away from the other fires that the sirens seemed distant, and the neighborhood was quiet despite fairly heavy traffic. I made a right turn onto Erin Avenue and slowed down, watching the house numbers and looking for the right one.

Chaos was coming from behind me. I pressed the brake pedal all the way down, bringing the truck to a jarring halt, and leaned out the window, listening. A lot of shouting joined by fresh sirens. A car behind me honked, and I pulled forward about twenty feet before making a hard left turn into a narrow alley. I put the truck in reverse and looked in the rearview mirror, waiting for an opportunity to back out and change directions, but then I said the hell with it and threw the truck into park. I figured the police had more important things to deal with right now than worrying about towing a truck out of an alley.

By the time I reached the sidewalk I could see the smoke. It wasn't the house near the park, which stood somewhere to my left, but the house that was farther east along the avenue. I broke into a run.

It was a one-story house, smaller than any of the others that were already burning, and this time I'd arrived early enough to see the flames at work. They crackled and roared as they licked out of broken windows and through the eaves of the roof. Inside, something collapsed, and the noise of the flames swelled with a sound of ecstasy, a primal monster bent on destruction.

There were no fire trucks yet, just two cops working out of one battered cruiser, shouting at the crowd to stay back. One man was in the middle of the street, refusing to move, and when the cop ordered him to get back on the sidewalk, he shouted an angry response.

"That's my house next door, man! If this thing spreads, it's going to get my house!"

"The fire department will get it under control," the cop answered, placing a firm hand on the angry man's chest. "Now, sir, please go to the other side of the street."

"Hell with that," the man said, knocking the cop's hand off his chest and running back across the street and into the house that stood no more than twenty feet from the burning home. The cop swore and ran after him while his partner turned to the crowd, hands up. It was Jack Padgett.

I stood and stared at him as he shouted orders at the onlookers, his partner pursuing the man who'd run for the house. Padgett was in uniform, stalking about the street confidently, tall and strong and angry.

I moved back down the sidewalk and called Joe again.

"There's another house burning," I said when he answered, "and guess what cop is down here working the crowd."

A pause. "Padgett?"

"Uh-huh. Kind of strange, him turning up at the scene like this, don't you think?"

"You know how long he's been down there?"

"No."

Joe grunted. "I don't like this, Lincoln. If I were you, I'd get the hell out of there."

Padgett had calmed the crowd and was now gazing up the street. I was standing out in the open, and he saw me. For a moment our eyes were locked.

"Shit," I said. "He's looking right at me. I'm going to hang up now, clear out of here, and check on the other houses."

Joe was issuing another warning when I disconnected the call. Padgett was walking toward me, but his head was turned, looking for the other cop who'd been with him. I hesitated only briefly before turning and walking back down the street. Any confrontation with Padgett could wait. This fire was a lost cause; the house by the park might not be.

I had to dodge people as I moved down the sidewalk. Word of the fires was clearly spreading quickly through the neighborhood, drawing people out into the streets. I heard one man insisting the fires were the work of street gangs; another woman was screaming about a gas leak.

I went down the sidewalk and across the street, toward the park, my gun still holstered on my spine. I was counting the house numbers, and I saw I was getting close. There it was, two houses down. I approached the porch, slipping my hand along my spine, close to the gun. My eyes were locked on the dark windows at the front of the house, looking for movement.

Those windows blew out with a roar just as my foot touched down in front of the door.

A shower of glass rushed past me, hard pebbles that didn't feel sharp even as they opened up my flesh. I dropped to my knees as the first wave of heat followed the glass. Flames surged out of the broken windows and up the front of the house. I covered my head with my hands and began to roll backward, away from the heat.

I made two complete rolls and half of a third before I fell off the porch and onto the lawn. As soon as I hit the grass, I began to clamber away from the house, moving on my hands and knees but trying to keep my face as low as possible, close to the cool earth and unexposed to the terrific heat behind me. Across the street more people were shouting; the crowd that had turned out to see what all the commotion to the east had been about was now drawn to the west by the new house in flames.

I went about twenty feet on the ground before finally rising and running across the street. The neighbors parted as I arrived, keeping their distance as if I had sprinted out of a quarantined plague camp. They watched me warily as I dropped onto my ass on the sidewalk and sat facing the fire, breathing heavily. My forearms were covered with long scratches from the glass, and blood was beginning to soak portions of my shirt.

"You all right, fella?" one woman asked, concern in her face. I just nodded.

"What were you doing over there?" said another voice, this one heavy with suspicion. "That house is vacant. What's going on? There are fires going all over the neighborhood."

I twisted my neck and looked behind me at the speaker, an overweight man with red hair and a face covered with freckles. I could see the other bystanders react to his words; expressions changed from surprise and concern to suspicion and anger.

"What *were* you doing over there?" someone else

echoed. "That house has been empty for a year. How'd a fire start in it?"

I braced the heels of my hands against the sidewalk and pushed off it, getting back to my feet. As I did, my shirt slid up my back a bit, and the woman who'd asked me if I was all right screamed.

"He's got a gun! He's got a gun!"

Chaos. Half of the bystanders ran immediately, not bothering to look for the gun or linger long enough to see if there was true cause for alarm. Two or three others simply joined the first woman in shouting, and the man with the red hair and freckles made a clumsy lunge at me, arms outstretched like a child running to hug his mother. I spun away easily and dipped under him, came up with my shoulder in his solar plexus, a football lineman's move. All the breath left his lungs in one choked gasp and he staggered back as I stepped free.

"Somebody get a cop!" another man yelled, and then I heard a woman misinterpret this and shout that someone had just shot a cop. By the time the police *did* get there, they'd have a hell of a time extracting the truth of the situation from that group. But if one of those cops was Padgett, I had no desire to wait around. I began to run.

My truck was only a block or two away, still parked in the alley, but I was running away from the crowd, which took me in the opposite direction. I decided it would be best to stay on foot and try to move as fast as possible. Five houses were burning in the neighborhood now, and if the son of a bitch responsible stuck to the houses on my list, there were just two more to go. I wondered if Padgett would be turning up somewhere else along the list.

I ran back across the street and past the park, ducked in behind a house, and got the Neighborhood Alliance list from my pocket. My fingers left streaks of blood on the paper as I unfolded it.

I had a good idea of where to go next. The first fire had been the farthest east of any of the homes, and the two on Erin Avenue had also gone up in east-to-west fashion. Whoever was doing this was working for speed and efficiency, moving through the houses systematically, working his way west.

The closest house left on my list was to the southwest, on West Fortieth, between St. Mary's Cemetery and Trent Park. If I ran hard down Fulton to Clark, I might be able to make it.

If the second house on Erin Avenue was the smallest I'd seen on the list, the house on West Fortieth was probably the largest. According to the recorder's-office list Amy had faxed me, this was the last house Anita Sentalar had acquired. It was an old home, set back from the road a little deeper than the neighbors, composed of three stories of faded paint and broken windows. A front door looked out over a short porch, but after my last experience I decided to avoid the front steps and take a look around the back.

The house faced west, and the south side was bordered by a sagging chain-link fence. A narrow driveway led past the house on the north side, ending in a detached one-car garage.

I walked down the driveway, my legs trembling beneath me from the long, fast run I'd made. A streetlight was at the front of the house, but at the rear it was quite dark. I had a flashlight in the truck, but the truck was too far away to do me any good now. I approached the back of the house.

Everything about the property was still and quiet, and those qualities were accentuated by the commotion raging to the north and east. By comparison, this stretch of the neighborhood now seemed like a ghost town. I looked around the yard carefully and saw nothing. The back door looked solid, and there was no sign anyone had broken in. Maybe I'd been wrong in my assumption of where the next fire would be set, or maybe whoever was responsible for them had stopped at five. With the gathering police and fire attention, not to mention the crowds on the streets, it wasn't an unreasonable idea.

I had nearly convinced myself of that when I stepped closer to the back door and saw a single pane of glass was missing from the window that made up the top half of the door. I slipped my arm through it and found the lock easily. I twisted it and then tried the knob. It didn't turn, which meant the door had already been unlocked.

I took three steps back from the house and gazed up at the dark windows, looking and listening for any sign of movement, of someone inside. Nothing. I reached behind me and took the Glock out of its holster, then switched it from my right hand to my left and reached back inside to unlock the door.

Inside, the house smelled musty. I took a few tentative steps, shuffling my feet instead of lifting them and lowering them, because I couldn't see what lay ahead. Using this technique, I moved forward, out of the small entryway and into what appeared to be a kitchen. Here I paused for a few seconds and allowed my eyes to adjust to the lack of light. When I could see well enough to make out large obstructions, I began to move forward again. At the doorway I stopped and slid my palm up and down the wall, searching for a light switch. I found it, but when I flicked it up, nothing happened. The electricity was out in the house, probably killed by a long-inactive account.

I moved through an empty living room and came to the steps, started up them. The first flight of steps ended on a narrow landing, and above it a hall led away to what I assumed were bedrooms. I was on the landing when I heard a shuffling noise, a slight rush of movement, then a gentle thud. I knelt and listened for another sound. Just when I was convinced there would be no more, I heard another thud, this one even softer than the first, followed by a jingling noise.

I was halfway up the steps, staying low and leading with my left hand, when something rushed at me. I shouted and brought the Glock up, my finger tense on the trigger, as a large cat bounded down the steps. It leaped over my shoulder and landed gracefully on the steps behind me, turned and meowed loudly. A metal tag on its collar glinted in the thin beam of light from the street, no doubt the source of the jingling I'd heard. The cat gave me one more yowl, then cut left and disappeared.

"Holy shit," I said, taking a long, shaky breath and sagging against the wall, every muscle in my body trembling with tension. No wonder the thuds had been so soft—the cat probably weighed about ten pounds. I wiped my forehead with the back of my hand, the sweat stinging in cuts and scratches left from the glass shards, and then stood up, ready to move on now that I'd courageously driven the cat away.

I found the rest of the house empty, left, and went back out to stand in the yard. Now what? Should I wait to see if someone arrived or continue moving through the list? After a moment's debate, I chose movement over patience. Joe wouldn't have been surprised.

The last house on my list was on Newark Avenue, near Trent Park. Like the previous one, it was empty, dark, and still. The back door was locked. Until I kicked it in.

I cleared the lower level and walked for the stairs. This

was the darkest house yet, and I didn't see the steps clearly until I ran into the banister with my shoulder. Like the rest of the house, the steps were wooden and old, and when my weight settled on each one, there was a soft creaking, like farmhouse shutters swinging in a gentle breeze.

At the top, I moved quickly down a short hall and found two closed doors. I opened one and stepped in, cursing the darkness. There wasn't enough light from the street to help in this house. I felt around the wall until my hand hit a sink. This would be the bathroom. I stepped back into the hall and pulled the door shut, then tried the next one. A bedroom.

Something creaked beneath me, and I tensed up immediately, then relaxed and laughed softly. Hadn't I learned anything from the cat? No need to overreact. The laugh died fast as I heard more sounds from below and realized that someone had entered the ground floor of the house, walking confidently, without fear of making noise.

I stayed in the bedroom for a minute, listening to the clomping steps beneath me and wondering if the intruder would try to come up the stairs. Then I eased the door open, gently as possible, and stepped back into the hall. My night vision had adapted, and I could see the steps clearly. I moved toward them, my left hand searching the wall for the railing. Just as I found it, I became aware of something that scared me far more than the cat had—a heavy smell of kerosene coming from the ground floor of the house.

Fear is a product of the senses. I'd experienced fear many times, but before it had always been the result of something seen or felt physically. This new sensation, of standing alone in the dark and literally *smelling* danger, froze me for a moment. I stood on the stairs with my right hand on my gun, my left tight on the railing, feeling like an animal in a cave, sniffing the air for signs of hostility. Then my brain finally kicked my body into gear, and I started down the stairs much faster than I'd come up them. I was no longer worried about proceeding quietly; my only priority now was getting out.

I made it all of four steps before flame touched fuel somewhere below me. There was one loud puff, like a gust of air forced out of a plastic bag, followed quickly by a crackling roar. I reached the landing just as the flames crawled up the walls of the ground floor, and for the first time I saw the dark old house illuminated. The front door was partially obstructed by flames, but I knew that my best chance—my *only* chance—was to rush through them, hit that door, and pray I could find the lock and turn it quickly.

In the interest of speed, I tried to leap from the middle landing all the way to the bottom of the steps, intending to hit the ground running for the door. I didn't make it. My leap carried me down about seven of the ten steps, and it turned out to be a poor idea. The old, rotten wood that had creaked so ominously under me on the way up the steps broke with this much greater impact. My left foot slid across the surface, free, but my right foot plunged into the step between the shattered boards and sank up to the ankle. It caught and held as my weight and momentum continued forward, and I went down hard.

I hit the floor with my hands held out to keep me from landing directly on my face, and the Glock slid free and skittered across the floor toward the flames. My kneecap connected with the edge of the bottom step, and a current of pain rode through my leg, followed instantly by a numb sensation. The flames from the walls were spreading across the floor now, toward the stairs, and I was on my stomach, pinned by my ankle.

Rolling away from the flames and lifting my arms to

cover my face, I jerked my numb leg, trying to wrench my foot free. One of the broken boards cut a furrow in my flesh, but I didn't get loose. For the second time in just a few seconds I felt like an animal: first smelling danger in the dark, now caught with my foot in a trap.

Something moved to my right. I rolled back onto my left shoulder, sending another wave of pain through my ankle as it twisted against the pressure of the boards that held it, and tried to stretch my hand out for the gun. I couldn't see anything now because I couldn't bear to keep my eyes open this close to the searing heat of the fire. All around me was the smell of fuel and burning wood, and an incredible, oppressive heat.

A hand on my leg. Now I shouted and lashed out with my arms, trying to strike. I caught nothing but air. The hand twisted hard against my leg, and then my foot was free and I was sliding all the way to the floor. My hand brushed against my gun, and I'd wrapped my fingers around it and begun to turn back to the steps when I was suddenly lifted easily into the air, turned, and set back on my feet. The flames surged against us, closer now than ever, and I squeezed my eyes shut and began to move, one hand on my gun and the other clutching the shirt of the man who'd freed my foot. I had no idea who he was, but he was moving purposefully through the heat, pulling me along, and right now that was all I needed to know.

We went through the living room, stumbling and staggering, and then the other man pulled up short, leaned into my ear, and said, "Duck!"

He put both hands in the middle of my back as I dipped my chin against my chest and then he shoved me forward with such strength that I felt my feet leave the floor once again as I sailed out through an open door. Cool air rolled over me a half second before I fell forward onto the pavement.

The heat was behind me now but still close, and I got upright quickly and began to stagger away from the house. I opened my eyes again but saw only shadows and flashes of light, and just as I was thinking that I'd better slow down before I hit something, I hit something. My skull clanged against some object of much greater density—wood, stone, steel?—and then I was falling backward into blackness.

CHAPTER 21

Consciousness returned like an abrupt end to a long journey, as if I'd been deep in water swimming upward slowly and easily, then broken the surface without warning. I opened my eyes, but my vision was fading in and out, and the room I found myself in seemed to be on its own axis, spinning fast. Above me the ceiling went on forever into blackness. Two hard blinks later I realized the ceiling was the sky, and I wasn't in a room at all. I was on my back on pavement.

I started to move upright, but a quick surge of nausea and dizziness stopped me. I dropped back down and rolled on my side, feeling as if I was about to get sick. It was then I noticed the men with the guns.

There were two of them—both in suits, both with automatics in shoulder holsters, no attempt made to cover the weapons with their jackets.

"Probably shouldn't have sat up so fast," the taller one said conversationally. The shorter one just stood and glared at me. I didn't know what to make of them yet, but they didn't seem inclined to shoot me, so I just put my head back down on the pavement and closed my eyes, waiting for the sickness to pass.

It was a few minutes before I was able to stand. The suits had carried me away from the fire, probably as far as a few blocks, then dropped me in an alley. We were

beside a Dumpster, and the smell of garbage wasn't helping my nausea. On either side of the alley were tall stone
buildings, dark and quiet. None of the light from the fire
that had to be still burning was visible, and it was
strangely quiet here in the alley.

"Hell of a thing you did," the suit on my right said. He
was the taller one, with short dark hair and close-set eyes.
"Running right into a wall like that. Never seen anything
like it. You came out running like you had a gold medal in
mind, head down, and then—boom—right into the wall.
Hell of a thing."

It's always nice to have your athletic achievements
appreciated.

"Can you walk now?" the other suit said. He was looking around, shifting his weight, edgy. The taller guy was
relaxed.

"Yeah," I said, my tongue thick against my teeth.

"Great. We're going to walk down the alley and get
into a car. Then we're all going to go get you some water
and some painkillers and have a nice little talk."

My legs were unsteady beneath me, but they moved
well enough, and everything above my waist seemed fine
except for the pounding in my head. The lump on the top
of my skull went warm and then cool, warm and then
cool, like a coal fanned by a breeze. I winced against the
pain and then, slowly, started to walk. The nameless men
in the suits stayed on each side of me, standing close.

"FBI?" I said as we moved down the alley.

"Just me," the taller one said, his voice as lighthearted
as his springy, fast step. He was walking down the alley
with bouncing enthusiasm, as if he were coming out of
Jacobs Field after watching the Indians win on a walk-off
homer. "I apologize for forgetting the formal introduc-
tion, Mr. Perry. My name's Robert Dean."

The FBI agent who had requested Rabold's files. A

member of the RICO task force, according to Amos Lorenzon.

"And you?" I asked the other.

"Brent Mason, internal affairs, Cleveland police." He clipped the words off individually, as if he were counting. If I'd had to guess, I would have put them the other way around. Seemed like the guy with the rod up his ass would have been federal. Then again, the internal affairs guys can't help the rod—nobody likes them, and after a while that begins to affect your personality a bit.

We came out of the alley and I saw we were back on Fulton Road. They'd hauled me quite a ways.

"Didn't want to let me be rescued by the fire department or some other cops," I said.

"Oh, no," Dean said. "Couldn't have that. You might not believe it, Mr. Perry, but there are some cops in this neighborhood that wouldn't have had all that much interest in rescuing you."

They put me in the back of an unmarked Taurus that looked identical to the one Joe drove. Mason drove and Dean sat in the front beside him, so at least they trusted me not to leap from the car and flee. No handcuffs, no indication that I was a suspect in the fires. That was a plus.

"So I look all beat to shit," I said as we stopped at a red light on Fulton, "and you guys seem pretty fresh. No cuts, no burns—suits aren't even wrinkled."

"Uh-oh," Dean said. "I get the feeling he's deducing something."

Mason didn't say a word.

"I'm guessing you didn't pull me out of that fire," I said. "But it's just the three of us in here. So who did?"

Mason didn't answer, but I could tell from the way his shoulders tightened that he didn't appreciate the question.

Dean twisted around to face me and grinned broadly. "Can't tell you. Because we missed the son of a bitch."

"Missed him?"

"Sure did," Dean said cheerfully. Mason's shoulders tightened even more, as if someone were ratcheting up the tension in him with a wrench. "You came running out, and we both went after you. You stopped yourself with that header into the building next door, and, like a couple of jackasses, we were both there when you went down. The other guy bailed out right then, cleared the yard, and was long gone. It was, Mr. Perry, a serious drop of the ball on our part. And, oh, man, you do not want to imagine the response we're going to get when we offer this one up to the powers that be."

Dean concluded with a chuckle, and Mason looked at him as if he'd like to take his hands off the steering wheel and wrap them around the FBI agent's throat. He kept his mouth shut, though. He was good at that.

"But you saw him go in?" I said.

"We did."

"And?"

"And he was a big son of a bitch in a baseball cap," Dean said. "We were across the street, and you saw how damn dark it was behind that house. By the time we got across, things were burning. We probably would have been in fine shape if you hadn't come storming out when you did."

"Sorry. If I'd known burning to death would have helped you boys, I'd have stayed inside, of course."

"You say the guy pulled you out of the fire?" Dean said.

"That's right. I jumped down the stairs and put my foot right through one of the steps. Fell and got hung up, and then he came in and pulled me loose. Got me out of the living room and shoved me through the back door and I just kept going."

"So you were right next to him," Mason said, speaking

for the first time since we'd gotten in the car. "You got a good look."

"I got no look."

He shifted his eyes to the rearview mirror and gave me a hard squint, as if he thought I were lying. I stared back at the mirror and shook my head slowly.

"No lie, Detective. The place was on fire, and the guy was behind me. I had my eyes closed because of the heat for most of it, anyhow."

Mason grunted with disgust and dropped his eyes from the mirror.

They drove to Clark, then west to the intersection of Clark and Sixty-fifth, where Mason pulled into the narrow, steep parking lot of Mom's Restaurant. Mom's had been there forever; as long as I could remember and a few decades beyond that, at least. When I was a kid, my dad would take me to breakfast at Mom's on Saturdays. We'd make the walk up from the house—always a walk, never a drive, even if it was pouring rain or blowing snow—and then eat and talk. My dad would drink water and coffee, and I'd have orange juice and pancakes. He'd wince every time I ordered it—*orange juice and syrup,* he'd say, *your teeth will rot out.*

Mason shut off the engine and we all got out and went inside. The room was nearly empty, and I realized the place had to be close to shutting down for the night. When I'd gotten older and joined the force, I'd still meet my dad here sometimes, generally early in the morning when I got off the night shift. The last time I'd set foot in the place, a guy who'd known the Gradduks well had come over and talked to my dad at length without ever acknowledging me. Neither of us commented on it, but we never went back, either.

A waitress came around the corner, saw us, and raised her eyebrows. Dean said, "Enough time for coffee?"

"Always time for coffee," she said, and led us back to a booth along the front wall.

Dean had a first-aid kit with him, retrieved from the glove compartment. He found some aspirin in it and gave them to me with a couple of antiseptic cloths in plastic wrappers.

"Wipe those over your arms," he said. "You got some burns on the arms, and one across the back of your neck. Don't look too serious, but you might want to get them looked at. You're talking well enough that a concussion doesn't seem likely, but I don't want you suing us for denying you medical treatment, either. You want to get checked out before we talk, we'll run you down to the hospital."

I shook my head. "I'm good."

"Hell of a knock on the head he took," Mason said, looking unhappy, no doubt envisioning his ass on the line for losing an arson suspect and denying a victim medical treatment in the same hour.

"I gave him an aspirin," Dean said, and I had a brief recollection of some bad Harrison Ford movie where guys in a submarine are dying from radiation and Ford keeps screaming at the medic to give them some aspirin. It made me want to laugh, but I figured an outburst of laughter would probably convince them to take me to the hospital, after all.

"All right, guys," I said. "I want to go home, take a shower, and go to sleep with a bag of ice on my head. So let's get to it."

"Half of Clark-Fulton's on fire, and this guy wants to go to bed," Dean said.

"You think I set the fires, take me to jail."

"We know you didn't set the fires," Dean said. "But you've got a real knack for showing up in hot-action places lately, Mr. Perry. Thought we should discuss that."

"Is that why you were following me tonight?"

"Didn't start out following you," he said. "Started out following Jack Padgett. Then you showed your face and we got more than a little intrigued. Split with the two other guys we were with and went with you. Got a hell of a show, too."

I made a little bow that caused the lump on my head to pulse with heat and pressure, like a balloon filling with hot water. I gritted my teeth and leaned back in the chair. Tonight wasn't a good occasion for physical comedy.

"A few nights ago, Jack Padgett and Larry Rabold ran over a fugitive in Clark Avenue," Dean said. "You were there. Last night, Rabold was found murdered. You did the finding. Tonight, houses all over the neighborhood are catching fire, Padgett's patrolling the crowds, and you're sprinting through the streets."

"How'd you get in it, Perry?" Mason said. "And how, exactly, do we convince you to get out of it?"

I looked at Mason and then back at Dean. "I got in it when my friend got run over by Padgett and Rabold. I'll stay in it until I can explain why that happened."

"Anybody paying you?" Dean asked.

"Nope."

"Can we interest you in a government-funded vacation out of state for, say, three weeks?"

"Nope."

Dean laughed loudly.

"I don't know who set these fires," I said. "If you're expecting otherwise, you're going to be disappointed."

"We don't expect otherwise. Not at all."

"Do you understand the fires?" I asked. "What the purpose was?"

"We're not here about the fires," Dean said. "That's somebody else's case. A serious one, yes. But it's not ours."

"So why did you need to haul me off the property to assure yourselves of a private conversation?"

All the humor and charm slid off his face as he leaned forward. "To explain to you, Mr. Perry, that you are going to get yourself killed."

They explained that to me, and a few other things, as well. Although Mason contributed, it was still Dean's show all the way. There were four of them on the task force, I learned—two internal affairs detectives and two FBI agents from the racketeering and corruption squad. The task force had a simple purpose: explore the depths of police corruption in the department and its ties to Jimmy Cancerno's criminal empire.

"By and large, this department is clean," Mason said. "Any department of this size has its bad actors. It's inevitable. That's why you need guys like me. To keep it as clean as possible. And in this department, we've noticed a disturbing trend—most of the serious allegations keep coming up in the same district."

The Cleveland police department has eight districts. Clark-Fulton is in District Two, and Padgett and Rabold were District Two officers. Had been for a long time, it seemed.

"We've been hearing it for years," Mason said. "Complaints come and go all the time. But there have been too many in District Two. We noticed something else—there are a handful of officers who routinely turn down promotions that would place them in other districts, and fight transfers passionately. Why? We didn't know. And then these guys"—he nodded at Dean—"got involved."

The FBI's organized crime and RICO squad had gone through a turnover in Cleveland over the years. The Italian mob was once prevalent in the city, trailing only New York and Chicago in activity. That was decades ago, though. Then the Russians moved in, and the organized crime folks had—and still have—their hands full with them. The Russian mobs aren't like the Italians, though; they aren't interested in dominating a neighborhood. They've got their eyes on bigger projects, and they don't care about the street-corner shit.

"But we kept getting a sense of this network," Dean said, "on the near west side. Drugs, prostitution, swag, real estate scams, everything on down to low-level neighborhood hustles and bookkeeping. I'll be the first to admit we didn't dedicate a lot of attention to this. Didn't get really intrigued until we got more and more tips—every one anonymous—about corrupt cops, all in the same damn neighborhood. People feeding us tips about cops who'd been paid off, about detectives who drank with suspects, patrol officers who turned away when certain drunk drivers would roll up on the sidewalk right in front of them.

"So we ask ourselves," Dean continued, "who the hell is running this show? Like I said before, most of the serious forces left in organized crime are on to bigger and better things. We can't connect any of this shit around Clark-Fulton to a larger network. But then we began to get it. What if the show down there isn't about a larger network? What if it's a lot simpler—a crime throwback, you might say. What if it's just one cunning son of a bitch who wants to own a neighborhood?"

"Cancerno," I said.

Dean nodded. "Took us a while to get to him. The man is distanced, I'll say that. He runs his games with an exceptional blend of control and distance. You don't see a guy put it together so well very often. But it's him. No doubt about it. At the end of the day, almost everyone working any sort of hustle in that neighborhood is tied to Cancerno in some way."

"As are," Mason threw in, "a concerning number of cops."

"Right," Dean said. "And that's what we're doing here. We have to know how deep it goes. How far does it spread? He owns street cops, sure. A few detectives, maybe. And every indication says there's someone higher. But Cancerno's good—the left hand never knows what the right is doing. One bought cop may not know the next. The information chain is broken by design. But it was for damn sure that an insider could learn more than an outsider. We needed help."

"Larry Rabold," I said.

"Yes. We picked Mr. Rabold for two simples reasons: we had good evidence of his wrongdoing, and he had a family."

"Leverage," I said, thinking of Rabold's daughter, her blanched face and bloody shoes, and feeling sick. "Nice, Dean. Real nice."

"What happened from that scenario is a shame," Dean said. "A true and profound shame. But we were giving Mr. Rabold the opportunity to avoid jail. We believed it would have worked out better all the way around."

"Sometimes it doesn't," I said. "You should have checked with me first. I could have explained that to you."

"I'll keep that in mind," Dean said.

"What did he give you before he died?"

"Not nearly enough."

"Where does Ed Gradduk fit? That's all I care about, Dean."

"Listen," he said, "we're not here to answer your questions. It's not advantageous to us, and, frankly, we don't have any desire for you to get more involved than you already are. You're not law enforcement anymore. You don't even have a client. You are nothing more than a concerned friend in this case, Mr. Perry, albeit a concerned friend with some unusual abilities. But while our sympathies may lie deep for concerned friends, our loyalties do not."

"Rabold was in the car when they hit him," I said. "He had to know what happened. What did he tell you?"

"Did you miss everything I just said?" Dean asked.

Everyone was quiet for a minute. The waitress came back to refill the coffees and saw that we all had full cups. She frowned and disappeared again. Across the room, a kid was working with a mop. Closing time.

"It's personal to you," Dean said. "We understand that. But when you let personal problems carry you into the middle of something you don't understand, Mr. Perry, you're inviting disaster."

I didn't say anything. Dean's eyes were hard on mine, his jaw set. The comic partner of the duo was now making Mason look cheerful.

"The last time Larry Rabold made contact with us was the morning before he was killed," Dean said. "At that time, it seemed some people viewed you as a problem. Perhaps one that needed to be dealt with. It is my assumption that nothing about your activities in the past few days diminished that perspective."

"So Padgett's on his way, then? Cancerno's problem-solver out to clean up another mess like he did with Ed?"

"Cancerno's got more problem-solvers than Padgett." Dean had a leather-bound folder with him, and he reached inside it, withdrew a photograph, and slid it across the table to me. It was a color headshot of a mean-looking Hispanic guy wearing an orange jumpsuit. A prison photo.

"Recognize him?"

"His first name's Ramone," I said. "He works for Cancerno's construction crew."

Dean took the photograph back and smiled at me. "He's no master carpenter, Mr. Perry. Most of Cancerno's people are not."

"All of them?" I said, thinking of Jeff Franklin, the good vibe I'd had from him.

"He has to have some people who are legitimate on that end," Dean said. "He handles enough work that having a few good people would be a requirement. But many people on Cancerno's payroll, be they construction workers or pawnshop cashiers or warehouse laborers, are earning their keep in other ways. The gentleman in that picture is Ramone Tavarez. He's served time for assault on two occasions, but he's managed to rotate back to the free world pretty quickly each time, somehow. He's an enforcer. Violent son of a bitch. He also contacted Jack Padgett about you the day Larry Rabold was murdered. Seemed concerned, Larry thought. As did Padgett."

"Interesting that I'm the only person bothering these guys. Too bad they aren't distracted by dealing with, say, police or the FBI."

"It would be best," Dean said, "if they were left to dealing with the police and the FBI. Understand me when I say this, Mr. Perry—Cancerno is evil. People who piss him off? Bad things happen. Businesses burn down. Cars blow up. Arms are broken. Some people turn up dead."

"You know he kills people, why don't you arrest him?"

Dean smiled. "Right. Good thinking. Why *don't* we arrest him. I like that plan."

I waited.

"I think you're going to help," he said.

I raised my eyebrows. "By?"

"What do you think of the word 'bait,' Mr. Perry?"

"I've never been a big fan of the concept that it's associated with."

"Too bad," Dean said. "But while you might not be a

fan of that concept, you're putting it in motion for us right now, whether you realize it or not. And while we may be able to capitalize from the result, I'm afraid it won't work out nearly so well for you."

PART THREE UNDER THE BRIDGE

CHAPTER 22

They drove me back to my truck, past an inordinate number of patrol cars still cruising the streets of the neighborhood. If there'd been more fires, we didn't see any sign of them. None of us spoke much on the ride, although I had to give directions to my truck. When they pulled in behind it, Mason gave me my gun back, which he'd apparently claimed after they'd found me on the pavement. I climbed out of the car, and Dean put down his window.

"Cell number's written on the back," he said, offering a card. "You get into trouble, give me a call. But I'm hoping that isn't going to happen. I'm hoping you believed enough of what I said back there to just go home and sit the rest of this one out."

I took his card and put it in my pocket. "If I thought you guys honestly gave a damn about clearing Ed Gradduk, maybe I would, Dean."

I walked away from them, unlocked my truck, and climbed inside. I was suddenly so exhausted that I wanted to just lean the seat back and go to sleep, not even make the drive home. I'd left my cell phone in the truck, and when I picked it up, I saw I had more than a dozen missed calls. Joe, Amy, Joe, Amy, Joe, Amy, Amy, Joe. I stopped scrolling through them when the phone vibrated in my hand, another call coming in. Amy. I answered it as I put the key in the ignition and brought the engine to life.

"Where in the hell have you been?" she said, the words drawn out and spoken between clenched teeth.

"Detained."

"I was going to send the cops after you, but Joe told me to wait. He said to give you another hour."

"I knew he had confidence in me."

"Actually, he suggested you were probably already in custody. Was he right?"

"No. But pretty close, I suppose. I'm going home now."

"We'll both meet you there," she said, and hung up.

E asy, Ace." I gritted my teeth as Amy pressed a sponge soaked in ice water against my head. The water leaked through my hair and trickled down the side of my face.

"Sorry. I'm trying to be gentle, but that's not easy with the lump you've got up here, Lincoln. It's about the size and texture of a Twinkie."

That description didn't make me feel any better. I was back in my apartment, on the couch, with Joe sitting across from me, and Amy insisting on tending to my battered skull. The dull ache that had been there all through my talk with Dean and Mason had become an incessant throbbing. I'd taken a handful of ibuprofen, but I had a feeling it wasn't going to do the job.

Amy took the sponge away, grimaced, then held it out for me to see. There was a coppery smear across its surface. I'd already washed off the long cuts and abrasions on my arms and hands, but I couldn't see the head injury well enough to deal with it.

"A cut?" I asked.

"Looks like it's just scraped up. Nothing too deep."

"Great."

She set the sponge aside and then handed me a plastic bag filled with ice, guided my hand to the lump at the crown of my skull. Her fingers were cold from the sponge.

"So tell me again," Joe said, "who hit you in the head?"

"A building."

He smiled. "You really ran . . ."

"Right into it," I said. "Yes. Headfirst."

His smile widened. Joe is not a strong one for sympathy. At least not for people who run headfirst into buildings.

I took them both through my experience in the house and my talk with Dean and Mason, doing most of the talking with my eyes squeezed shut. The light seemed to exacerbate the headache.

"So you honestly have no idea who pulled you out of that fire?" Joe said.

"The same person who started the fire. So when I do figure out this guy's identity, I'll be torn between wanting to thank him and wanting to shoot him."

"No guesses?" Amy said.

I opened my eyes again. I'd thought about it some on the drive home, but I hadn't come up with anything substantial. Just possibilities that could be far, far from the truth.

"Mitch Corbett?" I said. "The guy's missing, and he's tied to Sentalar and these houses. But then there's Padgett, conveniently turning up at the scene of one of the fires, just like Larry Rabold did seventeen years ago. Only problem is, I have trouble imagining either pausing to help me out."

"Right." She was sitting close to me, and although I'd closed my eyes again, I was very aware of her, distracted by the faint smell of perfume. I haven't had much luck sustaining relationships with women, and a long time ago I'd decided that to preserve my friendship with Amy, I needed to keep it a friendship. I assumed that she felt the same way, because, while there was an abnormal amount of flirting in our relationship, she'd never instigated anything beyond that. At times the arrangement seems less than ideal to me, though, and for some reason this had become one of them. The good news was that if such thoughts were passing through my mind at all right now, the burns and the knock on the head hadn't damaged anything too critical.

We kept talking for a while, but Amy asked most of the questions. Joe was quiet, and I knew why. He was worried about what Mason and Dean had told me, about their suggestion that Cancerno's network of corruption went deep and was going to be worth protecting to those involved. In Larry Rabold's basement, Joe and I had likely seen an example of that protection, and I had a feeling he was thinking about that a lot. If I hadn't been so damn exhausted, maybe I would have had the energy to be worried, too.

Eventually, I threw them out. I needed sleep in a way I hadn't needed sleep often before. When they were gone, I stripped off my clothes and lay down on the bed, lights off. Tired as I was, the stench of smoke that was still attached to me, trapped in my hair and soaked into my skin, was too distracting. I got up and went into the bathroom, turned the water up as hot as I could stand it, and stepped inside.

There are plenty of problems with my building, the type of problems that are common in any structure that's stood for nearly six decades, but poor water pressure isn't one of them. The water hammered at me, and the power of it felt good, even against my burns and the swollen tissue on my head. I closed my eyes and tried to let the water pound away the mental grime, too. I didn't want to think anymore. Not tonight. I didn't want to see visions of Ed Gradduk's body, or Larry Rabold's, or burning houses. I didn't want to think about what it all meant, how it all fit. I didn't want to think about a son of a bitch named Mitch Corbett who could probably make sense of a lot of it for me if I could just find him.

It was then, in this moment of attempting to think not at all, that I began to understand something. I stood there under the water and tried to tell myself that I was wrong, that the idea was the product of fatigue and one hell of a crack on the head. I couldn't do it, though. It made too much sense.

I stood there until the water heater kicked into higher gear and what had been a tolerable temperature became closer to scalding. Then I shut the water off, wrapped a towel around me, and walked back to the bedroom to get dressed again. Sleep would wait. I needed a computer.

The avenue was quiet as I walked down to the office, the wind gentle and warm. My hair was still wet from the shower, and I spent most of the walk telling myself that I really needed to invest in a home computer.

I went upstairs, unlocked the office, and turned on my computer. I left the lights off and stood at the window while the computer booted up, watching the cars pass. The building felt lonely at this hour. Hell, the city did. Most people were home in bed with their families, or they were working night shifts surrounded by coworkers. One of these days I was going to have to get a normal life.

To cut the silence, I turned on the little television on the filing cabinet. It was tuned to one of the local news stations, and they were rerunning the news from eleven, which had focused on the outbreak of fires. A young male reporter was standing outside the burned house on Erin Avenue. Little was left but wreckage. A total loss, he told us. Fortunately, it had been vacant, as had all the other houses burned in a "wildfire of arson." I didn't think the term "wildfire" really applied to arson, but then I'm not a professional journalist.

The computer was finally ready to go. While the reporter told us that there had been no arrests made in the case and the police had yet to announce whether there were any suspects, I logged on to the Internet. I went to the Cuyahoga County Web site and searched it until I found what I wanted—a biography page on Mike Gajovich. It told me Gajovich had begun his career as a deputy prosecutor, then been promoted to chief assistant prosecutor, and gave the dates of service in those positions. He'd been chief assistant prosecutor seventeen years earlier. That settled, I left his bio page and found the bio for the current chief assistant prosecutor. Beneath the bio was a description of duties. Three sentences into it, I found what I wanted: *Among other responsibilities, the chief assistant prosecutor reviews all Cleveland Police Department internal affairs matters, including possible criminal conduct and the use of deadly force.*

Joe answered on the third ring, but his voice was gruff, choked with sleep.

"It's me," I said, and then got into it without wasting time on any apologies for the late call. "Dean told me there's someone big involved with the police. Most of the guys they've tied to it are bottom-feeders, street cops and patrol officers. But he said every indication is that it goes higher than that."

"I've got a bad feeling you have an idea," Joe said after a pause.

"Mike Gajovich."

This time the pause was even longer.

"Gajovich isn't a cop, LP. You said Dean indicated it was someone higher up within the department."

"You telling me Gajovich doesn't have any sway within

the department? Come on, Joe. You know better. The guy's one of the top law enforcement presences in this city, and he's popular with everybody at the department after that stink he raised last year when the mayor cut staff."

"And you think he's a player in this because he sent your friend home? Because he came at you a little cold when we talked to him?"

"Gajovich has been with the prosecutor's office for a long time, Joe. He started with them as a deputy prosecutor, worked his way up the ladder. Seventeen years ago, when my father made the complaint about Padgett, Gajovich was chief assistant prosecutor. According to the county's Web site, the chief assistant prosecutor reviews all internal affairs matters, criminal conduct, and use of deadly force. Remember how Amos explained that the complaint was serious enough that they bumped it right to the lawyers? I think this is what he meant."

I heard a grunt and a rustling, probably as he sat up in bed.

"So you think Gajovich went to talk to Alberta Grad-duk, and then, what, discouraged her from making a complaint?" he said.

"Could be. All I know right now is it looks like he went to see Alberta, the complaint never developed into a case, and Gajovich is sweating Ed's death and all the circumstances around it years later."

He sighed. "We've got to confirm it first, LP."

"Yeah. That's what the morning will be for. We'll go see Alberta first thing."

"Would look pretty bad for a mayoral candidate," Joe said, "if a harassment cover-up was exposed."

"Be the type of thing that would keep you awake nights," I agreed.

"Gajovich's brother has been with the department for years."

"I know."

"Do you know what he does, though?"

"Administrative, right?"

"He's a commander."

"Okay."

"He's the commander of District Two."

District Two. Clark-Fulton.

There was a period of silence. The lights were still off, but the computer monitor filled the office with a soft blue glow. Outside, a car blew its horn at the intersection, maybe at some drunk running the red light, or somebody so tired they'd sat through the change to green.

"If either Gajovich really is tied to Cancerno . . ." Joe let the sentence die.

"Yeah," I said, and it was enough. We both understood the rest. It wasn't the type of thing you wanted to put into words at this hour of the night, anyhow. Not if you had any hope of finding sleep.

CHAPTER 23

There was no car in Alberta Gradduk's driveway, but there hadn't been on any of our previous visits, either. Whatever Ed drove had been impounded by the police, and maybe Alberta didn't have a car. I wondered if she even had a driver's license, or if some medical issue prevented her from being on the road. After seeing her with her bourbon earlier in the week, that was more of a hope than a passing thought.

She was home, as I'd assumed she would be this early in the morning, and her face had an ugly expression as she pushed the blinds aside and peered through the window after Joe knocked on the front door.

"You've been told twice," she said. "Go away. Please, just go away."

"Mrs. Gradduk," I said, "you've got to understand that I am trying to help."

"Go away," she repeated, then let the blinds swing back in place and stepped away from the window.

I raised my voice. "I know about the cop that came to arrest Ed, Mrs. Gradduk. I know that my father made a complaint to the police about him years ago."

She came back to the door, opened it, and stood before me with naked hatred in her eyes.

"You don't know anything. Not a thing." Her eyes were still sunken and her skin was still tinged gray, but she'd changed clothes, at least.

"We know you had some problems with Sergeant Padgett," Joe said. "And we need you to talk about that. We think it's important."

"You know I had *problems* with him?" she said, spitting the word back at him. "That's what you've been told?"

"Am I wrong?"

She was holding on to the doorknob as if she needed the support to remain on her feet. "Problems with him," she repeated. "Yes. Yes, I had *problems* with him, if that's the word you want to use."

"Explain it to us, Mrs. Gradduk," I said, taking a step toward the door. "We didn't come here to upset you. We just want to understand."

"No, you don't."

"Can we come inside?"

"You don't want to understand," she said, but she moved aside and let us in. We went back into the living room, and I saw a cluster of fresh glasses on the coffee table, all of them empty, a half-full bottle of bourbon on the floor beside the couch.

She sat down on the couch and shoved the bottle to the side. I took a chair across from her and leaned forward, my elbows braced against my knees. Joe sat beside me.

"Please tell us about Padgett," I said. "What happened with him?"

The ceiling fan turned overhead, the blades shedding dust. I waited for her.

"I was the one who suffered," she said. "I was the *victim.*"

"I know," I said.

"Norm just felt sorry for himself."

"What do you mean?" Joe said.

"I don't want to talk about it."

"Mrs. Gradduk . . ." I tried to make my voice as soothing and sympathetic as I could without sacrificing a tone of command, the voice I'd used as a cop dealing with hysterical accident victims or witnesses to brutal violence.

She looked back at the empty glasses. "I won't talk about it. Not again."

"It's important, Mrs. Gradduk. I think it is very important."

She lifted her hands to her hair, tugged on the ragged gray ends, pulled until the skin lifted around her skull. She made a low hissing sound as she did it.

"You can tell us," I said. "It's just the three of us in this room, Mrs. Gradduk. You don't need to be scared."

"That's what the lawyer said," she told me, releasing her hair. "And he was lying, too."

I nodded. "Yes, let's talk about the lawyer. We know about him." I reached in my pocket and pulled out a folded piece of paper with Gajovich's picture printed on it. I'd made a copy before I'd left the office not too many hours earlier. "Was this the lawyer that came to see you?"

She looked at the picture with wary distaste, as if she wanted to spit at it but was afraid Gajovich might spring to life if she did.

"Was this the lawyer?" I asked again.

She laughed, a fast, breathless series of rasping chuckles that made the skin at the back of my neck prickle. It was the kind of laugh you might hear in the corridors of an asylum late at night.

"Oh, you know he's the one. Your father sent him. Don't pretend he didn't. They were the ones to blame, you know. Norm and your father, the both of them. Norm started it, and then, your father, he tried to make it worse. But I wouldn't let that happen. I wouldn't let that happen to us."

"So my father sent this man to talk to you," I said, pointing at Gajovich's picture. "But how did that make it worse?"

"I protected us," she said. "The lawyer wanted to make . . . wanted to make a *spectacle* out of us. He came here and told me to talk to him, just like you are. And I talked, and talked, and talked. And then when I was done, he told me what it would be like. I asked if it couldn't be handled quietly, and he laughed at me. Told me it was going to be a big story. Told me I'd have to be on TV and in the papers, in courtrooms and on the radio. Me and my son. As if we hadn't been through enough. As if *I* hadn't been through enough. That's what your father did for me." She smiled too wide, mouth open, blackened cavities visible along her molars. "But I didn't let it happen. I protected us. Norm couldn't do it, but I did it. I did it for my son."

Joe was leaning forward now, and I found myself doing the same, edging my chair closer to the coffee table.

"What happened with Padgett, Mrs. Gradduk? You've got to explain what you're talking about."

She shook her head and pushed back into the couch.

"Tell me."

"It's all so long ago."

"But it still matters," I said. "More than you can imagine, it matters."

"No."

"Explain it to me."

"I'm not doing this!" she shrieked, her hands back in her wild gray hair again, clawlike fingers locking on the strands. "I'm not!"

"Just tell me what happened," I said. "Tell me so I can know how to help."

"No!"

"Yes!" I shouted back, rising out of my chair. "Damn it, you are going to tell me, because your son is dead and I need to know why!"

She looked up at me and cowered against the couch,

then slumped and began to sob. She cried like a child, her
fingers tightening on her hair, her face shoved against the
couch cushion. Joe had reached up and put his hand on
my biceps, as if to restrain me, but Alberta Gradduk's reaction had frozen me more than any physical force could.
I looked at her and saw her the way she'd been once, a
beautiful young woman with a husband and a son and a
future, and I crossed to the couch and dropped to my
knees and put my arms around her. She resisted at first,
pushing at me, but then she gave up and pressed her face
into my chest and cried. I closed my eyes and felt her
dirty gray hair against my neck and jaw, and I knew that I
would not ask her again. I wanted to know, but I did not
want this woman to have to tell it to me.

The longer I listened to her cry, felt her skeletal body
heave beneath my arms, the more I began to wonder if I
even really wanted to know.

Back to the office, under a pewter sky that darkened
as I drove, heavy with the promise of rain. It was
hardly past eight, but the humidity was already
noticeable. The windows were down, and the air that
rushed in through them was thick, seeming to pass over
me like a soft fabric. At every stoplight sweat sprang from
my pores. The digital thermometer in the corner of my
rearview mirror gave the temperature at eighty degrees,
but the still, muggy quality made it seem hotter. This in
the early morning. I left the air-conditioning off, though,
preferring to feel the wind hard against my face, forcing
my eyes half-shut as I accelerated.

"You backed off pretty quickly," Joe said after we'd
been on the road for several minutes. "Quickly for you, at
least."

"She was my friend's mother, Joe," I said, and then regretted it. I'd just confirmed exactly what he was so wor-

ried about, telling him I'd changed my normal approach because of my personal connection to the case. He didn't say anything, though. Just drummed his fingers on the door panel and stared out the window.

"It was Gajovich," I said. "We got that much, and that matters. He went in there with his stories about television interviews and courtroom appearances and he scared her into silence. To protect Jack Padgett. And his brother's running the show in that district."

"We need to talk to someone," Joe said. "This morning. Cal Richards, maybe."

"Or Dean and Mason. Neither of them gives a shit about Ed, but they're on the corruption task force. If one Gajovich is involved, let alone two, they need to know about it."

"I want to start with Richards," Joe said. "He's the only guy in the mix that I really trust."

"Call him, then." I wanted Richards involved, too. The names we were connecting to this went too high now. We stood on the edge of an investigation that was going to rock the city's law enforcement community and horrify the public. I didn't want any part of it. All I wanted to do was pull Ed Gradduk's legacy away from the fallout zone.

We were on the interstate now, doing seventy-five, and the wind was too loud for conversation. Joe rolled up his window, and I followed suit, then turned the air-conditioning on. Once the cab was quiet, Joe took out his cell phone and made the call into police dispatch. He was told Richards wasn't available, so he asked the dispatcher to get Cal a message as soon as possible. It was urgent, Joe said.

The sky was still darkening—pale clouds skimming quickly across the horizon, heavier, purplish clouds trudging somberly behind. I'd had all of four hours of sleep—after surviving a fire and nearly splitting my skull open on a brick wall—and the fatigue hung heavy with me, tightening the big muscles in my back and shoulders and creeping into the small muscles with little bursts of pain. I rolled my neck and winced.

The thermometer in the mirror said eighty-two. Climbing. We didn't talk much until I was back off the interstate, on Lorain. Traffic was thin, and I caught green lights heading back to the office. As I drove, a few fat drops of rain broke free from the clouds and splattered the windshield. There was thunder, but it was faint, the heart of the storm still miles away.

I turned onto Rocky River, then made another immediate turn into the narrow parking lot behind our building. A few more unusually heavy raindrops fell, plunking off the hood of my truck like golf balls as I pulled into a parking space beside a green van. I shut the engine off, and the van's side door slid open. A short, muscular Hispanic man stepped out, holding a handgun down against his thigh. Ramone, the guy from Jimmy Cancerno's construction crew. He didn't look any friendlier today than he had in the picture Dean and Mason had shown me the night before. He tapped on my window with the gun, then nodded his head at the backseat of the van. Whoever was driving it started the motor.

"Richards may have to wait," I said to Joe. "I think we're on our way to see Jimmy Cancerno."

CHAPTER 24

Ramone didn't turn out to be the talkative sort. I was wearing a gun, and he took that, then waved me into the van without a word while he checked Joe for a weapon. He moved smoothly and professionally, not like a construction worker who had no experience at this sort of thing. That wasn't exactly comforting.

"You taking us to see somebody, or to kill us?" Joe asked while Ramone ran a hand over Joe's ankles, making sure there wasn't a gun holstered down there. It seemed like a fair enough question, and I was hoping for an answer myself.

"Get in," was all Ramone said.

I was already in the van, and Ramone had his back to me. It would have been the perfect opportunity to jump him, had there not been another guy in the passenger seat, pointing a SIG-Sauer automatic at my chest. This guy looked like he went about 250 pounds. Just in the shoulders.

Joe got into the van, and I slid down the seat to make room for him. Ramone climbed in behind him, then slammed the door shut and sat on the floor with his back against the door, the gun trained on Joe.

"Classy van," Joe said, gazing around with all the trepidation of a man settling onto a familiar barstool and scanning the room for friends. "Is this the one with stow-'n'-go seating? That always sounded like a hell of a feature. Don't know exactly what it means, but it sounds good."

"Shut up," Ramone said.

Joe frowned at him, then gave me a sidelong glance. "Not real friendly," he said.

"No."

I didn't recognize the lumberjack in the passenger seat, who had turned around once Ramone was inside, or the driver. I could see him only through the mirror, but that was enough to show that he was older, with gray hair and wrinkles across his forehead. He took us out of the parking lot and back onto Rocky River. From there we pulled onto I-90 and headed east. The van rode smooth. So smooth that Ramone's gun never wavered.

We were on the highway for a while before the driver slowed and pulled into the exit lane. We got off on West Forty-fourth, then turned onto Train Avenue, back in my old neighborhood—Jimmy Cancerno's empire.

The van driver pulled off the street at a place called Pinnacle Pawn Plus. Judging from the sign in the window, the "plus" referred to cash loans, tobacco products, and lottery tickets. Something for everyone.

Behind the store was an old warehouse. A pickup truck and a green Mercedes sedan were parked in front of it. When the van came to a stop, Ramone rose to a crouch and slid the door open. Then he waved at us with the gun.

"Out."

We climbed out and stood in front of the warehouse while the three of them gathered around us. Thunder rumbled overhead, closer now than before. A fat raindrop hit the back of my neck, slid down my spine with a chill that continued even after the water was gone.

"Inside," Ramone said.

I went first, opening the door and stepping into a small office, the main room of the warehouse empty and dark behind it. Jimmy Cancerno sat in the office, his feet propped up on a steel desk, watching a flat-screen television that hung on the wall. He turned as we entered, then scowled when he saw the gun in Ramone's hand.

"What the hell are you doing?" he said.

"You said make sure they come," Ramone replied. "You said don't give them an option about it."

"That doesn't mean you need to act like a damn fool," Cancerno snapped. He was wearing glasses today, and his gray hair was slightly tousled, not the perfect comb off the forehead I'd seen before.

Ramone just shrugged, not looking particularly chagrined, then led the other two past us and into the warehouse. Cancerno let them go without a word. He motioned at a set of chairs in front of his desk.

"Sit down."

We sat. He took his feet off the desk, turned off the television, and swung around to face us.

"Look, I didn't tell that idiot to bring you in here at gunpoint. I just told him to make sure he got you here."

"Well, he got us here," Joe said. "Efficient, if nothing else."

Cancerno took his glasses off, folded them, and set them on the desk. There was none of the irritable quality to him today, just calm and control.

"There are different sorts of problems," he said. "You got minor nuisances—a flat tire, leak in the roof, maybe a splinter in your ass. They're frustrating, you know? Annoying. But they aren't big deals, either. None of them is a crisis. Demands some attention, sure, but nothing serious. You address the issue, you move on. You forget about it."

Neither one of us responded.

"So you got your minor nuisances," Cancerno said. "And then you got your crisis. The flat tire blows out, rolls the car over. The leak in the roof spreads, rots out the wood, the whole damn thing caves in on you. The splinter in your ass gets infected, you can't even sit down, end up in the hospital."

Cancerno spread his hands. "You're wondering," he said, "which one you are. Right? You're thinking—*just how much of a problem have I become? Am I the splinter in the ass, or am I the infection?*"

Silence filled the room for a minute. Joe and I didn't look at each other, just held Cancerno's gaze, which alternated between us. His calm hadn't been disrupted, but that didn't make me feel any more comfortable. He was a man who liked his temper. Liked knowing just how much damage would occur when it was tripped. Right now he was toying with the trigger like a man enjoying the feel of a big gun in his hand, savoring the moment before the shooting began. I didn't enjoy feeling like the target at the other end of the range.

"You want us to guess?" I said. "And there's not a C, none-of-the-above, category?"

Cancerno smiled. "Nah, you don't need to guess. I'll go ahead and tell you." There was another pause before he said, "You're the splinter. The flat tire, the leak. For now."

He studied me. "You come off like a good guy. Working your ass off to help a dead guy out, I mean, shit, what better kind of friend is there than the one who looks after you when you're dead? Don't know that I got any of those kind, myself."

He leaned forward in his chair. "You got somebody to look after you when you're dead?"

I didn't say anything. Beside me Joe was completely still. Out in the warehouse everything was quiet, but I knew there were men out there, and that they all had guns. My gun, too.

"I understand," Cancerno said, "that you're just doing what you do. You're looking for answers. That's fine. I'd prefer to stay the hell out of it, but I can't anymore. Because the places you're looking for answers are, well, a little sensitive to me."

"We still need to go through them," I said. "Sensitive or not."

His eyes flashed at that, a brief, cold glimmer, but he nodded.

"Sure. That's what I like about you. No back-down quality in you, right? None. Aren't a lot of guys that I'll say that about. I respect that. And that's why I had my guys bring you down here. I'm going to give you all the answers you need. And they're the ones you want, too."

"Yeah?"

"Yeah. I'll give you your answers, and then you get the hell out of here, stay gone. Because I simply cannot have you doing this anymore. Those fires, they don't matter anymore. Terry Solich told you that, himself. No need to involve police or anybody else at this point."

So Solich had made the call. It didn't surprise me. By the time we'd left his house, I'd had the feeling he was worried, and pondering some damage control. Apparently, he'd decided reporting to Cancerno was the best option. Knowing Solich had made the call was good, though. It told me Cancerno was probably oblivious to my dialogue with Dean and Mason. The less he believed me to know, the better.

"You tell everyone all you're interested in is Gradduk," Cancerno said. "That's good. That's all you need to be interested in. You get too interested in me, it won't be any good at all. And at the end of the day, it's not about me."

"Who's it about?" Joe said.

"Mitch Corbett."

"Explain."

Cancerno braced his arms on the desk. "You said you want to know how it went down with Gradduk. I'm telling you it's all about Corbett. Son of a bitch dragged me into it, but it's not about me."

"Corbett killed Sentalar?"

Cancerno nodded. "Would be my guess."

"Why?"

"Because Gradduk was talking to her. Gradduk was trying to take Corbett apart."

"How do you know?"

"Because he told me that. The night before he died."

"I'd heard Ed and Corbett were friends," I said.

"They were."

"So what happened?"

Cancerno looked at the little window in the door, which was now covered with raindrops. "I told Gradduk about something that happened a long time ago. I don't know why. I shouldn't have told him, maybe."

A man told me a story. What story? The one he didn't want to tell.

"What did you tell him?" I asked.

"I didn't know Gradduk well, but I knew Scott Draper," Cancerno said. "Draper recommended Gradduk to me, said he needed work. I gave him work. This isn't unusual for me. Guys come to me needing a favor, I help them if I can."

"Friend of the people," I said.

Cancerno's face went ugly, and any sense of ease that had seeped into my body as he'd begun to explain things to us leaked right back out.

"You don't mock me, prick," he said. "You don't say a word. Not if you want to walk back out the door. That van outside doesn't have to take you home."

For a moment there was nothing but an electric silence. Then Joe broke it.

"I'm sure he's sorry. Didn't mean anything by it, did you, Lincoln?"

I shook my head slowly. "Didn't mean anything by it."

Cancerno's glare didn't lessen, but after a moment he began to talk again.

"I hired Gradduk. A few weeks passed, and I ran into him down at the Hideaway. We all drank together, shot the shit. I liked the kid. Later on I found out he was hanging around with Corbett. That bothered me. It wasn't right, not with Corbett's history. The next time I drank with Gradduk . . ." Cancerno shrugged. "I told him some things he probably shouldn't have ever heard."

"What things?" I was leaning forward now, Cancerno's last outburst all but forgotten. This is what I'd wanted to know days ago, what Ed might have said if he hadn't been killed in the street before he'd had a chance to tell it to me.

"I knew a guy used to see Gradduk's mother. It went on for a while, while she was married. Then she tried to end it. This guy, he's not the most stable son of a bitch you ever saw. Violent. Mean-tempered. Holds a grudge. Anyhow, he promised the Gradduk woman he was going to take her life apart. She laughed at him, told him to get lost. But, this guy, he's not the type that makes empty threats. The man settles his scores."

"What's this have to do with Corbett?" Joe said.

"I was getting to that. This is where I come in. I had Corbett do some work for me. A few . . . projects that I needed handled."

"You hired him to burn Terry Solich out of business and out of the neighborhood," I said.

Cancerno looked at me with empty eyes. "Corbett took care of these projects for me, then set Gradduk's father up. This was at the request of the guy I was telling you about. It wasn't my idea."

Thunder rolled close to the building, making the door rattle against its frame. Out in the warehouse, men were laughing. The smell of cigarette smoke drifted into the office.

"It was Jack Padgett," I said. "The guy you're talking about. He could make the setup happen because he was a cop."

Cancerno didn't speak.

"I want you to confirm that," I said. "Otherwise we'll go out and do it ourselves. But you know it was him, and so do we."

"You don't tell me what to say," Cancerno snapped. "I'll tell you what I damn well want to tell you, kid. And you'll keep your mouth shut. You understand that I'm doing this as a favor to you? As a courtesy? Believe me, I got other ways to deal with you. Didn't need to have you brought in here for a talk."

I met his cold eyes. For a long time he just sat and stared at me. The laughter from the warehouse had stopped as soon as Cancerno had raised his voice again. I had the feeling his voice could make a lot of things stop.

"So Norm Gradduk committed suicide, and Padgett was still harassing Alberta," I said softly, still meeting his stare. "Ed found out about it, probably. Then my father did. He made a complaint, and people scrambled to cover up for Padgett. Mike Gajovich came down and convinced Alberta not to go public with the complaint."

Cancerno's eyes narrowed. "You're talking beyond me now. I don't know what the hell happened after Gradduk gassed himself in the garage."

"That's what happened," I said.

Another clap of thunder, this one louder than the last. A gust of wind followed it, howling around the old warehouse. Cancerno leaned back again, put his feet back up on the desk.

"That's what I told Gradduk," he said. "And I shouldn't

have told him. But I didn't like it, knowing that he was becoming buddies with Corbett. It didn't seem right."

"And a woman died for this?" Joe said. "I'm not seeing the connection."

Cancerno shrugged. "Not my job to help you see it. But I can tell you Gradduk had a serious hard-on for Corbett after I told him what I did. Then the woman went down, Gradduk went down, Corbett took off. Last night he sets my houses on fire. You see what I'm saying about this guy being the center of it?"

"Corbett burned the houses?" I said.

"You're damn right he did," Cancerno said. "No doubt in my mind. He had access to all of them, too. Would've been easy for him."

"Why do it?"

Cancerno smiled, and it was one of the least appealing expressions I'd ever seen. "No," he said, shaking his head. "No more answers. I gave you the ones you needed. The ones you don't need stay with me."

"The one I need the most, you haven't given me," I said. "Why was Anita Sentalar killed? You said Ed was trying to take Corbett apart, but not how. You say Corbett killed her, but don't say why. That's not enough. I need to prove it. Right now it's still on Ed, and I'm not letting it sit there. Someone else is going to answer for it. Ed deserves his justice, whether he's alive or dead."

Cancerno slid his feet back off the desk, stood up, and walked around to face us. He looked hard at my face.

"You want justice for your friend?"

"That's right."

"You going to find Corbett?"

"Yes."

He kept staring at me, then nodded. "You find Corbett, and I'll see that your friend gets his justice. And when that's done, you can work out whatever story you want to give the cops and the reporters. I'll deal with it." His dark eyes were filled with fury. "But first you find him. You call me. Tell me where he is. And then I'll see that your friend gets his justice."

CHAPTER 25

He left us in the office while he stepped out into the dark warehouse. Joe and I didn't say much while he was gone. It wasn't an environment that encouraged conversation. Cancerno was gone maybe five minutes before he returned, trailed by Ramone and the mountain man. The old guy who'd driven the van wasn't with them, but I heard an engine start up outside.

"They'll take you back now," Cancerno said. "I hope this visit straightened some things out for you. Hope it made some things clear."

We got to our feet, and Cancerno pulled the door open and held it. Outside the sky was still dark, but the rain had held off. Warm air whipped around the parking lot, blowing dust and bits of fine gravel in our eyes. I squinted as I stepped through the door. Joe came out behind me, Ramone and the huge guy on his heels. The green van was running already.

When we were outside, Joe turned to Cancerno. "Tell you what, we're going to pass on the ride this time. Thanks, though."

"What?" Cancerno said.

"We'll take care of ourselves," Joe said. "Got a few stops to make around the neighborhood, anyhow. Then we'll catch a ride back. Don't need to trouble your employees here with the task."

Ramone, standing close to Joe, turned and looked to

Cancerno for instruction. Cancerno leaned against the doorframe and tilted his head, studying Joe.

"You don't trust me? I bring you down here, tell you things you want to know, and you don't trust me?"

Joe shook his head. "That's not the issue. But seeing as you're such a trustworthy guy, I expect you've got no problem letting us go on our way here. Don't take it as disrespect."

Cancerno considered it for a moment, then shrugged and stepped back into the office. "You got it. Go on and walk home in the rain, if that's what suits you."

The door closed behind him. Ramone gave us one last long stare, then turned and reached for the doorknob to follow Cancerno.

"Give me back my gun, Ramone," I said.

He didn't say anything, but walked back out to the van, leaned in the open window, and said something to the guy behind the wheel. Then he stepped back with my Glock in his hand. I walked toward him, hand outstretched. When I was almost to him, he gave the gun a toss. It sailed over my shoulder and clattered on the pavement.

"Thanks, asshole," I said. He smirked, walked into the warehouse, and slammed the door shut.

I picked my gun up, dusted it off on my pants, and placed it back in its holster. Joe was standing beside me, shoulders hunched against the wind, eyeing the sky.

He began to walk toward the street. "Interesting conversation, huh?"

"Damn interesting," I said.

"You buying it?"

"What he said about being the one who told the old story to Ed, maybe. It's the trigger that got all of this rolling. When Ed started to explain it to me, he said a man told him a story. I asked him what story, and he said, the one he didn't want to tell. Cancerno was regretting it today. Admitted he'd hesitated to tell Ed about it in the first place."

Joe nodded, walking fast as we rounded the corner of the building and came out on the sidewalk.

"Some bad blood between Cancerno and Corbett, that's for sure," he said. "And until this morning we didn't have a logical motive for last night's fires. But understanding there's conflict between Cancerno and Corbett, it might fit. Why's Corbett care if half the police department rolls out to look at those fires? They're just going to focus on Cancerno. Be a hard sell for someone like Cancerno to convince investigators he had nothing to do with it, you know? A guy like that is an ideal smoke screen for Corbett."

"And what does it gain for Corbett?" I said.

"Gives him a way to come at Cancerno. Because it seems the man is awfully scared of Cancerno. He's hiding, afraid to use his credit cards, afraid to go home. Cancerno didn't hide how bad he wants to find the guy—basically offered to kill him if you do the finding. So maybe Corbett's returning fire. Making a preemptive strike, rather."

We were walking east down the sidewalk, Joe moving fast and purposefully. I realized I had no idea where he was going. It certainly wasn't in the direction of the office.

"You weren't so sure the van's intended stop was the same as ours?" I said.

"Don't like being a passenger. Besides, we got places to go."

"Yeah?"

"You catch what Cancerno said when he got to explaining why he's so sure Corbett burned those houses?"

"That he had access to all of them."

"Uh-huh."

We reached an intersection but caught the light right, walked across the street without a pause.

"Well," Joe said, "suppose you were hiding from some people. Suppose you were so scared you wouldn't use your credit cards or bank accounts or seek help from friends. Where would you go?"

I turned to face him, slowed my pace. "You're thinking the houses?"

He shook his head. "No. There's work being done on them, people from Cancerno's crew going in and out, neighbors watching. And, hell, most of them burned down last night, probably at Corbett's hand. Think beyond that."

"The school."

He nodded. "Huge old building, sitting empty. Locked up, but Corbett's got the keys. No work scheduled to begin on it for months yet."

"That's where we're going?"

He shook his head. "No. First we're going to find a convenience store. I think we'll need a flashlight."

The ground-floor windows were securely boarded up, the doors fastened with heavy steel chains and new padlocks. Entry into the building wasn't going to be easy for someone without a key. And while Corbett might have had one, we did not.

Joseph A. Marsh Junior High had once been a gorgeous building—three floors of brick walls with limestone inlay around the doors and windows on the outside; on the inside, oak woodwork and tile floors built with a skilled craftsman's greatest care. Everything in the blocks around the building had been knocked down and rebuilt at least twice in the lifetime of the school, and I figured that would be true for several more cycles. As we circled the building, looking for a point of entry, I remembered trudging through the grounds in sun, snow, and rain, Ed and Draper generally beside me. We'd been part of the last classes at both Joseph A. Marsh and West Tech, and looking back on it, there seemed to be something damned appropriate about that—Ed and Draper and I were the last vestiges of the old neighborhood, in a lot of ways.

"Basement window," Joe said, coming to a stop and pointing. There was a narrow window just above the foundation, and while there was a piece of plywood over it, the corner was raised, showing that someone had pried it away.

I knelt beside it and hooked my fingers under the edge, gave it an experimental tug. The board rose easily, with a harsh scraping noise. I put both hands under it and yanked harder, and this time it came free.

"You know what's down there?" Joe said.

"The metal shop."

"Metal shop in a junior high?"

"This school fed into West Tech, so they had more trade offerings. Hell, Tech even had a foundry. There was a time when classes like that got some kids jobs when they came out of school."

"That time was a few decades ago, LP."

"You think it's an accident that the school closed?"

He passed me the flashlight. I stretched out on my stomach and extended my hand, shining the light into the dark room. A musty smell rose at me, but there was more to it than that—the scent of metal and stone and, somehow, of heat, even though it had been years since any activity had taken place here. I passed the beam of the flashlight around the room, saw nothing other than old boxes and bare walls.

"We're good," I said. "Little bit of a drop to the floor, but not bad. Six feet from the window, maybe. Think you can make it?"

"I can make it."

"All right." I went first, sliding my feet through the window, then shoving my upper body in and dropping. The floor came up faster than I expected, giving me a jarring landing. I turned the flashlight back on and showed the floor to Joe, who was leaning down, eyeballing his entrance. He slipped through the window and dropped down smoother than I had. Thirty years my senior and still he moved with an athlete's grace.

"You remember your way around here?" he said.

I nodded while I passed him the flashlight and freed my gun from its holster. "Well enough, at least."

"Lead the way, then."

It took us an hour to clear the building. We moved in silence through dark, musty corridors that I'd once walked through daily, past the classrooms where I'd devoted more time to studying girls than books and a principal's office that Ed and I had known better than our homerooms. We'd had fun, though, and at the end of the day I don't think we were the type of students that drove teachers to drink. Drove them to a bottle of Tylenol, maybe, but nothing stronger.

Even knowing that the building had been closed for years, the sight of the disrepair stunned me. Debris littered the halls, mice scattered at the sound of our footsteps, and dank puddles from countless leaks spotted the empty rooms. Looters had moved in once the building had been closed, tearing free everything of value. Most of the light fixtures were gone, faucets torn from the sinks, ceiling panels removed so people could get at the copper wiring.

In a room on the second floor, in what had once been the English department, we found the remains of several candles beside a filthy blanket, a broken bottle of Southern Comfort, and a few empty Campbell's soup cans not far away. A dented metal wastebasket had been pulled up close by, and old ashes were inside. Joe ran the light around it and shook his head.

"Very old," he said. "Some homeless guy sneaking in to get out of the snow, I bet."

That was the closest we came, though. We didn't speak at all on the third floor, just moved through the rooms in total silence, Joe scanning the floors with his flashlight, me standing behind him with my gun out.

Neither one of us felt much like attempting to climb back out of the basement window we'd used to enter. It was too narrow and too high. All of the double doors had been fastened from the outside with chains and padlocks, but the single doors had been locked only from the inside. We found one leading out of the back of the auditorium, unlocked it, and stepped back outside into the overcast day.

"Damn," Joe said as I locked the door behind me and let it swing closed again. "I thought we might have some luck with that."

"It was a good idea," I said. "As good as any other we've had with this guy, at least."

We walked out of the schoolyard and back to the street. Overhead, the clouds were roiling. Looking up at them was like looking down on an angry sea. The rain was light, though. Cold, teasing drops. Thunderclaps that were louder and closer.

"Been holding off all day," I said, looking at the sky.

"Humidity building, though. Bound to cut loose soon."

"We need to get a cab."

"What, you're not up for the walk? Can't be more than a hundred and thirty blocks."

"The rain's coming," I said. "Otherwise, I'd be right there with you. Good exercise."

"We'll take the rapid."

There was a Rapid Transit station maybe fifteen blocks away. We walked west down Storer Avenue, then south to the station, took the blue-line train back down Lorain. There was another station at Fairview Hospital, just down the street from the office.

We were upstairs and Joe had his key in the door when the office phone began to ring. He unlocked the door and got to the phone quickly, spoke in low tones for just a few seconds, and hung up.

"Richards," he said.

"He finally got the message?"

"Didn't say anything about that. Just told me he wants to see us immediately. Says your boys from last night are with him."

"Mason and Dean?"

"Yeah. They're in Berea."

"Why?"

"Didn't say. Just told me to get to Berea City Hall."

"City Hall?" Berea was a small, middle-class suburb just southwest of us, home to Baldwin-Wallace College. I wondered what had brought a Cleveland homicide detective and members of the corruption task force together there.

"Uh-huh. He didn't explain it other than to suggest we haul ass down there. He didn't sound particularly happy with us."

"Pissed off that I didn't call him after the fires, probably."

"Could be."

I'd turned to go back out the door when I saw Joe had taken the snub-nosed Smith & Wesson he favors out of his desk drawer and slipped it into a shoulder holster. While I watched, he pulled a light jacket on over that. The rain was beginning again, pattering against the window.

"Planning to shoot a cop today?" I said. Joe always

avoids wearing a weapon when he can, so to see him putting one on before we went to meet with police was damn strange.

"I've been put in the backseat of a van by an asshole with a gun in his hand once too often today. That kind of got under my skin."

He led the way out of the office and shut the lights off behind us. The stairwell was filled with an eerie green glow. When we opened the door and stepped out into the parking lot, the air seemed to hum with the building storm's energy, greenish clouds skimming across the gray ones as raindrops splattered against us. Joe moved to his Taurus, but I took my truck keys out of my pocket.

"I'll drive."

"No, thanks," he said. It was a control thing, for both of us. Anytime we were heading into unknown circumstances, we both wanted as much control of the situation as possible. Driving didn't give a whole lot of that, but it was better than nothing. Joe slid behind the wheel of his Taurus without allowing a chance for further debate.

He drove out of the parking lot and across Rocky River, hung a right on Lorain, heading west. Instead of following Lorain as it headed over the bridge, though, he slipped off onto Old Lorain Road, a two-lane offshoot that wound down into the park, past Fairview Hospital. It was the same route we ran together several nights each week. This road would tie into the Valley Parkway down in the river basin, and we could take that all the way into Berea. The speed limit was reduced, but there weren't the stoplights or traffic delays you'd get on the main roads. The rain was falling harder, and Joe clicked the wiper setting up a few notches, the blades sweeping rapidly across the windshield. The soft patter of raindrops abruptly turned to a harsh clatter.

"Hail," Joe said. "Great. Probably put dents all over the car."

His voice was almost drowned out by the pounding of the rain and hail on the car. Rivulets of water rushed alongside the road. A roll of thunder began with a slow rumble and built into a harsh, clattering crescendo, like sheet metal passed through the gears of a powerful machine. A strobelike flash of lightning followed, and for a moment the tree-lined road was bright. I saw that the leaves on some of the trees had rolled upside down, the way they will when responding to the energy of a severe storm. Then the thunder and lightning faded and the world grew darker again. This time, the darkness was heavier, though. The clouds were shifting again, the green glow gone in favor of blackness.

"Hell of a storm," Joe said. "Car behind us doesn't even have its lights on yet."

Joe's headlights had turned on automatically, the sensor telling them it was night even though it was midday. We wound down a series of S-curves that would eventually straighten out and point us at the river. Behind the trees outside Joe's window was one of the MetroParks golf courses, brief glimpses of bright green fairways showing when the lightning flashed.

"What the hell," Joe said, twisting around to look behind us as he eased the car around one of the steep curves. The car that had been running without headlights had suddenly swung into the opposite lane, just off our rear bumper. Now the driver hit the accelerator hard, and the car, a black sedan, pulled close.

"Shit," Joe said, then he pressed down on his own accelerator while I reached behind me and freed my gun from its holster.

The sedan had the head start, and the Taurus was no race car. Before we made it out of the last curve, the sedan pulled up beside us, and a clatter of automatic gunfire rang out. The sound was deafening, even over the rain and the hail. Glass and metal exploded around us as bullets tore through the car. I got the Glock up but didn't fire, because Joe slammed on the brake and if I'd managed to hit anyone, it would probably have been him.

The pavement was soaked, and we'd been accelerating just before he hit the brake. The Taurus was a sure-footed car, low and wide, but even it couldn't take that sudden adjustment. We fishtailed as we shot out of the curve and toward the straightaway that led to the bridge, the back end of the car whipping first one way, then the next, as the black sedan slid ahead of us. The driver tried to spin the car around and block us, but he soon discovered, as we had, that these weren't good conditions for fast maneuvering. Before the sedan could get sideways, it skidded across the wet pavement, popped over the curb, and plowed into one of the supports at the front of the bridge. The hood crumpled and the windshield ruptured and spiderwebbed, but that was the last I saw of it, because we were spinning off the road ourselves.

Joe's abrupt braking had put us out of control, but he'd also done it just early enough to keep us from sliding into the bridge, as the sedan had. Instead, we slid onto the steep embankment on the opposite side of the road. Joe's foot was still on the brake, but it didn't matter now—any end to our slide was up to physics, not the car.

We scraped down the embankment at a dramatic angle, and I was sure the car was going to overbalance and roll. Outside my window I could see only grass. Below us was a shallow pool formed by excess river water. Before we went into it, though, we thumped against the slender trunk of the one young tree that stood on the hill. It bowed but didn't break, holding us perched halfway up the hill.

"You okay?" I said, turning to Joe. I saw then for the first time that he'd been shot.

He was slumped back against his seat, his head at an angle, his face a mask of pain. Blood was running down his jacket, spotting his tie underneath.

"Joe!" I unfastened his seat belt and leaned across the console, trying to see how badly he was hurt. Blood seemed to be coming from his left shoulder and his chest. It was flowing quickly from the chest wound, and his eyes were distant, his face white.

"We've got to get out of the car, Joe. They're going to come down here and kill us if we don't."

His answer was a ragged, shallow gasp. His head rolled sideways.

"Shit!" I took off my own seat belt and twisted in the seat, keeping my gun in my right hand. Leaning across Joe, I peered out of his shattered window, up at the road. I saw nothing but a glistening curtain of rain. They'd be on their way, though. I couldn't imagine that the crash would have killed the car's occupants, and if they could move, they'd come down here to make sure their task was complete.

I lunged over the center console and into the backseat. There were bullet holes through the door, and the back windows were broken. This entire side of the car had been riddled with gunfire. Joe's demand to be in the driver's seat when we'd left the office was the only reason I hadn't taken the shots instead of him. I didn't waste time trying to open the door, but just rolled onto my back and kicked at the remnants of the window, knocking the jagged glass away. Then I braced my hands—one still wrapped around the butt of the Glock—against the seat and pushed my legs through the window. A piece of glass raked across my ass, but then I had my feet on the ground and twisted my torso out of the car.

For a moment I paused, leaning against the side of the car and looking up at the road. I could see the wrecked sedan now, crumpled against the far side of the bridge, and I heard a bang. Someone closing a door, or kicking one open. I spun and grabbed the handle of Joe's door. It had been shot up, but it was intact and should open. When I tugged, though, it stuck. I reached through the broken window, ready to try to pull him out of it, but then I saw the lock was down. I pulled it up and tried the door again. This time it opened.

The door immediately began to swing shut because of the angle we were on, but I got my hip in front of it. Then I slid the Glock back into its holster and put both arms around Joe. He groaned when I lifted him, but I couldn't take the time to worry about being gentle.

Lurching backward, I got his upper body out of the car. His knees hit the edge of the steering wheel and stuck, though. He shifted, kicking weakly against the seat, and then he was free, falling out of the car and onto the hill. I set him down as gently as possible, then let the door swing shut. There was more noise from the wreck on the bridge, and when I looked up, I saw a man moving through the rain.

I got my gun back in my right hand, then wrapped my left arm around Joe. He wasn't heavy, maybe 170 at best, and I could drag him easy enough with one arm. His blood ran over my biceps as I pulled him, and he let out a gasp of agony. Slipping and stumbling down the muddy decline, I pushed us into the trees. As soon as I'd heard the door open up on the bridge, I'd known there was no point in attempting to use the car as shelter, or in trying to find a secure position around the trees. The guys on the road had automatic weapons. If they were in good enough condition to climb out of the car, they'd be in good enough condition to sit at the top of the hill and strafe us until there was nothing left for them to worry about.

We had to get into the river.

CHAPTER 26

The rain was still pouring down, turning Joe's blood from crimson to pink as it flowed over my arm and slid down his jacket. His heels plowed furrows through the mud as I pulled him toward the river. Behind us, a burst of gunfire opened up, shredding the Taurus. The sound was tremendous, so loud I wanted to drop Joe and cover my ears. There was nothing discreet about this hit; the men on the hill cared about nothing other than the efficiency of their murder attempt.

The muddy bank was slippery, and the river shallow close to it, maybe three feet deep at best. The only deep water here would be in the pool out in the center, where the current was strongest, but any attempt to hide in the river was going to be suicide. They'd stand at the top of the bridge and fire down on us. Our best chance—only chance—was to use the bridge against them, get directly beneath it and force them to come down to the bank to have a shot at us.

I lowered Joe onto the bank, dropped to one knee, and turned to face the bridge. Then I fired six shots as quickly as I could get them off, shooting up at the car. I couldn't see the gunmen, so I had little hope of hitting them, but I wanted them to hesitate as long as possible before crossing to the other side of the bridge where they'd have a clear shot at us. We needed every precious second if we were going to stay alive.

As soon as I got the shots off, I dropped to the ground beside Joe, pressing my cheek against the mud. It was a good decision. Hardly had I gotten prone before another burst of automatic gunfire, long and sustained, tore through the trees above us, blasting bark loose and shredding the leaves. When it was done, I counted off five seconds of silence before I sat up again. I put the Glock back in the holster but didn't fasten it, then turned and lifted Joe in both arms. His face was ashen, but he grimaced and hissed between clenched teeth when I lifted him. It was as good a sign as I could hope for. You have to be alive to feel agony.

"I'm sorry," I told him. "But I don't know another way to do this."

That said, I used my heels to push us both off the bank and into the river. It was a clumsy way to enter the water, but we needed to stay low. I moved in a sort of backward shuffle, crablike, holding Joe with one arm and using my heels and free hand to push down the river bottom, staying in the shallow end close to the bank. I'd gone only ten feet when I sank into a pool, the water rising dramatically without warning, and Joe floated free from my grasp. I tried to kick my way back to the surface, but by the time I made it, he was several feet away, out in the deeper water, and sinking. I floundered toward him, going with the current, my soaked clothing and shoes dragging me down. My hand found his jacket. I heaved him upward and rolled onto my back, using my legs to kick against the soft bottom, and one arm to pull. I rolled Joe so he was on his back, too, his mouth and nose clear, and then I concentrated only on keeping him above water as I struggled for the bridge.

The torrential rain had the river rushing faster than normal, but it was still wide and sluggish here, the current lazy, and that meant it took a hell of a lot of effort just to get us under the bridge. We passed under the shadow of it just as gunfire riddled the trees where we'd been before. Joe wasn't even attempting to kick or use his arms. He simply floated along, kept above water only by my efforts. That troubled me, and not just because his dead weight was making my struggle more difficult. Faced with disaster, instinct forces you to respond. You fight to stay alive, to the absolute limits of your physical ability. Joe's complete lack of effort told me he was close to dead.

Gunfire again. This time I could hear only the reports, no sounds of impact. That meant they were shooting into the water. I'd pulled us back to the same side as we'd started from, and now I regretted that. When they realized we'd gone under the bridge, they'd make their way down the bank, and this side offered an easier approach. The opposite bank was much steeper, lined with trees and heavy underbrush, and coming down it would be difficult. After a moment of hesitation, I decided I had to try to get us across while they were still up on the bridge.

I pushed my heels hard off the river bottom and sent us back into the current, using my free arm in long, sweeping strokes. Halfway across, the water deepened so that I could no longer touch the bottom, and the strength of the current took me by surprise. What had seemed like such a sluggish water flow had some real power, and with Joe limiting my mobility, I was having trouble fighting it. If we got swept out from under the bridge and into the open on the other side, the decision to move for the other bank would become fatal.

I sucked in a breath of wet air and swept harder with my right arm, the muscles in my shoulder screaming, pulling us back against the current and toward the other bank with everything I had. Several weeks without much rain were all that saved us. Had the water been deeper, I wouldn't have been able to pull us across before the current swept us into the open, but because it was shallow, I was able to cross the deep part of the pool and find footing on the bottom again. Once I could plant my feet, we were fine. I slogged us through the shallows until we reached the other side of the bridge, leaned against the cold stone, and gasped for breath.

Above us all was silent. I wrapped my left hand in Joe's shirt and tugged him through the water, edging out a bit so I could get a look up at the bridge.

I saw them through the steady, shimmering rain—two men in black jackets, ski masks over their heads, weapons in their hands. They'd come down from the bridge and were standing behind the wrecked Taurus, searching the nearby trees. The only thing keeping us alive right now was the storm. It was always dimmer down here in the bottom of the valley, and with the heavy black clouds, it was especially dark. They couldn't stand on the bridge and see the tree-lined banks well enough, so they'd been forced to come down to shoot accurately, and they'd started with the side where we'd wrecked, as I'd expected. Once they cleared that bank, though, they'd be coming this way.

Colored lights danced across the dark water around us. I rolled to my left slightly, and for a moment Joe's face dipped beneath the water. That was enough to let me see the source of the lights, though. A Crown Victoria with an overhead light bar had pulled off the Valley Parkway and crossed the bridge, heading toward the wrecked cars. I got a glimpse of the side of the car as it passed and saw the MetroParks Ranger logo on the door. MetroParks rangers weren't naturalists or park security—they were cops. They went through the state academy just like the city police, worked assaults and drug cases and the occasional murder like any other cops, but their jurisdiction was limited to the thousands of acres of parks in the system. He'd have a gun, and a radio.

Coming out from under the bridge was a gamble, but this was the time to take it. I braced my hand against the rough edges of the stone wall that bordered the bank, then pulled my body upright. I slid my right hand under Joe's arm and pulled him toward me, clearing him from the water and dropping him on the muddy bank.

Now I had a good vantage point to see across the river, but the gunmen were gone. A crackling, rushing noise from the trees told me someone was on the move. I squinted and peered through the rain. One of them was running away from the bridge, stumbling through the trees. I couldn't see the other. Maybe they'd both fled.

The ranger was out of his vehicle now, trudging across the bridge toward us. His head was down, his full-brimmed hat shedding rain. Water splashed with each step he took. I looked away from him and scanned the opposite bank again, searching for the shooter who hadn't been running away. I didn't see him. The rain fell harder, stinging my face, rivulets of water running into my mouth as I took gasping breaths. Fighting the current and Joe's clumsy bulk had taken a toll.

The ranger was close now, halfway across the bridge. He was searching the water and talking into a radio. By now he'd seen the wrecked cars and found them empty. But had he heard the gunfire before he'd arrived? It had been so loud, I couldn't imagine him *not* hearing it, though if he had heard it and had made the decision to walk out in the open like this, he was either a courageous son of a bitch or a damn fool.

Closer still he came, and now I could see that he held a gun in his right hand, down against his leg. He'd heard the shots, all right. And he was no fool, either, just brave. He hadn't waited for backup, because he'd known someone might be in the river. Maybe close to dying.

I waited until he came to our end of the bridge before I stood up and shouted.

"Hey! We need help down here!"

I waved my hands, but even so it took him a few seconds to locate the source of the shouting. All my back muscles were tight, braced for a shot that might come from the opposite bank. When the ranger saw us, he moved forward at a jog, around the edge of the bridge and down to the stone wall that shored up the bank. I left Joe and struggled around the wall and up the muddy slope, trying to get high enough to talk to the ranger. That was when I saw the gunman who hadn't fled through the trees.

He'd taken off his ski mask and climbed back onto the bridge. He was running up it now, closing fast. His footsteps slapped loudly off the wet concrete. The ranger turned at the sound of his approach and raised his gun.

"Stop! Put your hands in the air and get on the ground!"

The man kept coming, but he lifted one arm. Something glistened in his hand, and then I saw that it was a badge.

"Cleveland Police Department!" he shouted in response. "Relax, I'm a cop. Now stand down."

It was Jack Padgett, and in the hand that didn't have the badge was a gun.

The ranger lowered his weapon slightly, his shoulders relaxing.

"Don't listen to him!" I shouted. The ranger turned his head a fraction to the left, looked at my face. "He shot my partner," I said. "He's going to kill us."

The ranger's eyes snapped back to Padgett, who was still running toward him.

"Get on the ground!" the ranger yelled. "Now!"

"Cleveland Police!" Padgett said again, still running.

"I don't give a shit. Get . . . on . . . the . . . ground!"

Padgett kept running. The ranger's eyes slipped back to us, took in Joe's ashen face, my desperation. I dropped back down from the bank, knelt over Joe, and reached around for my gun. My fingers found the holster, empty. I'd lost the Glock in the river.

Padgett was ten yards away. The gun was still in his hand.

"Shoot him!" I screamed at the ranger.

"Cleveland Police!" Padgett yelled for the third time. The hand with the gun was coming up, the barrel moving toward the ranger.

I reached inside Joe's jacket, hoping his gun was still in the shoulder holster, but even as I did it, I knew it was too late. We were dead. The ranger wouldn't shoot a cop, and Padgett was going to kill us all.

The ranger shot Padgett.

He fired once and caught him in the thigh. Padgett's right leg spun away from his body, and he hit the pavement in a whirling tumble, banging against one of the iron bridge supports. For a moment he stayed down. Then he rolled over onto his shoulder and lifted his gun, aiming at the ranger. The ranger fired again. Padgett dropped and stayed down.

The ranger keyed his radio microphone and shouted into it, "Shots fired on the bridge at Rocky River. Repeat, shots fired, need backup immediately, and paramedics." Then he turned to us. He dropped to his knees and stretched out his arms. Rain cascaded off the brim of his wide hat.

"Let's get him up here," he said.

It wasn't easy. A sheer wall of at least ten feet was in front of me, and I couldn't shove Joe up to the ranger against that. Instead we had to move upstream, into the thickets and small trees that lined the riverbank. The ranger fought down through the brush until he reached me, then hooked his hands under Joe's arms and lifted him clear, dragged him back up the hill and set him on the grass. I clambered up the bank after them, using small trees for handholds, thorns tearing at my skin. My entire body was shaking. Sirens were wailing somewhere up above the valley, playing sorrow's anthem, this time for my partner.

The ranger left us there, walked back to the bridge, and crossed to Padgett. He knelt beside him and stayed there for a while. Then he returned to stand in front of me. His wet face was drawn and grave.

"Mister," he said, "I hope you're an honest man. Because I believe I just killed a police officer."

CHAPTER 27

The hospital room was cool and dark. I sat on the tile floor with my back against the door. I'd been here for a while now. At least ten minutes had passed since I'd told the cops I needed to go to the bathroom, when all I'd really needed was to get away from them, from the lights, from the world. I'd needed to close my eyes. It was a small thing, closing your eyes. But I needed it badly.

I'd made a few random turns through corridors that smelled of pungent cleansers until I found an empty room. Joe was in the building, somewhere. I couldn't see him, though. He was still in surgery. Eight hours of it now.

I wondered how long they could keep him in surgery. At what point did they just give up? Eight hours seemed like a lot of it. I wondered who the surgeon was, how steady his hands were, how much experience he had with gunshot wounds. I wondered if Joe was already dead.

If I'd gotten him killed.

I slid my heels back so my knees were raised, crossed my arms over my knees, and rested my forehead on my arms. Kept my eyes closed. He hadn't wanted to get involved. Not even at the beginning. I'd gone out to his house in the middle of the night, sat in his living room, and pressured him into helping me. He'd hesitated, and not because he was worried about his own safety, or about lost money on the paying cases, or about the media attention surrounding Ed's death. He'd hesitated because he knew that I was on a fool's mission. Because in the end, what could I accomplish? I could alter a dead friend's legacy. But was that enough? The answer wasn't as resounding in my mind tonight as it had been all week.

Eight hours Joe had been on the table. They would have parts of him opened up, blood running down his skin, tubes inserted into his nose, wires fastened to his flesh, computers monitoring his life, if indeed he still had life.

Ed Gradduk was my demon, not Joe's. If anyone was going to be hurt trying to help a dead man, it needed to be me.

Voices in the hall. Someone inquiring about me. A nurse saying she hadn't seen me. I kept the door shut until I heard the man thanking the nurse, and then his voice registered. It was Cal Richards. I'd seen nothing but cops for hours now, but not Richards. I'd been wondering when he'd show up.

I slid sideways far enough to clear myself from the door, then reached up for the handle and pulled the door open.

"Richards."

He was halfway down the hall when I spoke, and at the sound of his name he turned and looked one way, then the other, seeing nothing. I stuck my hand into the hall and waved it at him. He saw me and walked down to my room. When he stepped inside, he turned on the lights. I winced against the harsh brightness, and he flicked them back off. He closed the door softly. A chair was at the foot of the empty bed. He slid it across the floor and sat down.

"You okay?" he said.

I looked at him, but in the dark room I saw nothing of his face, just an outline.

"He's still in surgery," I said.

"Yeah." I couldn't see his mouth move when he talked, and his voice seemed to float out of the blackness, soft and strong. "I've asked about him. First thing I did when I got here, in fact, was talk to the doctors."

"And?"

"It's a bad one. Two gunshot wounds."

"I know that, Richards. I was there. What else, though? Nobody around here will give me details."

"I'm not a doctor, Perry. I can't tell you what's happening in there."

I leaned my head back against the wall and shut my eyes again. "What can you tell me, Richards?"

"I can tell you that Jack Padgett's not dead yet, but he's also in no condition to talk. I can tell you that the car he drove was stolen, and I can tell you that we don't know who the second shooter was."

"Have you found Corbett?"

"No."

I shook my head. "That son of a bitch matters. Corbett's the guy who makes everything go, Richards."

"You seem a lot more convinced of that than you were two days ago."

"He matters to everybody," I said. "Living and dead. Mattered to Sentalar, Ed, Rabold. To Padgett and Cancerno. You've got to find him, Richards."

"We're going to." He shifted in his seat and I saw his silhouette lean forward. "But first you've got to tell me what you did that made it all escalate so damn fast, Perry. What you did that made a cop decide it was worth the risk to try and take you out. You have to have an idea about that."

"I've got one."

"I need to hear it."

"Okay," I said. "It starts with Mike Gajovich."

Richards let his breath out in a long, low exhalation. "Yeah."

"You're already there, huh?"

"Started that way this morning," he said.

"In Berea?"

"Uh-huh. While I was looking into Sentalar, I learned she wasn't the first choice for director of the Neighborhood Alliance. A Berea city councilman was. He took the job, then backed out. Seems Mike Gajovich was pretty heavily involved in the whole project. Seems this guy from Berea was guaranteed a job on Mike's staff when he became mayor. Guaranteed the job if he'd look the other way on some funding issues with Cancerno's contracting company and the Neighborhood Alliance. Guy had long ties to Gajovich, and I'm sure he's a crooked bastard, but he was wise enough not to like that setup and he backed out. The way things are shaping up, it looks like Cancerno's kicking back a lot of the cash from that organization to Gajovich, funding his campaign, most likely."

I wanted to care. I wanted to ask for the details, try to tie it all back to the puzzle pieces I'd spent a week assembling, make it fit, make it neat. I couldn't, though. I couldn't find it in me to give a damn about any of it anymore. Not with Joe stretched out on some cold steel table, scalpels and forceps being used on his body.

"You gonna tell me how you got to Gajovich?" Richards said.

"His brother's going to be involved, too," I said instead of answering his question. "Dean and Mason are probably already on it. His brother's the commander of District Two. Rabold and Padgett's boss."

"That did come up," Richards said.

"Have you brought Cancerno in yet?"

"Looking for him. Missing in action, for now."

"Him and Corbett," I said. "Wonderful."

"I'm going to need you to tell me what you know in some detail. But not now."

I was already shaking my head. "You're right, not now.

I'm done talking to cops for the night, Richards. I'm done until someone lets me see Joe."

He was quiet for a minute. "I wanted to come earlier. Soon as I heard. But with all this shit going down, the prosecutor involved now, I spent the whole afternoon meeting with the brass."

"It's fine."

He looked up. "I'm just trying to tell you," he said, "that it matters to me, too."

I nodded. "All right, Cal. I understand."

Twenty minutes later, Richards was gone, off to consult with his superiors yet again. I didn't envy his job. The department would already be sweating the damage control of Padgett's shooting by the MetroParks ranger. Adding it to a day in which they'd learned one of their own commanders and the county prosecutor were likely tied to major corruption had probably sent them into cardiac arrest.

Let them see it through, I thought. Let them deal with Cancerno, and find Corbett, and fire Gajovich or impeach him or whatever the hell it was you did with a prosecutor. It didn't matter anymore. Ed Gradduk was dead, and my partner was headed that way.

With Cal Richards gone, I sat alone on a vinyl chair in a waiting room for something like the urology department at MetroHealth. The doctors and nurses in this ward were long gone, and it was basically empty. They'd wanted to keep me out of sight, though. The media was swarming, and they all wanted me. The cops had wanted me to go to the police station; the MetroHealth administrators had simply wanted me to get out of their building. I'd refused.

"Lincoln!"

I turned my head to see Amy rounding the corner of

the hallway, walking fast, her face pale. She crossed the room and knelt in front of me, rested her hands on my knees, and looked hard at my face.

"Is he okay?" she said.

"I don't know."

"What happened? I didn't find out till about two hours ago, when my editor called to see if I could get in touch with you for a quote. I didn't even know what he was talking about. It took me forever to figure out where you were."

She slid into the chair beside me, and I told her what I could tell her. What she most wanted to know—Joe's status—I could not provide.

"He was alive when they put him in the ambulance, and he was alive when they got him to the hospital," I said. "All I've heard since then is that he's in surgery. They're not telling me more. But it's been a hell of a long time, and nobody's come out to say he'll be okay. He can thank me for that. I put him into it."

She shook her head. "Don't do that to yourself, Lincoln," she said, her voice soft. "Don't."

"It's true, Amy. This one had nothing to do with him, and he's on an operating table while I'm out here. It's not right."

She leaned down, looked into my eyes. "Why did you start investigating this to begin with?"

I waved her off and turned away. I didn't want to have the conversation where someone told me it wasn't my fault.

"Well?" she insisted.

I sighed. "Because Ed had been my friend once, Amy. Because he'd been a good friend."

"Same thing Joe would say about you. You wanted to help your friend; he wanted to help his. So it's okay for you to use that as motivation, but not okay for him?"

I braced my elbows on my knees and ran both hands over my face, took a deep breath, but didn't speak.

"Don't blame yourself for what happened to Joe. It's not going to help anything. And it's stupid."

Blunt. That was Amy.

"I heard it was Padgett?" she said after a moment's silence.

I nodded. "Another guy with him, as yet unidentified."

I told her about Cancerno then, and about Gajovich, and Alberta Gradduk. It felt good to talk, better than I'd thought it could after so many rehashings with police already. Maybe that was because talking gave me a break from thinking. Made the minute hand on the clock on the wall slide by a little quicker, a little easier.

"So you believe what Cancerno told you?" she said.

I shrugged. "It made sense. Some of it has to be true, I think. It fit well."

"Joe agreed?"

"He thought the truth was probably somewhere in the middle. That's where it usually tends to be."

"Cancerno will kill Corbett if he can find him?"

I nodded again. "I got that feeling, yes. But he was hoping I'd find him. Save him the trouble."

"Mr. Perry?"

The voice came from behind me, and I sat up and turned around to see a doctor standing there. He was wearing surgical scrubs and glasses, and he put his hand out when I turned to him. When I shook it, I saw his hands were long and thin, and strong. He was maybe sixty, with gray hair and perfect posture.

"James Crandall. I've been attending to your partner for the last eight hours." He nodded at Amy.

I got to my feet, searching his face for an indication of what news he'd come to share. It displayed no emotion.

"He is not," said Dr. James Crandall, "in good shape.

That said, he is in rather remarkable shape for what he has endured. There were two gunshot wounds, and both were serious. They alone might have killed him, even had medical attention been immediate. Instead, he was plunged into a polluted river."

It seemed there was nothing anchoring me to the ground. I could feel my feet on the floor, but the rest of me seemed disconnected, like a balloon pulled free from its tether. I forced myself to keep my eyes on Crandall's.

"The chest wound caused some serious blood loss," he said. "There was arterial damage, massive trauma. We've stabilized it, but there's no guarantee his body will be able to respond. Sometimes, they simply cannot recover from trauma like that."

I tried to nod.

"The second wound," he continued, "was in the shoulder, and also quite serious. The bullet lodged between the upper and middle branch of the nerve trunks—they're called the brachial plexus—that give movement and sensations to the muscles of the chest, shoulders, and arms. It also damaged an artery in his shoulder. I was able to remove the injured portion of the artery and perform an artificial graft. That was a five-hour process, in itself. If it works, it may save his arm."

"May," I said.

He nodded. "The arm could be lost. That is a possibility I have to acknowledge at this point. I hope it won't be the case."

"But he'll live."

Crandall's eyes never left mine. "He might. As I said, the chest trauma was massive. The blood loss was severe. His heart is strong for a man of his age, but it has still been around for sixty years. Sometimes, they simply cannot take the trauma."

I didn't come close to managing the nod this time.

"I'm going back to him now," Crandall said. "They told me he has no family, but that you were here. I wanted to talk to you directly."

"Thank you," I said, but my voice was not my own.

He gave a curt nod, turned on his heel, and moved back down the corridor. He walked confidently and with purpose. He was a man of gifts, a man who could save lives. But he had lost lives before, too. Even the best surgeons did.

More hours passed. I stayed in my chair, and Amy sat with me. We talked less. The police had not come to find me again, and I had not heard from Richards. Amy was struggling to stay awake. I told her to go home and get some sleep.

"No way, Lincoln."

"I'll call you as soon as I hear something. It's almost two in the morning, Ace. Go get some rest."

"What about you?"

"I'll fall asleep eventually."

She didn't want to go, but she also didn't want to argue with me. After a minute, she got to her feet.

"Call me as soon as you hear anything new," she said.

"I will."

She leaned down and gave me a hug, kissed me on the forehead, and then left. I was alone again in the empty waiting room, watching the clock.

My thoughts returned to Mitch Corbett. Had he set us up? If Cancerno was to be believed, Corbett and Padgett had worked in tandem before. But trusting a guy who made a life running every hustle in the book was a big if.

I found myself hoping Cancerno knew where Corbett was. Hoping someone else had been able to succeed where I had failed, and that Cancerno had already finished his own task. I'd believed his sincerity about that more than any other part of his story. If he found Corbett, he would kill him.

It wasn't going to be easy to find him, though. Joe and I were good, and we hadn't come close. And knowing Corbett's relationship with Cancerno changed things. Maybe he had more money than anybody had known. Maybe he'd swindled a cool million off Cancerno and bailed, and that was why Cancerno wanted him dead. That could change things dramatically. Explain why even our gifted spook in Idaho hadn't been able to help us. Money changes everything. The two hardest people to find are those with plenty of money to run with, and those with none at all.

Joe's idea about checking Joseph A. Marsh had been a good one. Assuming Corbett didn't have money, it had been perfect. Where else would he go without any cash, with no family to take him in? His options would have been slim, and finding someplace—anyplace—to wait the storm out while he tried to come up with a plan would have been hard. The Neighborhood Alliance properties offered him that, and the school was the best option of the lot. Remove that from the list, and who the hell knew where he'd gone.

The thought of the list stopped me cold. The night of the fires, I'd tried to get ahead of Corbett by moving through the list of Neighborhood Alliance properties. Where had the list come from, though? Amy. And she'd gotten it from the county recorder's office. The houses had nothing to do with Cancerno's crew until they were instructed to begin working on them. One house, the big one on West Fortieth, had been purchased just a week before Sentalar died. It was almost certain Cancerno's team wasn't ready to work on it yet, and quite possible that they didn't even know about it. But Corbett had been with Sentalar in that last week, touring the neighborhood. He might have known.

"Shit," I said aloud. "I saw it. I *saw* the damn thing."

Mitch Corbett had a cat. There'd been a litter box in the furnace room at his house. The door to the furnace room had been closed. If he'd left the cat in the house, he would have left that door open. Wouldn't want the cat pissing all over the rug.

There hadn't been a cat in Corbett's house, but I'd seen one in the vacant house on West Fortieth. Hard to forget the little beast, considering I'd damn near shot it. It hadn't been a stray, either, but healthy and well fed, with a collar that had reflected a glitter of light when I'd leveled my gun at it.

t was five past two when I left the hospital to find Mitch Corbett.

CHAPTER 28

I didn't have my truck at the hospital, so I had to walk it. The house was about two miles from MetroHealth. I walked down the empty sidewalks, keeping my hands in my pockets and my shoulders hunched against the light chill the storms had left in the night air. A car cruised past me slowly, a couple kids sticking their heads out of the windows and yelling at me. I didn't look up. One of them tossed a bottle that hit ten feet away and shattered. They laughed and drove on.

Although I was feeling confident that Corbett had been in the house, I wasn't sure he'd still be there. The day after the fires, the cops would have had to put some scrutiny on the Neighborhood Alliance. They would have checked the other houses, probably accompanied by an arson team. If they'd flushed Corbett out, would he have returned? All I could do was hope that he had.

The house on West Fortieth looked just as it had the last time I'd visited it in the night—dark, lonely, and forgotten. A neighborhood lived on around it, but this house was no longer part of that. I approached the back door.

I didn't have a gun. My Glock had been lost in Rocky River, and I hadn't gone back to the office or to my apartment before making this trip. I wasn't in a mood to let that worry me, though.

The door wasn't locked. The knob turned freely in my hand. I pushed the door open about six inches, then stepped to the side, and listened. There was no sound of movement. I gave it a few seconds longer, then pushed the door all the way open and stepped inside. I remembered the layout and moved fairly quickly through the kitchen and into the living room. As I entered, I heard a soft thump and moved to the side again. A car passed outside, and light slid over the room momentarily. It was enough to show me a familiar gray-and-white cat on the floor, looking up with wide eyes that shone in the darkness, and a large man stretched out on the floor under a thin blanket, a handgun beside him.

I shuffled close to him, and the cat meowed loudly. The man didn't stir. I felt along the dirty floorboards with my left hand, searching for the gun. I touched something else and discovered it was a metal-handled flashlight. I took it in my right hand, then kept searching till I found the gun and put it in my left hand. When I picked the gun up, the cat yowled again, louder this time. The man on the floor grunted softly and sat up. I hit the flashlight button and shot the beam into his eyes.

"Rise and shine, Mr. Corbett."

He covered his eyes with one arm and swept the other across the floor, searching for the gun.

"I've already got it," I said, and he stopped moving. His eyes were shielded and he squinted, and still he couldn't see me, because I was standing behind the light.

"I'm Lincoln Perry," I said. "And we're going to do some talking. Talk well enough—and that means honest enough—and you might not die tonight, Corbett."

He sat on the floor with his back against the wall while I stood in front of him. He was a big man, over six feet and carrying probably 220 pounds. He wore grimy jeans and a T-shirt, and a new growth of beard covered his face. The cat had curled up beside him, and he stroked its fur absently while he talked.

"Whatever Cancerno told you is a lie. The only thing he knows about the truth is how to avoid it. Ed was my friend. You think I had anything to do with what happened with him, you're out of your mind."

"You know what did happen, though?"

"Most of it."

"Then what the hell are you doing here, instead of down at a police station trying to help before more people die?"

"You just told me," Corbett said, "that it was a cop who shot your partner."

"Yes."

He laughed softly. "So there you go, man. There you go. First Anita went down, then Ed, and I knew it was time for my ass to clear out. Not that I expected to make it long. I got no money, no place to go. And Jimmy Cancerno is not going to let me stay gone for long. When the man finds me . . ." He shook his head. "Dying isn't going to be easy for me. He'll make damn sure of that. Take his time."

"Why?"

"Why? Because I put it all in motion, man. I told the old stories. And he knows that. Everything that's happened since? Jimmy's holding me personally responsible. I guarantee that."

"Explain it. If you put it all into motion, I want to know how. Every last detail, Corbett."

He ran a hand over his scruffy beard and sighed. My night vision had adapted to the point that I could see him even without the flashlight. The empty living room smelled heavily of dust and mold.

"It goes back a ways," he said. "For you to understand what Eddie got into, you got to listen a bit."

"I've been through a lot to hear the story. I'm sure as hell not going to get impatient now."

His eyes searched for me in the darkness, and he nodded once. "Okay. Then I'll get to telling it."

◆ ◆ ◆

I t started, Mitch Corbett told me, when Norm Gradduk
lost his job. It hadn't been in April, which was what
Norm had offered to his family. It had been the previous October. For six months, Norm had left the house
every day pretending he was on his way to work. In reality, he was on his way to the Hideaway or another drinking establishment of choice. Norm had gone through a
handful of jobs in the two years leading up to that, and at
his last firing Alberta had hit the roof. He didn't want to
deal with that scene again, so he decided he'd just keep
things quiet till he found another job.

"Problem was," Corbett said, "he didn't find another
job."

So Norm needed cash, and a steady supply of it.
Didn't want to go for unemployment, though. There was
pride at stake, and of course it was more likely Alberta
would find out the truth if he did go on the county. Maybe
even leave him. One of Norm's friends, maybe Scott
Draper's dad, maybe somebody else, introduced him to a
neighborhood guy named Jimmy Cancerno. Told him this
was a man who could give him some cash, a short-term
loan, a long-term loan, whatever he needed. Cancerno
was more than cooperative when the two men met; he
was downright friendly. Slapped Norm on the shoulder
and told him the money was his. They'd work out terms
of repayment later, he said with a wink. At first, Norm
borrowed as little as possible, just enough to keep the
electric bill paid and food on the table. But the money was
given so freely, without hassle or heartache, that it also
became easier to ask for it. The weekly loans increased.
So did the debt. And Norm's drinking and gambling.

"You know much about Cancerno?" Corbett asked me,
his voice low and quiet in the dark.

"Big player in the neighborhood, I understand."

Corbett laughed that unamused laugh of his again. "He runs this neighborhood, man. Owns it. And the loan-sharking was just a different sort of investment plan for him. He wasn't counting on getting the cash back. What he wanted was favors. He wanted to have guys who owed him so bad, they'd be willing to do a lot of things for him. Do things that would make Jimmy a hell of a lot more in the long run than what the guys owed him on the loans. He liked to set the hook, Jimmy did. Still does."

"I believe it."

Winter came and went, and Norm started to pull himself together again, Corbett explained. Got off the barstool and back out looking for work. Fessed up to Alberta about his employment status, but didn't tell her how long it had been since he was fired. Didn't mention his arrangement with Jimmy Cancerno. Norm found a job. Awful pay, but the best he could do at the time. Then summer rolled around, and so did Jimmy Cancerno.

By then Norm owed Cancerno somewhere in the neighborhood of twenty-five grand. Not an astronomical sum, but a lot to a guy whose new job paid about four hundred a week. And Cancerno wanted repayment immediately, with value added. When Norm confessed that it would likely be a few years before he could cover all of the debt, Cancerno made him an offer—he could work the debt off. Clear thousands owed in one night, by setting a few fires. A guy named Terry Solich was really beginning to cramp Cancerno's business style, and Cancerno had decided it was time for Solich to go. Solich hadn't proved agreeable, so now the matter was going to be taken out of his hands. And for Norm Gradduk, it was a chance to get out from under. One night's work with a can of gas and a book of matches, one loan cleared. Simple as that. Cops wouldn't even be an issue, Cancerno said. He'd take care of that end. All Norm had to do was light the matches.

"But Norm didn't agree to it," Corbett said. "He drew his line, and drew it hard. He said he wasn't going near Terry Solich's pawnshop, and if Jimmy asked him again, Norm was going to the cops. Jimmy asked him how he was going to pay the loan back then, and Norm told him he'd pay it back when he got good and ready. Then he made some more threats about the cops."

Corbett stopped talking for a moment. The cat rose beside him, stretched until it seemed to have doubled in length, then wandered away from us. Corbett shifted position, hooking his arms around his knees.

"Back then people were just getting to know the sort of man Jimmy was. A guy like Norm Gradduk, well, he had no idea. Not really. But the one thing *nobody* was going to get away with was threatening Jimmy. Especially by talking about bringing in the cops. Jimmy always knew that owning a piece of the neighborhood police was important, and by then he had a couple guys on payroll. One of them was Jack Padgett."

"I saw him take a bullet today," I said. "And it was one of the nicer things I've seen in a long time."

Corbett just nodded. "Well, Jimmy decided it was time to make a statement. Norm needed a lesson, right? So Jimmy rounded up Padgett and they went down to pay a visit to Norm at his house."

Corbett's voice was quieter, his tone softer. He didn't like the topic he was discussing. He didn't want to have to tell this story again, I could tell.

"Jimmy told Norm he had a choice—burn Solich out or pay up right then. Norm told him to go to hell. His wife was at the house, and she had no idea what was going on."

"What about Ed?" I said.

"Wasn't there. I don't know where he was, but I know it wasn't the house."

If he hadn't been home, it was a safe bet he'd been

with me. I wondered what we'd been doing the night Cancerno and Padgett had paid their visit to the Gradduks.
Having fun, probably. Laughing our way through another
summer night. That was the way they all went, back then.

"Norm came on like a tough guy," Corbett said. "Giving them hell, telling them to get out of his house. He
didn't know what he was dealing with. Padgett slapped
him around a bit, kicked his ass in front of the wife.
Laughed and showed them his badge when Gradduk's
wife screamed about calling the police."

Silence. I waited, but he didn't continue.

"Well?" I said eventually.

Corbett's head was down, eyes on the floor. "Jimmy
was screaming at Norm, telling Norm that he owned the
cops, owned the neighborhood, owned Norm. Nobody
threatened Jimmy the way Norm had, and he was going to
make that point. With Norm's wife."

I looked away as a car passed the house again, another
brief shaft of light filling the room.

"They held a gun to Norm's head," Corbett said. "Then
Padgett and Cancerno . . . well, they made her perform.
In front of him."

I was rubbing my thumb in small, circular motions
across the butt of the gun, my finger tense on the trigger.

"When they left, they promised Norm they'd be back.
Said unless he did what Jimmy wanted, when Jimmy
wanted, they'd be back. Padgett was the key to the whole
night. He's been the key to a lot of nights like that. It's
one thing going up against Jimmy, but when you know
he's got cops on his team, too, particularly an evil son of
a bitch like Padgett . . . well, it makes a guy feel helpless,
you know? I think that's how Norm felt."

"That's why he killed himself," I said, my voice hollow. "He thought he was protecting the family. Severing
the tie between Cancerno and Padgett and his family."

"I'd expect so. But it didn't work out that way. Jack Padgett is one of the meanest men I've ever known, and I've known some that would turn your stomach."

"Cancerno said you two were tight."

"What did I tell you about Jimmy and the truth?"

I nodded.

"Jimmy's a ruthless son of a bitch, but only when he's got something to gain," Corbett continued. "With Jimmy, when Norm was gone, it was done. No value left for him. But for Padgett, that wasn't how it went. He'd taken a liking to Norm's wife, and he came back for more."

"And Ed found out."

"Yeah. I don't know when he got wind of it, exactly, but he did. And he went looking for someone to help." Corbett lifted his head. "He picked your father."

I took a deep breath and nodded. "I understand this part. My dad made the harassment complaint, and Mike Gajovich swept it under the rug. He went down and intimidated Alberta, scared her out of it by telling her she and Ed would become part of a humiliating public spectacle."

"That's close to the sum of it. Jimmy wanted to protect Padgett, because Padgett was so valuable to him. He also knew Gajovich's brother, an asshole of the first order. You were a cop?" When I nodded, he said, "You know him?"

"Not really."

"Lucky, then. Anyhow, Cancerno went through the brother to the lawyer, the one who's prosecutor now. Mike. He took some cash from Jimmy and played his role, maybe thinking it was one and done, I don't know. If he was hoping that'd be it, then he didn't realize he'd just made as bad a mistake as Norm Gradduk had. Making a deal with Jimmy is like the kind of arrangement some men have made with the devil on a lonely highway. You get what you want, but then, brother, you're gone."

I was suddenly tired of standing. I slid down the wall

until I was sitting on the floor like Corbett, angled to face him. I set the gun down beside my leg.

"You said you were the one who put things in motion," I said. "I'm assuming you told Ed the story, and he went after Cancerno."

"Uh-huh. Ed figured he had a score to settle with Jimmy. He knew what was going on with the Neighborhood Alliance houses, so he—"

"What *is* going on with those houses?"

"I don't know the details, man. I just ran the crew. My job was to do shit repairs and fleece the HUD grant for four times what we'd actually put into it. Where's the excess going? Maybe right back into Jimmy's pockets, maybe somewhere else."

According to Cal Richards, the excess was going into Gajovich's campaign fund, Cancerno making a down payment on owning a big piece of the city.

"When Ed went to see Gajovich, what was he trying to do?" I asked.

"Bargain with him. Or blackmail him, whichever you'd prefer. He wanted Gajovich to look at the Neighborhood Alliance scam and throw Cancerno in jail. Ed figured Gajovich owed him that much."

"So he went to Gajovich and came up empty," I said. "What happened then? How'd Anita Sentalar get involved?"

"She was always involved. She and Gajovich go way back. He handpicked her to run the Neighborhood Alliance because he trusted her to look the other way. She knew if he got elected mayor, she'd have a high-level position on his staff."

"Who killed her?"

"Cancerno had it done, though I couldn't tell you for sure who pulled the trigger. And that was our fault. Ed's and mine. He needed a strong witness if he was going to bring it down, and he thought she could be it. He was pressuring her to go to the attorney general and roll on Cancerno. She wouldn't. That's when Ed and I decided to go in two different directions."

"Meaning?"

"He decided to start burning the houses down. Figured that would force the cops to take a hard look at the Neighborhood Alliance. And I think he liked the idea, too, saw some element of sweet justice in that. Jimmy had wanted Ed's dad to start some fires, right? Well, Ed was coming through on that, with fifteen years of interest payments, to boot."

"And what direction did you take?"

"I was still working on Anita. I showed her around the neighborhood, introduced her to one of the kids who was being put in an Alliance house. They were the people who were losing, you know. Sure, the mortgages were insured, but they thought they were moving into dream houses when they were really hovels with fresh paint and some new drywall. That made an impression on Anita, too. I think she was ready to go with us on it. Cancerno must have thought so, too. Because she got killed."

"So they set Ed up, and then Padgett and Rabold were sent down to kill him," I said. "Or at least Padgett was. Rabold was working undercover by then. Which is why he ended up dead, too."

"Came close to working perfectly for Jimmy," Corbett said, "except Ed got a few minutes to talk to you. Otherwise, it might have gone without a hitch."

"You think Cancerno ordered Padgett to try to take us out today? Or could that have been an enterprise project for Padgett?"

"He wouldn't have rolled out till Jimmy took him off the leash."

I was thinking about that, wondering what the trigger

had been. Why not just send Ramone to kill us right away? Why drive us down for the meeting, then let us go? To find out exactly what we knew. But we'd seemed to buy his story. So what made him send Padgett out to hit us?

"I mentioned Gajovich by name," I said. "I told Cancerno that I knew he'd been the one to make my father's complaint about Padgett disappear."

"Could have mattered," Corbett said. "Or it could not. I can't tell you that."

"Whatever the reason, he definitely wanted us killed."

"Cancerno'll kill me, too," Corbett said matter-of-factly. "He blames me for all of this, and after what he told you, it's clear he's also hoping to use me as a fall guy. Wash his hands of the Neighborhood Alliance and put it all back on me. Once I'm dead, I'll become awfully important. Time this is all done, it'll be me that was running the books on the Neighborhood Alliance, me who took the cash, me who killed Sentalar. I guarantee it."

"You helped him out by burning the rest of his houses down."

Corbett coughed and shook his head. "I didn't burn those houses down, Perry."

I frowned. "Be honest, Corbett. You were finishing what Ed started."

"No. I didn't set those fires. But I can tell you who did. I was checking out some of the houses that night, thinking maybe I needed to relocate. Instead, I saw one of them burn."

"Who did it?"

"The guy who owns the Hideaway," he said. "Draper."

CHAPTER 29

The name rocked me, but it shouldn't have. After all, until that day I'd never seen Cancerno without Draper at his side. It explained the phone call I'd gotten from Scott the morning after Ed died, too, the sudden change of heart he'd shown. Cancerno had probably ordered him to bring me down so they could see how much Ed had shared before Padgett had crushed him under the Crown Victoria.

"You're sure?" I asked Corbett, even as all of the facts supporting it slid through my mind.

He nodded once. "Trust me, I got a good look at the man. No doubt in my mind at all. Jimmy sent him out because Jimmy wants to use me to explain his way out of everything surrounding the Neighborhood Alliance. Burn down the houses, blame it on me, and he's done. Well, he's got to find me and kill me, first. But then he's done."

I stood up. A muscle in my back clenched hard at the movement, stopping me before I got upright. I winced and pushed past it, taking a deep breath that made the muscle ache worse. I'd been in a car accident, dragged a lifeless man through a river, and had no sleep. No wonder my body was protesting.

"You've got to talk to the police, Corbett. I've already got them looking at Gajovich, and Padgett's dead. You can't just hide here, waiting for other people to figure it out."

He didn't say anything.

"People have been murdered," I said. "No one is going to care about what you did with the Neighborhood Alliance. They're going to care about taking Cancerno down, and Gajovich. Not about you."

He was scared, though. A guy like Corbett, who'd spent years working cons and scams, seeing corrupt cops and prosecutors, did not like the idea of solving things through official channels. But he was going to have to do it.

"I'm calling a detective named Cal Richards," I said. "And you're going to talk to him. You can trust this one."

He nodded, slowly. "All right."

"One more question—how the hell did you know so much about what happened between Cancerno and Padgett and Alberta Gradduk, anyhow?"

For moment, he didn't respond. Then he lifted his head and looked at me.

"Remember how I told you they put a gun to Norm's head while Padgett and Cancerno had their fun?"

"Yes."

"I held the gun." He did not drop his head. Did not look away. "By then, I owed Jimmy a hell of a lot more than Norm Gradduk ever did. And I'd been working for him for a while. And before Norm killed himself, I burned Solich out of business, like Norm was supposed to."

"And told the cops it was him," I said.

"Yes."

I exhaled loudly and shook my head. "Did Ed know?"

"Yes. It's how I started the story when I told it to him."

I stood and stared at him.

"I changed a lot over the years," Corbett said softly. "Never forgot that night, Perry. And then when Ed started working with us . . . and, man, we got along. He was a good guy. One of the best I've ever known. And loyal. If you were his friend, he'd break his back to help you. No questions asked."

"Yes," I said. "He would."

"A time came when I knew I had to tell him. Had to. Man was my friend, and he didn't know. And he was working for Jimmy, and didn't know. And that wasn't right."

It had been a hard story for Corbett to tell, all right. Ed hadn't been exaggerating when he'd told me that.

"He listened to it all, and he didn't turn on me, not right then, and not after," Corbett said. "Can you imagine? The things that happened to his family, you know? The things that I was a part of. And all he did was thank me for telling him."

I watched the shadows on the opposite wall. "Could be he'd learned something about holding grudges."

"I thought it was the right thing to do," Corbett said. "But now? Shit. I'd do anything to take it back. Because look what it started. Look what it did."

I shook my head. "No. You needed to tell him, Corbett. It needed to be settled. Ed started to settle it, and now we're going to finish it. You and me. You're talking to Cal Richards. Telling him everything you told me. You're going to do that because you're too much of a man not to. You can't hide from it anymore."

"Okay," he said, his voice low and sad. He snapped his fingers, and out of nowhere the cat emerged again, purring. It sat beside him, and he scratched its head.

"You know," I said, "you should have left the cat at home. It certainly wasn't helping you hide."

"He's fifteen years old," Corbett said, as if that explained everything. "Couldn't leave him."

"I'll have someone come to get you."

He shook his head. "No. I'm not going to do it that way. You say I can trust this guy, Richards, then I'll trust

Richards. But you're not going to send them out to get me, put me in handcuffs. You set up a meet with him, and I'll be there."

I thought about it, then nodded.

"Tomorrow morning, Richards and I will come here. Just the two of us. You'll be here?"

"I'm not going anywhere."

I believed him. He was not a man who had any energy left to hide, or to run.

"I'm leaving now," I said. "And I'm taking your gun."

"Where you going?"

"To see an old friend."

The neighborhood was silent when I stepped out of the back door of the house on West Fortieth Street with Corbett's revolver tucked in my waistband. There was a pay phone up the street. I could use it to call Cal Richards. I could send him down to the Hideaway, let him pick up Draper.

I walked past the phone, though, moving north toward Clark Avenue at that time when the night seemed to have forgotten to which day it belonged. The police would get their chance at Draper soon enough. Right now, I wanted my own. I wanted to hear him explain it. To understand how he'd let it happen.

It was past three when I got to the Hideaway, and even Clark, usually an active street, was still. The bar would have been closed for nearly an hour now, but I was hoping to find Draper there, anyhow. People in the bar business typically go to bed about the time most of us wake up.

I walked up the sidewalk to the front door, over cracked stone steps where I'd once sat with Ed and Draper and watched the regulars drift in and out of the bar. Now I stood on them alone and tugged on the heavy door, found it locked. I pulled my hand back and knocked several times, the enormous piece of wood soaking the sound up even when I pounded hard with a closed fist.

Nobody came to the door. It was hard to make a good, loud knock on that front door, though, and if Draper was in the back, it was no surprise that he hadn't heard it. I walked around the building and down the alley that ran beside it. The back door was familiar to me; when Ed and Draper and I used to snag a couple bottles of booze from Draper's old man's supply, that was how we made our exit.

The back door was open. I stepped through it and into a narrow, musty corridor with rubber mats on the floor. A couple empty kegs were stacked along the wall to my right, and it was dark. I started to yell out for Draper, but stopped. Something felt wrong about the place.

I moved slowly down the hall, sidestepping the kegs, and trying to keep quiet. I didn't hear anything from the bar, and that bothered me. If Draper was still here, it seemed he'd be cleaning up from one day and getting ready for the next, moving chairs and adjusting kegs and filling the coolers with bottles of beer. Instead it was completely still.

There was a door to my left that would take me out of the hall and into the back portion of the dining room. I passed it up and continued until the hall took a sharp, ninety-degree turn and opened out behind the bar. I had Corbett's revolver in my hand now, held against my thigh. I stepped around the corner of the hall and raised the gun as Scott Draper came into view.

He was sagging forward in front of the tall shelves that stood behind the bar, his hands over his head, cuffed to the heavy wooden shelves that were lined with bottles of liquor. He'd been cuffed just high enough that when he fell forward, his knees hung a few inches off the floor, increasing the pressure and pain in his wrists. He hung there now, his body limp, head down, and I could see blood dripping off his face and onto the floor. His T-shirt was soaked with sweat and blood, and even from ten feet away I could see swollen knots rising on his face. While I watched, Jimmy Cancerno stepped forward with a gun in his hand and swung the butt of the gun into Draper's face. It connected without the hard crack of metal hitting bone that I'd expected; instead, it was more like the sound of someone stepping on a wet sponge. That gave me an immediate idea of just how swollen Draper's face already was.

The scene in front of me was wildly different from anything I could have expected when I stepped around the corner, but I didn't pause to consider it. Instinct took over. Draper had been a friend once, and moving to help him wasn't a decision so much as a reflex action.

"Not surprised you had to put him in handcuffs before you had the balls to hit him, Cancerno," I said, taking another step forward and pointing the revolver at his head.

It wouldn't be like Cancerno to travel alone to take on somebody like Draper, but I couldn't see anyone else yet, so pointing the gun at him was my best bet. I stepped forward some more, clearing the edge of the wall so I could see into the rest of the room. That was when Ramone came around the corner and lifted a shotgun at me.

I switched the revolver's muzzle quickly from Cancerno to Ramone, bringing it to bear on his chest before he could get his gun high enough to fire, and he froze for a moment, just a few feet away with the shotgun at his waist. Even while I stopped his advance, I knew I was screwed. He and Cancerno were positioned at opposite angles from me, and they were close. Keeping both of them at bay was going to be difficult.

"Get out of here, Lincoln," Scott Draper said, the

words sounding as if they'd been spoken through a mouthful of newspaper as he spit them out through busted, bloodied lips.

"I'd prefer it if he stays," Cancerno said, and there was a flash of motion as he turned to face me, reversing the gun in his hand so it was no longer held by the barrel.

"Keep the gun down, Cancerno," I said, taking a step back, close to the wall, and shifting the gun quickly from Ramone to Cancerno and then back to Ramone as he started to raise his gun again. I had to get at least one of them disarmed, fast, or this was going to be over all too quickly. My choice was Ramone—he would be the better shooter, the better fighter, and he was closer.

Keeping an eye on Cancerno, who was walking around the bar toward me, I took a few shuffling steps toward Ramone. All the lights were off in the bar except for one thin fluorescent lamp above the mirrors, and behind Ramone the dining room was dark. I hoped they didn't have more backups waiting there.

"Put it down, Ramone," I said, and he stood completely still, looking unconcerned. In Ramone's eyes, I had already lost this fight because I hadn't shot him as soon as I'd seen him. He was a killer, and his mind worked in a kill-or-be-killed fashion. I had failed to kill him, and now he was sure that I would die before this was over.

I was about to repeat my command when I saw Cancerno lift his gun quickly to shoulder level. I jerked the barrel of the revolver away from Ramone and fired a quick snap shot at Cancerno almost exactly as he fired at me. Both of us missed. Even as I was pulling the trigger, through, I was diving to my left, into Ramone, knowing that I had to prevent him from getting that shotgun up and firing at close range.

I hit him in the chest with my shoulder, but he'd been prepared for my lunge, and rather than attempt to bring his gun up, he dropped it, wrapped one arm around my head, and went with my momentum. We fell together, Ramone clutching my head and neck, and landed painfully on the floor of the bar. I tried to roll onto my right shoulder immediately and bring my gun around on him, but Cancerno was running toward us, trying to get a clear look at me, so I leaned back and fired two rounds into the glass mirrors behind the bar, making him drop. That was too much time to give Ramone, though, and he was on his knees, swinging his fist at my face.

He caught me high on the side of my head, as I had just enough time to turn my face away. It was a hard punch, and the next one was even harder. I swung the gun at his mouth, but he blocked it with his forearm and the gun flew from my hand. I grabbed at his chest with both hands as he threw another punch, and another, both connecting with my forehead.

Then it was over, Cancerno standing above me with a Beretta 9 mm pointed at my face. Ramone threw one last punch, this one splitting the skin above my right eye, then climbed off me and retrieved his shotgun.

"Thanks for coming by," Cancerno said, and kicked me in the ribs. I rolled onto my stomach and tried to push myself up, but he kicked me again and pushed the Beretta against my skull.

"Stay down," he said, and then to Ramone, "Get him over with Draper."

"No more handcuffs," Ramone said.

"That's all right."

Ramone lifted me off the floor by my hair, pushing the barrel of a gun I assumed was Mitch Corbett's revolver in my spine. He shoved me past the bar and then kicked me behind the knees, making me fall forward. I caught myself with my palms out, but he ground his boot into my back, shoving me down on my stomach again.

I looked up at Scott Draper, and it took a great deal of effort to keep my eyes on him. His face was a pulpy mess of blood and bruises. I saw his front teeth hanging loose and chipped behind torn lips, and his nose had been smashed flat against his face. Blood dripped from various areas of his face and fell onto the rubber mat below him in slow, steady drops. His eyes, though, were remarkably clear. Clear, and angry. More than once while we were growing up—and even a few times in the last week—I'd had the passing thought that Draper was a man who could take a hell of a lot of punishment before he stayed down. Now I had proof of that hanging in front of me.

Draper coughed, and a fine spray of blood flew from his lips and landed on the back of my hand, covering it with tiny crimson droplets. Ramone stepped away and Cancerno stood over me and kicked me again in the side. He hit me directly in the ribs, but he wasn't a powerful man, and the blow didn't do the damage he'd hoped to inflict.

"Glad you made it, Perry," he said. "You're the other one I wanted to see tonight."

"You're done, Cancerno," I said, not bothering to twist my head so I could see him. "Padgett got shot, and the half of the police department that you *don't* control is going to see Gajovich right now."

"No shit?" he said. "Well, then, I guess that makes this encounter all the more important. Because I'd hate to go to jail with unsettled scores."

Cancerno paced to the end of the bar where Ramone stood, then whirled back to Draper and me.

"You guys like fires, right?"

He reached up with the hand that wasn't holding the gun and grabbed a bottle of vodka from the shelf above Draper. I started to get to my hands and knees when he did it, but Ramone stepped forward and pointed his gun at me.

"I know Draper likes fires," Cancerno said, smashing the top of the vodka bottle against the bar and shattering the glass. He turned it upside down and poured the alcohol out on top of us. It splattered the floor and my legs and Draper's bloody face. Draper rose up higher on his toes, the handcuffs still binding him to the heavy oak shelves. It was a massive, one-piece unit filled with shelves for liquor, with mirrors set behind the shelves, and stood at least eight feet tall. Draper's cuffs were looped around one of the solid crosspieces that separated the two sides of shelves. The wood was not going to break, no matter how hard he pulled.

."Draper likes fires more than he likes his life," Cancerno said, breaking another bottle and emptying it around us. "That seem like a good trade to you, Perry?" When I didn't say anything, he said, "What about you, Ramone?"

"Doesn't sound like a good trade," Ramone said.

"I didn't think so, either. But it appears this prick"— Cancerno threw a bottle that just missed Draper's head before breaking on the shelves—"thought it was a good one."

Cancerno stopped picking up bottles and stared at me. "I own this neighborhood. But I was done with it. Bigger things in mind. So you bastards had real, real bad timing. Gradduk could have been the only one to die. I didn't need to send his friends to join him."

"It's done, Cancerno," I said again.

"Exactly." He nodded. "It is done. But I'm going to be the one to finish it. Understand that, Perry? And Draper here just designed your own graves. Because with all the fires in this neighborhood last night, one more isn't going to stand out." He poured a bottle of Crown Royal in a circle on the floor at my feet.

Ramone stood behind the bar, keeping the revolver pointed at us. Cancerno was still working his way down the length of the bar, grabbing bottle after bottle, breaking them, and then pouring the liquor on the floor.

I'd kept moving, still trying to turn my body and prepare to get on my feet when the time came, and apparently I'd gotten too close to that for Ramone's liking. He fired a round into the shelves just above my head, the bottles exploding, glass and liquor landing on the floor around me.

I stopped moving, and Ramone smiled, showing his teeth.

Ramone's round was one more in addition to those Cancerno and I had fired earlier, but I wasn't too hopeful that they would have attracted the attention of the neighbors. The Hideaway's ancient, thick walls absorbed noise better than the most expensive soundproofing panels. Draper's dad used to brag about how loud he could turn the jukebox up before you'd hear a bit of it on the sidewalk.

Beside me, Draper shifted position again, sliding his heels across the floor until they actually rested against the bottom of the shelf unit. The chain on his handcuffs jingled softly as he pulled it tight on his wrists. I looked away from him, feeling pity. When Cancerno lit this place, Draper had nowhere to go. Not that I'd make it far—Ramone stood just ten feet away, and his gun was trained on me. At this distance, he'd kill me before I even came out of my crouch.

Cancerno had assumed a position at the far end of the bar, his back to the hallway that led out to the back door. He'd finished spreading alcohol and stood with a bar rag in one hand and his revolver in the other. Watching him, Ramone set the revolver down on top of the bar and lifted his shotgun again, leveling it across the surface of the bar, the ugly muzzle pointed right at me. No need to worry about accuracy now; the shotgun would cut me in two if I tried to move.

"You're right, Perry," Cancerno said. "It's all done." He shifted the bar rag so he held it in the same hand that was clenched around his revolver. He reached into his pocket with the other hand, and when he withdrew it, a steel Zippo was in his fingers. He flipped the top off the lighter and flicked the wheel with his thumb. A short flame appeared, and he touched it to the edge of the bar rag, which began to burn slowly.

I shifted my weight forward, onto my toes, preparing for a rush that would end with a shotgun blast, and behind me I could hear Draper tensing, the handcuffs scraping against the wood that held him.

"I don't think so," Ramone said, following my movement with the barrel of his gun. My fingers brushed against glass, and I squeezed them around the shattered neck of one of the bottles Cancerno had broken. My opportunity would come thanks to Cancerno, although he didn't realize it yet. The fire wouldn't kill me as fast as Ramone's shotgun would, and the initial burst of flame might be more distracting to the shooter than to me. When Cancerno dropped that rag to the floor, I was going to be moving with the flames, right at Ramone's throat, with that jagged glass in my hand.

"I hope this hurts like hell," Cancerno said, holding the now-burning rag high in the air, grasping it with just two fingers, and I tensed every muscle, ready to spring forward when that rag hit the floor. That was when I heard Draper let out a grunt that sounded like an explosion as he suddenly lurched forward.

I am a strong man. I own a gym where many stronger men come regularly to hoist obscene amounts of weight. During my time on the narcotics beat, I saw men riding methamphetamine highs kick down doors and punch through walls as if they were not even there. Never, though, had I seen a display of raw strength comparable to the one Scott Draper offered in that moment at the Hideaway. With a single, swift-but-massive effort, he lunged forward and jerked with all his power at the handcuffs that held him to the shelves. Because Draper was so tall, they were fastened fairly high on the cabinet, well above the central point of balance. When Draper leaned into that savage jerk forward, the several hundred pounds of oak shelving and liquor bottles leaned with him, overbalanced, and fell forward.

Ramone had time to shoot. He had time, but the shelving unit was at least eight feet tall, and it was coming down right at his skull. He'd been focused on me because I'd been the only one with freedom to move, and when Draper lunged forward Ramone had to pivot to his left to bring the gun around to this new threat. By that time the massive wooden cabinet was falling, and when Ramone pulled the trigger, he took a full step back, trying to avoid taking all that weight on the top of his head. The combined pivot and step backward were enough, and the slug he fired missed us both, splintering through the cabinet about a foot to the right of Draper's head as it came crashing down.

The bar saved us. The weight of the enormous cabinet would probably have killed us both, crushed us, if it had fallen directly onto our bodies. But because it was so tall, it landed against the bar, shedding glass and booze all over us, and held there, wedged at about a forty-five-degree angle.

Ramone was hidden from my sight now, but Cancerno had screamed something and jumped backward as the cabinet fell, throwing the rag at the same time. It caught the edge of the new obstruction provided by the fallen shelves and dropped to the floor. There was some alcohol there, but it missed the large pool Cancerno had spread earlier, and the eruption of flame was smaller than it might have been.

Staying on my hands and knees to avoid braining myself on the shelves that lay angled over my head, I scrambled for the end of the bar and Cancerno, bits of broken glass slicing into my flesh. I cleared the shelves as Cancerno brought his Beretta up, and I sprang forward, hitting him around the waist as he fired over me. The tackle drove us both down, and he landed on his back, his head snapping against the floor with a crack like a dropped cinder block. By the time I lifted myself off him he was already unconscious.

Behind me the fire was spreading. I had turned back to the flames, searching for Draper, when there was motion in the hallway behind me and a shot was fired through the air over my head.

I ducked and grabbed Cancerno's Beretta as another shot was fired, this one blasting off part of the wall above me. Ramone must have found the revolver, because these shots were clearly rounds from a handgun and not slugs from his shotgun. I rolled onto my left shoulder and brought the Beretta up, looking for him. A shadow moved along the dark wall that separated the bar from the dining room, and I fired several shots in that direction. Then the shadow was gone, and I didn't pursue. Draper was still pinned behind the bar, with the fire surging closer.

Crawling back to him from the way I'd come out was impossible now; the flames had devoured that end of the bar, the heat so intense I could only look with a sidelong glance, holding my arm up to shield my face. I ran around the front of the bar, switching the gun from my right hand to my left, then put my right palm on the surface of the bar and leaped, swinging myself over it, and onto the floor.

Draper was pulling furiously at his handcuffs, straining away from the fire that was now almost upon him. I ducked my head under the angled shelves and crawled to him. It was almost impossible to see anything now because I couldn't keep my eyes open against the heat.

Relying on touch instead of sight, I felt for the handcuffs. The metal was hot when my fingers finally found it. I slid my free hand away, pressed the barrel of Cancerno's Beretta against the thin central portion of the chain, and squeezed the trigger. Shards of metal and wood flew away, and I tugged at Draper's hands, expecting them to come free. The cuffs held.

I put the muzzle of the gun back against the chain and fired again, and again. I was screaming until I choked on the acrid air. Unable to stand the heat anymore, I fell away, my hand still wrapped around Draper's wrist. It took me a second to realize his wrist had come free with me.

Then we were on our feet and running out of the bar as flames surged behind us. Draper's knees buckled and he started to go down, but I caught him and lifted him and then he seemed to find his balance. Clutching on to one another, we staggered out of the bar and into the dining room, which was also beginning to fill with smoke. The heavy front door loomed in front of us, and I hit it with my shoulder, but couldn't get it to open. Draper found the bolt with one of his bloody hands, turned it, and then we fell forward, out of the bar, and onto the cool concrete of the front steps.

By now smoke was pouring out of the building, and windows ruptured with a soft popping noise that sounded harmless compared to the crackle of the flames. Draper and I scrambled out to the sidewalk on our hands and knees, gratefully gasping in breaths of fresh air. I tried to speak to him, but instead I fell onto my stomach, my chin bouncing off the concrete. I twisted onto my side on the cold, rough pavement of the sidewalk, watched the Hideaway burn, and waited for the sirens to begin.

CHAPTER 30

Joe and I saw the press conference on the television in his hospital room. Mike Gajovich had been relieved of duty pending a criminal investigation, his brother jerked from command of District Two along with him. The chief of police delivered the message with a firm voice, but he didn't look at the camera. The mayor stood awkwardly next to him, trying to look grim and reassuring at the same time.

Beside me, Joe's breathing was shallow but steady. His face matched the white sheets on the bed, except for his eyes, which were red and rimmed with dark purple circles. A handful of tubes ran from his body, and monitors hummed behind the bed, keeping watch. He could talk, but it took a lot out of him, so we didn't say much. He kept his head on the pillow, but his eyes followed the television closely. When the press conference had concluded, I stood up and turned the television off. Joe spoke while my back was to him.

"No Richards." The words came out in a rattling whisper, a hell of a lot of effort behind them, and I turned and nodded at him.

"They wouldn't let him speak at a press conference," I said. "Too much risk he'd tell it like it is."

It was the first time I'd been alone with Joe since his condition had stabilized, and I still had trouble looking at him without feeling awash with guilt. The first thing he'd said when he saw me was "Thanks for the swim."

He didn't remember much of it. I'd talked him through it, but there had been a dozen cops in the room for that, it seemed, spilling out into the hallway, all of them taking notes and whispering to one another. We'd talk about it again sometime when it was just the two of us. But not today.

Jimmy Cancerno had died inside the Hideaway. Ramone Tavarcz had been picked up four hours after the fire, and four hours after that he'd offered a confession to the murder of Anita Sentalar. Jack Padgett had handled the details of the setup, and recruited Jerome Huggins, but Ramone had fired the killing shot. He'd been paid fifty thousand dollars for the hit by Cancerno. Ramone said he was planning to buy an SUV with the cash. One with leather seats.

Ramone would still be charged with first-degree homicide, but his confessions carried value. He offered Padgett up for the murder of Larry Rabold and said word of Rabold's involvement with the corruption task force had spread to Mike Gajovich's brother, the District Two commander. There was no telling exactly what the Gajovich brothers would be charged with by the time it was all done, but it was safe to say they'd run neither the city nor the police department.

"If I've ever seen a more beat-up pair of guys, I can't remember the boxing match."

Amy stepped into Joe's room and regarded us with a frown and raised eyebrows. I would have raised my own in response, but they were gone. The fire had taken care of that and left mild burns across my face, neck, and arms. I'd spent an hour in the shower trying to lose the smell of smoke and still hadn't succeeded.

Amy took Joe's hand and squeezed it, smiling at him as she studied the tubes leading from his body.

"Great to have you back with us," she said.

"Thanks."

You could tell he wanted to say more, but he was fading again, the medication and the trauma beating him back into sleep even as he tried to fight out of it. Amy kissed the back of his hand and placed it gently back on the bed, then stepped across the room to face me. She ran the tips of her fingers lightly over my burns.

"Make me look rugged, don't they?" I said. "Sexy."

"Keep on telling yourself that, soldier."

She dropped her hand, glanced at Joe, whose eyes were closed now, then spoke in a hard-edged whisper.

"So you want to explain why the hell you needed to call me at five in the morning and make me drive out to see some lunatic living in an abandoned house?"

"You told him what I asked you to?"

She nodded. "That he should tell Cal Richards everything he told you, but leave Scott Draper out of it."

"And he seemed agreeable?"

"Absolutely. I drove him to meet Richards. He said he didn't want to see any other cops until he'd seen Richards."

"Good. That's what I told him to do." I dropped into one of the chairs at the foot of Joe's bed, and Amy took the other. She leaned forward and rested her hand on my knee.

"What happened last night, Lincoln? Three hours after I left the hospital, you'd found Corbett, killed Cancerno, and burned down a building. I've got to hear the story."

"Hear it, or write it?"

"Hear it."

So I told it. I'd had some practice—Cal Richards alone had made me go through it a half dozen times, and he'd been the third detective to get to me.

"And what, exactly, was with the message to Corbett?" she asked.

I'd stolen a cop's cell phone and called her from the bathroom as dawn broke over the city.

"Cancerno was at the bar to kill Draper," I said. "I was at the bar because I thought Draper was working with Cancerno. If he ever had been, the partnership no longer seemed to be amicable. I don't want to drop the hammer on Draper for those fires until I hear why he did it."

"Do you know what he's told Cal Richards?"

"Draper?" I shook my head. "No, I don't. But Cal was still asking me about the fires this morning."

"And what did you say?"

"Not much. Just pointed out that Cancerno was ready to burn the Hideaway last night. Let him take it from there."

"The story will be all over the front page tomorrow," she said. "I only wrote some of it, but I did offer a headline suggestion for the sidebar: 'Gradduk Not Guilty.' "

"Got a hell of a good sound to it."

We sat quietly for a while and watched Joe. His chest rose and fell under the blankets, his heart thumping away, smooth and steady.

"He's going to be okay," Amy said.

"Yes. Dr. Crandall's eight hours of surgery got it done."

She kept her hand on my leg. "So it's over."

"Yes," I said again. It was almost over.

Sometime that afternoon, while I talked to police and doctors attended to my partner and Scott Draper, Ed Gradduk was buried without ceremony, at his mother's request.

I t was late the next day before I saw Draper. He called me as soon as he was released from the hospital and asked me to meet him outside. I walked out of Joe's room and down the steps, came out into a hot, bright day with a sky so blue it seemed artificial.

Draper was standing at the corner. When I got closer, I saw his face was a ghastly collage of bruises and stitches. There was a cast on his nose and a bandage over his right eye. But the rest of him looked fine, strong and sturdy.

He put out his hand. "Thanks for coming down. Now, and the last time."

I shook his hand. "Thanks for pulling me out of the house fire a few nights ago. Too bad you didn't stick around at the time. Maybe some things would have gone a little easier on a lot of people."

"Let's take a walk," he said.

We walked north on West Twenty-fifth, the cars buzzing past us. It was late in the afternoon, the heat as intense as it would get all day, and after only a block of it I could feel my pores begin to open up. The storm that had cooled things off was forgotten now, the sky clear, the air still. The heat would continue to build till the next storm blew through. August in Cleveland.

"Cops cut me loose," Draper said eventually. "A lot of questions first, sure, but at the end of the day it seems I'm just a victim to them. They seem to think Cancerno was punishing me for helping you, and I didn't discourage that line of logic. Problem is, I know it's not the truth, and you know it's not the truth. Corbett came by to see me in the hospital. Told me what he told you."

I walked on without saying a word, head down.

"So you know Cancerno came after me because he found out I set those fires," Draper said.

"I got that impression. But how did he know?"

"One of his guys was in my bar that night. I came in through the back, went into the bathroom, and was running water over my arms. I had some burns. Smelled of smoke. I should have gone home, but there were so many cops out that I just wanted to get off the streets for a while. This guy walked in the bathroom and saw it. I guess he reported back to Cancerno the next afternoon, once he heard whose houses had been lit."

"How'd you know which houses to burn?"

"Not too hard—all the ones they were working on had signs in the yard. I drove around the neighborhood and found a half dozen without much trouble."

"I see."

"Uh-huh. And now I got a question—you knew I set the fires, but you didn't tell the cops that, and you got your friend to find Corbett, make sure he didn't say anything." Draper turned to look at me. "Thanks for that, Lincoln. I could be in jail right now. But I'm wondering . . . if you knew I'd burned those houses, and you thought I was working with Jimmy, why the hell did you come down to the bar? Why didn't you just call the cops and let them finish me off?"

"I wanted to hear you explain it. I just wanted to understand why the hell you would've done it."

"Well, I'm damn lucky you did. Because you saved me down there."

"Were you working with Cancerno, at any point?"

He shook his head. "Not in the way you're thinking. Reason I set the fires was simple—it was what Ed had in mind when he went down. And I owed him. So I decided I'd finish his job."

"Did you know what had happened between Cancerno and Ed's family?"

He nodded. "He told me the night he ran from the cops and hid at my bar."

"So you knew all of it? Why the hell didn't you tell me?"

"I didn't know all of it. I just knew the old stuff. Didn't know anything about the houses and Anita Sentalar and Mike Gajovich. Cops explained all that to me yes-

terday. All I knew was that Ed was out to settle a score
with Cancerno."

"And you didn't tell me."

"I pointed you at him," he said. "I brought him down
and introduced you to him, I told you about Mitch Corbett, and later I reminded you about the old fires. I got you
started. I figured you'd do the rest. And you did. I just
didn't know . . . I had no idea how bad it would all get."

Two women were walking toward us. When we got
close, they looked at Draper's face with undisguised horror and stepped off the sidewalk to get away from him.
He didn't blink.

"So you directed me," I said. "When you could have
just told me from day one. And people got shot, and people died, and you got your face beat to shit, and half the
neighborhood burned down." I shook my head and looked
away, across the street.

"Like I said, I didn't know what would happen, and I
didn't know how deep it all ran. I only knew what Ed had
told me about Padgett and Cancerno." Draper ran a hand
over his bald head and sighed. "And there's something
else to it, Lincoln. Something that made it a little difficult
for me to really talk to you, bring you into it."

"What?"

He stopped walking, turned to face me. I didn't want to
stop moving, but I had to when he did. I looked at him
and waited.

"When Ed went to jail, he wasn't protecting Antonio
Childers. He was protecting me."

"What . . ." I didn't even finish the question. I just
stood and stared at him. A city bus roared by beside us,
belching a cloud of exhaust smoke. The sun was harsh in
my eyes.

"I was in serious money trouble," Draper said. "I was
going to lose the bar. Less than two years after my old

man died and left it to me, and already I'd run it into the ground. I couldn't let that happen. I talked to Jimmy Cancerno. He was the guy you talked to in the neighborhood with something like that, or so I thought at the time. He told me he could definitely help. Said a guy in my position could be useful as hell. He had the connection to Childers. Offered serious cash if I'd run some stuff out of the bar. Said I needed one good guy I could trust, though, to handle the transactions."

His eyes flicked down, seeming lost in the swollen, bruised tissue that surrounded them.

"I picked Ed."

I stood with my arms at my sides and didn't speak. After a while, I turned away from him and looked out at the street, watched the cars go by. Then I began to walk again.

He followed. "That's why he wouldn't tell you anything. That's why he took the fall. He was protecting me. Ed didn't know anything about Antonio Childers; I did."

I spoke for the first time in a while then, my voice tight. "So when the neighborhood was cursing my name for being such a traitor, you kept quiet."

"No," he said. "I led their cheers."

I shot him a hard look at that, and he met my gaze evenly. I held his eyes for a moment and then looked away.

We came to Clark and turned left, walking west, toward Ed Gradduk's old house and what was left of Draper's bar.

"I know it went rough on you," he said.

I gave a short laugh and shook my head. "You know it went *rough* on me? Good call, man."

We walked on together, but it was different now. Our steps were falling in sync, but it seemed as if they shouldn't be, as if we both thought maybe we should change our pace, let the other fall behind or pull ahead.

We stayed together, though, through several blocks of silence.

"You hear people talk about going home all the time," I said eventually. "Every Christmas, people from out of state, from across the country, tell me they're going back home. I've lived ten minutes down the damn street for years, Draper, and I couldn't go home. So much as walk in this neighborhood, and anybody who knew me would tell me to leave. My father, who it turns out was the only guy who tried to fix anything the right way, moved out a year after Ed went to jail. It wasn't because he wanted to leave the neighborhood, either."

Draper didn't say anything.

"But, yeah," I said. "It went rough on me. Yes, it did. Thanks for understanding, buddy."

"I was a coward," he said. "I know that. You took the heat for trying to help, and I kept my coward's mouth shut and let Ed do his time and you pay the rest of the price. I was looking at more time than Ed if they really investigated me, and I used that to tell myself it was all right. Ed was just weighing it and making the best decision for both of us, right? That's what I told myself."

"You ever visit him in jail?"

"Every week."

"You look him in the eye when you were there?"

He didn't say anything to that. We went another block before a red light brought us to a halt.

"Ed knew what you were trying to do," Draper said. "I'm not saying he appreciated it, the idea you and Allison cooked up, but he understood. He told me that, himself. You were trying to help. You were a bigger man than me. Without question."

I shook my head. "Ed was. You were the coward and I was the fool who wanted to be the hero. Ed was the man."

We kept walking, but didn't say anything more for a long while. We went for many blocks. Past Ed's house. I looked up when we went by, wondered about Alberta. Should I go see her? What would I say? None of it would matter now. Not to her.

"I'd give anything for a chance to talk to him," Draper said. "Just one more conversation. To be able to tell him that it's done. That you finished it for him."

"It was done for him five days ago."

We reached the Hideaway and stopped. We stood together on the sidewalk and looked up at it. The fire department had done a hell of a job, but then they'd had a hell of a lot of practice in the days leading up to the fire. They'd managed to save the building, though the interior was demolished. The sturdy old stone remained, though, the ancient walls and that massive door standing strong and steadfast.

"You gonna get it back up and running?"

"Hell, yes," Draper said quietly. "No doubt, Lincoln. It'll be back. I'm one of the only people on this block who actually had fire insurance."

"Good. You belong behind that bar."

"It'll be a while before I can work the bar without turning people's stomachs. I've got plastic surgery ahead, it seems." He snorted. "Plastic surgery, and me a guy from Clark Avenue. What do you think my regulars will say when they hear that?"

"Probably tell you to spring for the boob job while you're at it."

He laughed. "You know, it'll be a surprise if one of them doesn't say something close."

I nodded and turned away. "I'm going to take off, man. Get back up to the hospital, see how my partner's doing."

"Wait."

I turned again and looked at him expectantly.

"Lincoln, I owe you . . ." he began, but I waved him off.

"Don't say that. I don't want to hear it. Not about owing people, about debts and balances and making amends. It can't be about that, Scott."

He frowned, shifted his weight, and hooked his thumbs on his belt, then took them off again. I'd never seen Scott Draper look so awkward.

"Listen," he said, "I was thinking, maybe you and Allison could drop by later this week. We could grab a drink, have some dinner or something. Hang out again."

I gazed up the street. "That group's one name short, don't you think?"

"Yeah. But that can't be helped anymore. The others can."

Cars buzzed back and forth along the avenue, crossing over the pavement where Ed Gradduk had died, nobody slowing. I watched them for a while before I nodded.

"Yeah, Scott. We can do that."

He put out his hand. "I hope so, Lincoln. When I get the bar open again, I want to see you down here. And not just because I owe you."

I took his hand. "I'll be down," I said.

I left him there in front of his bar and walked up Clark Avenue, the sun warm on my back. Joe had been asleep when I'd left, but he'd wake up again soon. I wanted to be there when he did.

READ ON FOR AN EXCERPT FROM THE
NEW MYSTERY BY **MICHAEL KORYTA**

A WELCOME GRAVE

COMING SOON IN HARDCOVER FROM
ST. MARTIN'S MINOTAUR

1

Sometime after midnight, on a moonless October night turned harsh by a fine, windswept rain, one of the men I liked least in the world was murdered in a field near Bedford, just south of the city. Originally, they assumed the body had only been dumped there, that Alex Jefferson had been killed somewhere else, dead maybe before the mutilation began.

They were wrong.

It was past noon the next day when the body was discovered. A dozen vehicles were soon assembled in the field—police cars, evidence vans, an ambulance that could serve no purpose but was dispatched anyhow. I wasn't there, but I could imagine the scene—I'd certainly been to enough like it.

But maybe not. Maybe not. The things they saw that day, things I heard about secondhand, from cops who recited the news in the distanced way that only hardened professionals can manage . . . they weren't things I dealt with often.

Jefferson was brought from the city with his hands and feet bound with rope, duct tape over his mouth. A half mile down a dirt track leading into an empty field, he was removed from a vehicle—tire tracks suggested a van— and subjected to a systematic torture killing that was apparently quite slow in reaching the second stage. Autopsy results and scenarios created by the forensic team and the medical experts suggested Jefferson remained breathing, and probably conscious, for fifteen minutes.

Fifteen minutes varies by perspective. The blink of an eye, if you're standing in an airport, saying good-bye to someone you love. An ice age, if you're fighting through traffic, late for a job interview. If your hands and feet are bound while someone works you over slowly, from head to toe, with a butane lighter and a straight razor? At that point an eternity isn't what the fifteen minutes feel like— it's what you're begging for. To be sent to wherever it is you're destined, and sent there for good.

The cops were preoccupied with the basics for most of the first day: processing the crime scene, getting the forensic experts from the Ohio Bureau of Criminal Investigation involved, identifying the body, notifying next of kin, and trying to piece together Jefferson's last hours. The locals were interviewed, the field and surrounding woods combed for evidence.

No leads came. Not from the basics, at least, not from those first hours of work. So then the investigation extended. The detectives went looking for suspects—people whose histories with Jefferson were adversarial, hostile. At the top of that list, they found me.

They arrived at ten past nine on the day after Alex Jefferson's body was discovered, and I hadn't made it to the office yet, even though I live in a building just down the street. Below my apartment is an old gym I own and from which I occasionally make a profit. I've got a manager for the gym, but that day she had car trouble; she called me at seven-thirty to say her husband was trying a jumpstart, and if that didn't work, she might be late. I told her not to worry about it—no rush for me, so none for her. I'd open the gym and then leave whenever she made it in.

I'd gone downstairs with a cup of coffee in hand and

unlocked the gym office. There's a keycard system that allows members to come and go twenty-four hours a day, but Grace, my manager, works the nine-to-five in the office and at the cooler. We make most of our money off energy drinks and protein shakes, granola bars, and vitamins, not the monthly membership dues.

There were two women on treadmills and one man lifting weights when I opened the office, our typical crowd. One nice thing about working out at my gym: You never have to wait on the equipment. Good for the members, bad for me.

I checked the locker rooms to make sure there were fresh towels, and found Grace had taken care of that the previous night. I was on my way back through the weight room when I saw the cops standing just inside the office. Two of them, neither in uniform, but I caught a glimpse of a badge affixed to the taller one's belt, a glint of silver under the fluorescent lights that made my eyebrows narrow and my pace quicken.

"Can I help you?" I stepped into the office. Neither one was familiar to me, but I couldn't pretend to know everyone at the department, especially now, a few years since I'd last worked there.

"Lincoln Perry?"

"Yes."

The one whose badge wasn't clipped to his belt, a trim guy with gray hair and crow's feet around his eyes, slid a case out of his pocket and opened it, showing a badge and identification card. HAROLD TARGENT, DETECTIVE, CLEVELAND POLICE DEPARTMENT. I gave it a glance, looked back at him, nodded once.

"Okay. What can I help you with, Detective?"

"Call me Hal."

The taller one beside him, who was maybe ten years younger, lifted his hand in a little wave. "Kevin Daly."

Targent looked out at the weight room, then back at me. "You mind shutting that door? Give us a little privacy?"

"My manager's late. Don't want to close the office up until she gets here, if that's okay."

Targent shook his head. "Going to need some privacy, Mr. Perry."

"That serious?" I said, beginning to feel the first hint of dread, the sense that maybe this had nothing to do with one of my cases, that it could be personal.

"Serious, yes. Serious the way it gets when people die, Mr. Perry."

I swung the office door shut and turned the lock. "Let's go upstairs."

To their credit, they didn't waste a lot of time bullshitting around without telling me why they were there. No questions about what I'd done the previous night, no head games. Instead, they laid it out as soon as we'd taken seats in my living room.

"A man you know was murdered two nights ago," Targent said. "Heard about it?"

My last contact with the news had been the previous day's paper. I hadn't seen that morning's yet, and I get more reliable news from the drunk who hangs out at the bus stop up the street than I do from the television. I shook my head slowly, Targent watching with friendly skepticism.

"You going to tell me who?" I said.

"The man's name was Alex Jefferson."

It was one of those moments when I wished I were a smoker, just so I could have something to do with my hands, a little routine I could go through to pass some time without having to sit there and stare.

"You remember the man?" Daly asked.

I looked at him and gave a short laugh, shaking my head at the question. "Yeah. I remember the man."

They waited for a bit. Targent said, "And your relationship with him was, ah, a little adversarial?"

I met his eyes. "He was sleeping with my fiancée, Detective. I spent two hours working my way through a twelve-pack of beer before I beat the shit out of Jefferson at his country club, got pulled over for drunk driving, got charged with assault. Pled the assault down to a misdemeanor but got canned from the department. All of this, you already know. But, yes, I suppose we can say that my relationship with him was, ah, a little adversarial."

Targent was watching me, and Daly was pretending to, but his eyes were drifting over my apartment, as if he thought maybe I'd left a crowbar or a nine-iron with dried blood and matted hair stuck to it leaning against the wall.

"Okay," Targent said. He looked even smaller sitting down, as if he weighed about a hundred and twenty pounds, but he had a substantial quality despite that, a voice flecked with iron. "Don't take it personally, Mr. Perry. Nobody's calling you a suspect. Now, if I can just ask—"

"Were you there when she was notified?" I said.

"Excuse me?"

"Karen. His wife. Were you there when she was notified?"

He shook his head. "No, I was not. Lots of people are working—"

"I can imagine. He was a very important man."

Targent blew out his breath and glanced at Daly, whose eyes were still roving over my apartment, looking for any excuse to shout "probable cause" and begin tearing the place apart.

"I was out with a friend till about eleven Saturday night," I said. "We had dinner, a few drinks downtown.

I've probably got the receipts. Came back here, read for an hour, went to bed. No receipt for that."

Targent smiled slightly. "Okay. But you're getting ahead of us."

"Like he said, nobody's calling you a suspect," Daly said.

"Sure."

"Just covering bases," Targent said. "You were on the job not long ago, you know how it goes."

"Sure."

He leaned back and hooked one ankle over a knee. "So you had an admittedly adversarial relationship with Mr. Jefferson."

"Three years ago."

"And had you—"

"Seen him since? No. The last time I saw him he was on his back in the parking lot, doing a lot of bleeding, and I was trying to make it to my car."

That wasn't true. I'd seen him twice after that, but always from a distance, and always unnoticed. Once in a restaurant; he'd been standing at the bar, laughing with some other guys in expensive suits, and I'd walked in the door, spotted him, and turned right back around and walked out. The other time was the day he and Karen were married. I'd parked across the street and sat in my car, watched them walk down the steps as people clapped and whistled, and I'd thought that it was all kid stuff, really, the marriage ceremony, and that when people like Jefferson—nearly fifty years old and trying a third wife on for size—went through it in public, it was pretty sad. Pathetic, even. Almost as sad and pathetic as being parked across the street, eighty-eight degrees but with the windows up, watching another guy marry your girl.

That was during my bad phase, though. Fresh out of the job, shiftless and angry. Time had passed, things had changed. Alex Jefferson, while never really gone from my mind, no longer weighed on it, either.

"You're wasting time," I said. "I understand you've got to go through the motions, but this is a dead end, gentlemen. I hadn't seen him, I hadn't seen her, and I didn't kill him. Happy he's dead? No. Sad? Not particularly. Apathetic. That's it. He and his life were of no concern to me and mine. Not anymore."

Targent leaned forward, ran a hand through his hair, and looked at the floor. "They took their time on him."

"Pardon?"

He looked up. "Whoever *did* kill him, Mr. Perry? They took their damn sweet time doing it. Slow and painful. That was how he went. With forty-seven burns and more than fifty lacerations. Burns from cigarettes and a lighter, lacerations from a razor blade. Sometimes the blade was used to cut deep, like a knife. Other times, it was used like a paint scraper across his flesh. He had duct tape over his mouth, and at some point, trying to scream, maybe, or maybe just going into convulsions from the pain, he bit right through his own tongue."

I turned and stared out the window. "I don't need the details, Detective. I just need you to scratch me off the list and move on."